fun with 1001 ACTIVITIES

MOONSTONE

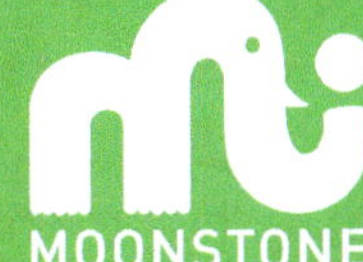

Published in Moonstone
by Rupa Publications India Pvt. Ltd 2023
7/16, Ansari Road, Daryaganj
New Delhi 110002

Sales centres:
Prayagraj Bengaluru Chennai
Hyderabad Jaipur Kathmandu
Kolkata Mumbai

P-ISBN: 978-93-5520-748-7
E-ISBN: 978-93-5520-755-5

First impression 2023

10 9 8 7 6 5 4 3 2 1

Printed in India

1. Find the bird names in the word search and circle them.

A	S	D	F	L	K	J	G	H	Q	P	T
V	P	E	L	U	E	T	C	O	O	T	U
I	A	O	O	T	H	P	A	S	T	E	R
C	R	O	W	O	P	Y	V	U	O	D	K
Q	R	P	L	O	I	F	I	S	N	U	E
H	O	E	N	T	G	L	T	A	G	C	Y
T	W	O	T	P	E	A	C	O	C	K	I
T	Y	C	A	A	O	M	T	O	E	T	H
S	A	T	E	R	N	I	R	N	T	I	S
P	L	A	Q	R	E	N	S	T	E	M	O
L	A	R	M	O	O	G	C	I	S	O	R
C	A	N	I	T	O	O	H	O	N	G	U

Turkey, Sparrow, Pigeon, Parrot, Peacock, Flamingo, Crow, Tern, Duck, Owl

2. How many frogs are there? Circle the right answer.

4 5 6 9

3. Spices make our food tasty. Match these spices with their names.

Cloves

Aniseed

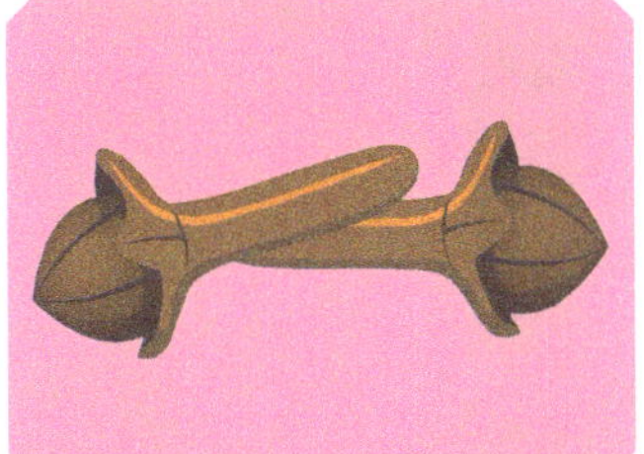

Cardamom

4. Count the number of squirrels and tick the correct answer.

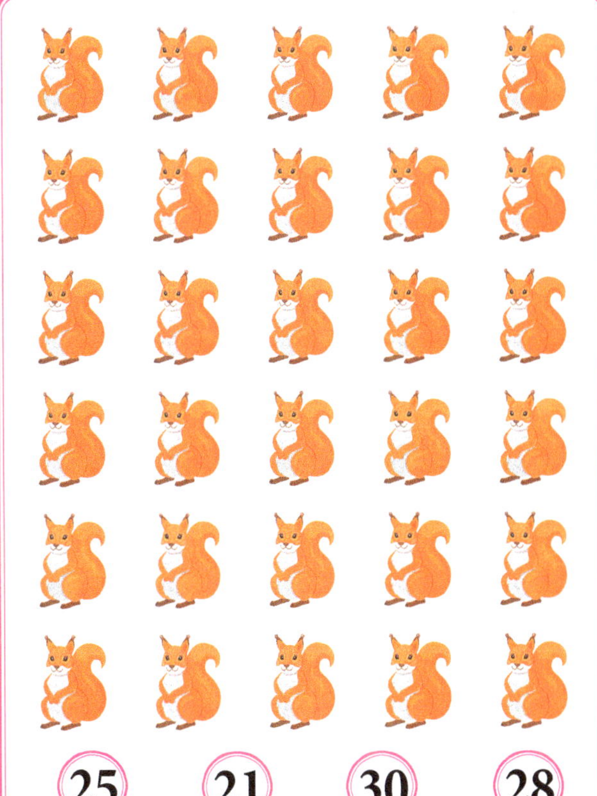

25 21 30 28

5. Write the numbers that follow.

6. Colour the rabbits with even numbers.

7. Read the number names and write their half as shown in the given example.

8. Circle the first letter these images begin with.

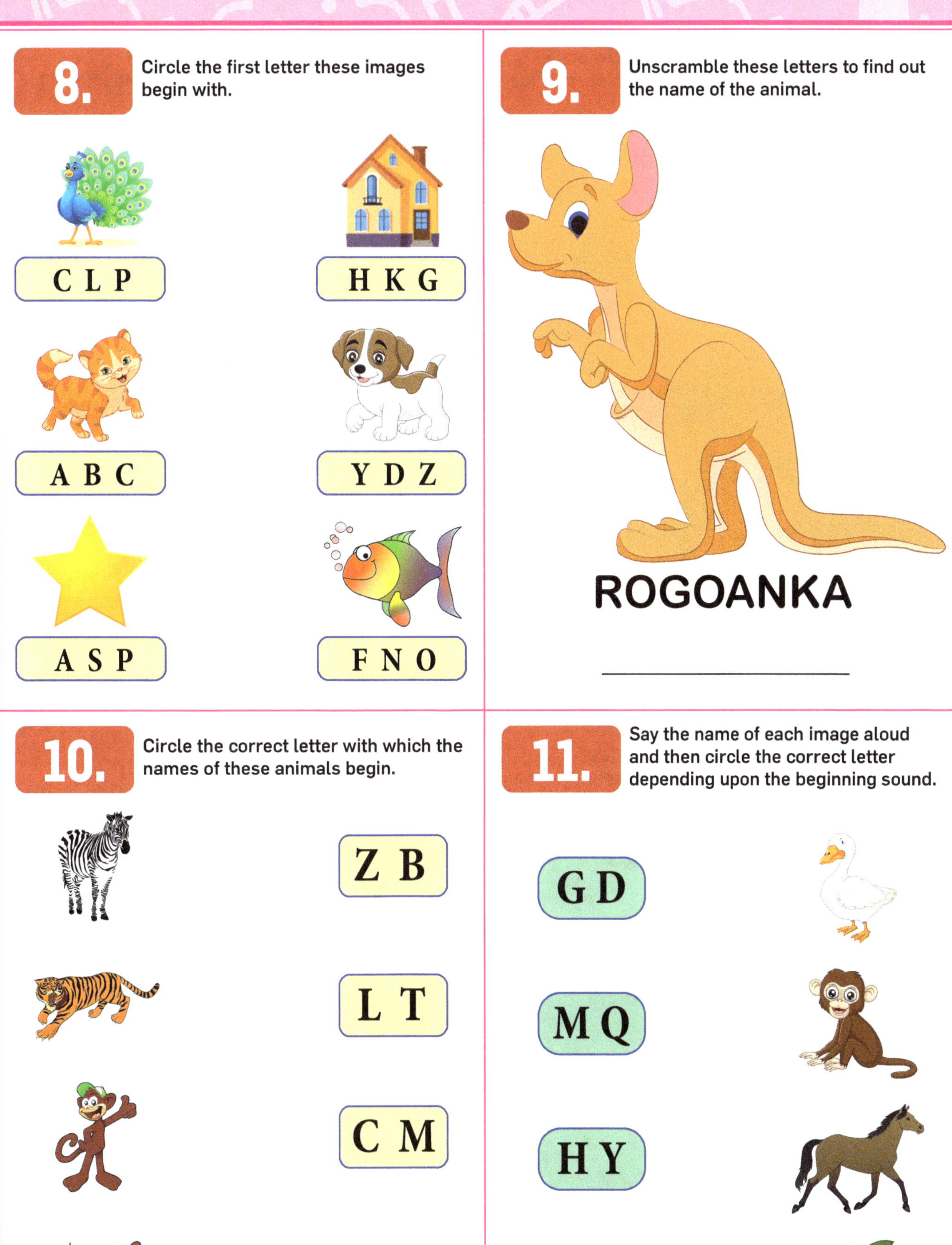

9. Unscramble these letters to find out the name of the animal.

____

10. Circle the correct letter with which the names of these animals begin.

11. Say the name of each image aloud and then circle the correct letter depending upon the beginning sound.

12.

Separate the citrus fruits from the non-citrus fruits and write them in the correct columns.

Pear

Grapes

Grapefruit

Orange

Pineapple

Apple

Citrus fruits	Non citrus fruits

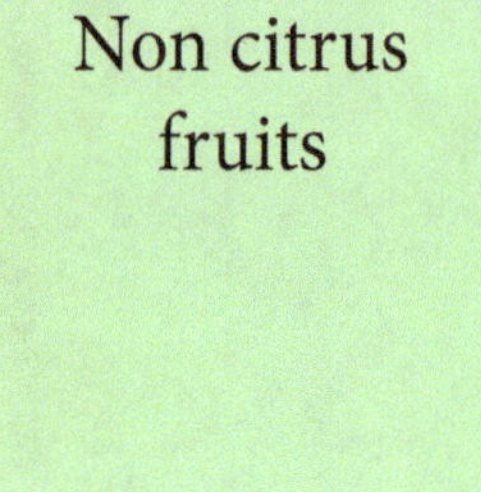

13.

Join the numbers and colour the bird.

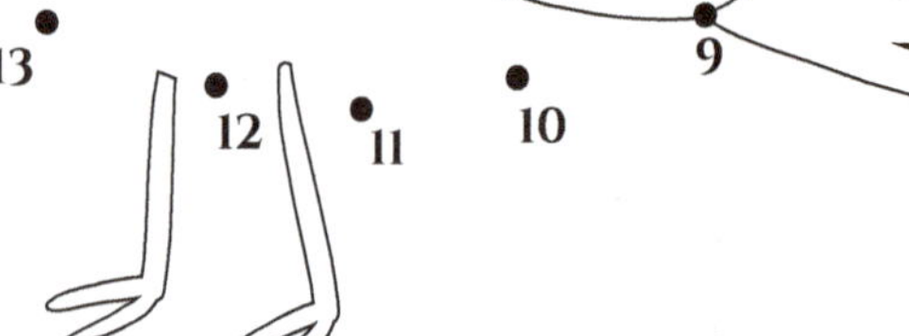

14.

Write the missing letters to complete the sentences.

usually did work worked got

1. I___________________ get up early but this morning.
2. I ___________________ up late 07.00 a.m.
3. We _________________ a lot of ____________ yesterday.
4. James has ________________ in a bank from 1999 to 2002.

15.

I am Danny and this is Daniel, my twin. Colour him the same as me.

16. Time to calculate!

4 + 4 =

3 x 3 =

9 ÷ 3 =

4 + 3 =

5 + 2 =

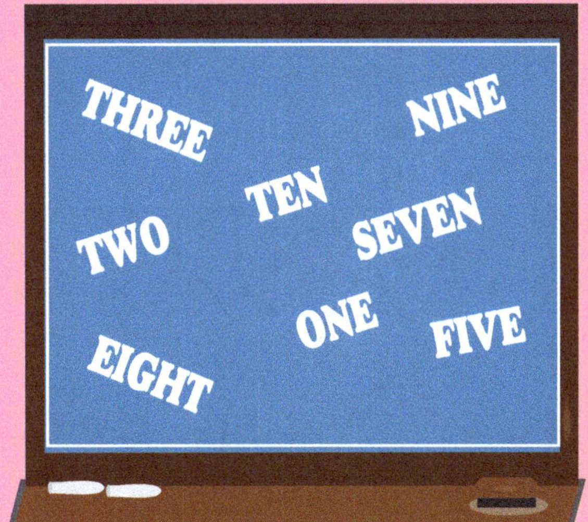

17.

Colour the numbers which adds upto the given numbers in the centre.

Centre 8: 2, 6, 3, 4, 5, 1

Centre 8: 3, 7, 4, 5, 6, 1, 8, 2

18. Can you spot all the words given in the word box in the grid below?

T	E	E	T	H	K	K	S	D	J	O	I
E	I	O	T	M	E	Y	E	P	I	N	S
K	E	E	T	H	K	K	S	D	H	A	I
E	N	O	T	M	E	Y	E	S	I	L	B
H	A	I	R	K	K	S	D	S	S	E	I
E	I	O	T	S	K	I	N	P	I	O	B
T	L	E	T	H	K	K	S	D	J	O	I
E	I	O	T	M	E	Y	E	P	I	T	B
T	E	E	T	N	O	S	E	D	J	H	I

HAIR SKIN NAIL TEETH NOSE EYES

19. Complete the series.

20. Colour the picture and write the name of the vegetable.

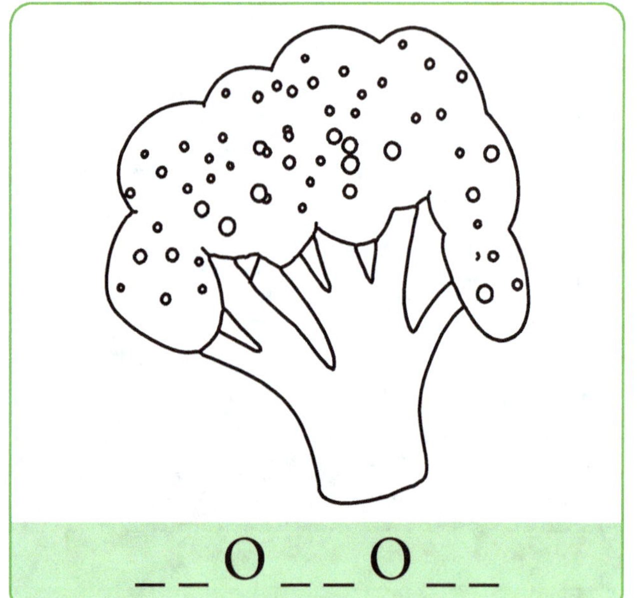

21. Match the word to the correct picture.

Giraffe

Goat

Key

Horse

22. Count the total number of objects and write the answer

23. Complete the following sentences.

1. The bird____________________ towards south.
   (Flat / Flew)

2. I had a glass of water since I was______________.
   (Thirsty / Think)

3. I _____________ to my best friend on the phone.
   (Walk / Talk)

4. The boat went very______________on the water.
   (Lost / Fast)

5. I like to eat popcorn when I watch a___________.
   (Movie / Move)

6. It is fun to go swimming in the_______________.
   (Pool / Poor)

24.

Help the tortoise reach the baby tortoise.

25.

Choose the best word to complete each sentence.

1.A ________ teaches the children.

2.A ________make us well.

3.A ________looks after our teeth.

4.A ________looks after the animals.

5.A ________drives a lorry.

6.A ________bakes bread.

Baker	Teacher	Doctor
Vet	Dentist	Driver

26.

Write the first letter of each picture.

____

____

____

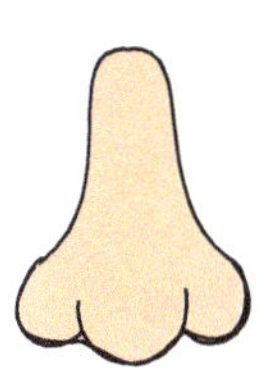

____

27.

Solve the sums given in each row.

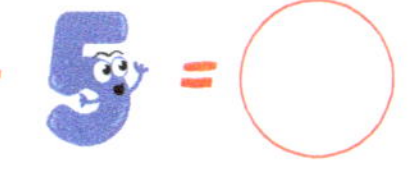

28. According to the weight, select the heavy or light animals. Write H for heavy and L for light.

W-300 grams [ ]

W-250 kilograms [ ]

W-10 kilograms [ ]

W-15 kilograms [ ]

W-300 kilograms [ ]

W-600 grams [ ]

29. Draw lines to join questions with their answers.

4x5	8+6	9-3	6+9

31. Match the animals to their feet.

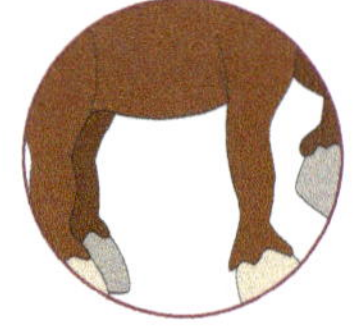

30. Match each object with either the recyclable or the non-recyclable bin.

32.

Unscramble the letters to find the name of each picture.

ORFG ____________

ITBBRA ____________

ERDE ____________

33.

Write the name of each water animal.

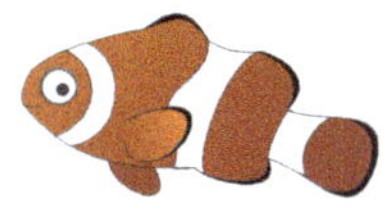

34.

Join these animals to their footprints.

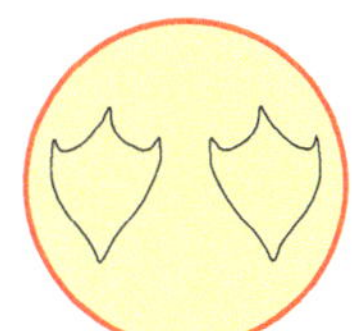

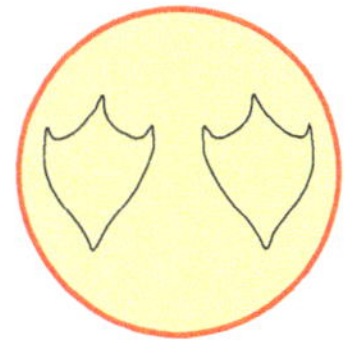

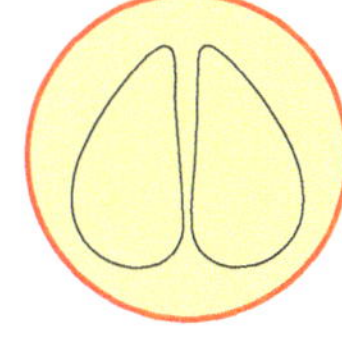

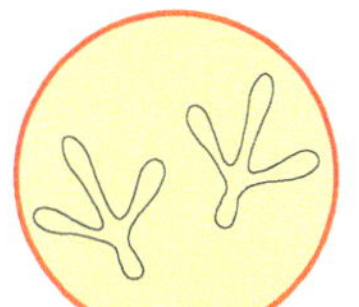

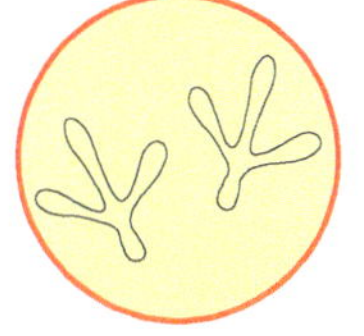

35.

Unscramble these letters to find out the names of these vegetables.

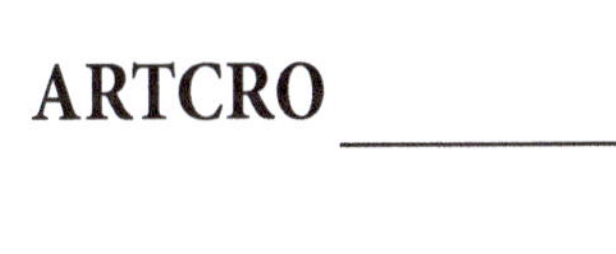

ARTCRO ____________

AEPS ____________

36. Match all the eyes below to their pairs.

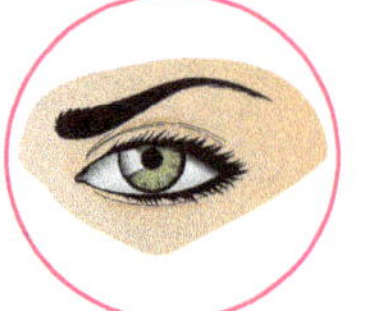
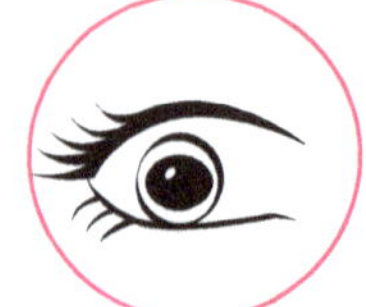

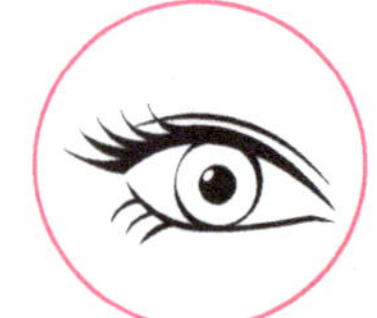

37. Find out the names of these fruits.

EPAPL

____

EATORMEWLN

____

EMPAONGRATE

____

38. I sometimes run, but I cannot walk. You always follow me around. What am I? Circle the correct answer.

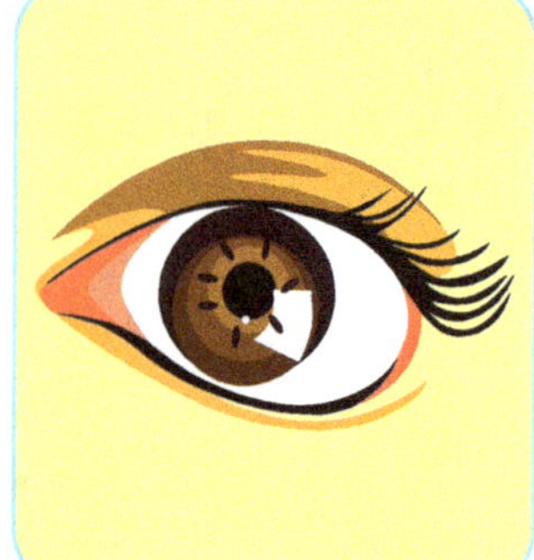
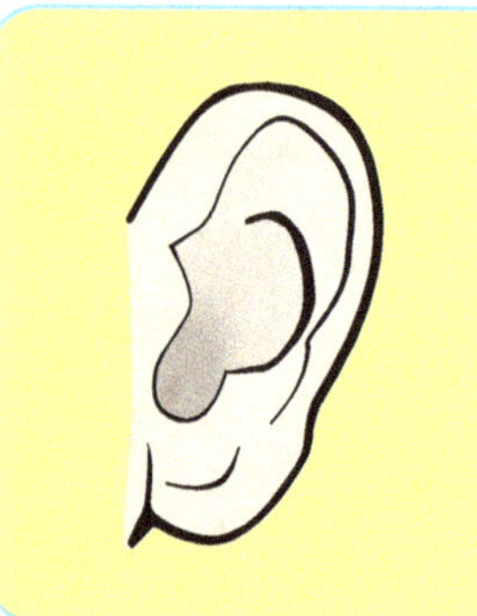
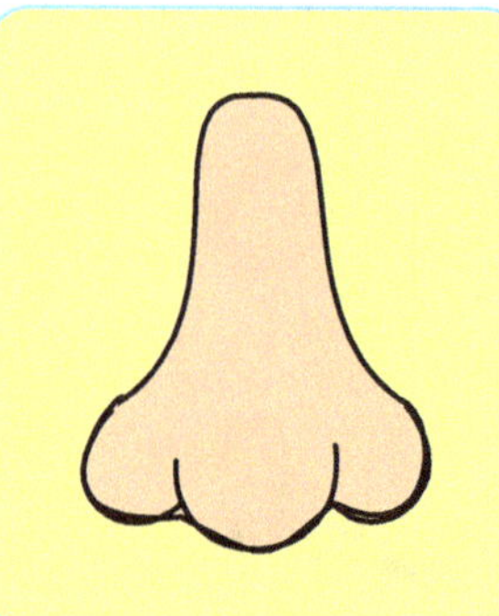

39. Fill in the blanks.

Jill had_____ bananas.

Mom gave her ____ bananas.

Now Jill has ______ bananas.

Mom

40.

If 5 bananas are deducted from the total number, how many bananas remain?

10-5= ◯

41.

Solve the multiplication sums.

5 x 2 = = ☐

7 x 2 = = ☐

8 x 2 = = ☐

9 x 2 = = ☐

6 x 2 = = ☐

42.

Solve the mirror sums.

☐ = 7+19

☐ 12+9=

☐ = 6+16

43.

Write the numbers that comes after.

44. Complete the puzzle.

3	+	9	=	
+		+		+
1	+	9	=	
=		=		=
	+		=	

45. Count the number of globes and tick the correct circle.

18 16 17

46. Match the following.

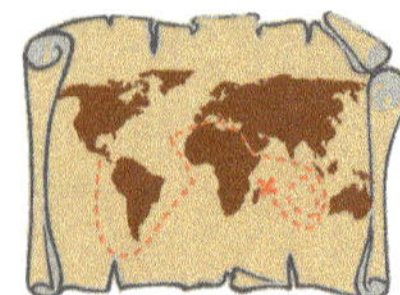

MAP

CAT

MAT

FAN

47. Draw a circle around the images that start with the letter C.

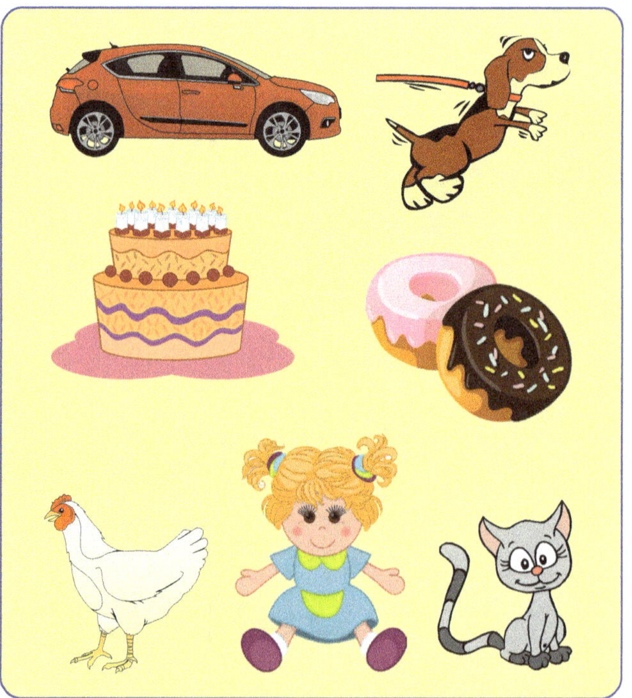

48. Complete the crossword with the help of the images given.

49. Complete the words.

50. Write the missing alphabets.

51. Trace the words and colour the pictures.

52. How many rockets do you see?

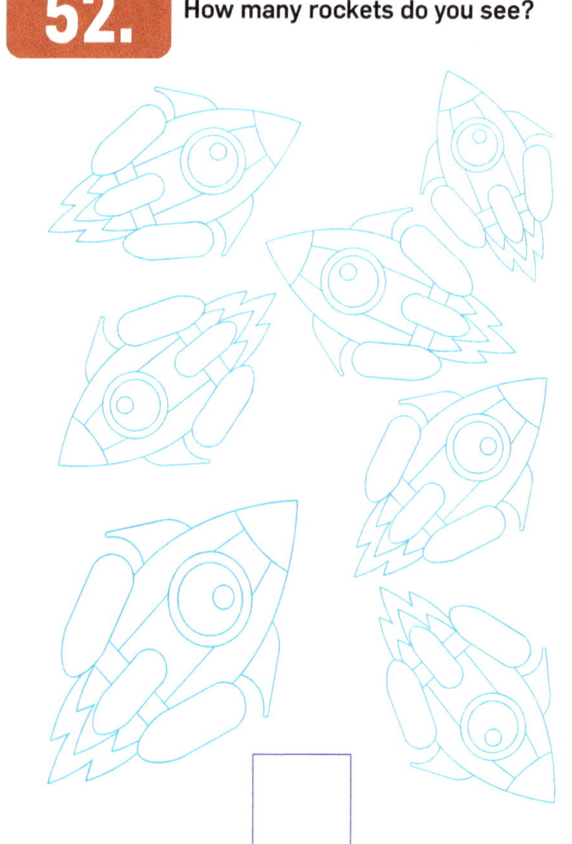
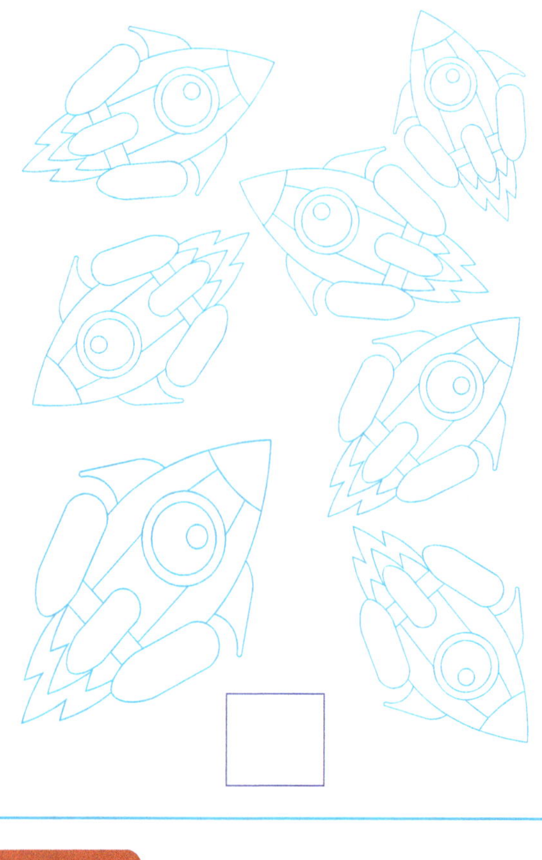

53. Colur the picture. It is used in the winter season. Name it.

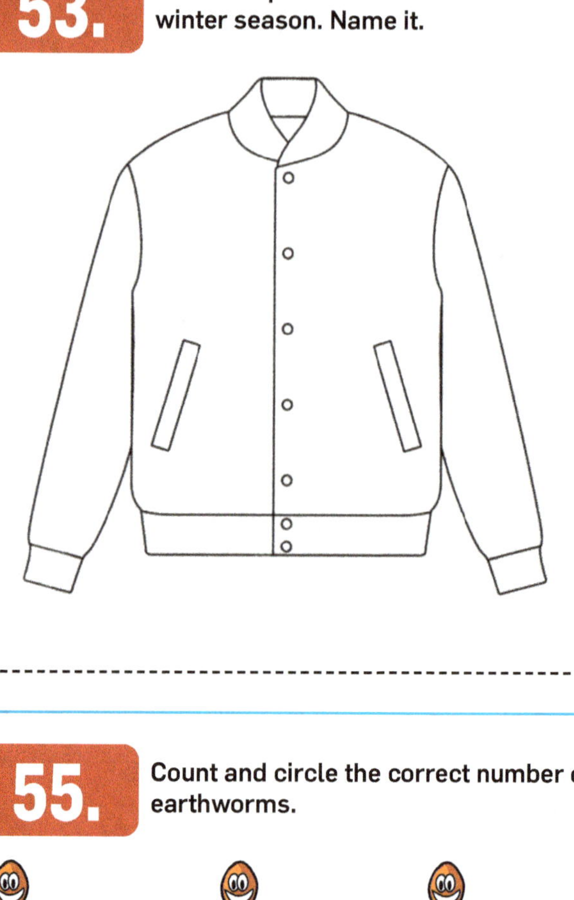

----

54. Calculate the sums using the given clues. Write the answer in the blank boxes.

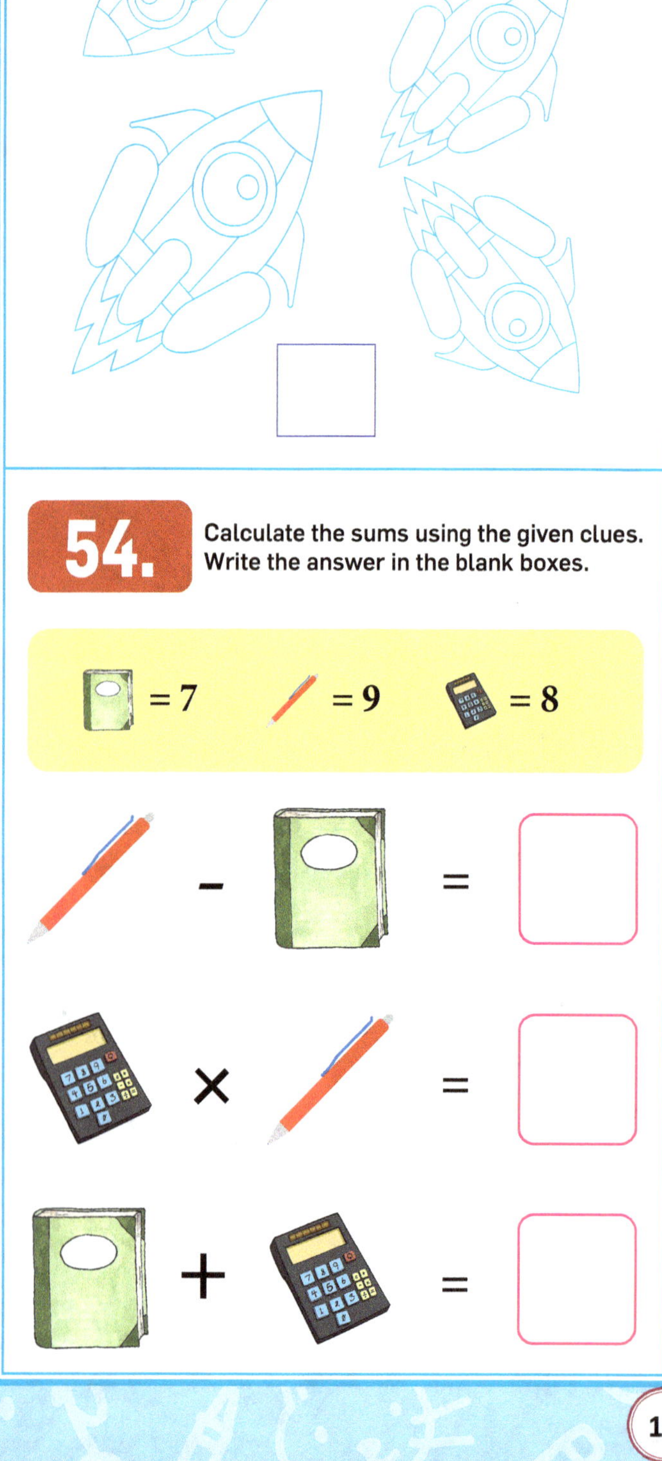

55. Count and circle the correct number of earthworms.

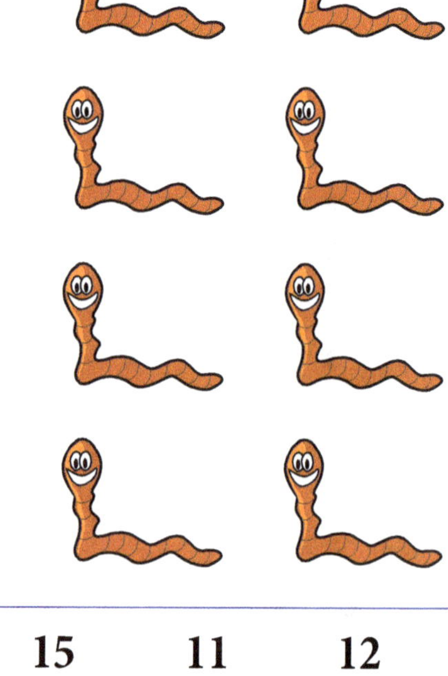

14	15	11	12

56. Our body is made up of three main parts. Match the words with the correct part of the boy's body.

57. Complete the christmas tree.

58. Write the number of objects you see in every card.

59. Count the images and write whether they're even or odd.

60. Match the following pictures with the appropriate senses.

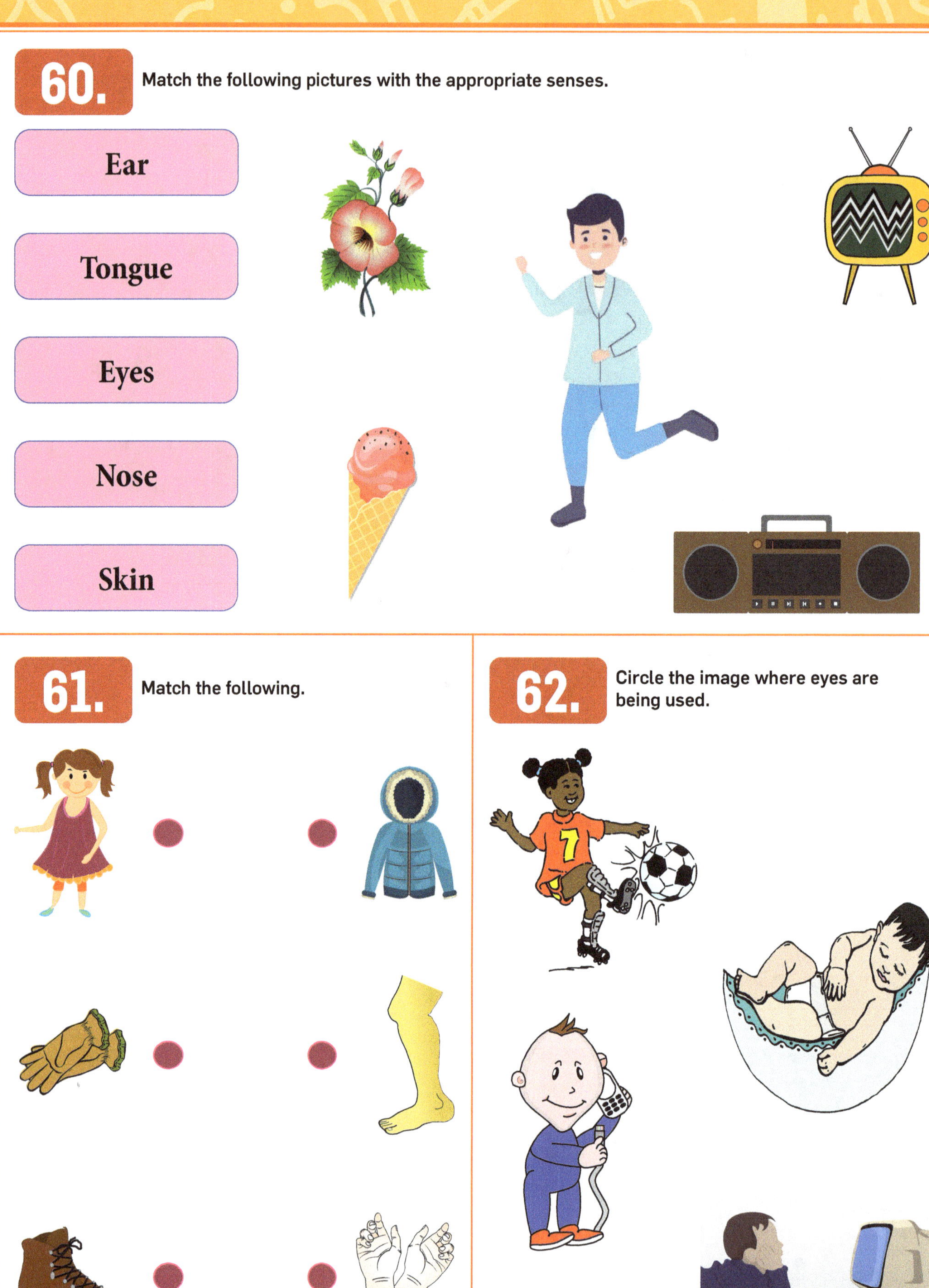

61. Match the following.

62. Circle the image where eyes are being used.

63. Solve the following multiplication sums.

$$\begin{array}{r} 4 \\ \times 7 \\ \hline \end{array} \quad \begin{array}{r} 6 \\ \times 6 \\ \hline \end{array} \quad \begin{array}{r} 2 \\ \times 5 \\ \hline \end{array} \quad \begin{array}{r} 9 \\ \times 4 \\ \hline \end{array} \quad \begin{array}{r} 3 \\ \times 5 \\ \hline \end{array}$$

64. Colour the cat that has the largest answer to the sum written on it.

65. Circle the animal that bleats.

66. Complete the series.

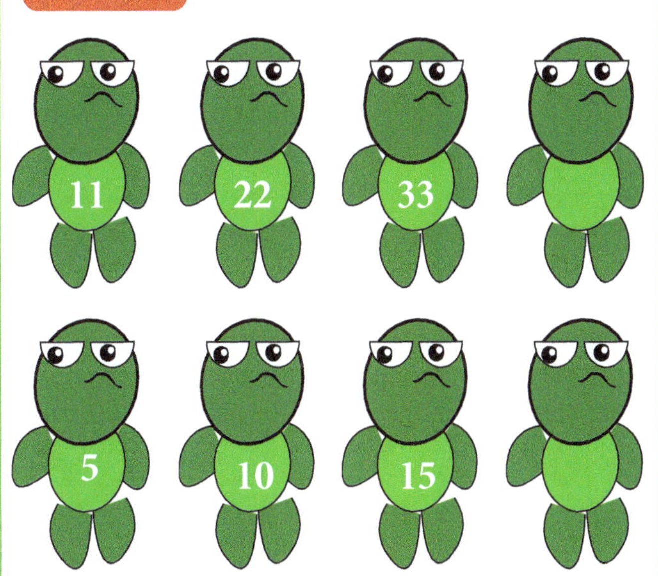

67. Colour the tree with the letter N.

68. Help the chick find its mother.

69. Say the names of the pictures in each row aloud. Colour the pictures that rhyme.

70. Circle the things that have the letter 'a' in their names and cross the things that have the letter 'e' in their name.

71. Complete the series.

72. Complete the sentences with This or That.

1. ____________ is a globe.
2. ___________ is a wall chart.
3. ____________ is a computer.
4. ____________ is a painter.
5. ____________ is my bedroom.
6. ____________ is my sister's bedroom.
7. ____________ is a helicopter.
8. ____________ is a plane.

73. Form a sentence using these words and colour the picture.

____

74. Look at the pictures and complete the sentences.

1. Our_________help us to see.
2. Our_________help us to hear.
3. Our_________helps us to feel.
4. Our_________helps us to smell.
5. Our_________helps us to taste.

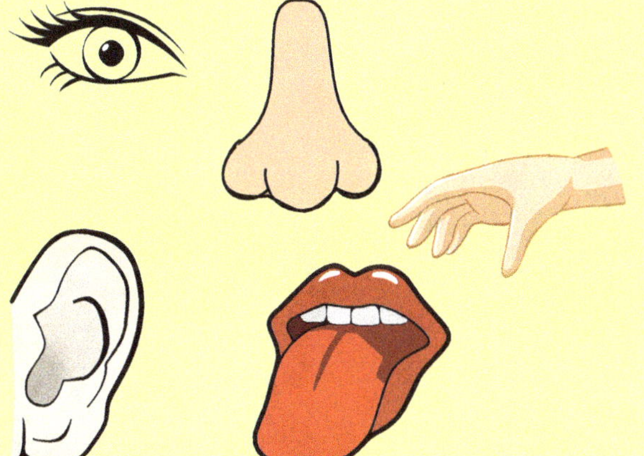

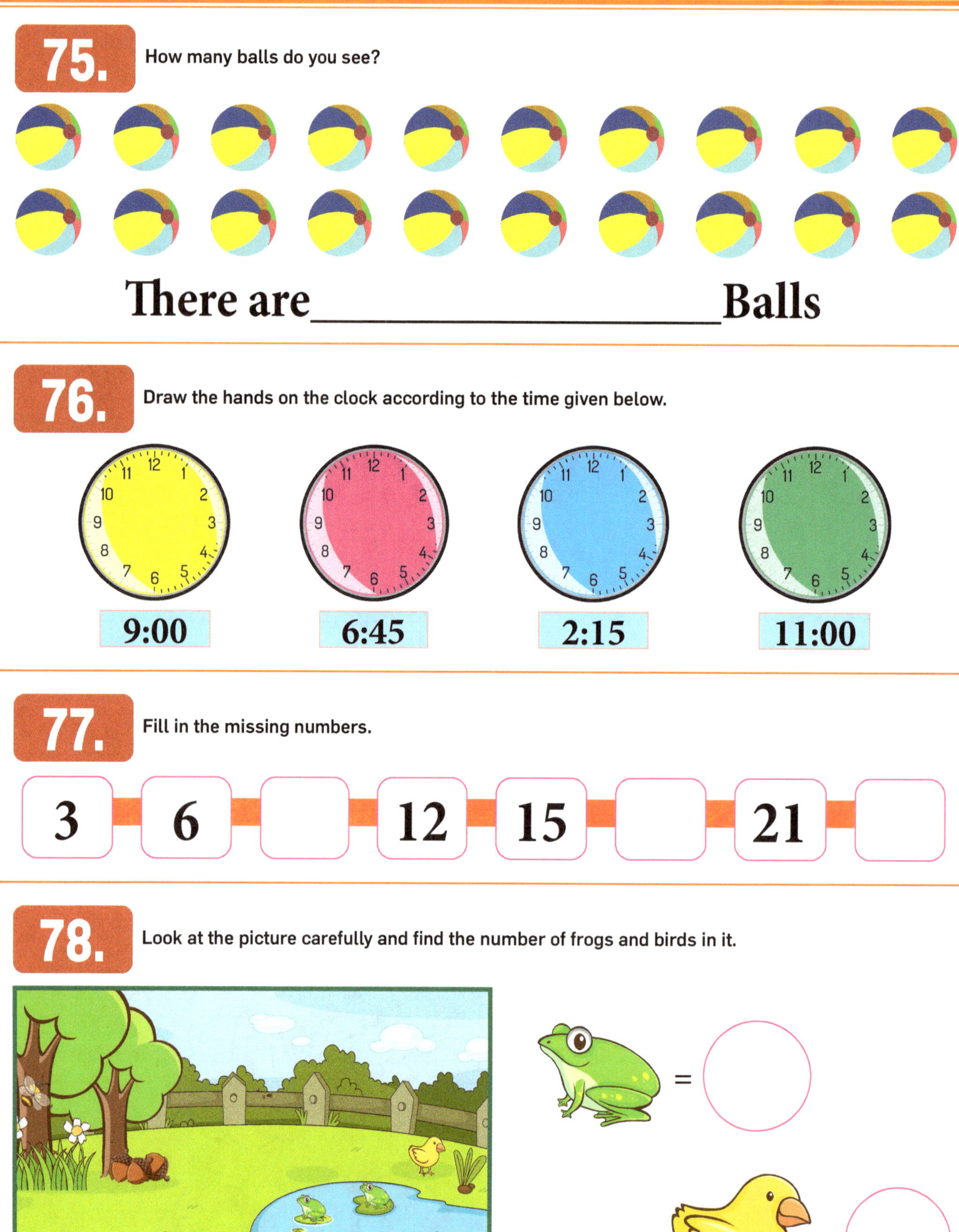

75.

How many balls do you see?

There are ____________________ Balls

76.

Draw the hands on the clock according to the time given below.

9:00 | 6:45 | 2:15 | 11:00

77.

Fill in the missing numbers.

3	6		12	15		21	

78.

Look at the picture carefully and find the number of frogs and birds in it.

=

=

79. Complete the sentences using 'is' or 'are' and arranging them in the correct order. One has already been done for you.

1. at school / your children?
2. the shops / open today?
3. interested in football / you?
4. at home / your mother?
5. this pizza/delicious?

1. Are your children at school?
2. ______________________________
3. ______________________________
4. ______________________________
5. ______________________________

80. The sky changes colours at different times. Read the sentences and colour the sky accordingly

A clear sky with lots of kites flying.

Sky on a rainy day with the sun hidden behind the sky.

81. Fill the blanks with words that rhyme with 'CAN' and 'NET'. Say all these words out loud.

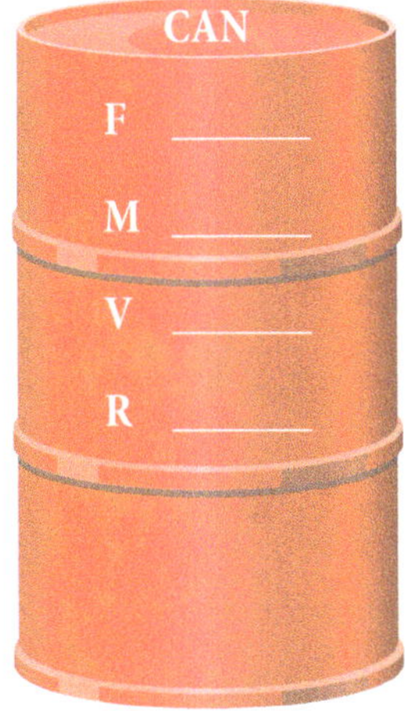

82. Write the beginning letter of each word.

_OOK

_OAT

_OOR

_OX

_AT

83.

How many creatures do you see?

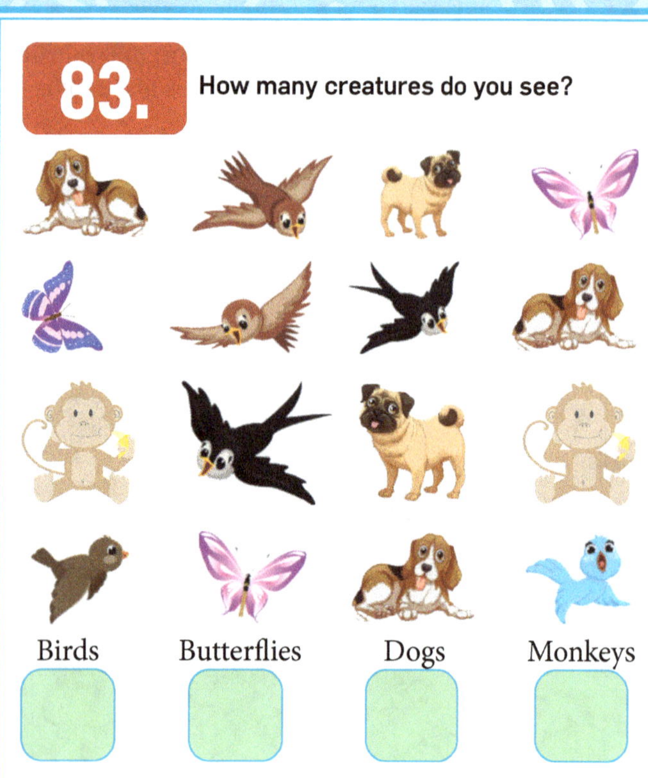

84.

Spot the biggest star and circle it.

85.

Next, circle the smallest candy.

86.

Lastly, circle the biggest pencil.

87.

Help the animals get their ears back.

88.

Circle the correct sound associated with the pictures.

89. Complete the sequence of numbers.

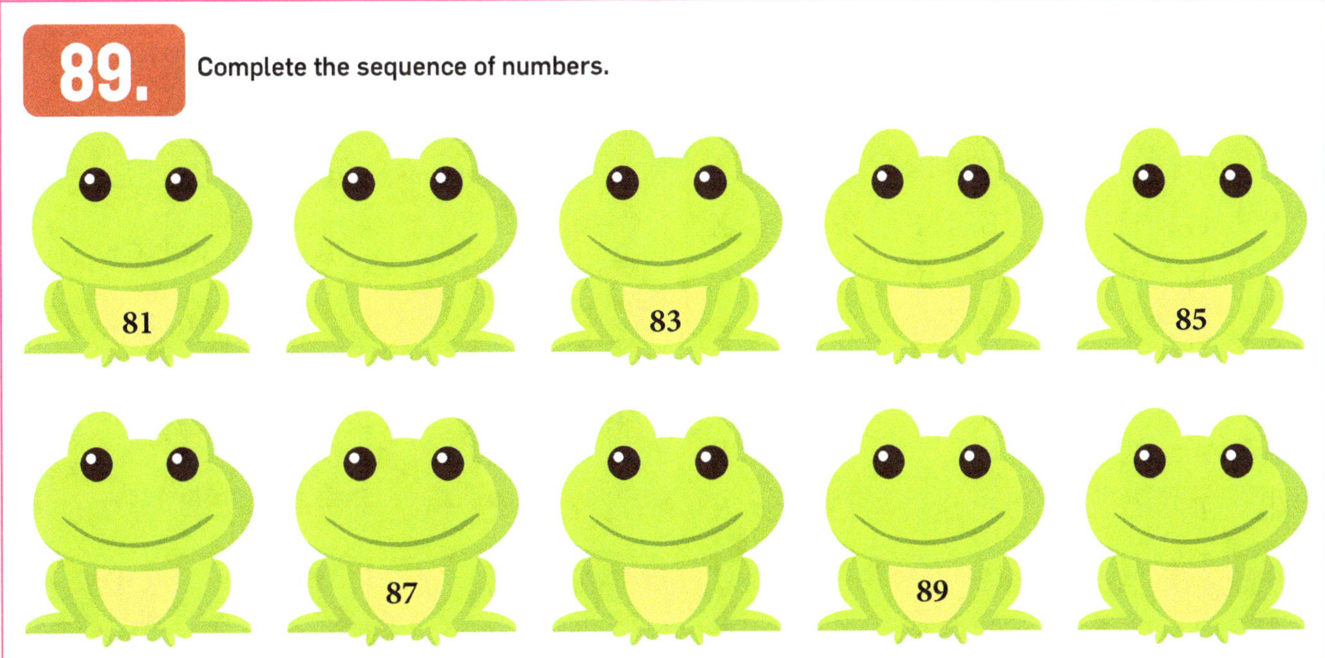

90. Count the images below and tick the correct answer.

91. Circle the Santas holding even numbers.

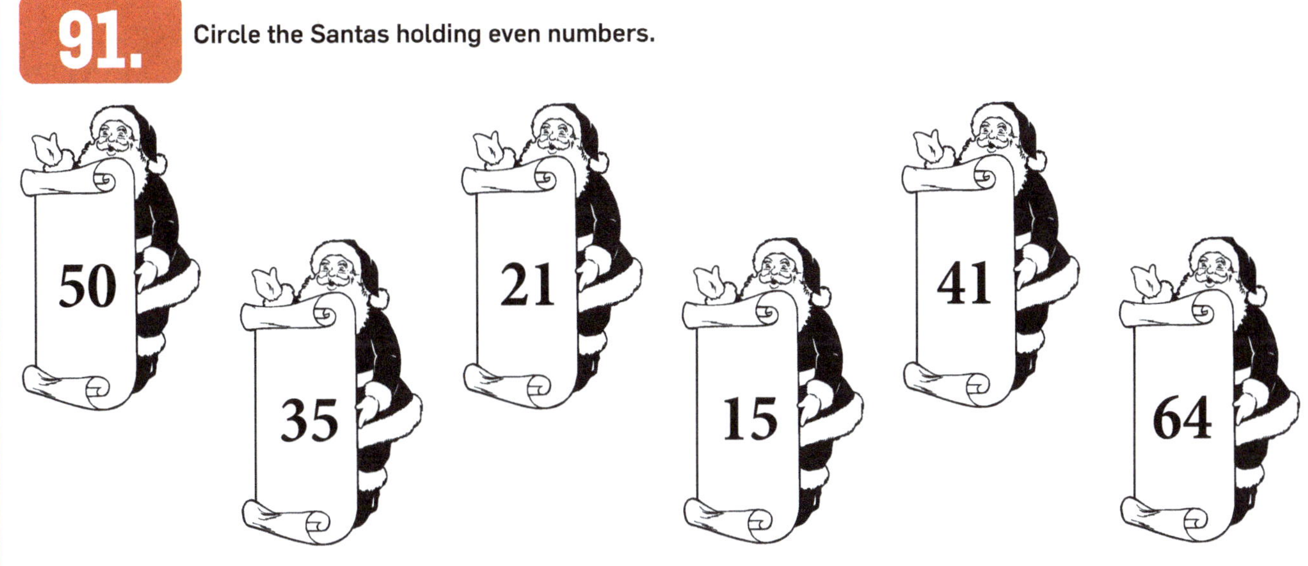

92. Find the words given in the orange box in the yellow grid.

S	T	U	V	W	R	Y	Z	A
F	G	H	I	B	E	E	V	X
N	K	P	E	N	D	K	L	M
S	G	I	N	W	I	Y	Z	S
J	R	L	T	N	P	H	Q	R
A	A	C	D	E	S	C	D	E
T	P	G	H	I	H	O	Z	X
S	E	U	F	W	X	Y	Z	S
J	S	L	M	N	O	P	Q	R
A	B	I	R	D	S	C	D	E

KITE PEN BEE SPIDER
FISH BIRD GRAPES

93. Look at the pictures below and fill in the blanks.

1. The monkey is eating _______________.
2. The _____________ is playing with a mouse.
3. The _____________ is singing.
4. The _____________ is sitting on the tree.
5. The _______________ is in the kennel.

94. Write the first letter of each picture in the box next to it, and rearrange the letters to form a new word.

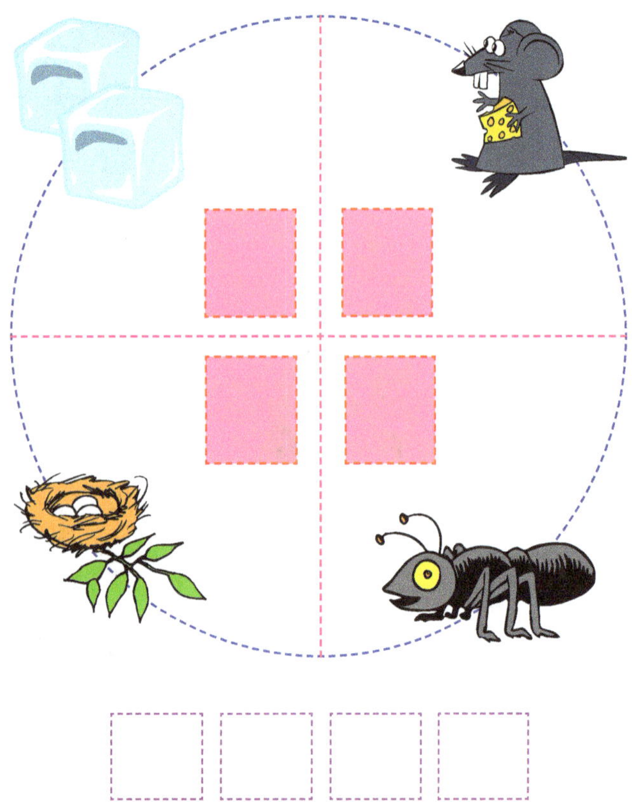

95. Look at the picture and fill the blanks using vowels.

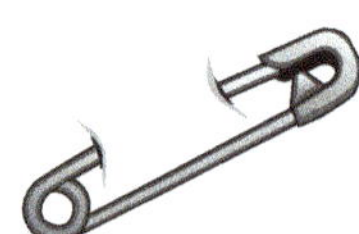
p n

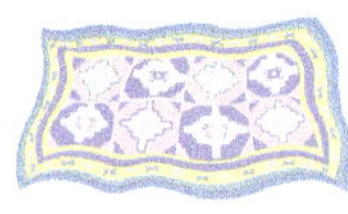
m t

n t

b n

p t

l ck

s n

h n

h ll

96.

Colour the picture according to the shades assigned to the numbers mentioned.

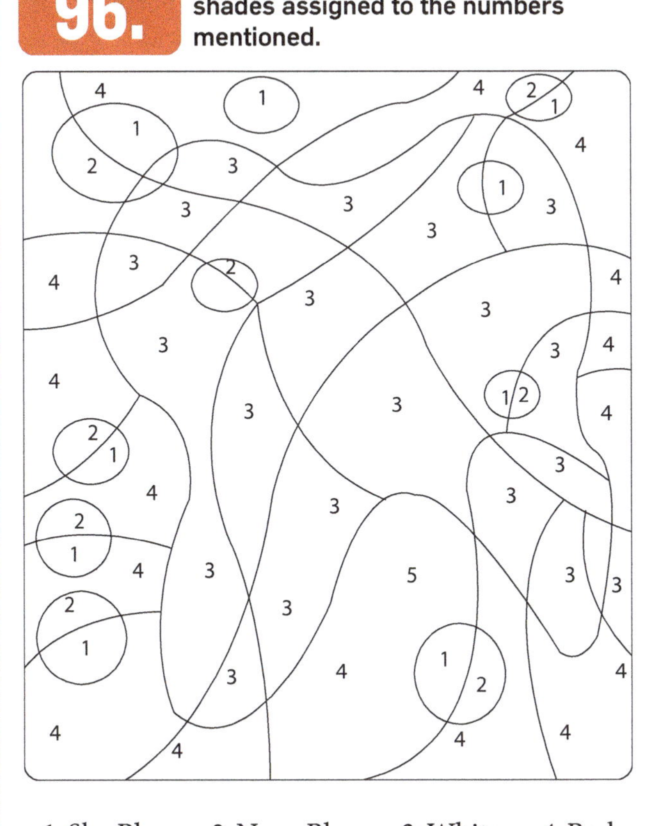

1-Sky Blue 2-Navy Blue 3-White 4-Red

97.

Look at the pictures and complete the crossword.

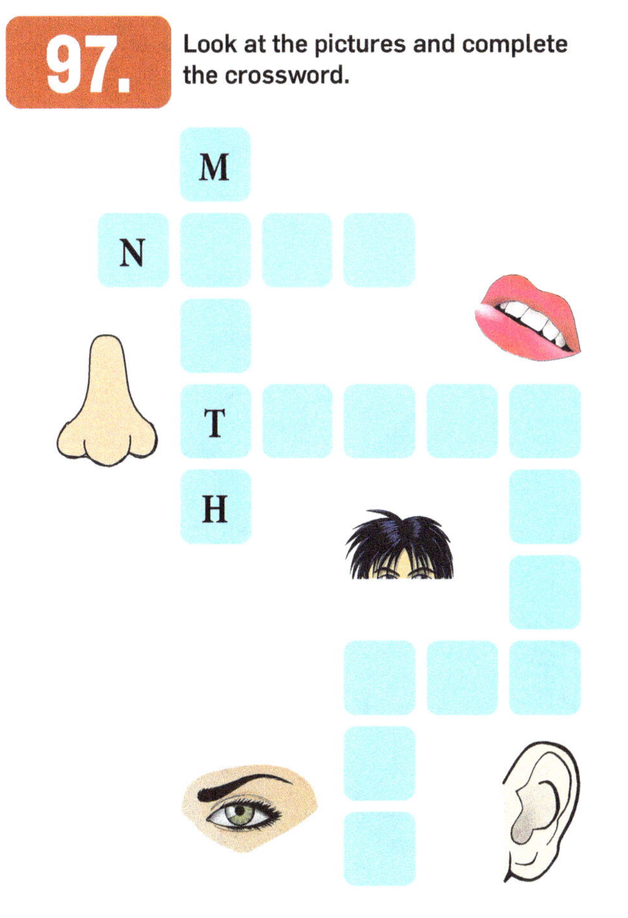

98.

Look at the picture and circle the odd one in each row.

99. How many papers, books, and pencils do you see?

100. Colour the car with even number on it.

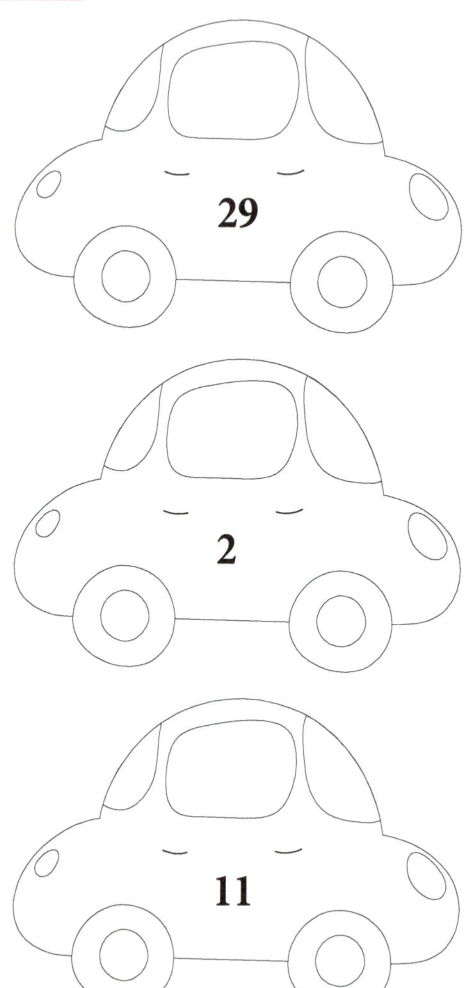

101. Which number comes before 19 and after 22?

102. Tick the words that show the correct movement of these living beings.

Swim Crawl

Hop Walk

Fly Swim

103. Fill in the correct initial letter.

104. Read the story. Then write the correct noun in the blank.

Tony and his family arrive at the lake. A boat takes them to sea. They catch many fish. Tony's family enjoy fishing very much. They are happy.

1. Tony and his family arrive at the ______________.
2. A ______________ take them to sea.
3. They catch many ______________.
4. Tony and his family enjoy __________ very much.
5. Tony and his ______________ are very happy.

105. Help the astronaut get back to the rocket.

106. Add '-es' to the words given below to change them into their plural forms.

Fill in the blanks with the plurals of the following.

Fox ________________________

Mango ________________________

Watch ________________________

Brush ________________________

Dress ________________________

Glass ________________________

Zero ________________________

Wish ________________________

107. Colour all the unhealthy foods.

108. Take away or add letter in the problem below to spell the name of the animal.

TEA-EA+URN-N+TLEA-A

= ______________________________

109. Help the brush reach the tooth through the maze!

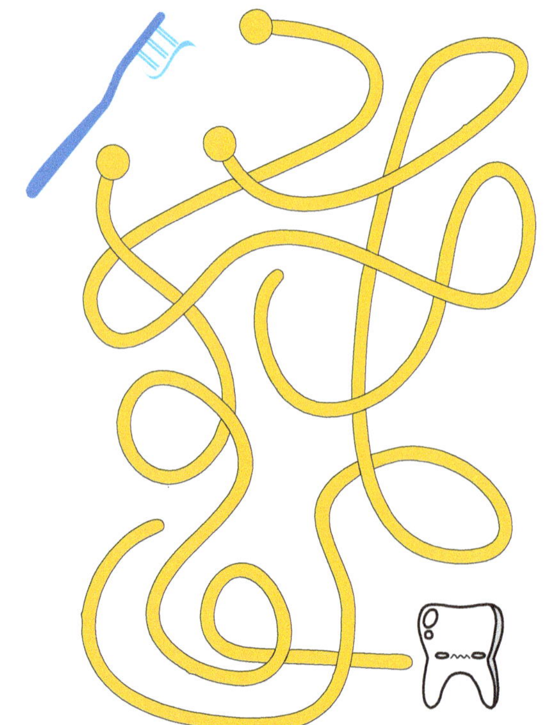

110. Name and colour the fruits below.

____

____

111. Solve the sums.

112. Solve the mathematical operations and circle the ones whose answer is 30.

4 + 8 =

19 x 5 =

15 x 2 =

16 + 3 =

13 + 17 =

113. Trace the grey line and find an animal that no longer exists. Can you name it?

114.

A pronoun is used to replace a noun. Use the pronouns in the given word box to complete the sentences.

We, I, They, or You.

1. Maria and I are going to the playground. _________ will be walking till there.
2. Ron is in the park. Will ____ be going there too?
3. Harry is getting the mop for me. _______ am going to clean the floor.
4. Martin and Jamie are so hungry! ________ will eat a watermelon.

115.

Complete the names of the vegetables given below.

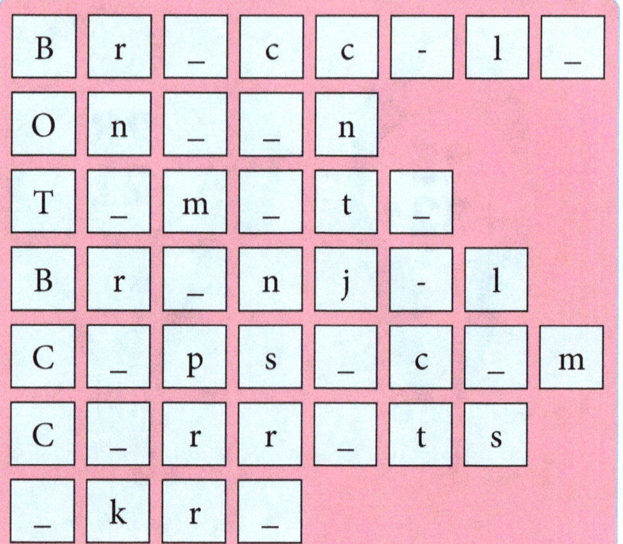

B	r	_	c	c	-	l	_
O	n	_	_	n			
T	_	m	_	t	_		
B	r	_	n	j	-	l	
C	_	p	s	_	c	_	m
C	_	r	r	_	t	s	
_	k	r	_				

116.

We use 'this' when we refer to a single object that is near and 'that' when we refer to a single thing that is far away. Can you use this and that in the sentences below?

1. _______________ is a cat.
   _______________ is a dog.

2. ____________ is my House.
   ____________ is a hospital.

3. ___________ doll belongs to me.
   __________ airplane belongs to my sister.

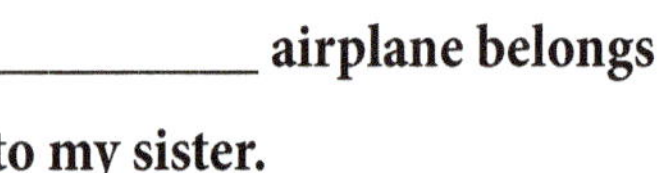

117.

How many words can you create by joining the given words?

COW	HOUSE
	HAT
	BOY
WIND	BALL
	MORE
	MOVE
FOOT	CAKE
	HOPE
	MILL
RAIN	DANCE
	FALL
LIGHT	COAT

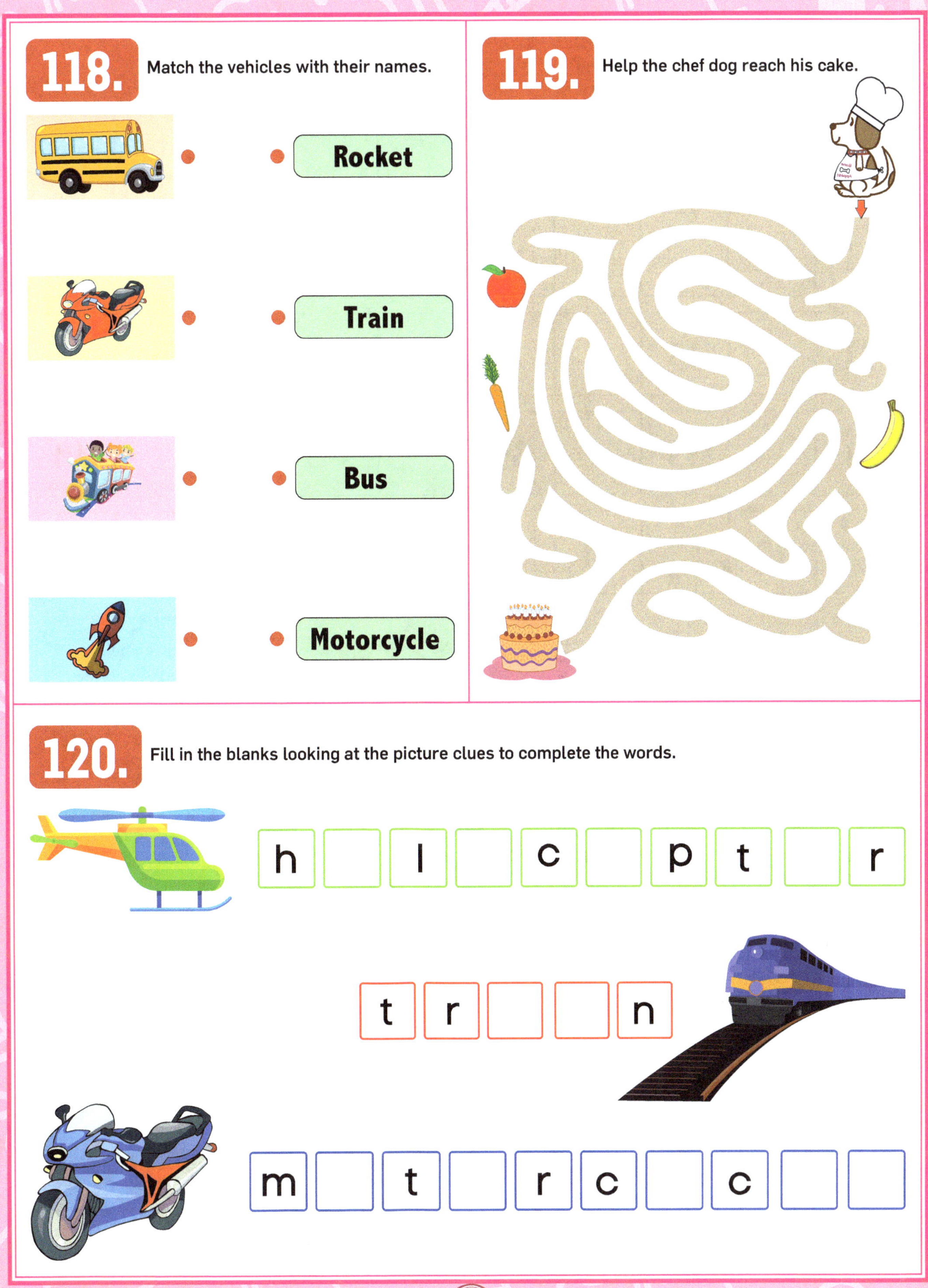

118. Match the vehicles with their names.
Rocket
Train
Bus
Motorcycle
119. Help the chef dog reach his cake.
120. Fill in the blanks looking at the picture clues to complete the words.
h l c p t r
t r n
m t r c c

121. Write the missing numbers.

1		3		5			8		10
11				15		17	18	19	
21		23			26			29	
31		33		35			38		40
	42		44			47		49	

122. Count the frogs, circle the correct number and then colour them.

7

8

5

6

123. Add 6 to the apples given below and circle the basket with the correct number.

14

12

124. Find the days of a week in the word search puzzle below.

S	F	R	I	D	A	Y	Z	S
F	A	H	I	B	E	E	W	A
N	T	T	E	N	D	K	E	T
S	G	I	U	W	I	Y	D	U
M	O	N	D	A	Y	H	N	R
A	A	C	D	E	D	C	E	D
T	U	E	S	D	A	Y	S	A
S	E	U	F	W	X	Y	D	Y
J	S	U	N	D	A	Y	A	R
T	H	U	R	S	D	A	Y	E

125. Circle the correct number of dinosaurs you see below.

8 12 9 10

126. Find the following words in the word puzzle.

Sand Towel Seaweed
Sun Birds

d	f	h	i	t	a	b
b	i	f	u	o	x	i
q	c	s	o	w	z	r
s	e	a	w	e	e	d
u	c	n	h	l	o	s
n	v	d	j	k	p	i
q	m	s	x	d	e	a
p	i	u	f	n	k	q

127. Write the vowels in the flower petals.

128. Match the word that describes the activities shown in the photos.

Running

Walking

Dancing

129. Unscramble these letters to find the names of insects.

TAN	
EBE	
SRDEPI	
MRWO	
NLISA	
ETLEBE	
LLRACPETRI	

130. Match the picture with its respective leg.

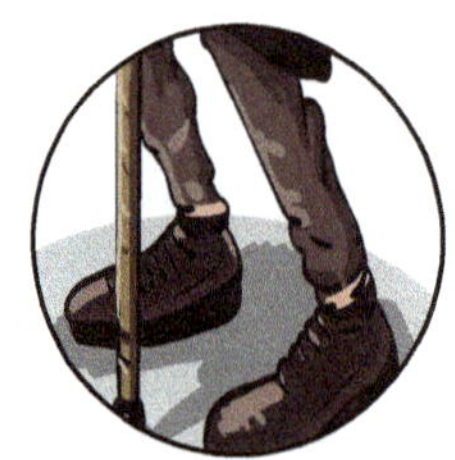

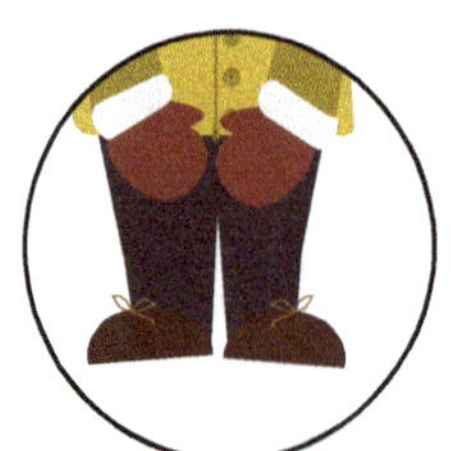

131. Match each picture with the correct sentence.

I allow you to walk without getting hurt.

I protect your head from harsh weather.

I allow you to listen to the music.

132. Arrange the picture according to the sequence.

				1

133. If we add 9 more into the group of 6 cups, how many cups will we have?

6+___=

134. Colour the cows containing odd numbers.

135. Colour the deer using the given numerical codes.

1 2 3 4 5 6

136. Help the bee reach her honeycomb.

137. Plants that grow along the ground are called creepers. Such plants have weak stems. Match the following creepers with their names.

PUMPKIN PLANT

POTATO PLANT

WATERMELON PLANT

138. Fill in the blanks with vowels.

s____n

t____n

m____g

b____n

b____g

p____t

c____n

b____d

p____n

139. Say the sounds of the letters shown on each brush. Make new words on the cans with the sound.

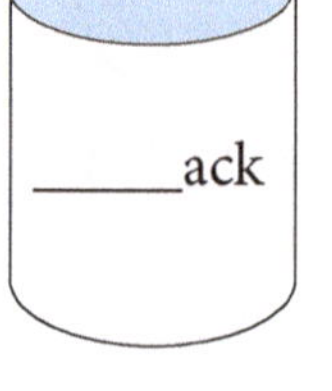
_____ack

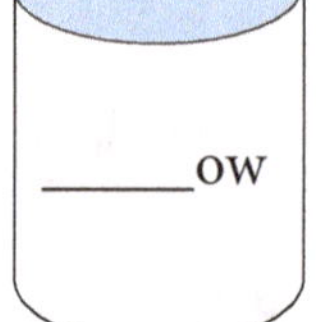
_____ow

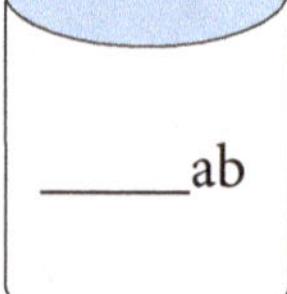
_____ab

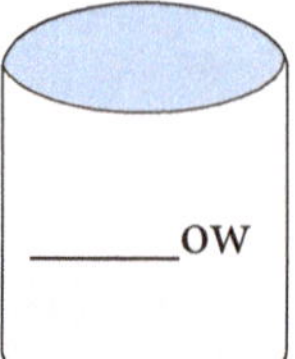
_____ow

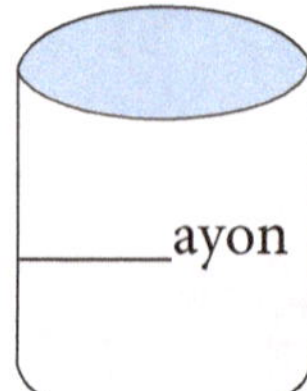
_____ayon

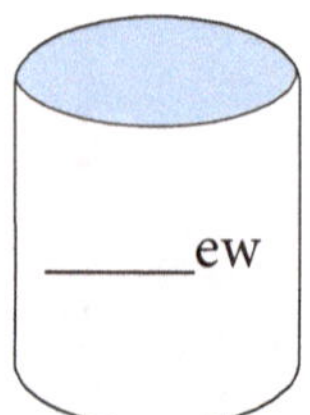
_____ew

140. Colour the picture according to the shades associated with the given numbers.

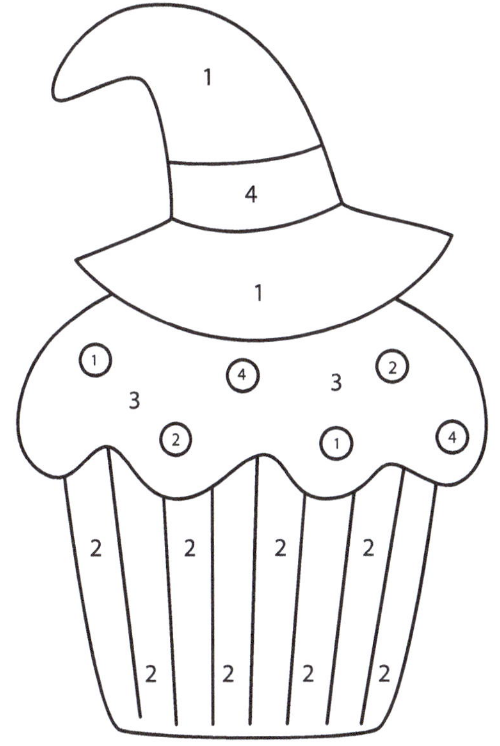

1 - 2 - 3 - 4 -

141. Help James figure out which fruit he will be able to find his way to.

142. Unscramble the letters to write the names of these body parts.

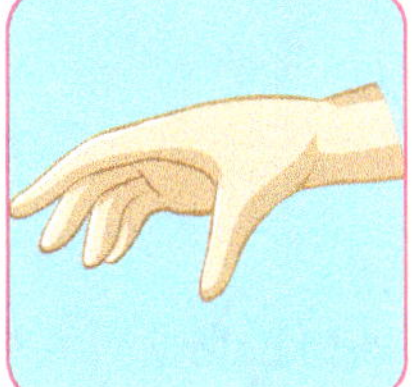

nahd

____

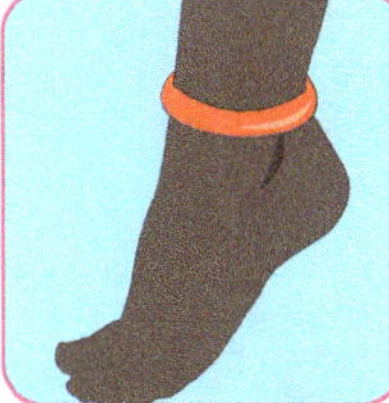

otof

____

boen

____

143. Write the first letter of each picture and find the two body parts.

1. __ O __ E

2. __ O __ E

144. Count the total number of bears and subtract the ones which have a cross on them to solve the sum.

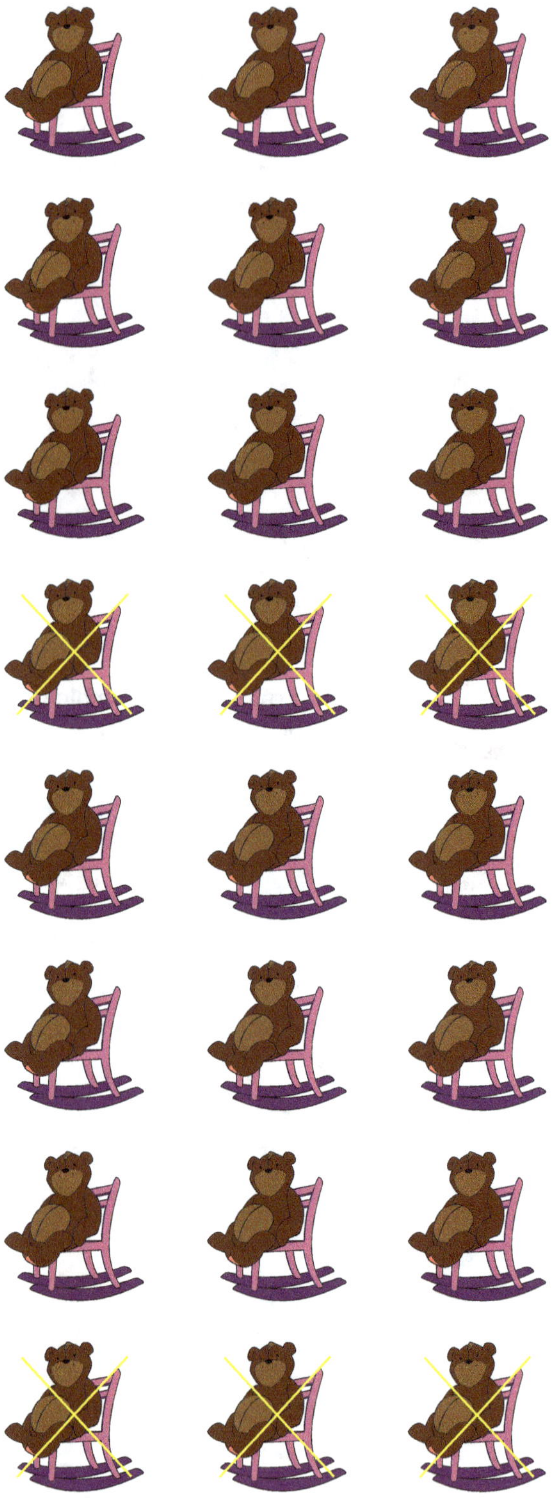

24 - 6 = ○

145. How many different kinds of flowers do you see?

146. Use red to colour the circles with even numbers.

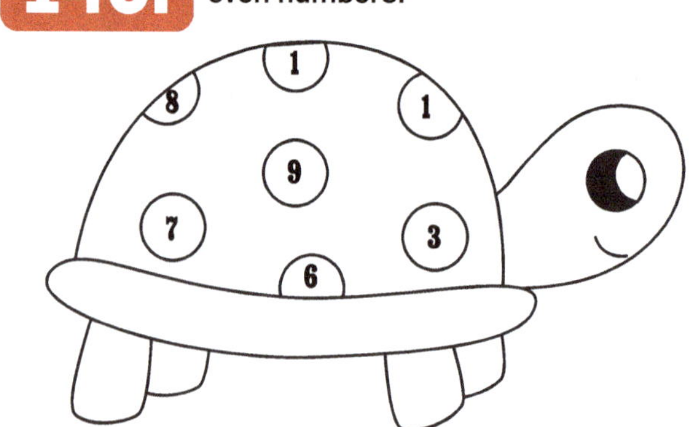

147. Solve the sums in the grid below.

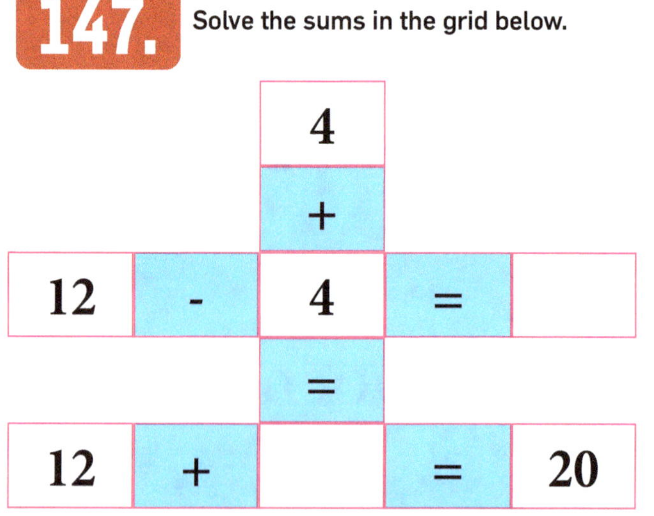

148.

Colour the house according to the shades given for the mentioned numbers.

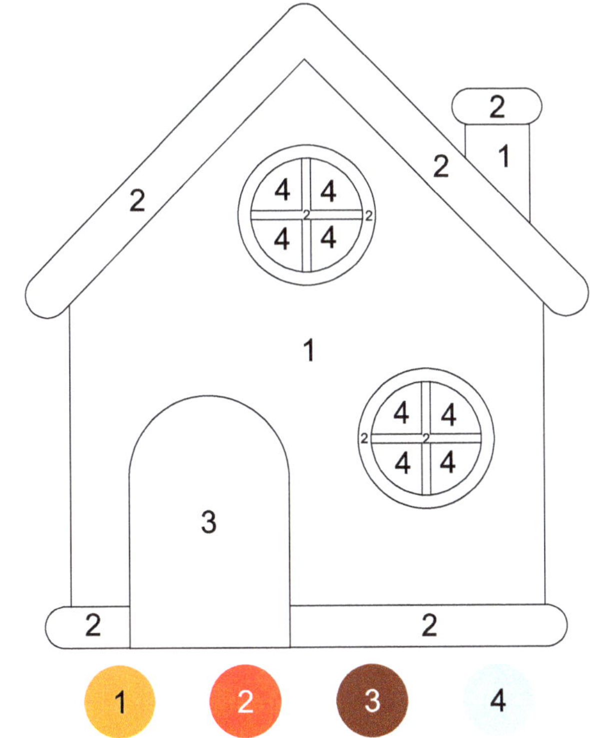

149.

Complete the crossword

Seat Rules Maths Grades

Reading Playground Locker

150.

Learn how a seed transforms into a big plant.

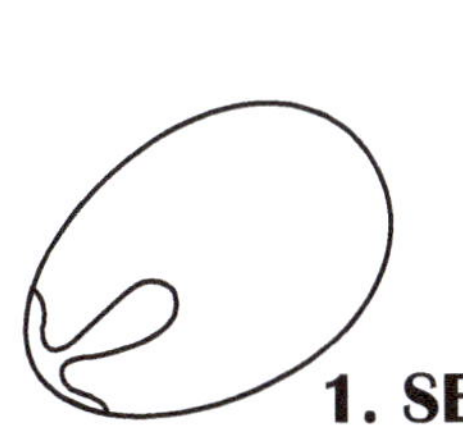

1. SEEDS

2. BUD

3. SPROUTS

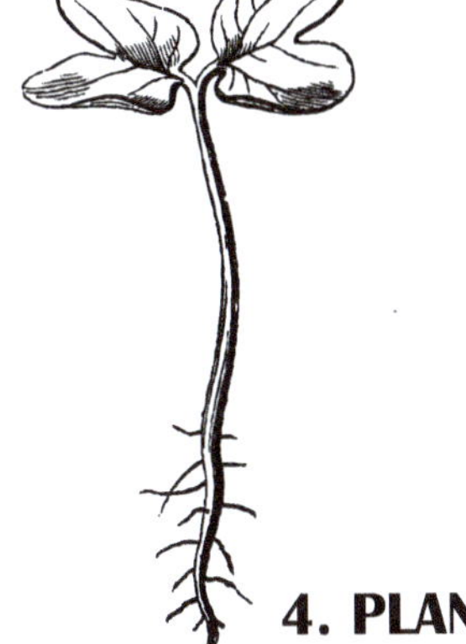

4. PLANT

151.

Write and match the correct words to its picture.

152. Rearrange the letters of these images to make a word.

LPSIEGNE ____________

PAML ________

ALMUBELR ____________

EIKT ______

153. Write the names of the body parts and match them with the correct image.

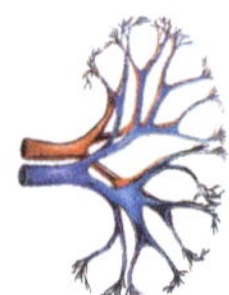

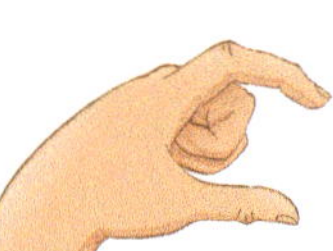

CENK ____________

ENKE ____________

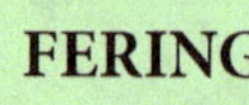

FERING ____________

SNIVE ____________

WOBLE ____________

HFDEAOER ____________

154. Fill in the blanks with the correct helping verbs.

is

are

am

Hi! I __________ Sam. This _____ my home. My sister's name _____ Martha and, these ____________ my parents.

My father_________ a scientist and, my mother _______ a teacher.

They both _____ very kind and, smart. I ______ always learning a lot from them.

We_____________ so happy to meet you!

155. Name the different parts of an arm using the word bank.

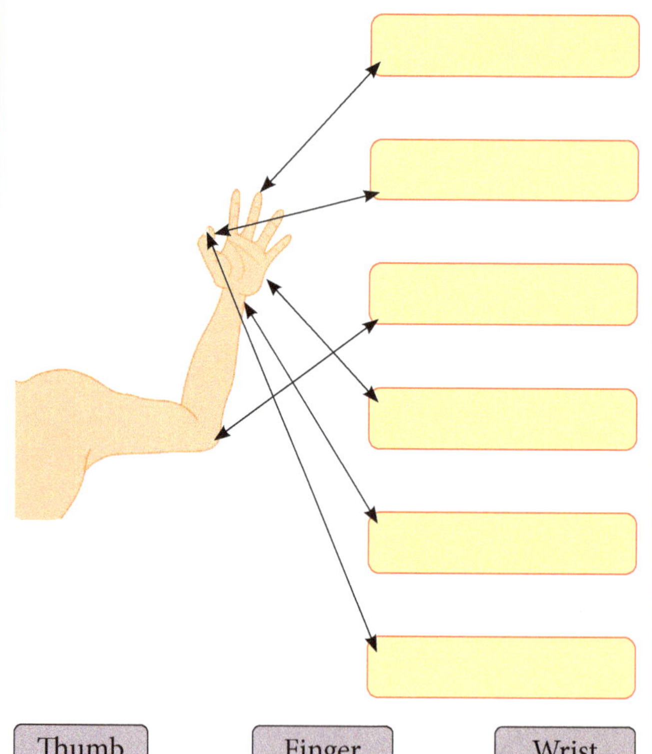

Thumb	Finger	Wrist
Nail	Elbow	Hand

156. Match the word with the correct sense.

SEE

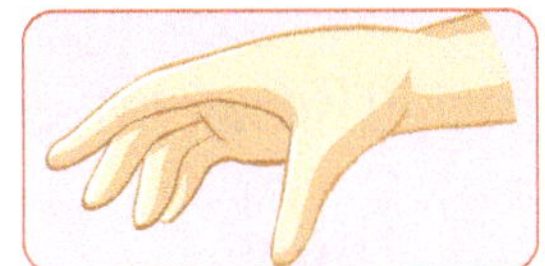

TASTE

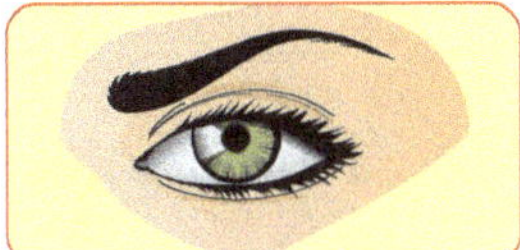

TOUCH

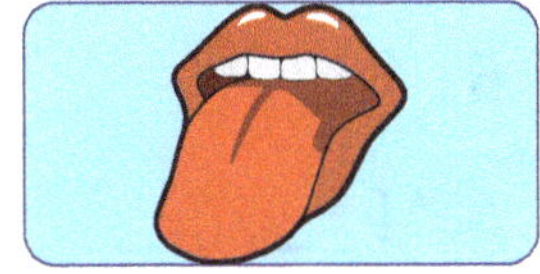

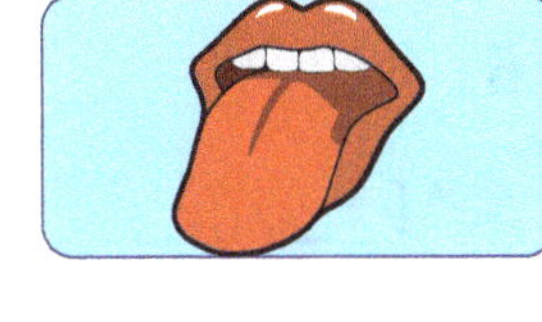

157. How many toy soldiers do you see?

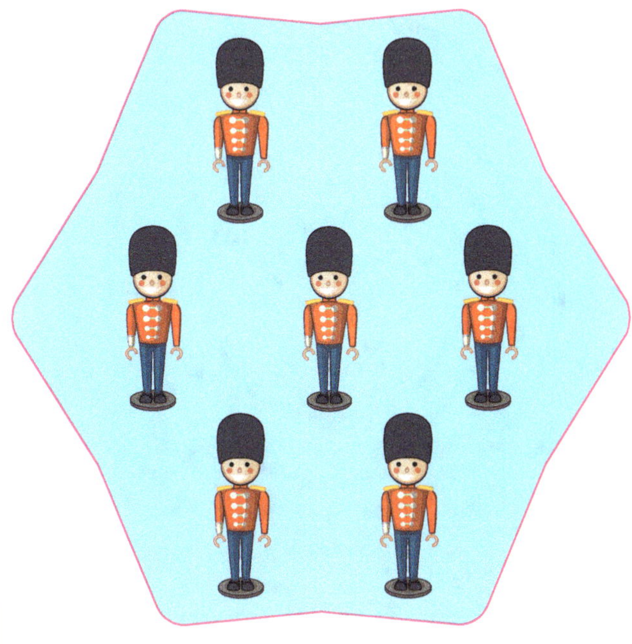

Total soldiers ◯

158. Count the total number of each image.

159. Join the numbers in decreasing order and colour the fish.

160. Find out the path you can take to set the bird free.

161. Use is, am, are and complete the sentence.

1. The weather ____________ nice today.
2. I __________ not tired.
3. This book ____________ heavy.
4. I ______________ a taxi driver.
5. These __________ my toys.
6. I _____________ a pilot.
7. My sister __________ a teacher.

162. Match the rhyming words.

ten	pan
fan	mug
rug	boy
toy	hen

163. Rearrange these letters and form the correct word.

poen	____________
art	____________
bear	____________
reap	____________
tear	____________
shore	____________
raw	____________
rage	____________
care	____________
arc	____________
heart	____________

164. Find the hidden names of body parts in the grid below.

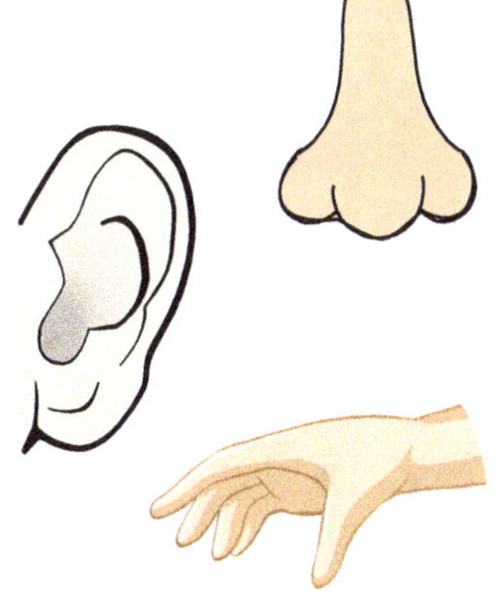

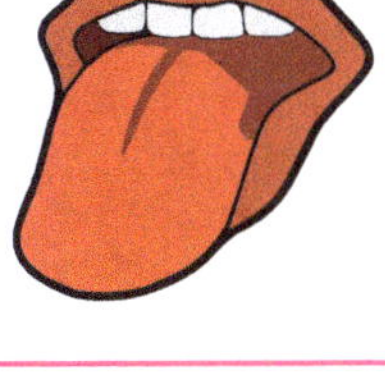

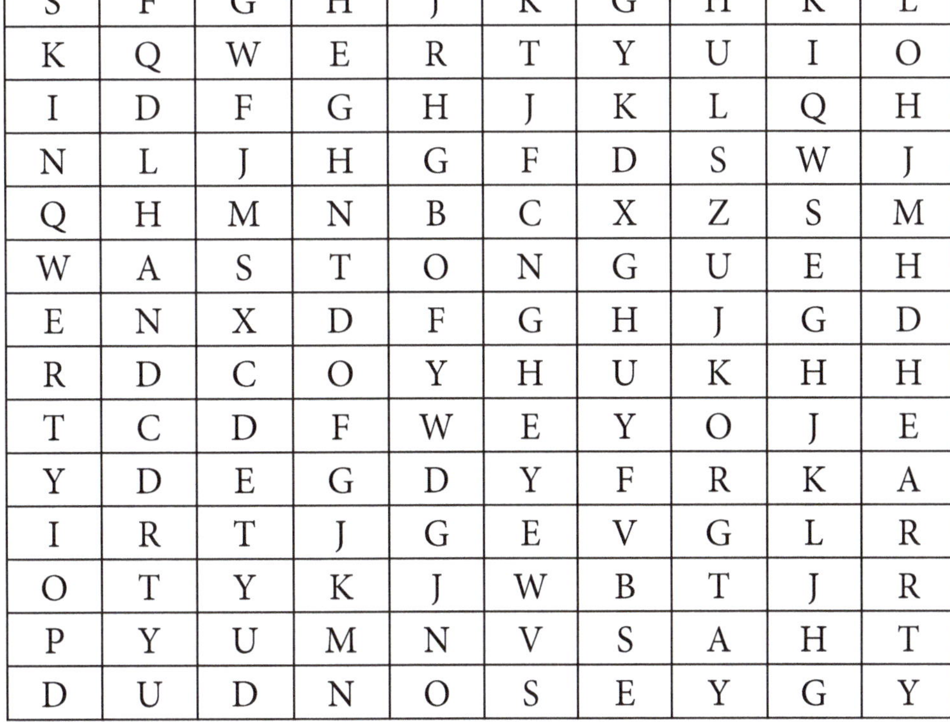

S	F	G	H	J	K	G	H	K	L
K	Q	W	E	R	T	Y	U	I	O
I	D	F	G	H	J	K	L	Q	H
N	L	J	H	G	F	D	S	W	J
Q	H	M	N	B	C	X	Z	S	M
W	A	S	T	O	N	G	U	E	H
E	N	X	D	F	G	H	J	G	D
R	D	C	O	Y	H	U	K	H	H
T	C	D	F	W	E	Y	O	J	E
Y	D	E	G	D	Y	F	R	K	A
I	R	T	J	G	E	V	G	L	R
O	T	Y	K	J	W	B	T	J	R
P	Y	U	M	N	V	S	A	H	T
D	U	D	N	O	S	E	Y	G	Y

165. Match to complete each sentence.

I can smell — the TV with my eyes

I can hear — the flower with my nose

I can see — the phone with my ears

166. Map out a baby's journey with the help of these images.

BABY
YOUNG
OLD

______

______

______

167. Our eyes help us to see shapes and sizes of the objects.

1. Circle the bigger insect

2. Circle the bigger object.

3. Circle the small animal.

168. Colour any three numbers so that their sum is 10.

5, 4, 3, 2, 7, 8, 10, 6

10

169.

Multiply and find the answer.

170. Match the number of images in each group to their correct number.

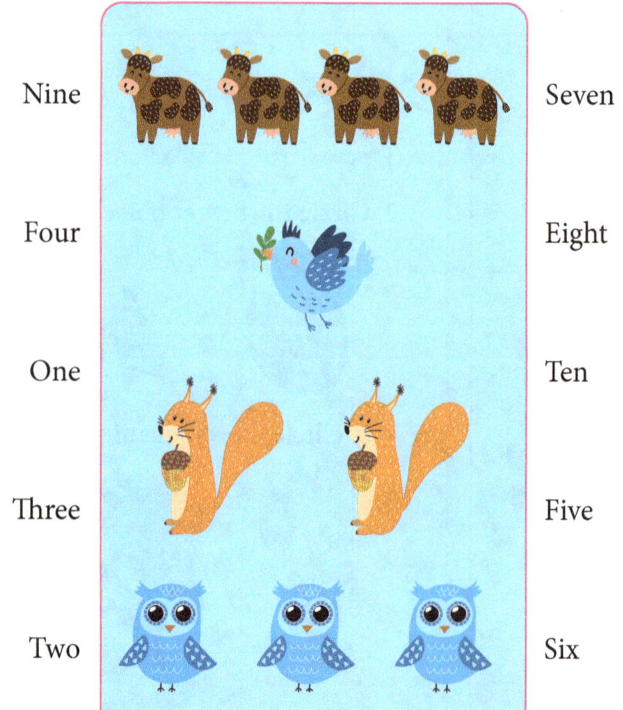

Nine	Seven
Four	Eight
One	Ten
Three	Five
Two	Six

171. Complete the sentence with the help of the given pictures and colour them.

1. Mother boils soup in a __________.

   Plate

   Pan

   Pot

2. Father bought a __________ for my study room.

   Bicycle

   Table

   Pillow

3. The water in the _________is hot.

   Toaster

   Kettle

   Jar

172. Let's colour the pictures brightly.

Rainy

Sunny

Windy

173. Colour the countable pictures given below.

174. Tick the sentences that contain non-living entities.

○ 1. The kitten is playing.

○ 2. The babies are crying.

○ 3. Humpty Dumpty fell down.

○ 4. The windows are open.

○ 5. The door is closed.

○ 6. The sea is hot.

○ 7. My sister likes chocolates.

○ 8. The ice-cream is cold.

○ 9. The sky is blue.

○ 10. Take this chair.

175. Write a sentence using the words next to the picture.

the

rat cat

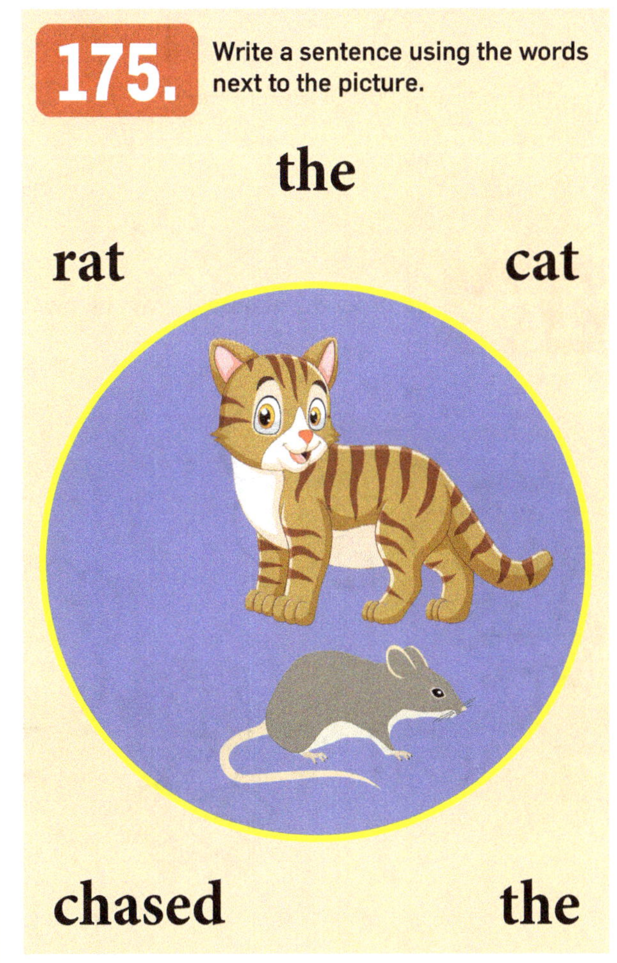

chased the

176. Colour all the circles yellow, all the squares blue, and, all the triangles green.

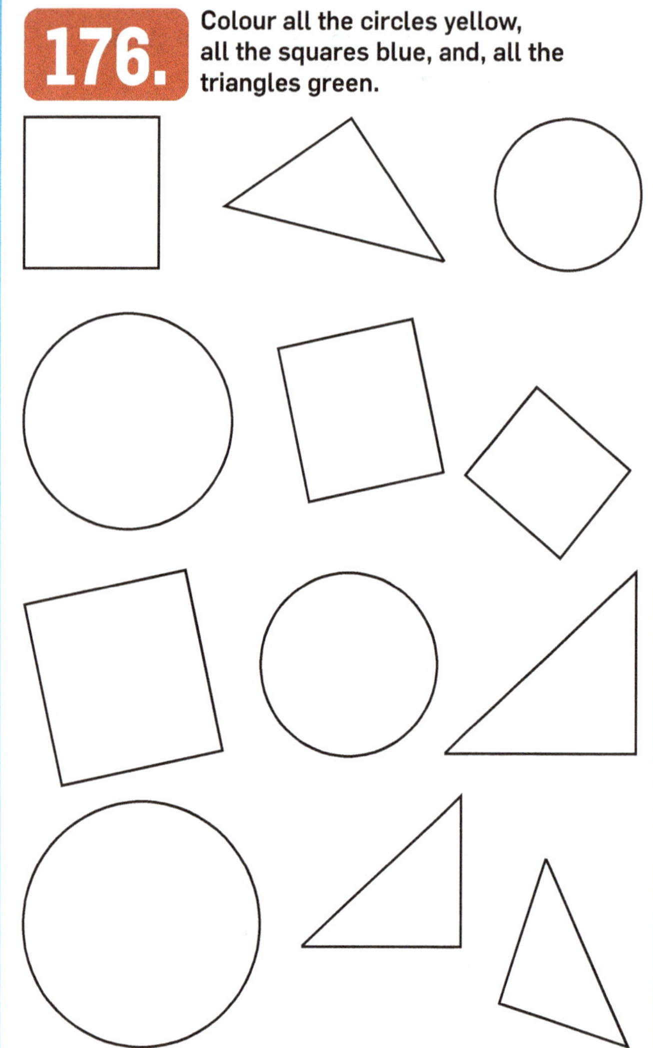

177. Answer the sums according to the picture codes given below.

178. Subtract the numbers given below.

179. Match the animals with their coverings.

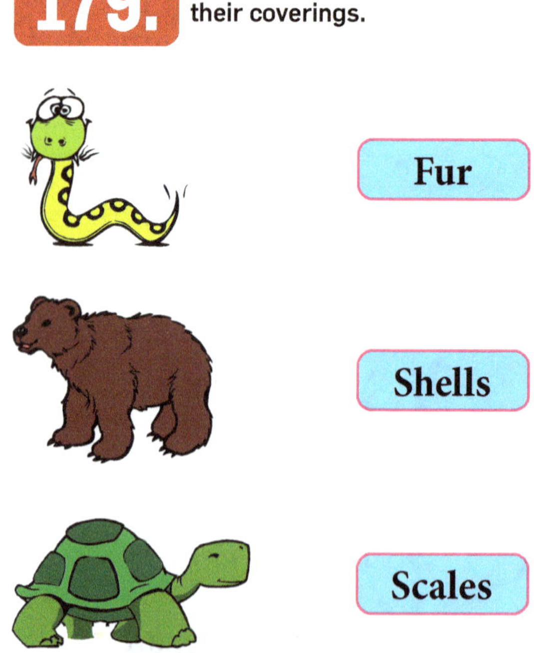

180. Circle and fill in the correct word.

1. Trees help keep the air__________.
   (fresh / dirty)

2. We get ____________from trees.
   (wood / plastic)

3. ____________ live on trees.
   (rats / squirrels)

4. Trees are home to the____________.
   (foxes/monkeys)

5. Paper is made from ____________.
   (wood / rubber)

182. Match the bird with its correct shadow.

181. Unscramble these letters to find the name of the colourful bird.

AUOTCN

____

183. Match the sums with their correct answers.

184. Trace the grey lines and find out the name of the sea animal.

185. Use the correct articles to complete the sentences.

a an the

1. There was once ___ duck and ____ his wife.
2. Mom and I bake __________ chocolate cake.
3. Mary likes to dance in ________ morning.
4. There are many bees in ________ hive.
5. What is __________________ time now?
6. I am painting __________ landscape.
7. The children are washing _________ dishes.

186. Match the following.

	CLOUD
	SHIP
	CHAIR
	SHEEP

187. Write the letters in alphabetical order. One example is given.

abcdefghijklmnopqrstuvwxyz

x z s	s x z
c s m	_____
b v c	_____
h d f	_____
a b i	_____
e r k	_____
e q t	_____
g b m	_____
r v x	_____
n b m	_____
u z c	_____

188. Fill in the missing letters to complete the names of the images given.

B_ _

T-S_i_ t

B_o_

F_o_ _r

F_s_

P_n_ _ _p _ e

189.

The following words are written in a tricky code where each letter is equal to the letter that comes after it. For example:

A=B, B=C, C=D, D=E,

Try to figure out the human organ names using this code. The first one is done for you.

ANMD B O N E

KHUDQ _ _ _ _ _

KTMFR _ _ _ _ _

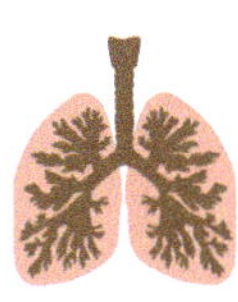
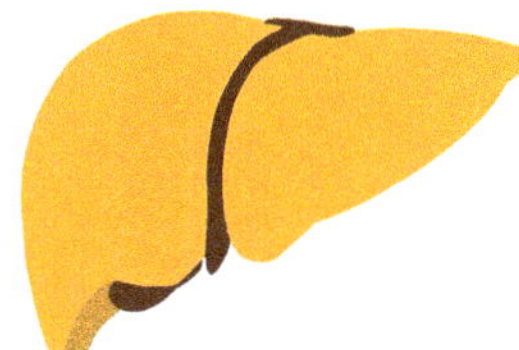
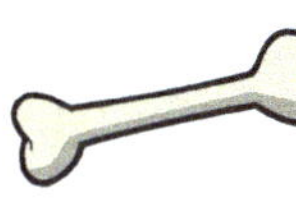

190.

Can you find your way through the puzzle to reach the end?

191.

How do the following things feel? Circle the word that describes them the best.

Smooth/Rough

Hot / Cold

Blunt / Thorny

192.

Fill in the missing alphabets to complete the names of the things below.

W_it_

U_bre_la

W_te_ mel_n

K_t_

O_a_g_

193. How many crabs can you see? Circle the correct number.

194. Count the butterflies and multiply with 8. Write the answer in the box given.

195. Put each noun under its own group.

apple,	toy,	sock,	skirt,
rice,	ball,	book,	bell,
coat,	story,	bread,	shorts,
game,	carrot,	comic,	cake,
jigsaw,	hat,	magazine,	newspaper

Things to eat

____
____
____
____
____

Things to wear

____
____
____
____
____

Things to play with

____
____
____
____
____

Things to read

____
____
____
____
____

196. A noun is a word that represents a person, place or, a thing. Read the words in the pink box below. Next, write them under the correct category.

Desk	Doll	Norway	Jason
Chicago	Mary	Kathy	Book
Window	India	Kate	Japan

PERSON	PLACE	THING
__________	__________	__________
__________	__________	__________
__________	__________	__________
__________	__________	__________

197. Use the suffix-ick to complete the words.

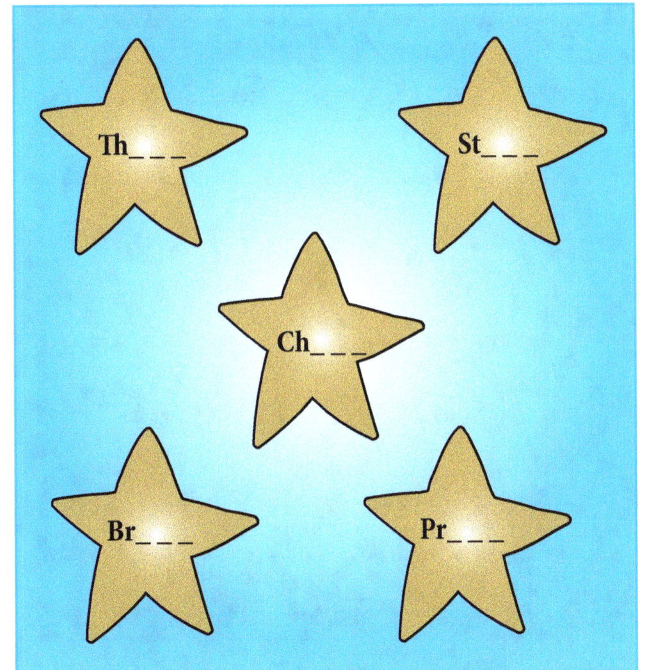

198. Match the images with the words given in the word box.

NOSE LEAF MAT POT BROOM

199. Think of a *vowel* to complete each word.

1. H--------p
2. Z--------p
3. J--------t
4. M--------ss
5. S--------ng
6. Ch--------mp
7. Th--------n
8. W--------P
9. C--------t
10. B--------n
11. L--------g
12. C--------ll
13. L--------st
14. Sh--------rt
15. Cl--------P
16. St--------r

200. You leg has many different parts. Can you point and name them with the help of the given word bank?

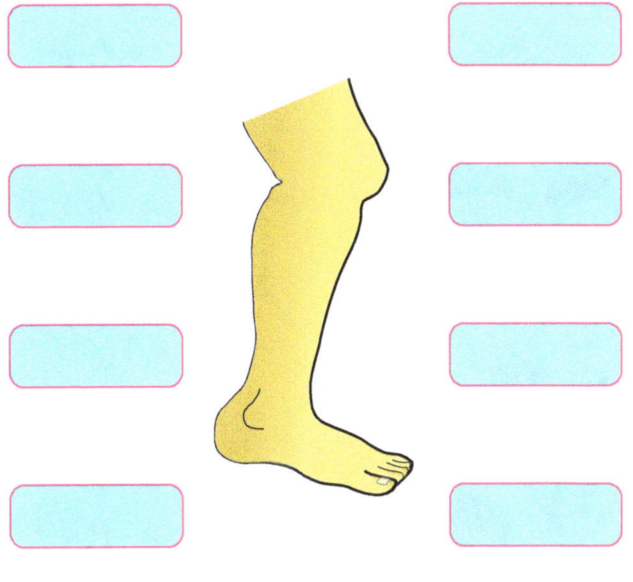

Knee	Foot	Calf	Heel
Toes	Thigh	Ankle	Shin

201. Can you spell the name of a flower by rearranging these alphabets? Colour the images.

202. Colour the kites with singular nouns in red and with plural nouns in blue.

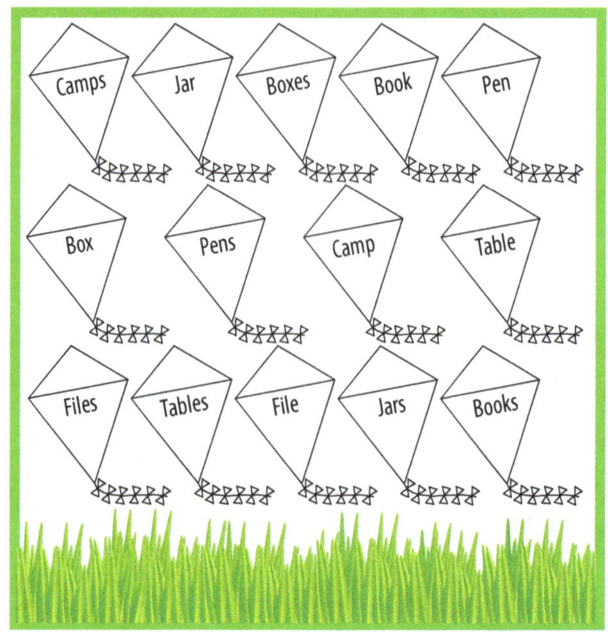

203. Match the pictures with their pronouns.

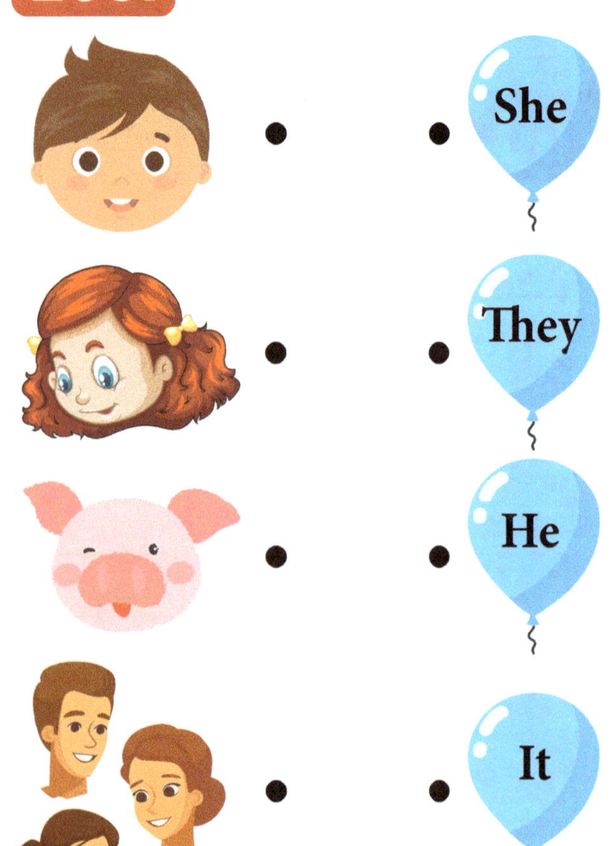

204. Look in the word search grid for the names of eight different birds and find them in the puzzle given below.

O	S	T	R	I	C	H	E	O	M
G	O	S	O	C	A	A	R	U	S
E	D	A	T	W	R	I	X	C	H
P	U	F	K	F	L	N	C	E	O
P	E	N	G	U	I	N	Q	W	E
W	U	L	P	F	U	C	N	G	T
O	A	F	S	R	I	T	R	O	C
H	A	W	F	K	D	O	S	O	G
E	M	U	P	I	F	D	I	S	W
N	O	T	R	I	N	X	H	E	O

Crow	Emu	Goose	Hawk
Ostrich	Owl	Penguin	Puffin

205. Fill numbers in the caterpillar's body by adding 2 to the previous number.

207. Number the pieces of the picture in the correct order.

206. What number comes between these numbers?

88		90
35		37
48		50
63		65

208. Draw a line to match the objects to the appropriate senses used for them.

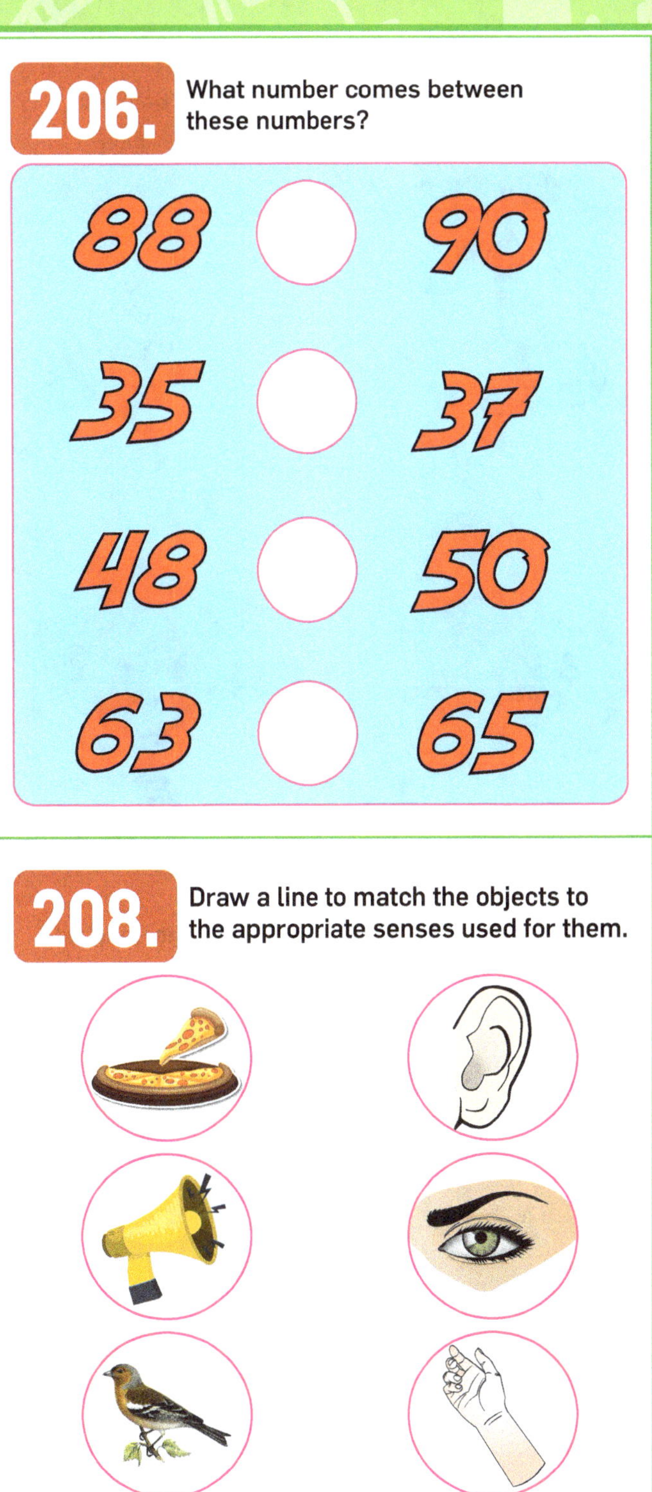

209. Tick the images of trees below.

210. Encircle all the nouns in the sentences below.

1. My brother is going for a vacation.
2. Sam is going to the beach.
3. My mother cooked fish curry for dinner.
4. The King likes to paint with bright colours.
5. My sister likes to dance.

211. Fill in the blanks using the images as hints.

1. I trim my ____________________ 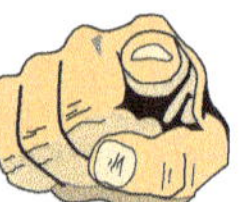

   with a ________________________ 

2. I brush my ____________________ 

   with a ________________________ 

3. I wash my ____________________ 

   with ________________________ 

212. Tick the words that do not match with the given pictures.

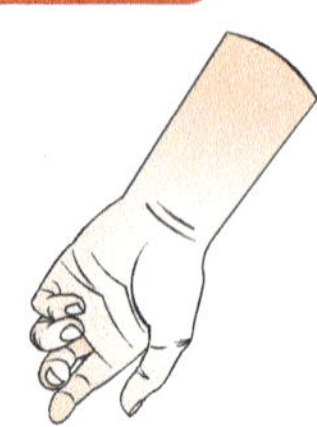

Hand **Jam**

Ring **King**

Queen **Nail**

Jump **Jug**

Kite **Tent**

Girl **Quilt**

Colour the picture.

Encircle the words of the wordbox in the following grid.

A	S	D	F	L	K	J	G	H	Q	P	T
V	C	E	L	U	E	T	C	O	O	T	P
I	T	O	O	T	H	P	A	S	T	E	G
G	U	M	S	O	I	Y	V	U	O	N	M
Q	E	P	S	O	P	A	I	S	N	O	N
H	D	E	N	T	I	S	T	A	G	U	V
T	O	O	T	H	B	R	Y	D	U	H	I
T	Y	C	A	B	V	I	T	O	E	T	H
S	A	T	E	R	Y	P	R	N	T	I	S
P	L	A	Q	U	E	A	S	T	E	M	O
L	A	R	M	S	O	L	C	I	S	O	R
C	A	N	I	H	O	T	H	O	N	G	U

TOOTHBRUSH	TOOTHPASTE	PLAQUE
DENTIST	TOOTH	TONGUE
CAVITY	FLOSS	GUMS

Tick the plants that will grow up healthy.

216. Can you place the correct name of the flower next to its picture with the help of the word box?

Lotus **Rose** **Tulip** **Daisy** **Hibiscus**

217. Can you solve these multiplication problems?

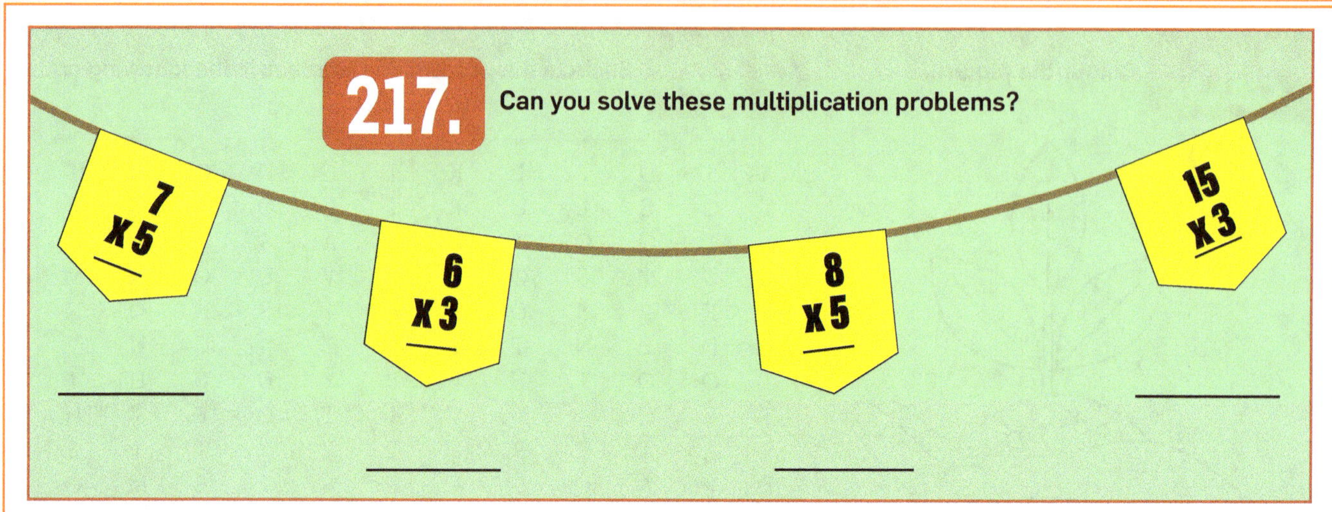

218. Fill in the missing numbers and then colour the parrots with even numbers.

219. Complete the crossword puzzle using the images as hints.

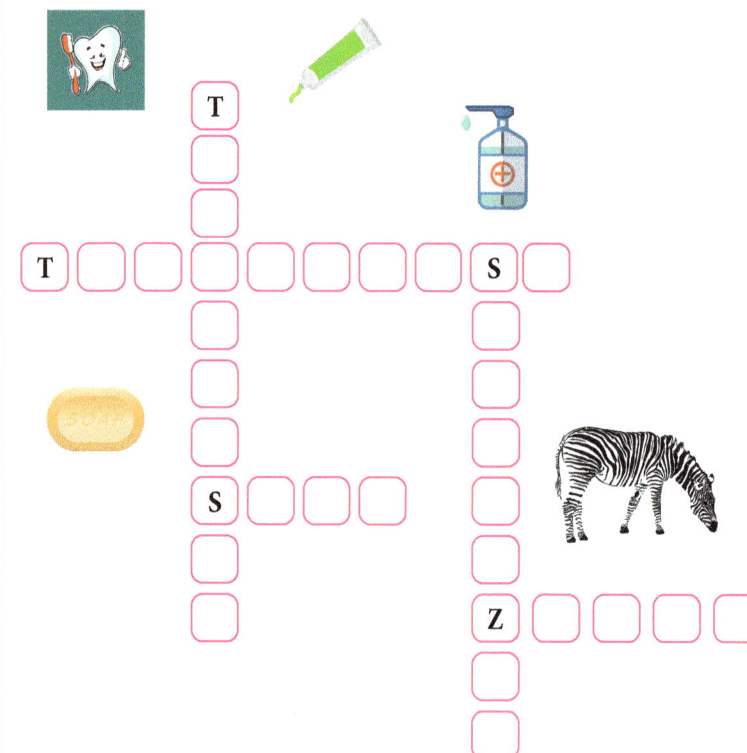

220. Solve the sums.

221. How many objects from the word box can you find in the picture? Circle the images and colour the picture.

HUT	GLASS	PIG	FIRE	COCK	CROW	BALL
WELL	COW	SMOKE	CHAIR	WHEEL	UTENSILS	

222. Complete the words by adding 'ace' to the blanks.

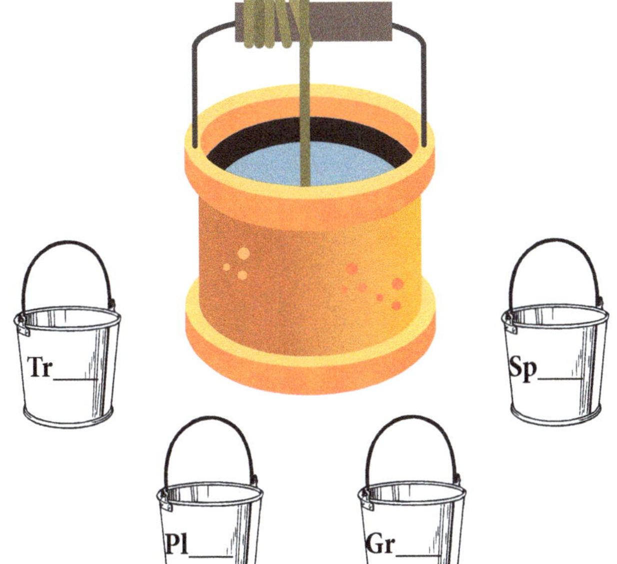

223. Write the correct plural forms of the following words.

Fish

Week

Tree

Lamp

Man

224. Colour the penguin.

225. Match the words with the correct expressions.

Sad

Happy

Angry

226. Number the images correctly, keeping in mind the process of a seed growing.

227. Choose one option from the alphabets given below to complete each word.

an at am ap

Bo____

C____

B____

M____

H____

R____

228. Write the number in place of tens in the images given below. The first one is done for you.

229. Match the following.

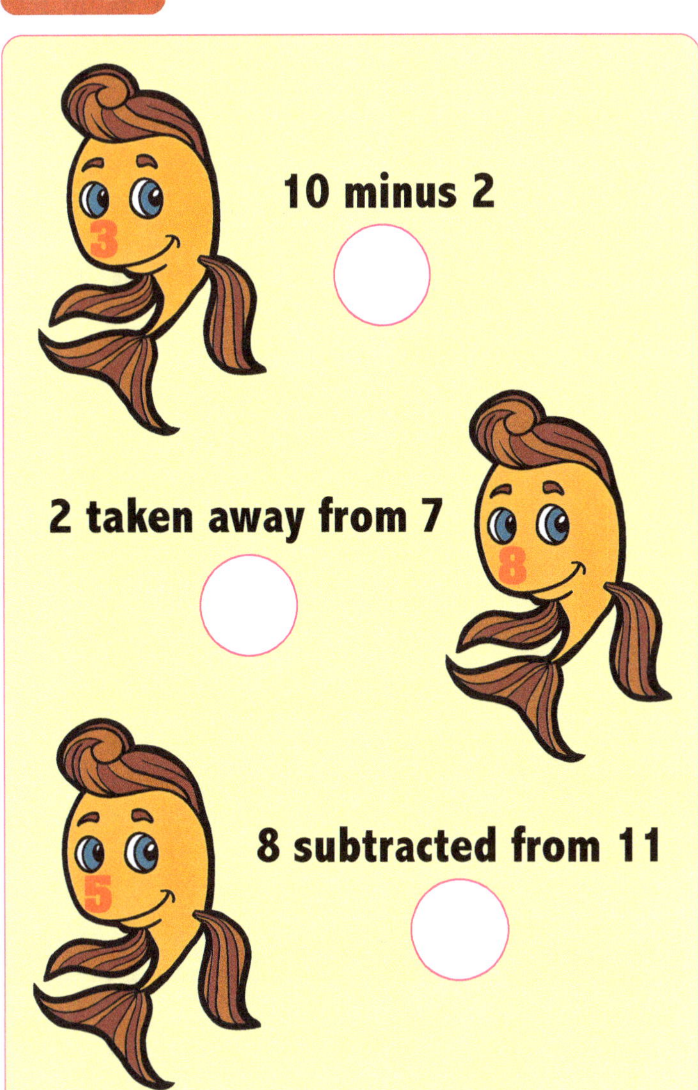

230. Add +3 and +5 to each number and find the total.

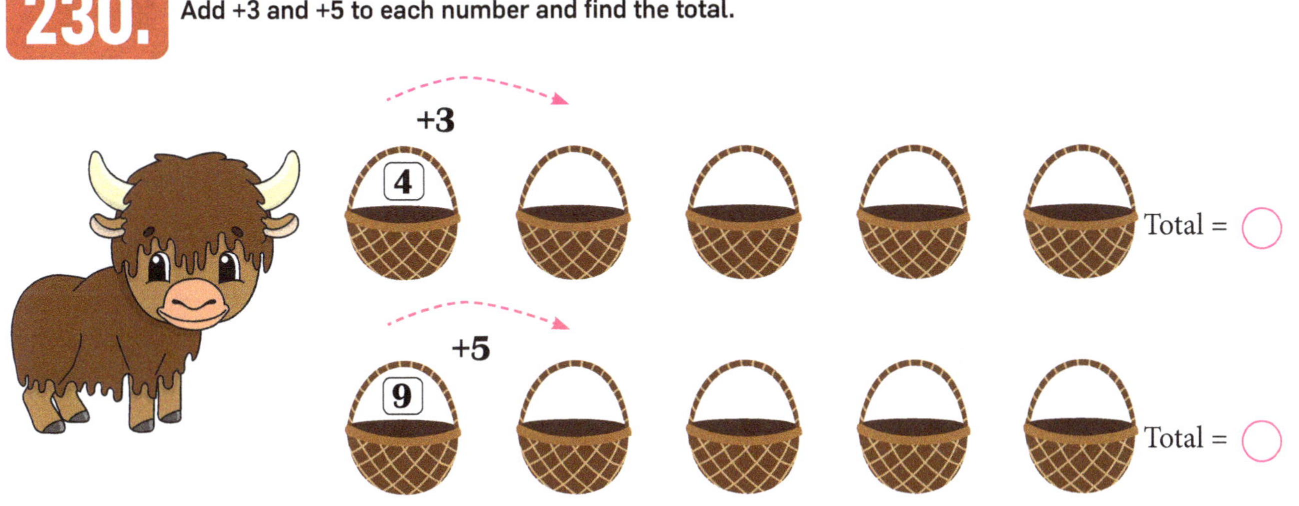

231. Match the objects with the vowel sounds they begin with.

232. Match the letters to complete the name of the images given.

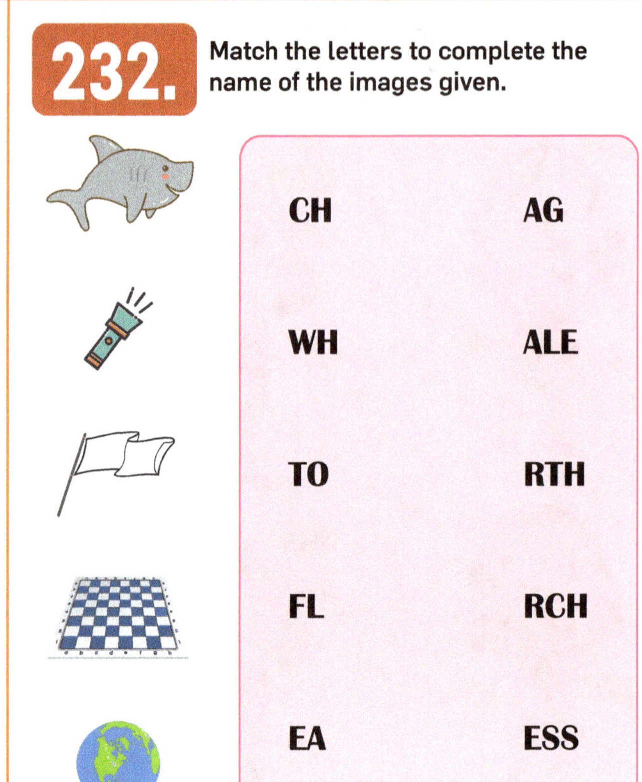

233. Can you label all the pictures correctly with the help of the word box?

House Hospital Hotel Barber Cinema Hall Pizza Place

____

____

____

____

____

____

234. Find the names of the different colours in the box below.

P	O	R	A	N	G	E	Z	S
I	A	H	I	B	L	U	E	A
N	T	B	E	N	D	K	L	T
K	G	L	U	W	I	G	S	W
M	O	A	D	R	Y	R	I	H
A	A	C	D	E	D	E	L	I
T	P	K	H	R	H	E	V	T
V	I	O	L	E	T	N	E	E
J	S	U	N	D	A	Y	R	R
T	H	Y	E	L	L	O	W	E

Pink	Yellow	Black	Orange
White	Green	Blue	Red
Violet	Silver		

235. Write the mising numbers to complete the table of ten.

1	x	10	=	10
__	x	10	=	20
__	x	10	=	____
4	x	10	=	40
5	x	____	=	____
6	x	10	=	60
7	x	10	=	70
__	x	____	=	____
9	x	10	=	90
10	x	____	=	____

236. Count the number of fruits and flowers.

Fruit ☐ Flower ☐

237. Solve the addition sums given below.

15 + 2 = ________

18 + 9 = ________

12 + 6 = ________

238. Look at the codes to colour the butterfly.

1	2	3	4

239. Write the numbers in sequence on the wheels of the train and colour it.

240. Using the table of 2 take the worm to the apple.

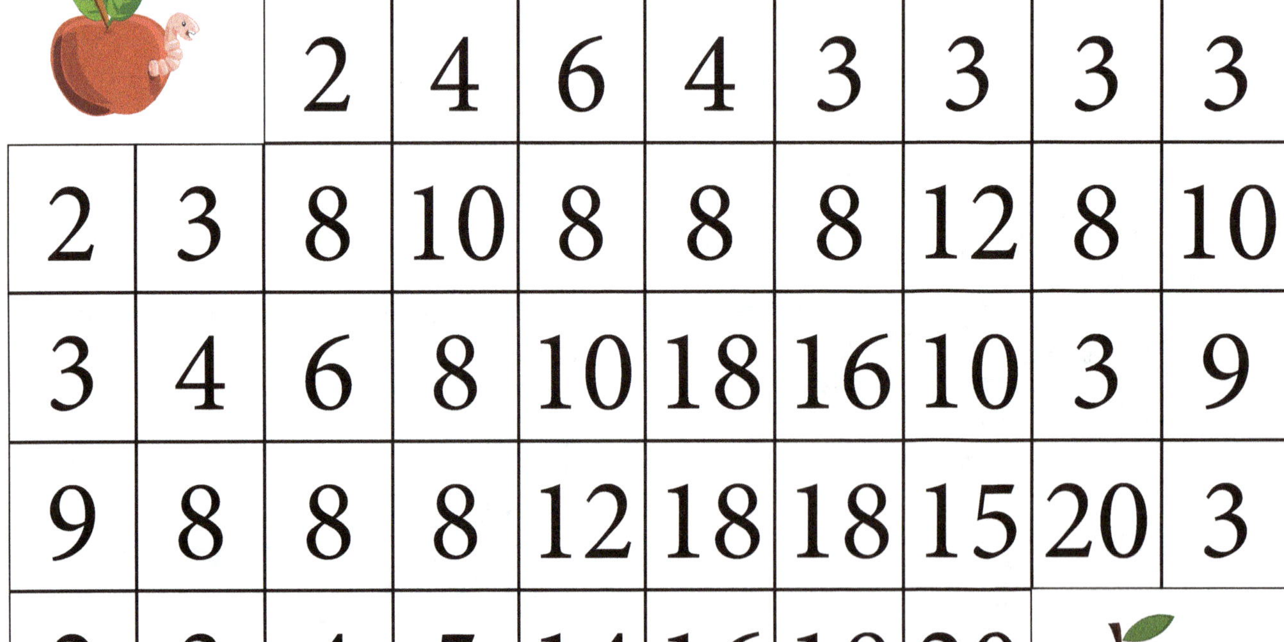

		2	4	6	4	3	3	3	3
2	3	8	10	8	8	8	12	8	10
3	4	6	8	10	18	16	10	3	9
9	8	8	8	12	18	18	15	20	3
2	3	4	5	14	16	18	20		

241. Choose the correct pronouns from the options given and fill in the blanks.

it | you | her | me | him | us | them

1. This is Miss Jane, our teacher. We all like_______________.
2. My mother drives__________________ to school every day.
3. John, here's a present for ____________.
4. Hold the vase carefully, don't drop____________.
5. Karl's dad helped________________ with his home work.

242. Can you find all the fruits' names hidden in the box below?

G	R	A	P	E	S	S	O	E	P
F	P	F	I	G	Z	F	Y	D	I
L	I	M	E	B	B	R	E	R	N
H	N	C	B	A	N	A	N	A	E
M	E	H	M	I	A	W	L	O	A
E	A	E	A	P	P	B	E	R	P
I	P	R	N	L	P	E	M	A	P
O	P	R	G	U	L	R	O	N	L
N	L	Y	O	M	E	R	N	G	E
P	E	A	R	B	X	Y	K	E	X

LEMON ORANGE APPLE PEAR
LIME GRAPES BANANA PINEAPPLE

243. Choose words from the box to fill up blanks.

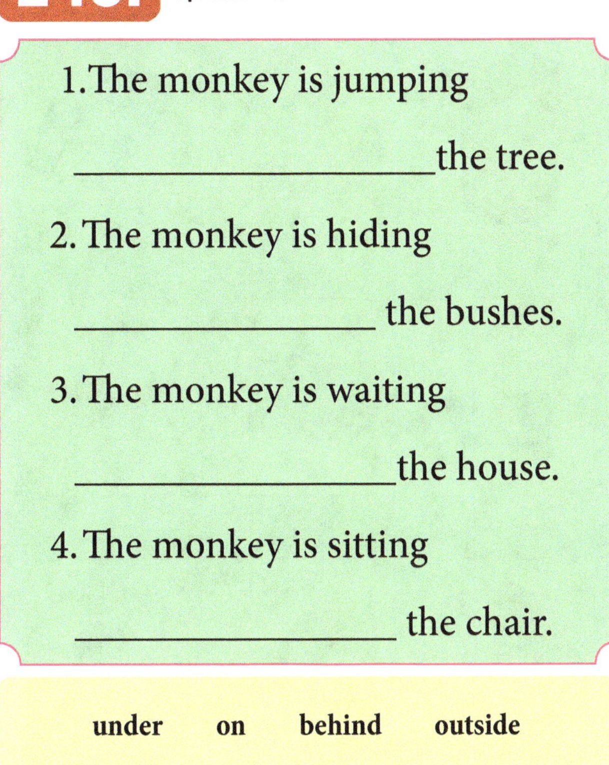

1. The monkey is jumping __________________the tree.
2. The monkey is hiding ________________ the bushes.
3. The monkey is waiting _________________the house.
4. The monkey is sitting _________________ the chair.

under on behind outside

244. Look at the pictures and fill in the blanks with in, on, or, under.

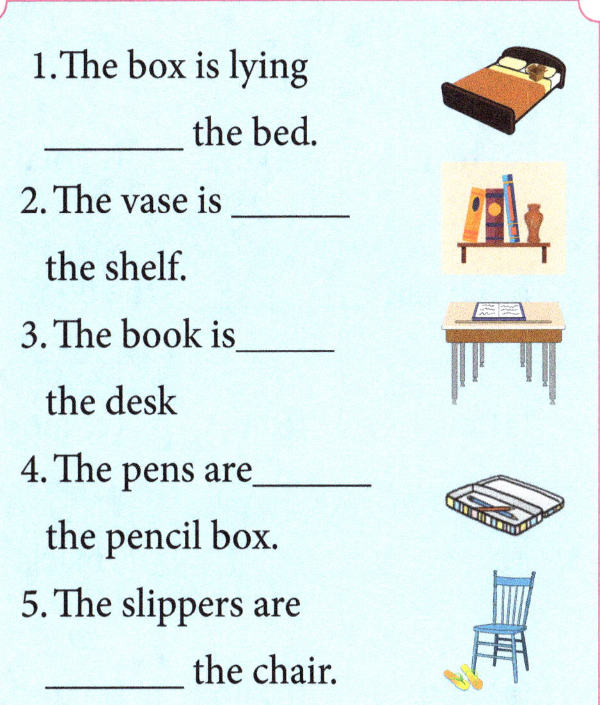

1. The box is lying _______ the bed.
2. The vase is ______ the shelf.
3. The book is_____ the desk
4. The pens are______ the pencil box.
5. The slippers are _______ the chair.

245. Use this colour-coded box to colour the kettle below.

246. Match the small letters to their capitals.

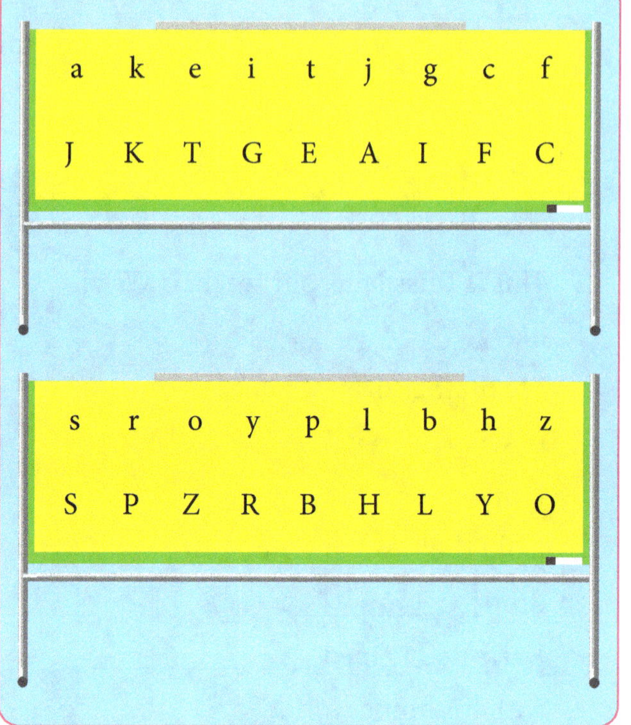

247. Circle the correct word.

1. We can ring the ______________

   (a) bad (b) bed (c) bell

2. Mom can ___________ the floor.

   (a) map (b)met (c) mop

3. My _________________ is black.

   (a) dog (b) dug (c) dot

248. Mark the odd one out in each column.

249. Count the pictures and solve the subtraction problems.

250. Colour the kettle containing the biggest number.

251. Label the body parts of a fish. Use the words from the box.

Mouth Tail Gills

Scales Eye Fin

252. Solve the subtraction sum and cross the correct answer.

253. Fill the white boxes using the codes below to find out where the boy is going!

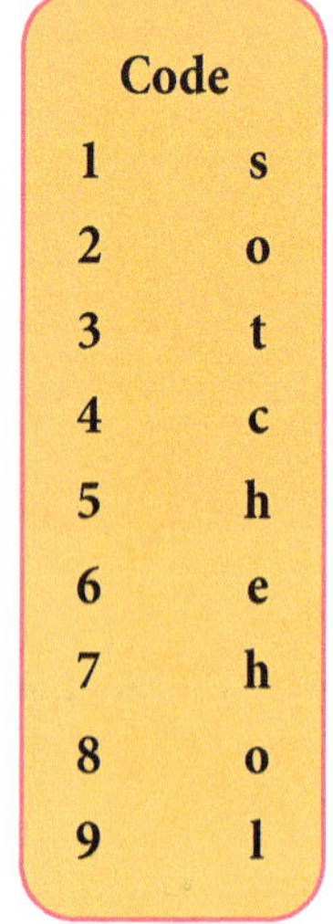

Code	
1	s
2	o
3	t
4	c
5	h
6	e
7	h
8	o
9	l

3	5	6	1	4	5	2	8	9
☐	☐	☐	☐	☐	☐	☐	☐	☐

254. Tick all the things you will find in a kitchen.

255. Can you write the names of these places correctly with the help of the word box?

Clinic **School** **Field** **Library** **Airport**

_______________ _______________ _______________

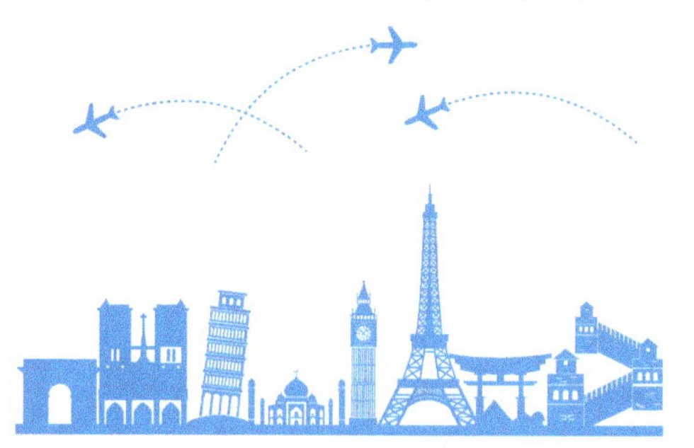

_______________ _______________

256. Circle all the trees out of these images.

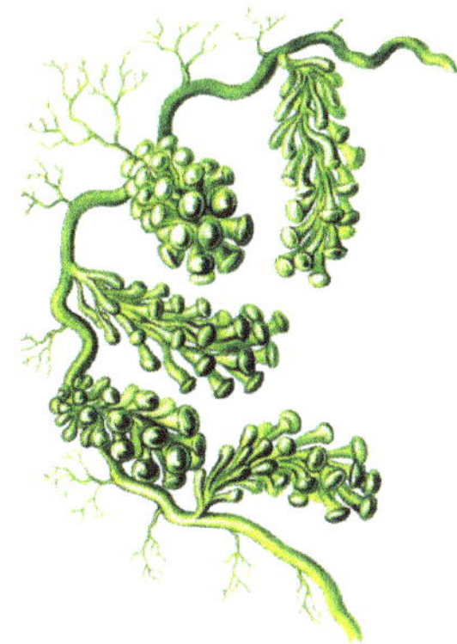

257. Tick the fruits that have one seed and circle the fruits that have more than one.

Apple

Watermelon

Peach

Cherry

Pear

258. Colour the trees as you wish.

Apple Tree

Date Tree

259. Count the pictures and write the number under the even or odd headings.

260. Solve the following sums.

261. What comes after these numbers?

262. Cross out the required number of objects in each row and solve the sums.

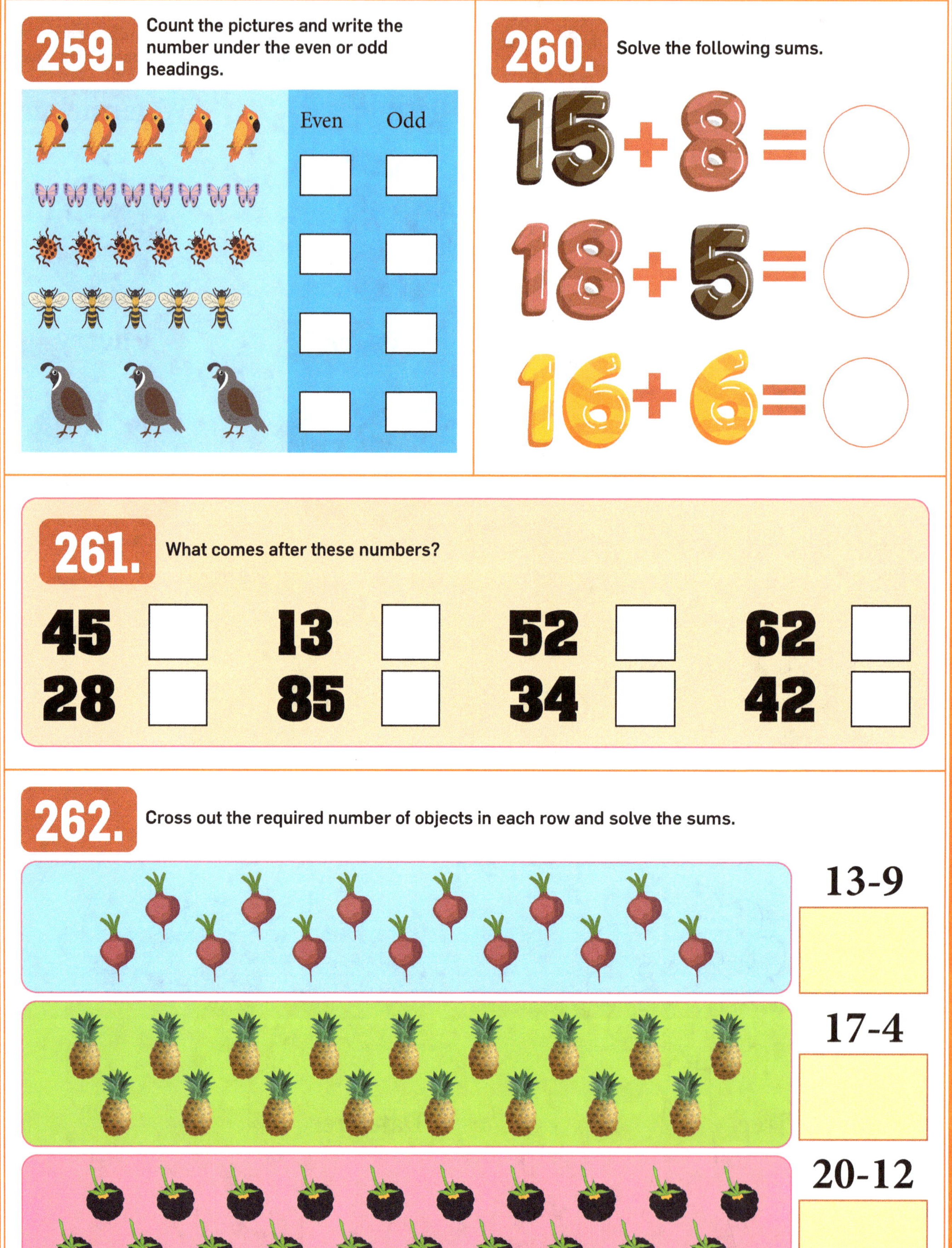

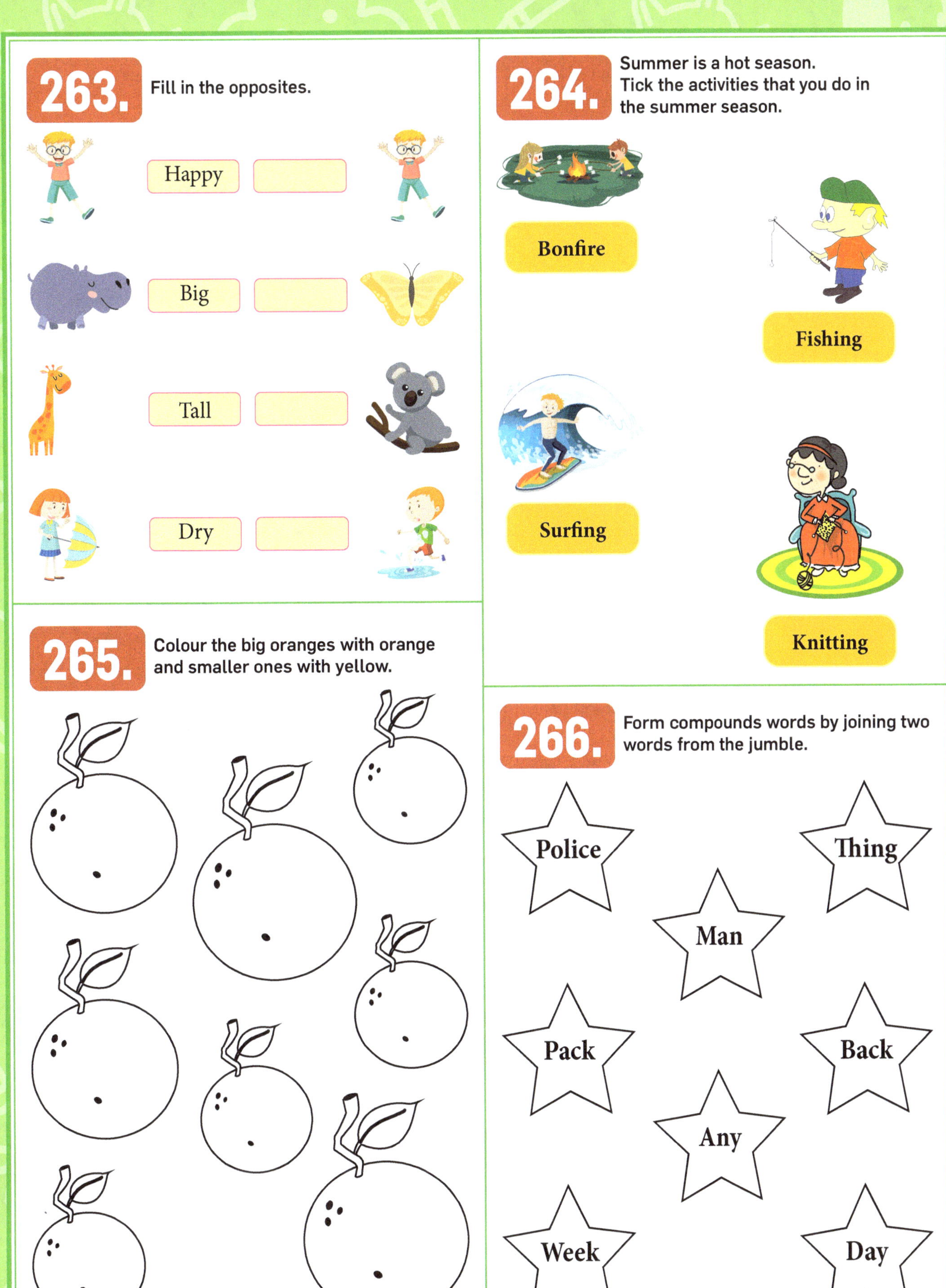

263. Fill in the opposites.

Happy

Big

Tall

Dry

264. Summer is a hot season. Tick the activities that you do in the summer season.

Bonfire

Fishing

Surfing

Knitting

265. Colour the big oranges with orange and smaller ones with yellow.

266. Form compounds words by joining two words from the jumble.

Police

Thing

Man

Pack

Back

Any

Week

Day

267. Colour the biggest rose in red and the smallest rose in blue.

268. Can you help Mary find her way to the rose?

269. Encircle the correct names of the following flowers.

ORCHID
ROSE
HIBISCUS
LILY

TULIP
LOTUS
IXORA
DAISY

SUNFLOWER
MARIGOLD
LILY
HIBISCUS

270. Colour the flowers below.

271. Circle the numbers whose difference is the number in the centre.

14		1
11	2	6
9		4

14		6
11	6	5
10		13

8		6
1	5	3
12		10

272. Colour the boxes in yellow that show a sum of 16 and help the dog to reach the house.

	15 + 5	12 + 4	18 + 6
12 + 4	8 + 8	5 + 9	21 + 6
9 + 4	12 + 4	6 + 10	19 + 5
9 + 6	12 + 14	11 + 5	4 + 12
5 + 6	14 + 2	7 + 19	

273. Count the correct number of pots and write the answer.

274.

Solve the word problem to name the organ.

BAT - AT + RAN - N + THIN - TH

= ____ ____ ____ ____ ____

275.

For the given words, choose the correct category and write them accordingly.

Desk	John	Table	Chair
India	Jimmy	Pen	Watch
Cindy	Tim	USA	England
Taj Mahal		Germany	

Person	Place	Thing
________	________	________
________	________	________
________	________	________
________	________	________
________	________	________
________	________	________

276.

Look at the pictures. Write down the words for the pictures. Then match each word with the one that rhymes with in the words in the middle column.

____

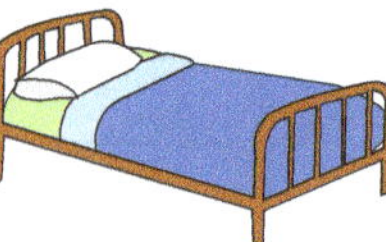

____

____

____

____

____

____

____

frog

rat

bun

chick

pen

shed

fox

pan

277.

Use **ON, IN, AT, BY** in each blank.

1. James goes to school ____ bus.

2. My mother was born ____ October.

3. We are going to the play ____11.00 pm.

4. We have an art class ________ Monday.

278. Join the trees with their correct names.

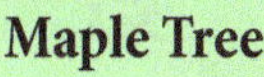

Maple Tree

Banyan Tree

Coconut Tree

Pine Tree

280. Can you help the bee find its way to the flower?

279. Can you draw a beautiful eye within the grid? Also, colour it.

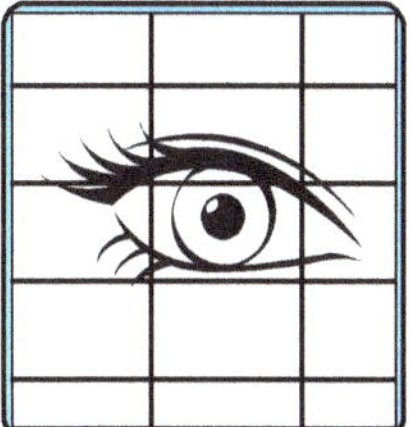

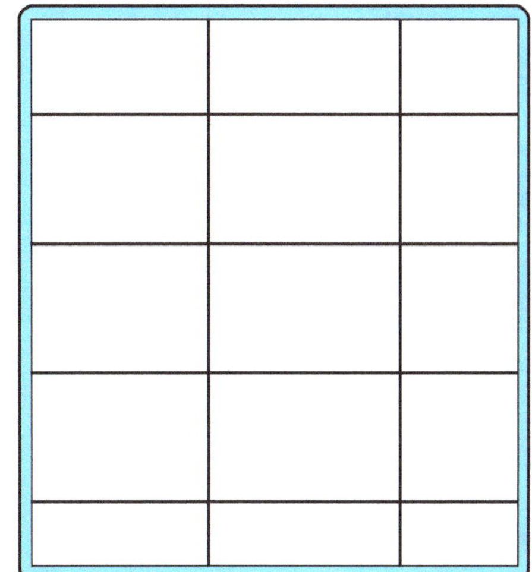

281. Match the fruits with the correct tree.

Apple

Mango

Banana

282. Match the following images with the correct numbers.

10

12

11

4

8

283. Fill the missing numbers to complete the counting.

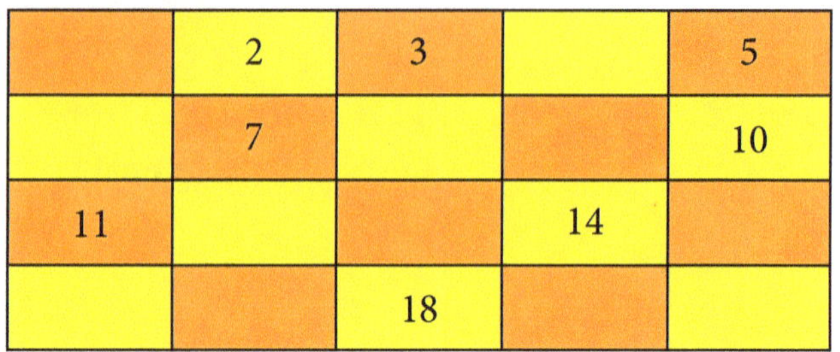

	2	3		5
	7			10
11			14	
		18		

284. Can you complete these multiplication sums?

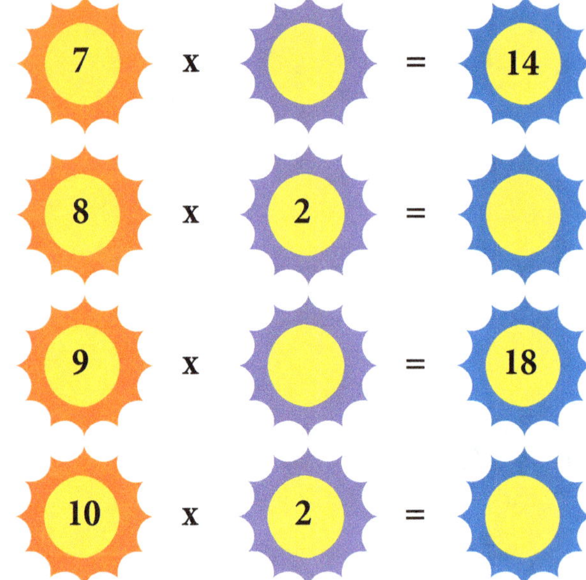

285. Connect the dots according to the pattern to complete the image.

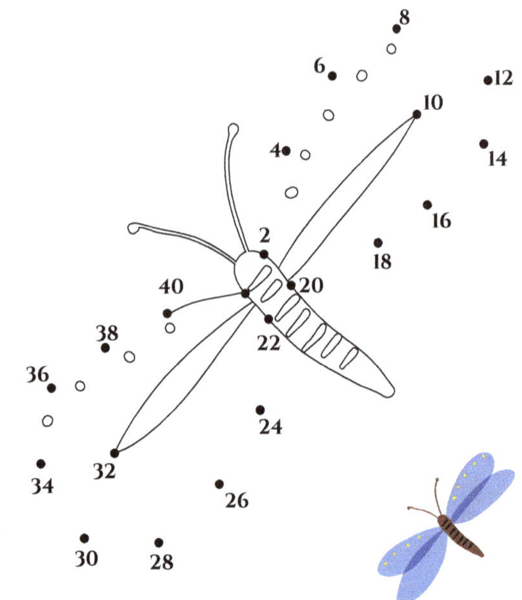

286. Find the biggest and the smallest number from the set.

Biggest

Smallest

287. Match the pictures with rhyming names.

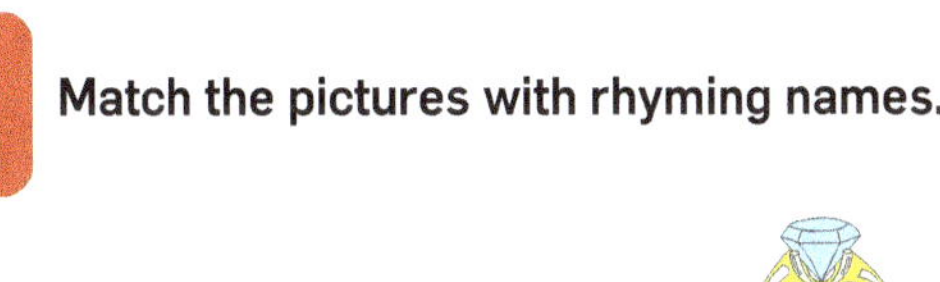

288. Spell the following words correctly using the pictures on the left.

C__a__r

__ o __s __

B__a__

S__nd Ca __t__e

289. Tick the right noun.

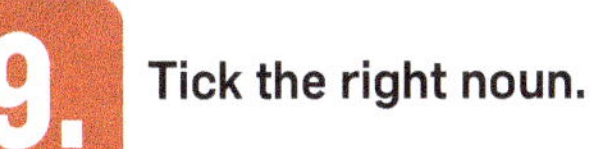
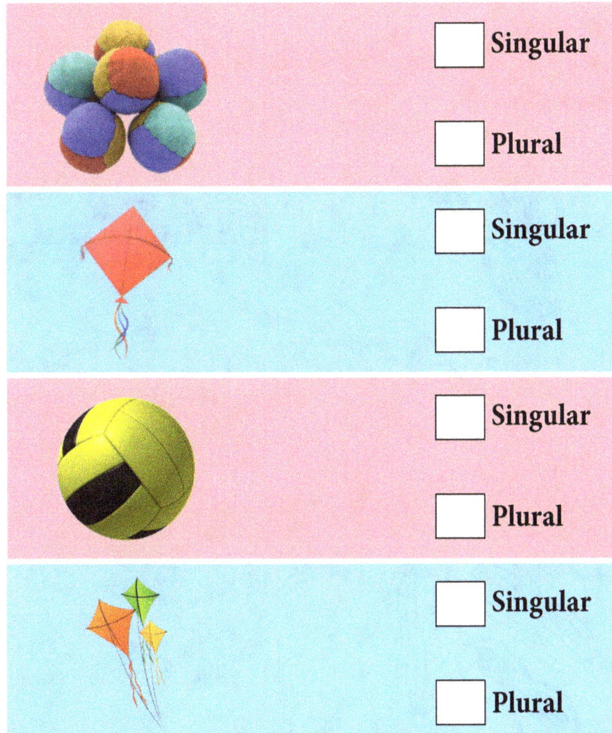

☐ Singular
☐ Plural

☐ Singular
☐ Plural

☐ Singular
☐ Plural

☐ Singular
☐ Plural

290. Fill in the letters to find out the means of transportation the girl wants to use.

Code

1 = a	10 = j
2 = b	11 = k
3 = c	12 = 1
4 = d	13 =m
5 = e	14 = n
6 = f	15 = o
7 = g	16 = p
8 = h	17 = q
9 = i	18 = r

__ __ __ __ __ __ __ __ __
1 5 18 15 16 12 1 14 5

291. Match the leaves which look similar.

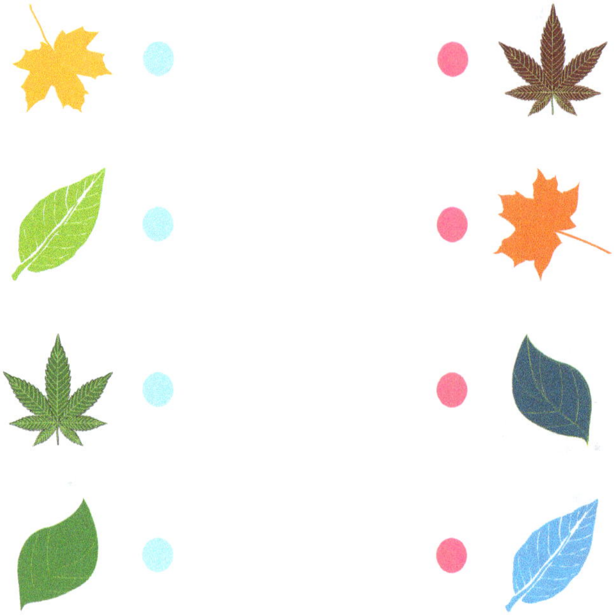

292. Circle the leaf.

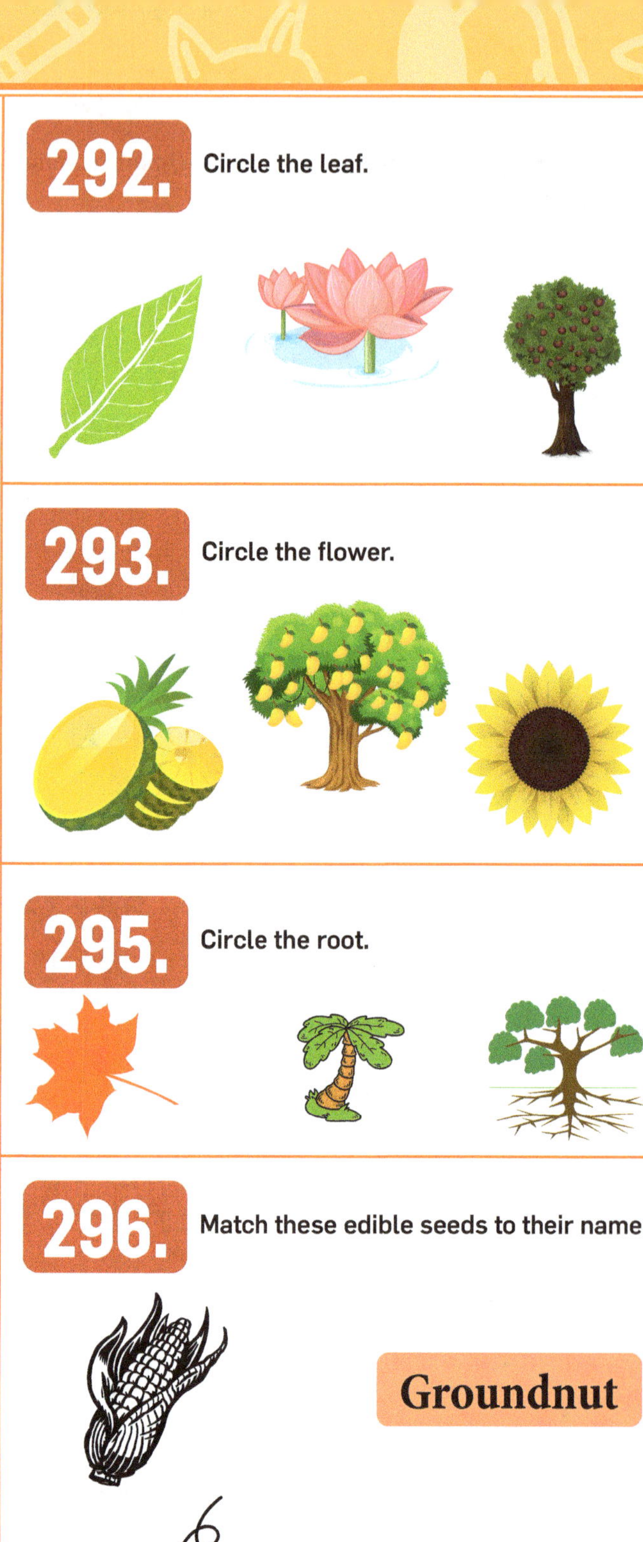

293. Circle the flower.

294. Find out the names of the different parts of a tree.

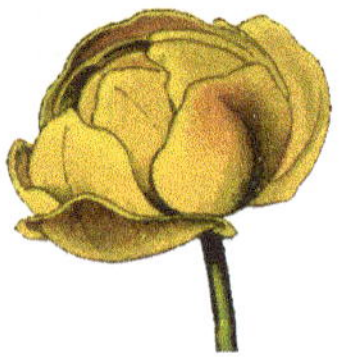

O W L E F R

____

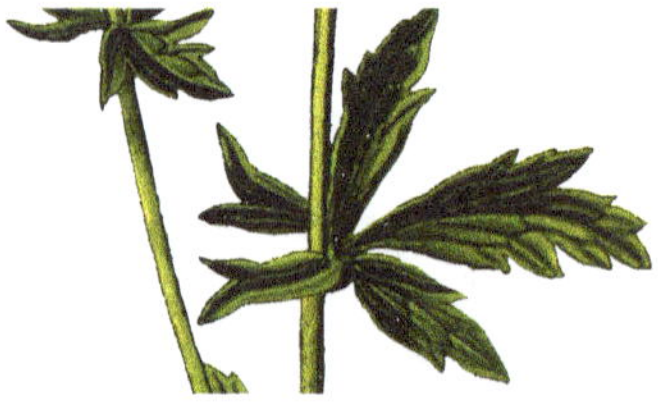

F L E A

____

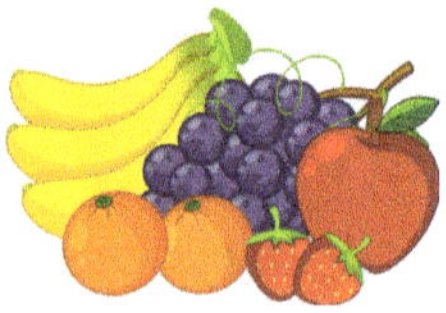

T I R F U

____

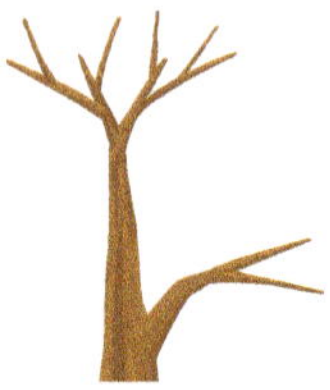

R T N U K

____

295. Circle the root.

296. Match these edible seeds to their name.

Groundnut

Sweetcorn

Pea

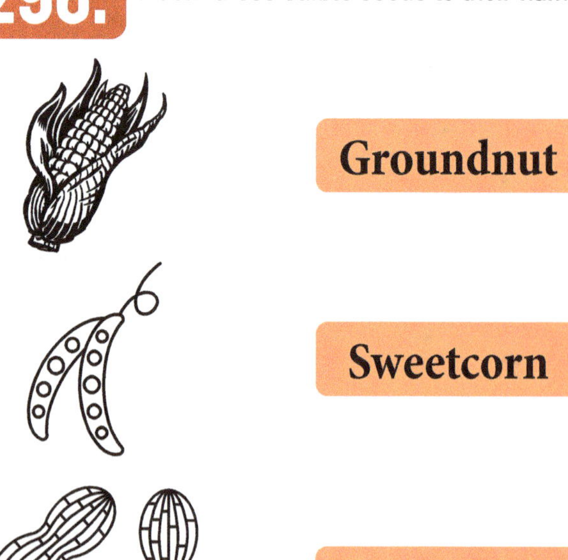

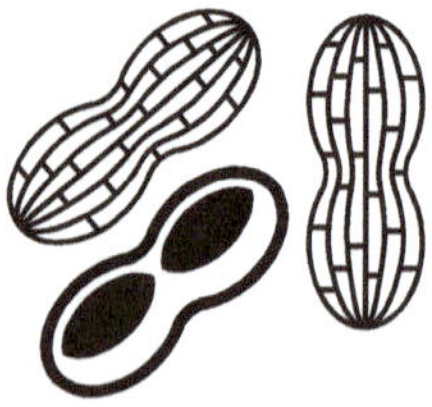

297. Fill the missing numbers in the empty boxes to complete the pattern.

100	200	300	400	
100	99	98	97	
11	22	33	44	
100	105	110	115	
151	152	153	154	

298. Solve the grid.

16	+	8	=	
+		-		+
4	-	4	=	
=		=		=
	+		=	24

299. Can you solve the sums below?

1x2= 2 =

2x2= 2 + 2 =

3x2= 2 + 2 + 2 =

4x2= 2 + 2 + 2 + 2 =

5x2= 2 + 2 + 2 + 2 + 2 =

300. Colour the given number of objects.

301. Fill in the missing numbers.

302. Solve the sum.

303. Can you count the number of toys these three trains are carrying?

__________ x 3

304. How many toys do you see?

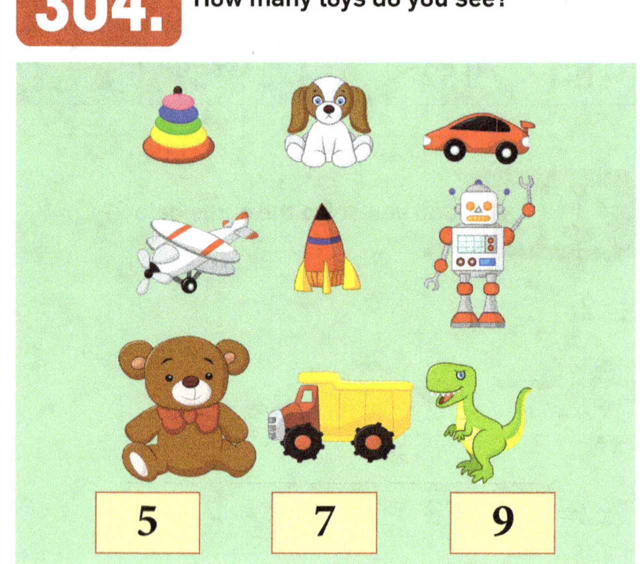

305. Count and write the number of images in each blue box.

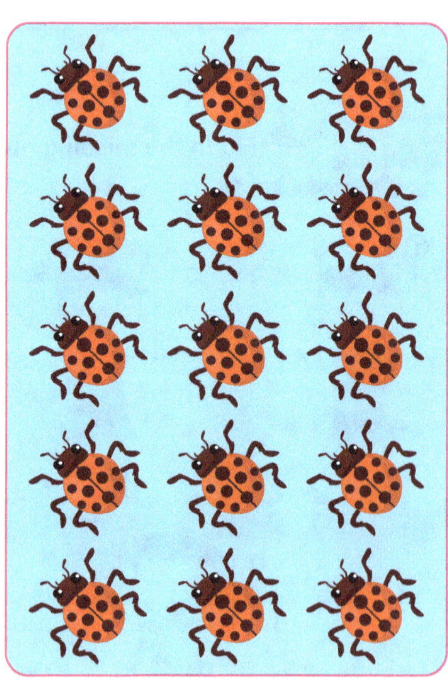

306. Join the dots and colour the picture.

307. What is the name of this plant?

ACUCTS

308. We are farm animals. Find us in the grid below.

goat, sheep, rooster, donkey, hen, cow, horse, duck

s	x	t	v	i	f	r
h	h	d	o	n	k	o
d	g	e	u	h	e	o
c	o	w	e	c	n	s
k	a	n	o	p	k	t
u	t	g	k	e	y	e
h	o	r	s	e	t	r
e	n	s	h	r	y	o

309. Colour the picture with the help of the reference.

310. Fill in the blank spaces.

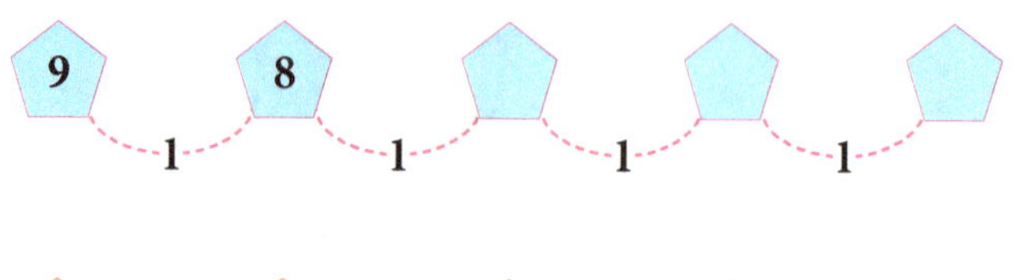

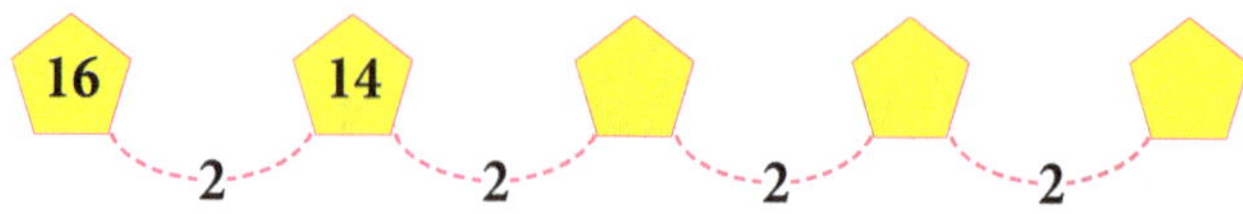

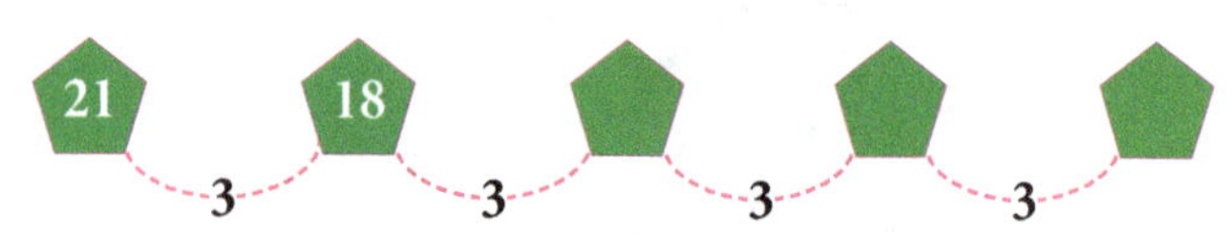

311. Solve the mathematical problems in the grid by filling in the missing numbers.

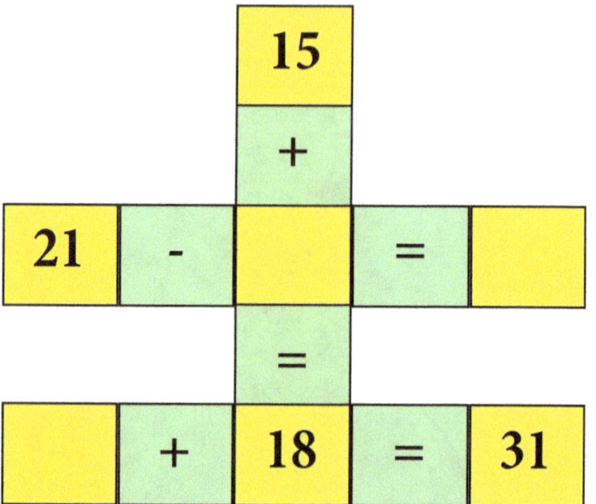

312. Add the numbers.

313. Match the mathematical operations to their answers.

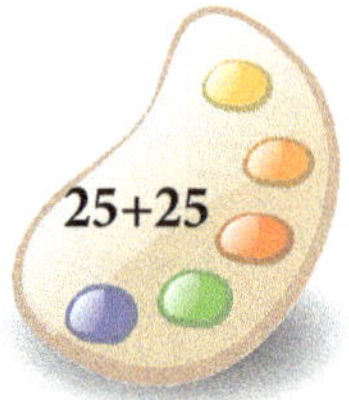

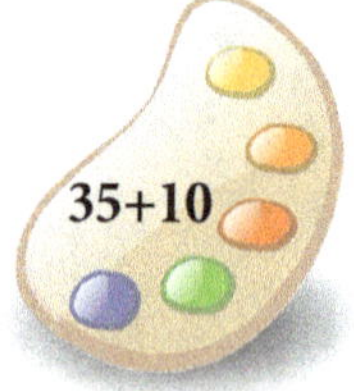

314.

Draw a line to join the masculine nouns with their feminine ones.

TIGER ○	○ VIXEN
COCK ○	○ SOW
LION ○	○ DOE
PEACOCK ○	○ COW
GANDER ○	○ TIGRESS
STALLION ○	○ HEN
BUCK ○	○ LIONESS
BULL ○	○ GOOSE
FOX ○	○ PEAHEN
BOAR ○	○ MARE

315.

Look at the picture and write the plural form by removing 'y' and adding 'ies' at the end of the word.

Pupp___

Bab___

Lad___

316.

Make a word by adding 'ace' in the given spaces on each apple.

317.

Write the first letter these images begin with.

_______ _______ _______

_______ _______ _______

318. Circle the leaves out of these images and colour them.

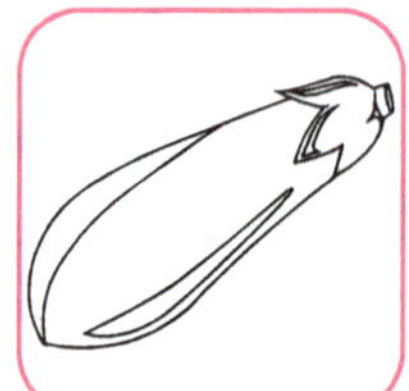

319. Draw a line from the letter to the image that starts with that letter.

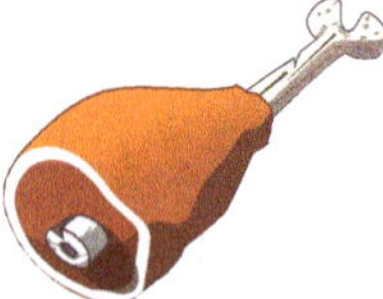

320. Fill in the blanks below by taking help from the given clue pictures.

1. This is a ____________________.

   It is ______________ in colour.

2. These are ____________________.

   They are ____________________.

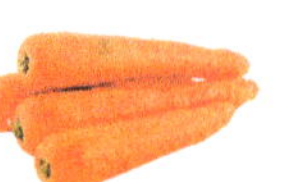

3. This is a ____________________.

   It tastes ____________________.

4. This is a ____________________.

   It is a ____________________.

5. This is a ____________________.

   It is ________________ in colour.

321. Colour the odd one out in each row.

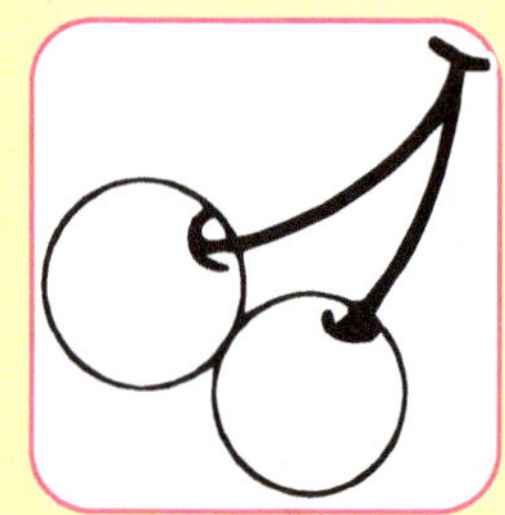
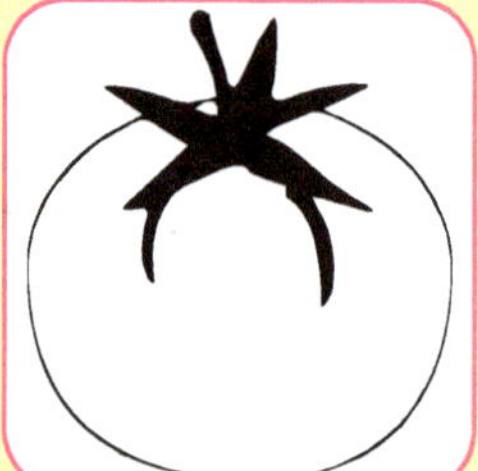

322. Create a number pattern by joining the rockets through a line.

323. Colour in accordance with the codes.

324. Specify the tens of each number given below.

37 = ________

15 = ________

78 = ________

62 = ________

325. Colour the picture that is marked with an even number.

326. Colour the fruits.

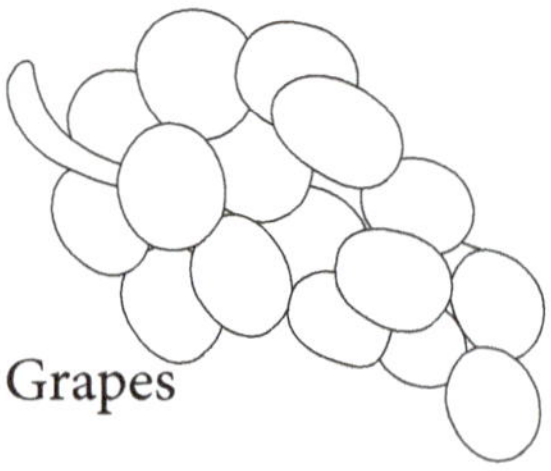

Grapes

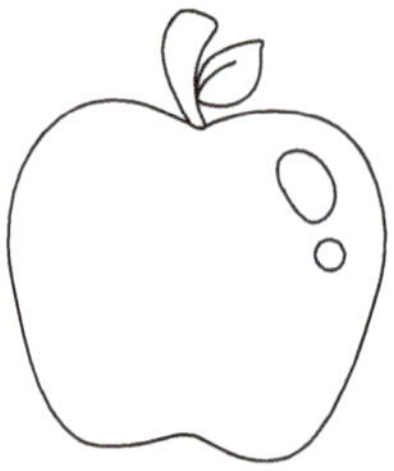

Apple

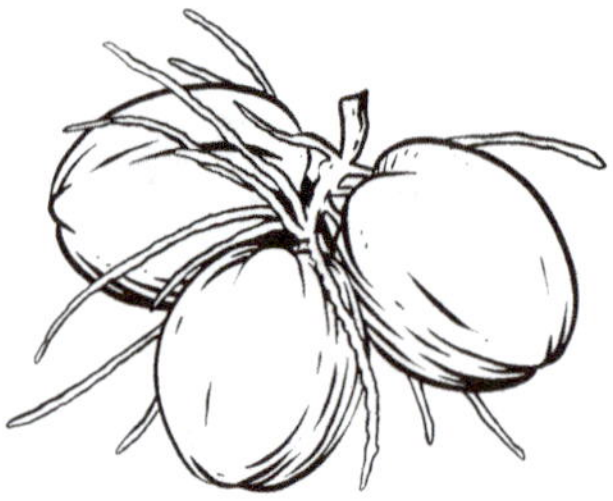

Coconut

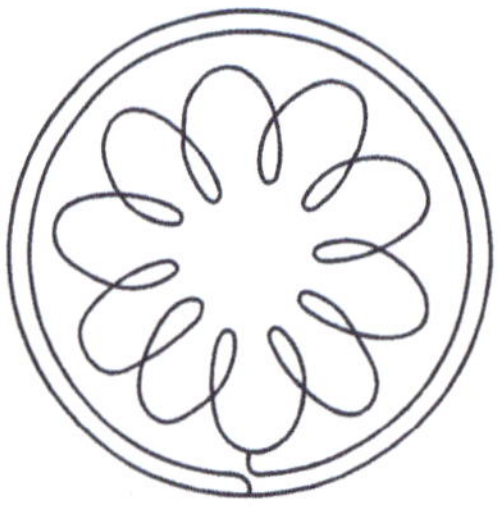

Cantaloupe

327. Match the picture with their names.

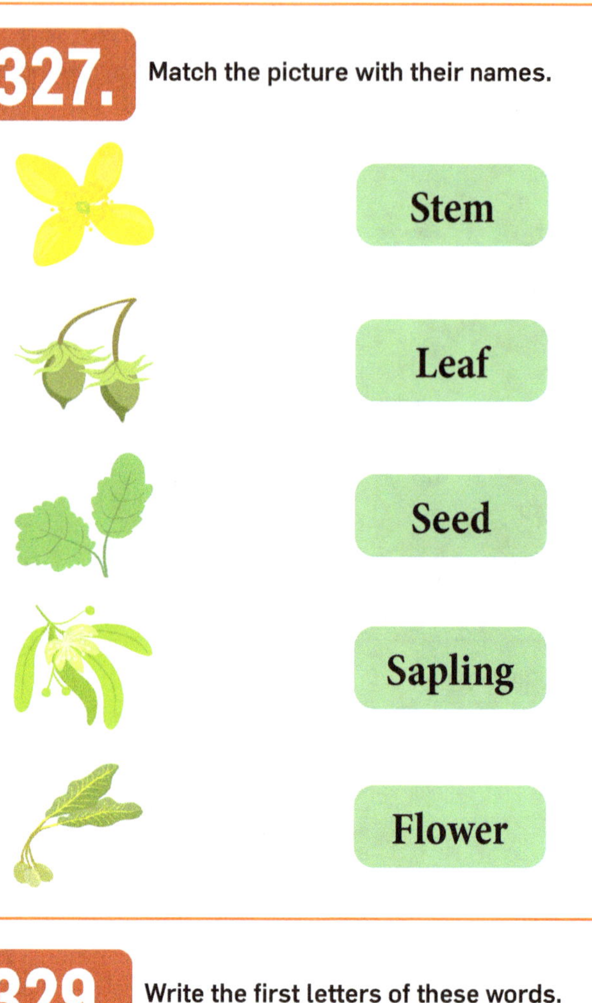

328. Colour the picture with their natural colour and write their names.

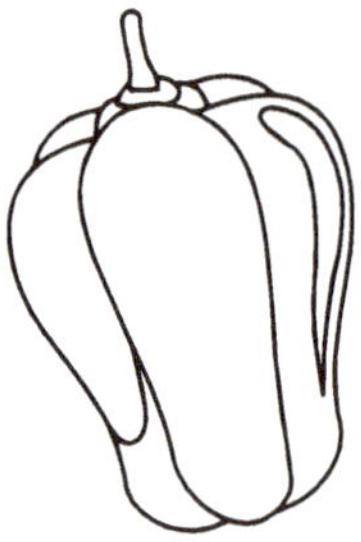

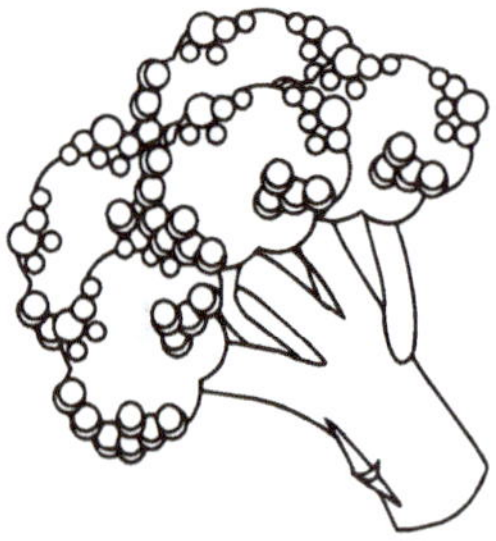

______________ ______________

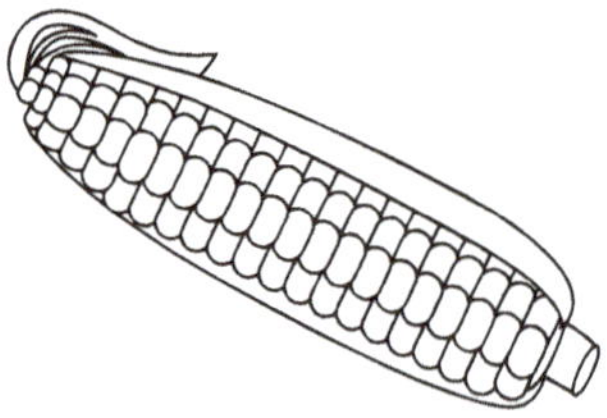

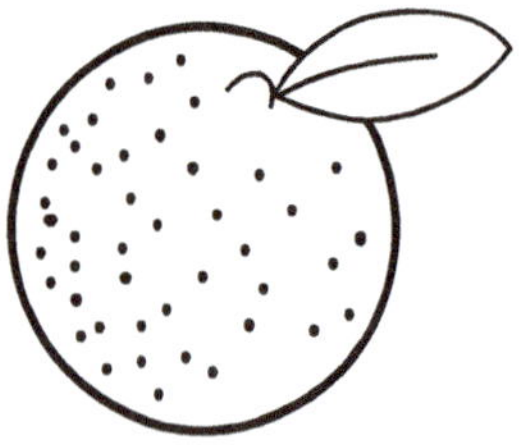

______________ ______________

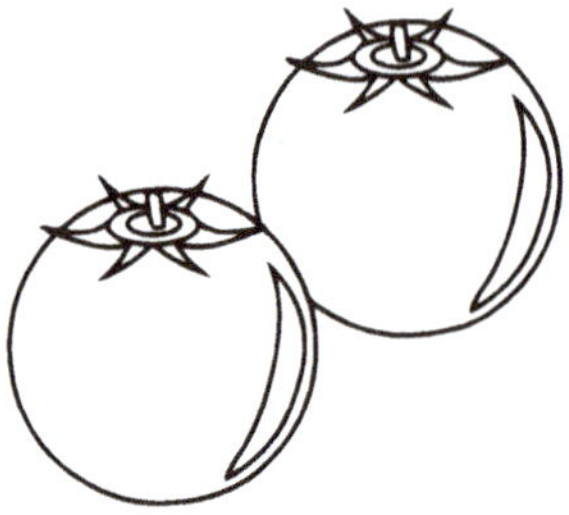

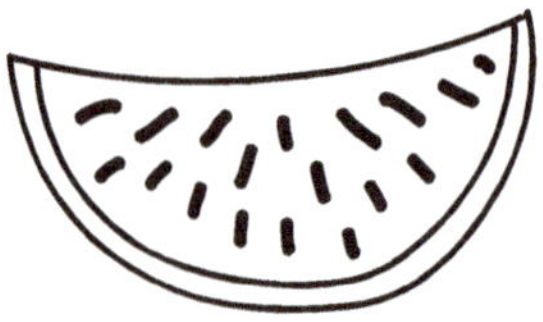

______________ ______________

329. Write the first letters of these words.

330. Circle the countable nouns and cross out the uncountable nouns.

331. Help the lamb reach the house and watch out for the wolves in the way!

332. Read the story and answer the questions given below.

It is Jaden's birthday. He is celebrating his 11th birthday with his best friends Teddy and Monica. Jimmy. They have brought a cake for Jaden, and are singing a song for him. He blows out the candles and cuts the cake.

1. What day is it today? It is________
2. How old is John? He is___________
3. Who brought the cake for John? _____

333. Fill in the blanks with 'a' or 'an' words.

1. The man has ____ tie.

2. There is ____ lizard on the wall.

3. This is ____ bat.

4. Sharon is playing with ____ doll.

334. Circle the even numbers out.

1

2

7

18

17

14

15

4

1

3

335. Solve the following sums.

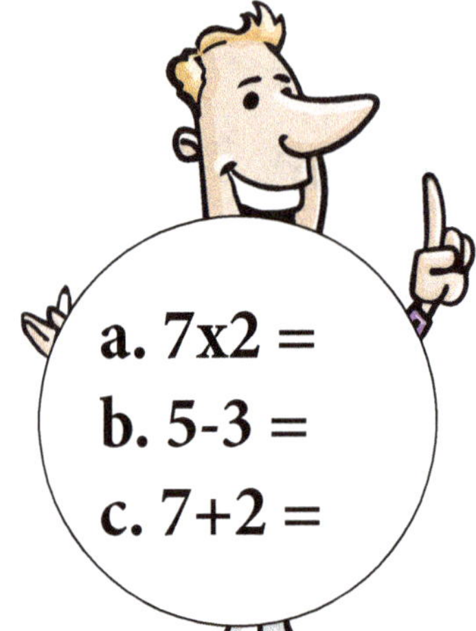

a ______

b ______

c ______

336. How many times does 5 appear within the blue circle?

4	5	2	5	2	1
5	3	5	5	1	5
3	3	1	5	5	2
5	1	3	3	5	4
3	4	5	5	2	1
3	5	1	1	5	4
3	5	2	3	4	2

337. In each of the sets given below, write the total number of objects and what their half will be.

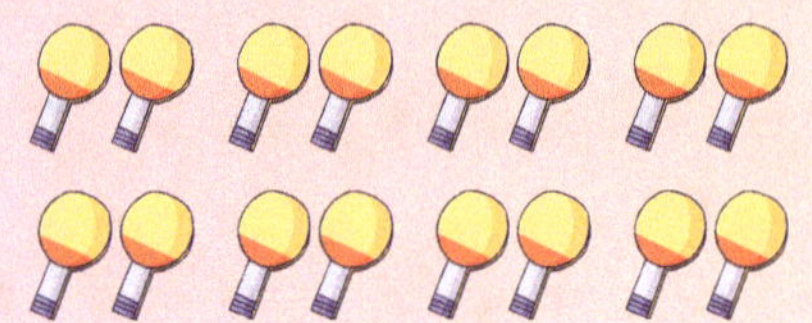

Total objects are______.
The half of the total number of these objects is ________.

Total objects are______.
The half of the total number of these objects is ________.

Total objects are______.
The half of the total number of these objects is ________.

338. Draw lines to match pictures and the sounds they begin with.

339. Write the beginning and ending sounds for each picture.

 ____u____

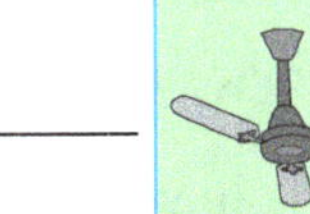 ____a____

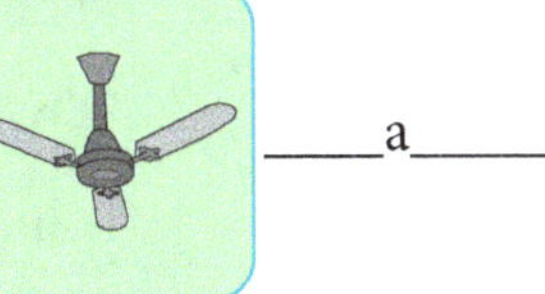

 ____a____

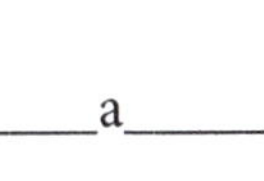

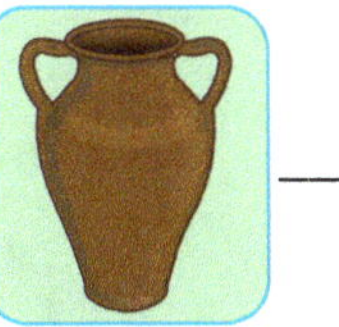 ____o____

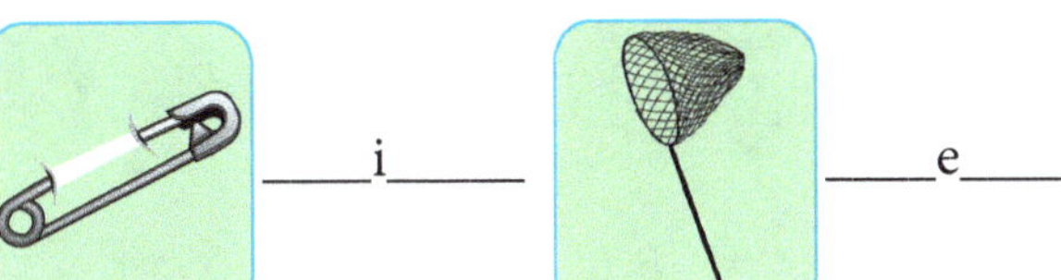 ____i____ ____e____

340. Colour the identical sequence among the 3 options.

341. Complete the alphabetical series.

342. Circle the correct spellings from the word sets given below.

Garden Gardin Gardene Gardenn	Shoval Sovel Shovel Shovehl	Boud Bund Bood Bud
Rake Raek Rak Raeke	Flower Floerher Flowr Flowere	Bie Beee Bea Bee
Spring Springeg Sprineg Spning	Fruite Fruit Fruiet Fruet	Watr Waeter Water Watere

343. Unscramble the letters to find the names of the following objects.

PLEPA

OSRE

GROF

----

344. Help the Rabbit find his way to the carrot.

345. Colour the picture and take or add a letter in the problem below to spell the name of the animal.

BEK - BE + OAA - A + La

= ______________________

346. Fill in the blank with 'has' or 'have'.

1. Tina__________three apples.
2. Sarah_________ some mangoes in her basket
3. Tom and Jane____ four mangoes and a pineapple.
4. All the children______ fruits in their baskets.
5. Jason _________some grapes.

347. Write 'C' beside the countable nouns and 'U' beside the uncountable nouns.

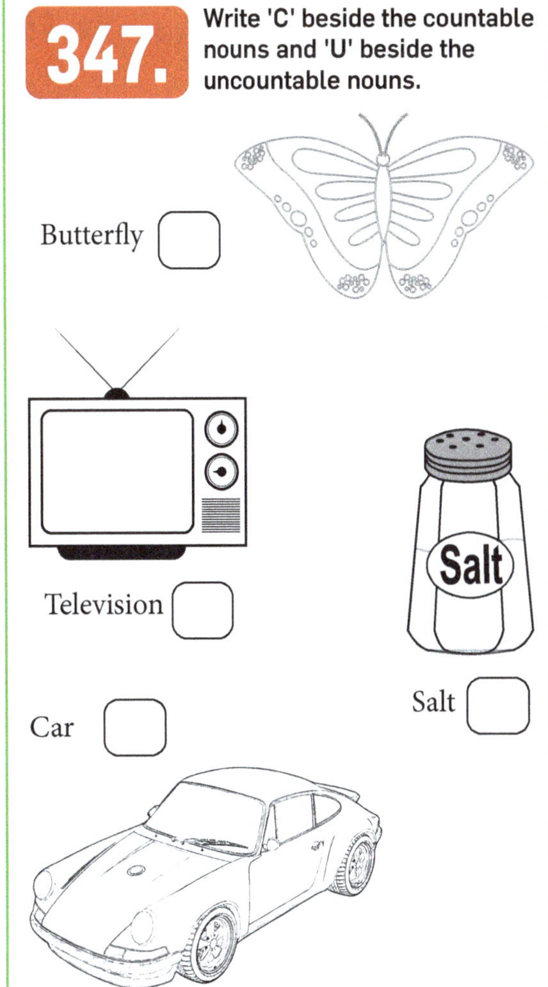

348. Circle the correct verb.

1. Sheila **(read, reads)** a book.
2. Alex **(eats, eat)** a cake.
3. The hungry babies **(cry, cries).**
4. Tracy (wears, wear) a blue dress to office everyday.
5. The man (drop, drops) some eggs.

349. Take help from the picture clues and solve the crossword.

1 2 3 4

350. Rearrange the words below to form sentences.

1. six am I old years.

____

2. is box heavy This.

____

3. I eating am pizza a.

____

4. are There rainbow in a colours seven.

____

5. is James boy tall a.

____

351. Circle the correct answers.

1. Amy is playing __________.

table tennis, lawn tennis

2. She brushes her __________ everyday.

face, teeth

2. The rainbow has beautiful __________

shapes, colours

352. Encircle the nouns from the words given below after looking at the picture. Also, colour the picture brightly.

Peter	is	playing	in	the	garden

353. Write the difference stages of water. Use the words from the box.

Solid, Liquid, Gas

354. Colour the leafy vegetables from the pictures given below.

Spinach

Potato

Ginger

Cabbage

Peas

Tomato

355. Write the names of the plants.

-------------------- -------------------- --------------------

-------------------- -------------------- --------------------

356. Write the correct Collective Noun from the box in the blank.

Bunch Library Collection Flight School

1. A ______________ of stamps.
2. A ______________ of stairs.
3. A ______________ of keys.
4. A ______________ of books.
5. A ______________ of fish.

357. Fill in the blanks with the given words.

Him Her She They We

1. My cat has three kittens. _____ are so cute.
2. My sister is a kind girl._______ is helping me to paint my room.
3. My family wants to do some housework. _________ want to keep our house clean.
4. Aunt Lisa wants some tea. Go and give _________ a hot cup of tea.

358. Can you recognize the pattern of these number series and fill in the blanks?

9,18,____, 36,	45,____, 63
7,14,____, 28,	35,____, 49
5,10,____, 20,	25,____, 35
2,4,____, 8,	10,____, 14
8,16,____, 32,	40,____, 56

359. Fill in the missing number.

45		47		49
81		83		85
34		36		38
65		67		69

360. Follow the codes and colour the cat's head accordingly.

2= 3= 4= 5= 6= 7=

30-24 10-4 50-48 50-43 4-1

361. Find the answers to the problems on the pot and colour the correct option.

362.

Find the opposite words from the word box and write them next to the given words.

day	safe	small	inside
short	fat	slow	

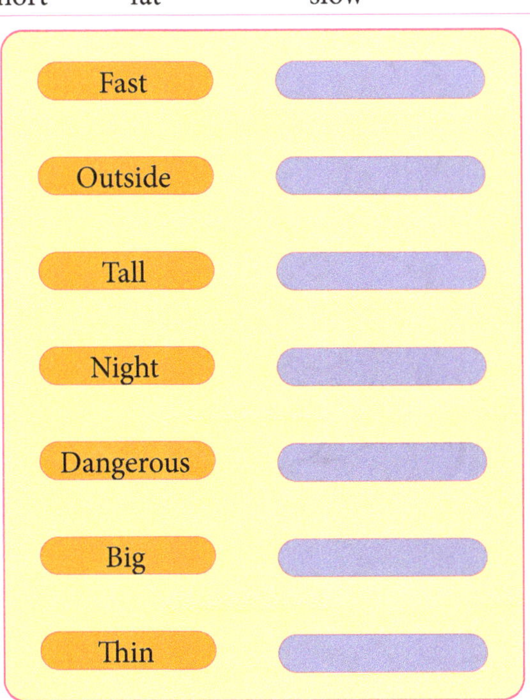

363.

Fill in the blanks with the correct occupations from the box.

Doctors **Postmen** **Firemen**

1. They deliver letters.
   They are__________.

2. We go to them when we are ill.
   They are__________.

3. They put out fires.
   They are__________.

364.

How many professions can you find within the grid?

Q	W	E	R	T	Y	U	C	I	P	O	F
D	O	C	T	O	R	E	A	C	O	Z	I
P	A	S	D	F	G	H	R	J	L	K	R
O	Z	X	C	V	B	N	P	M	I	J	E
S	P	O	I	U	T	Y	E	R	C	E	M
T	Q	C	E	T	G	M	N	J	E	I	A
M	Y	G	P	I	L	O	T	Q	M	S	N
A	M	H	R	W	D	A	E	C	A	B	U
N	N	U	R	S	E	Y	R	L	N	S	M

Doctor **Fireman** **Pilot**
Policeman **Nurse** **Carpenter**

365.

Match each professional with the correct object.

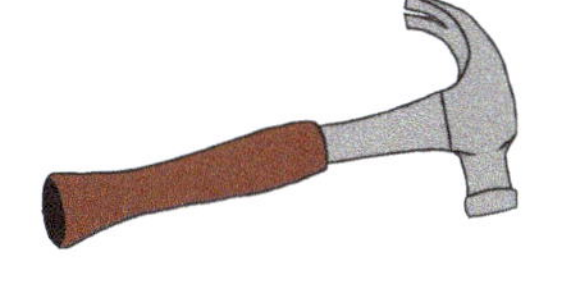

366. Circle the plants that can grow flowers on them.

367. Colour the picture like the image given.

368. Name the food items.

369. Solve the following sums.

370. Count the number of igloos and subtract the canceled ones. Write down the total number of remaining igloos.

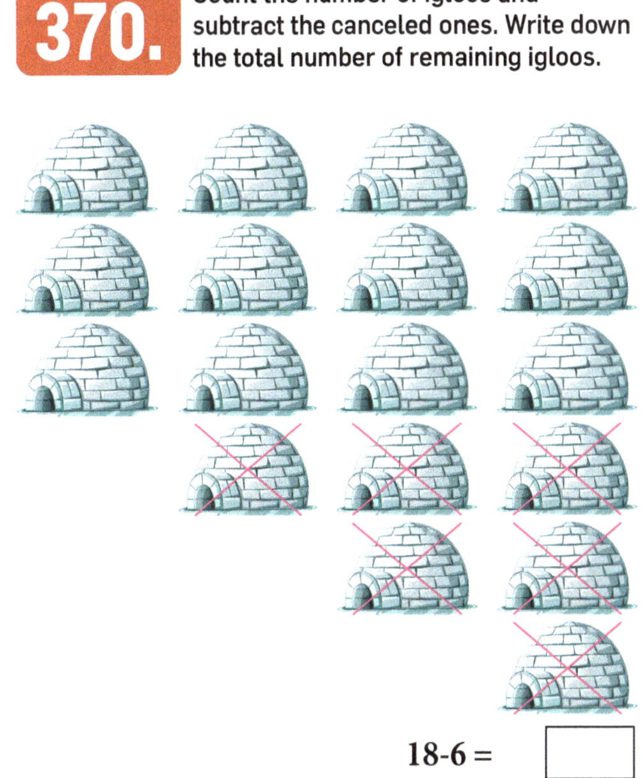

18-6 = ☐

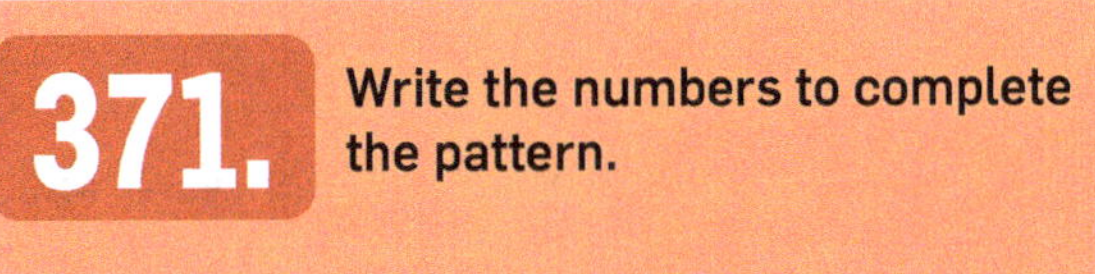

371. Write the numbers to complete the pattern.

8 __ 12 __ 16 __ 20 __ 24

372. Fill in the brackets to complete the grid.

8	+		=	12
17	–	5	=	
	+	5	=	12
16	–	12	=	
5	+		=	12

373. Solve the sums and colour the fish according to the colour codes.

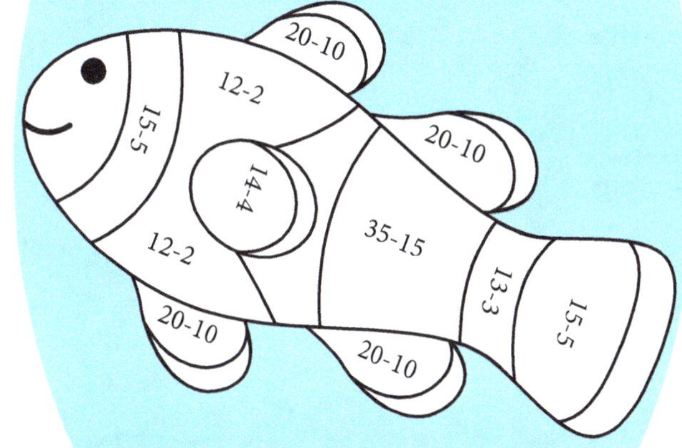

20 = Yellow
10 = Red

374. Look at the picture. Choose the correct answer and fill the blanks up.

How many pet _______do you have?

1. Dogs
2. Hamsters
3. Fish
4. Cats

I talked to my friend on the _______.

1. Television
2. Torchlight
3. Mobile
4. Computer

The elephant raised its ____________.

1. Leg
2. Trunk
3. Trumpet
4. Ear

375. Join the group of words to the correct picture.

1. A swarm of

2. A litter of

3. A flock of

376. Look at the images and unscramble the letters to fill the blank boxes.

noeb	
tike	
gip	
aisln	
mdru	
uckd	

377. Find all the vowels in each word, and write them in the boxes below.

1. Dictionary ☐ ☐ ☐ ☐ ☐
2. Photograph ☐ ☐ ☐ ☐ ☐
3. Flute ☐ ☐ ☐ ☐ ☐
4. Winter ☐ ☐ ☐ ☐ ☐
5. Computer ☐ ☐ ☐ ☐ ☐
6. Diamond ☐ ☐ ☐ ☐ ☐
7. Playground ☐ ☐ ☐ ☐ ☐
8. Kitchen ☐ ☐ ☐ ☐ ☐
9. Koala ☐ ☐ ☐ ☐ ☐
10. Sandwich ☐ ☐ ☐ ☐ ☐

378.

Trace the line and find the name of the tree.

Name of the tree ____________________________

379.

Plants called climbers need support to grow. Colour the climbers given below.

GRAPEVINE MONEY PLANT

380.

Draw the remaining half of the leaf and colour the complete image.

381.

Circle the odd one out from the lot.

Pomegranate

Pea

Mango

Apple

Corn

Cherry

382. Colour each number with different colours.

383. Circle the hidden numbers from 1 to 6.

384. Solve the picture equations below and write the answers in the blank boxes.

+ =

+ =

+ =

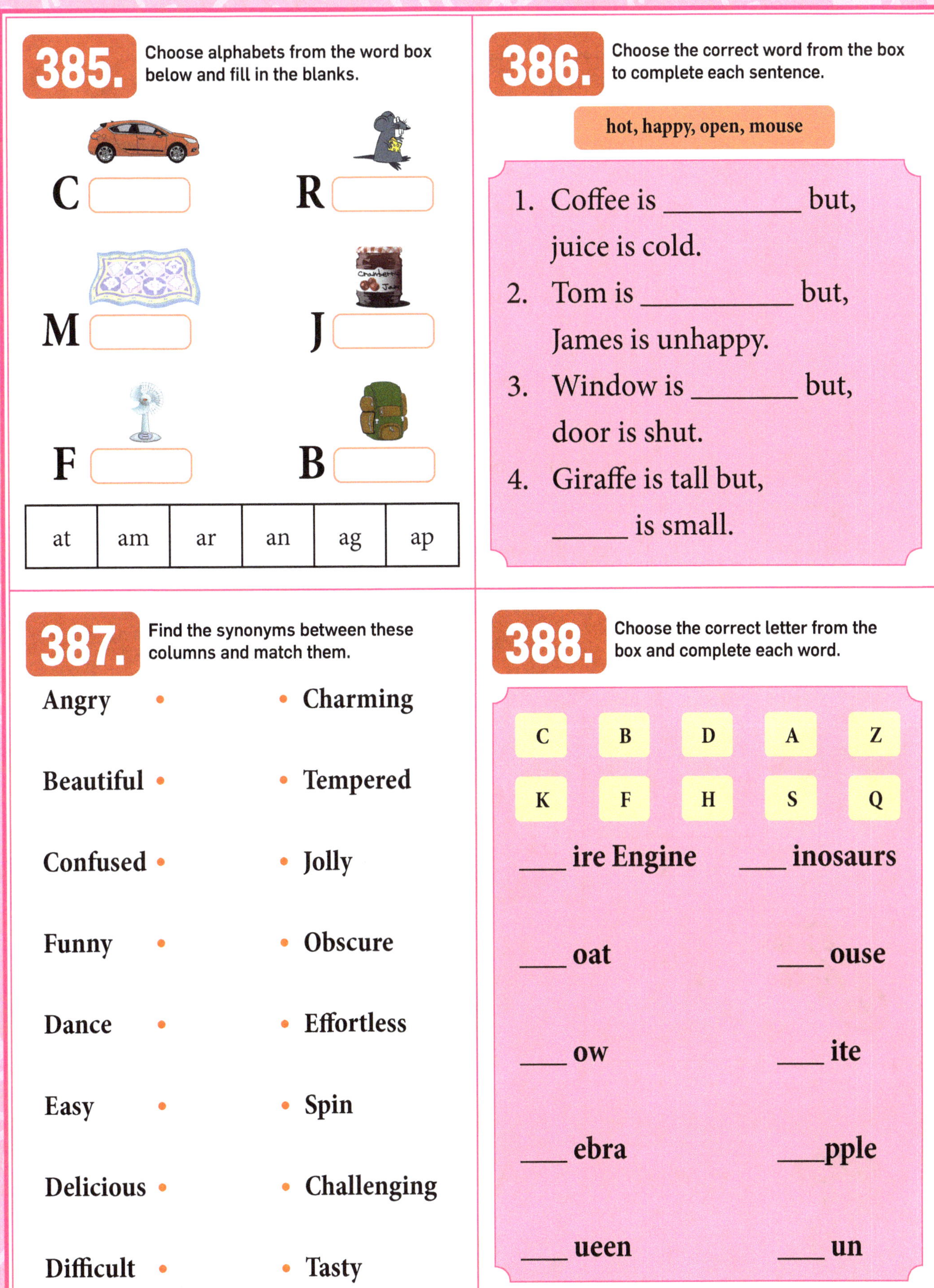

385. Choose alphabets from the word box below and fill in the blanks.

C ______

R ______

M ______

J ______

F ______

B ______

at	am	ar	an	ag	ap

386. Choose the correct word from the box to complete each sentence.

hot, happy, open, mouse

1. Coffee is __________ but, juice is cold.
2. Tom is ___________ but, James is unhappy.
3. Window is ________ but, door is shut.
4. Giraffe is tall but, _____ is small.

387. Find the synonyms between these columns and match them.

Angry •	• **Charming**
Beautiful •	• **Tempered**
Confused •	• **Jolly**
Funny •	• **Obscure**
Dance •	• **Effortless**
Easy •	• **Spin**
Delicious •	• **Challenging**
Difficult •	• **Tasty**

388. Choose the correct letter from the box and complete each word.

C	B	D	A	Z
K	F	H	S	Q

___ ire Engine **___ inosaurs**

___ oat **___ ouse**

___ ow **___ ite**

___ ebra **___pple**

___ ueen **___ un**

389.

Do you know how useful trees are for us? Match the images with the given pointers to know about them.

A. Trees give us wood.

B. We make paper from trees.

C. We get pulses and spices from trees.

D. Trees keep the air fresh.

E. Trees give us rubber.

F. We get fruits and vegetables from trees.

390.

Look at the pictures and unscramble the letters to find out the names.

IGGERN

____

RELEYC

____

CCOLIBRO

____

391.

Unscramble these letters to find out the name of the biggest flower in the world!

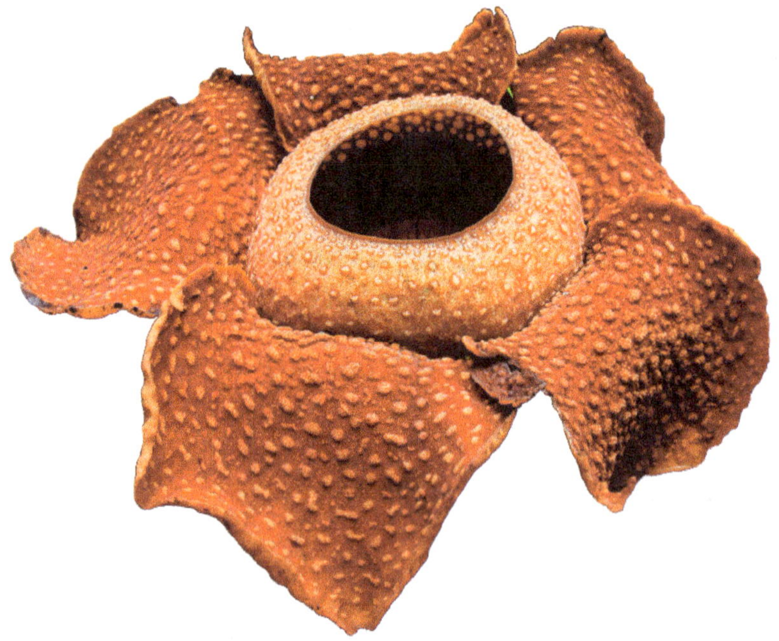

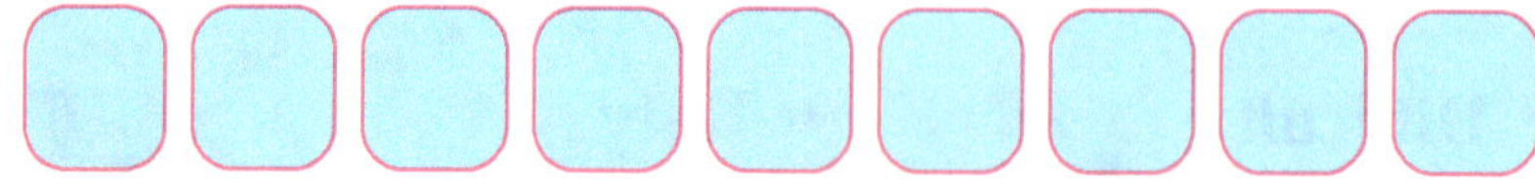

392. Trace the dotted letters and learn the concept of big and small simultaneously.

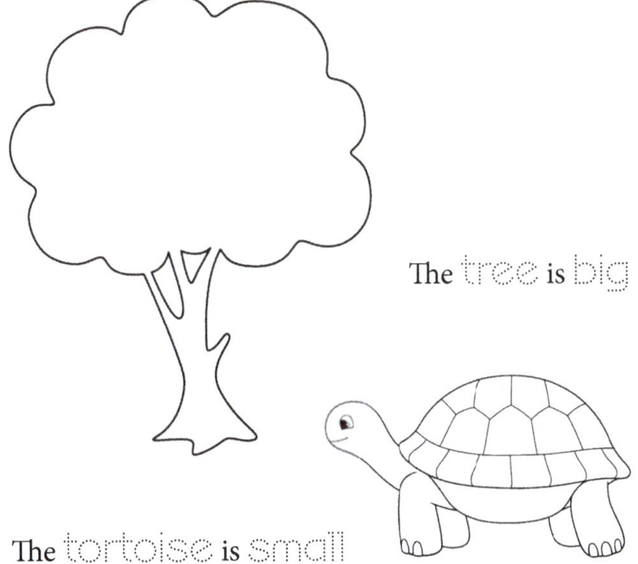

393. Complete the crossword.

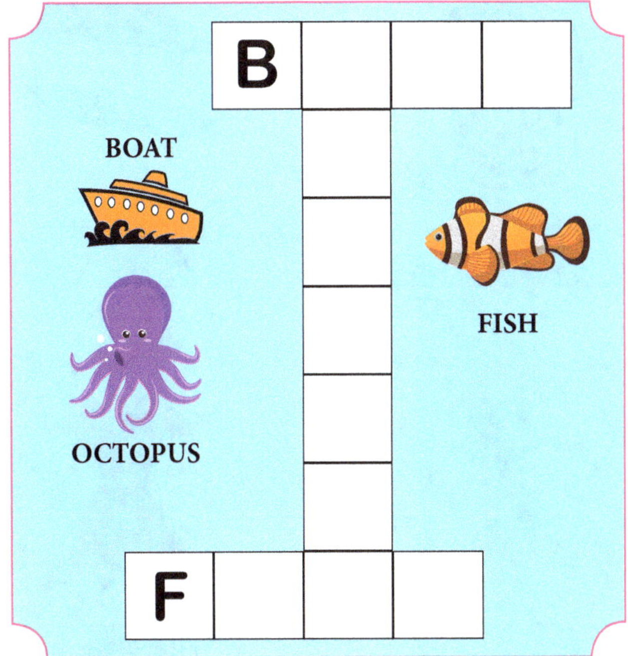

394. Choose the correct word.

1. A dog — moos / barks
   ____
2. A spider spins a — web / house
   ____
3. Fish swim in — mud / water
   ____
4. Some rabbits eat — candles / carrots
   ____
5. A car goes on a — road / rail
   ____
6. The lady sat on a — chicken / chair
   ____

395. Join the beginning to the correct ending to make sensible sentences.

1. A baby cat is called a__________
2. A baby chicken is called a_______
3. A baby duck is called a ________
4. A baby horse is called a ________
5. A baby goat is called a ________
6. A baby sheep is called a ________
7. A baby dog is called a ________
8. A baby cow is called a ________

chick	calf	kitten	puppy
lamb	foal	kid	duckling

396. See each picture carefully and complete the word.

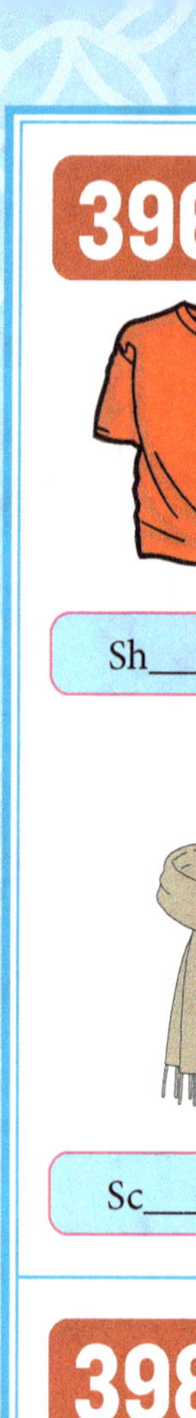

Sh________

Sk________

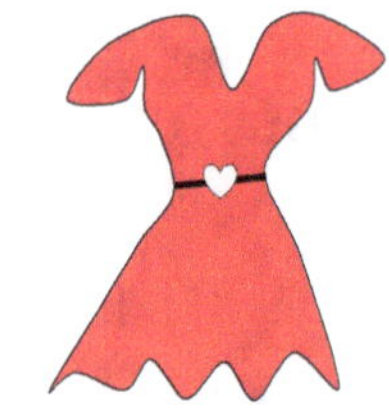

Sc________

Dr________

397. Fill in the blanks with correct word from the box.

Sunday	Monday	Tuesday	Wednesday
Thursday	Friday	Saturday	

1. ______________ lies between Tuesday and Thursday.
2. The day after Wednesday is____________.
3. ______________ comes after Thursday.
4. The first working day of the week is____________.
5. The day that comes before Wednesday is ________________.
6. Which is your favourite day of the week?______________

398. Look at the picture and circle the pair of rhyming words in each sentence.

The free boat is beside the tree.

The fat cat is dancing.

I want to bake a cake.

399. Look at each picture and fill in the blanks with the correct option.

a. I took out a tray of_________ from the freezer.

1. Ice
2. Lollipops
3. Chocolates

b. My aunt bought me this __________ on my birthday.

1. Net
2. Racket
3. Rod

400. Can you recognize these fruits and vegetables?

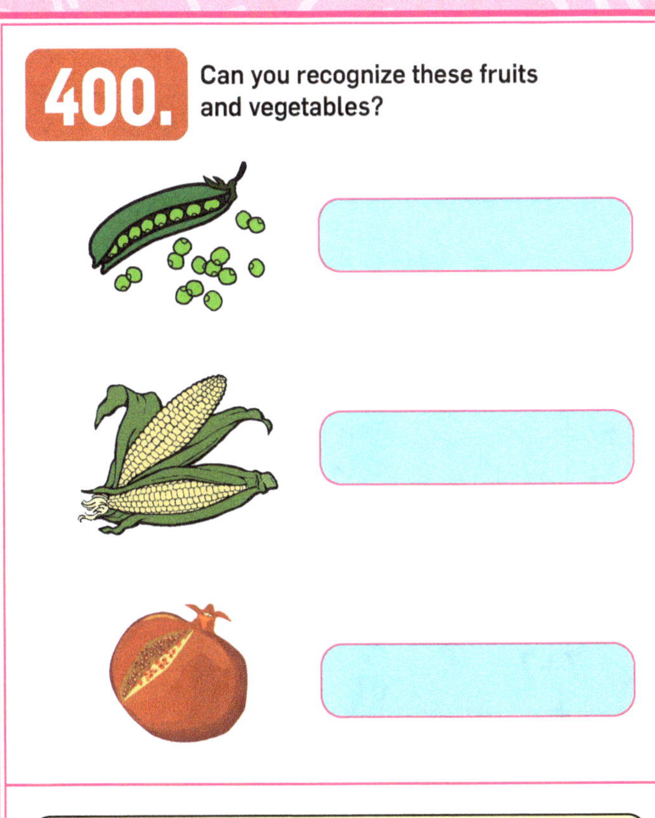

401. Trace the grey line to find the shape of each leaf.

402. Write the name of each fruit in correct column.

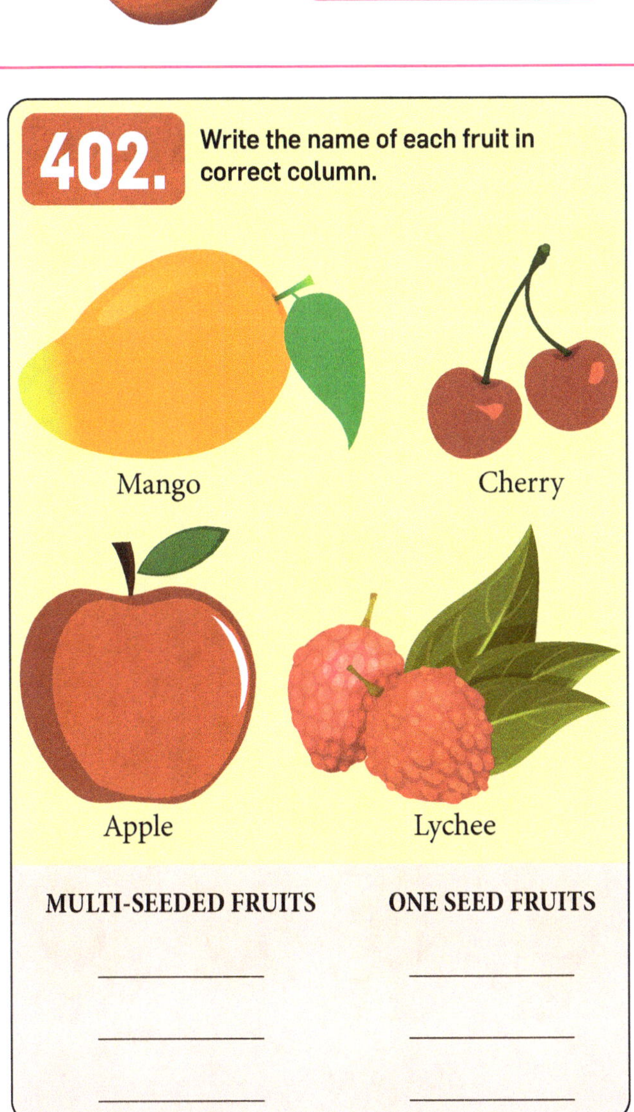

MULTI-SEEDED FRUITS	ONE SEED FRUITS
________	________
________	________
________	________

403. Trace the grey line and colour juicy fruit. Say its name aloud.

____

404. Bit by bit, follow all the sums that equal to 10 to clear the path and reach the dog.

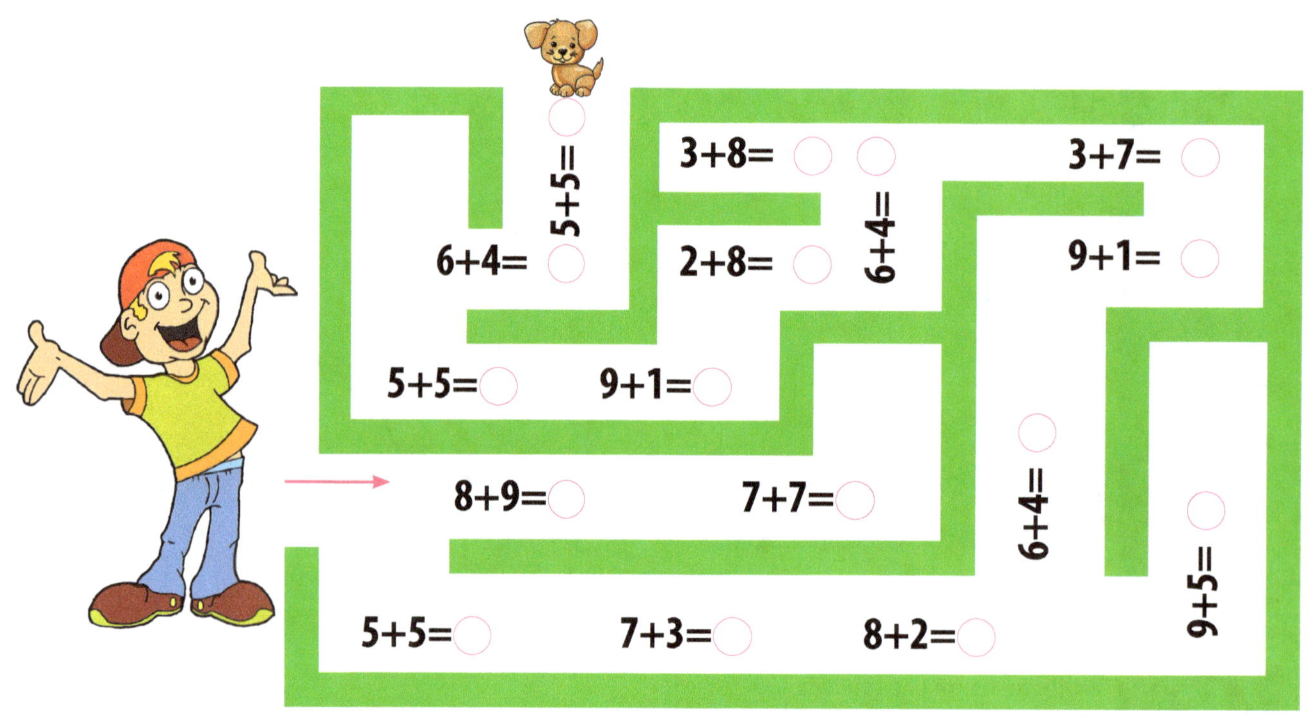

405. Find the answers of these sums.

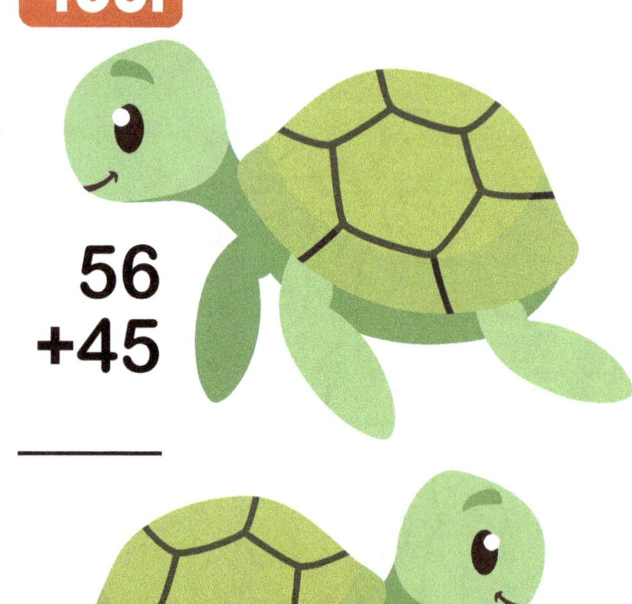

$$\begin{array}{r} 56 \\ +45 \\ \hline \end{array}$$

$$\begin{array}{r} 86 \\ -25 \\ \hline \end{array}$$

406. Count the number of suns and write your answer in the circle.

Total Suns

407. Take the help of the clues and hints in the word bank to solve the crossword.

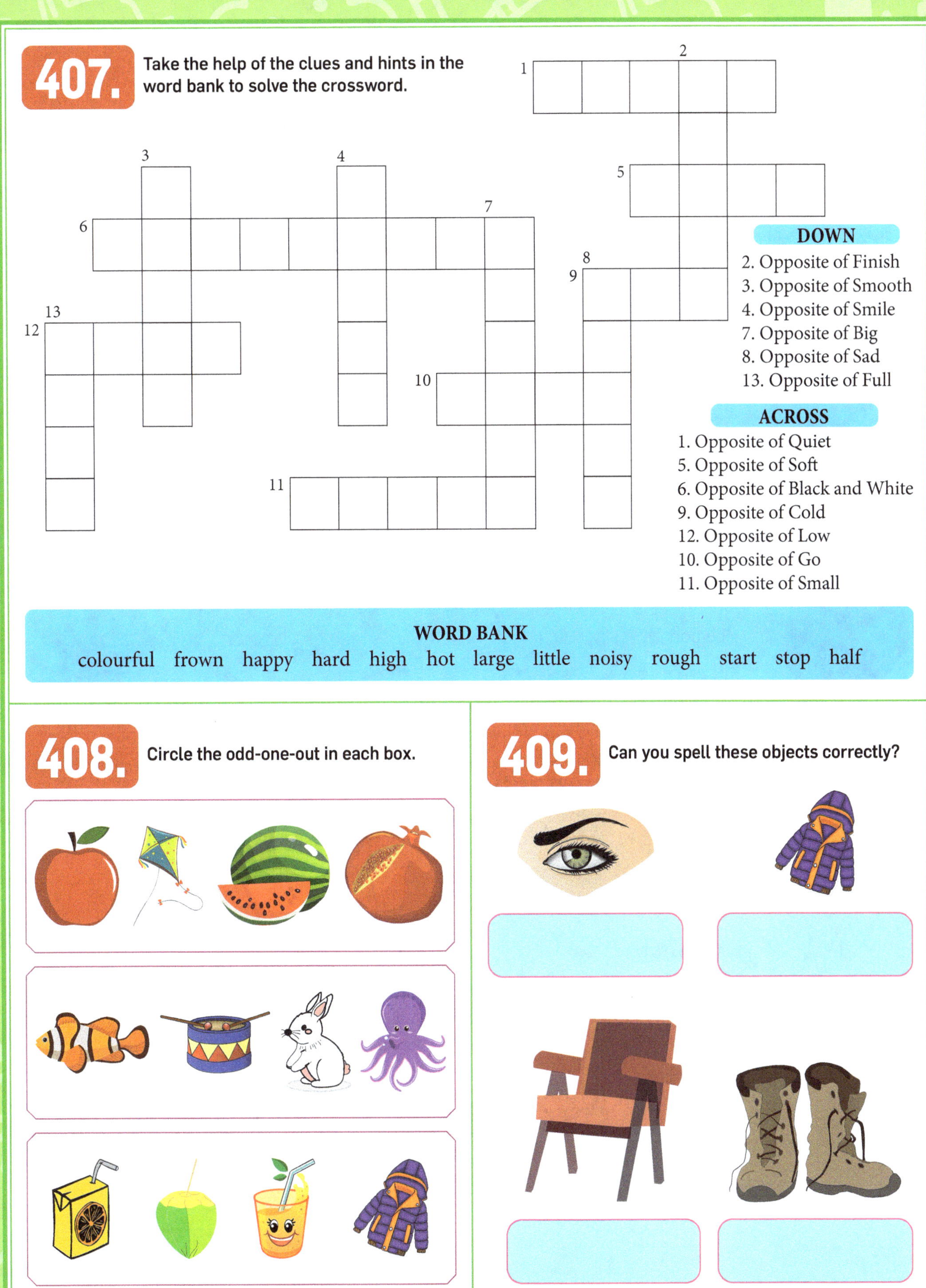

DOWN

2. Opposite of Finish
3. Opposite of Smooth
4. Opposite of Smile
7. Opposite of Big
8. Opposite of Sad
13. Opposite of Full

ACROSS

1. Opposite of Quiet
5. Opposite of Soft
6. Opposite of Black and White
9. Opposite of Cold
12. Opposite of Low
10. Opposite of Go
11. Opposite of Small

WORD BANK

colourful frown happy hard high hot large little noisy rough start stop half

408. Circle the odd-one-out in each box.

409. Can you spell these objects correctly?

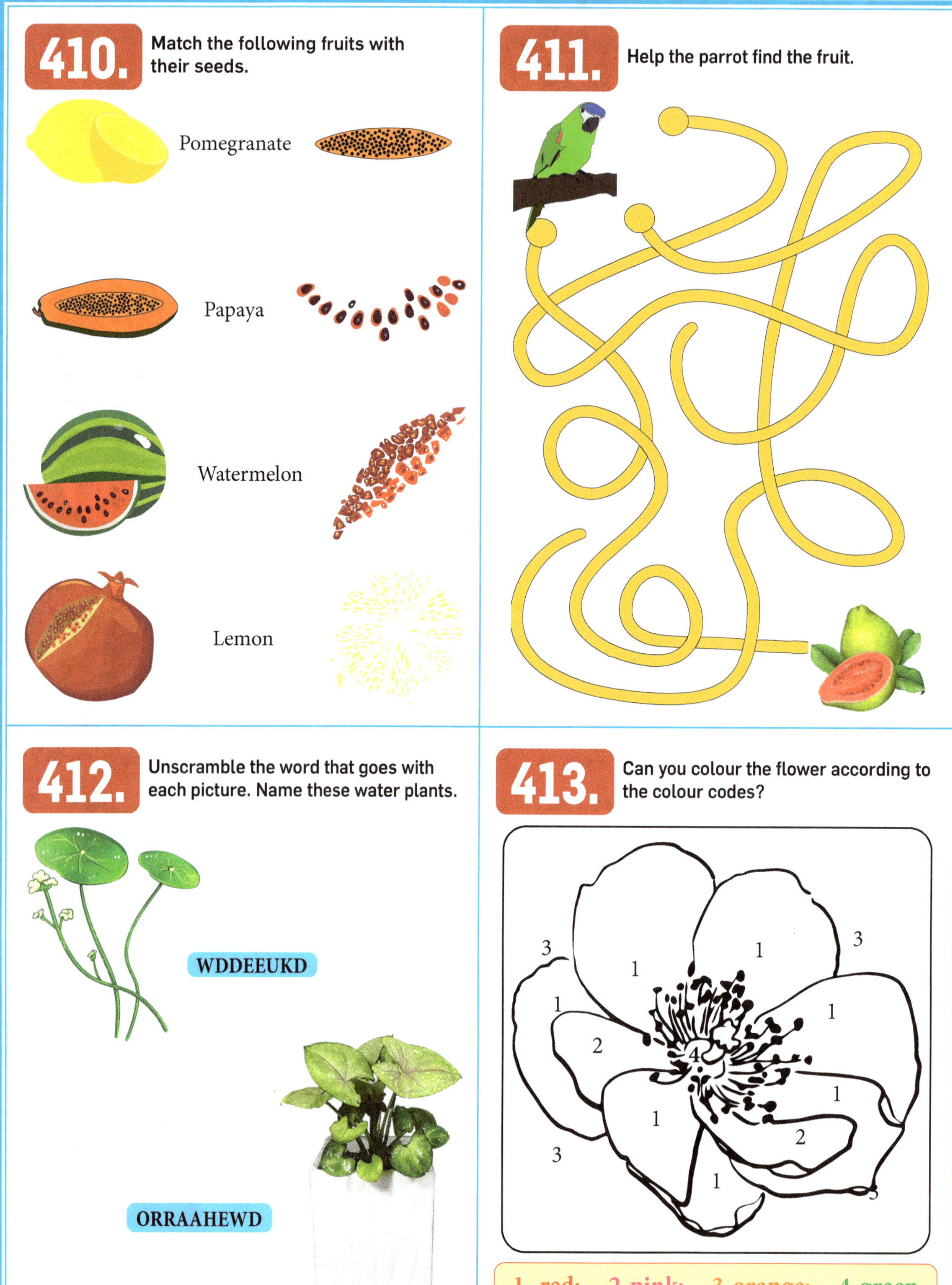
410.
Match the following fruits with their seeds.
Pomegranate
Papaya
Watermelon
Lemon
411.
Help the parrot find the fruit.
412.
Unscramble the word that goes with each picture. Name these water plants.
WDDEEUKD
ORRAAHEWD
413.
Can you colour the flower according to the colour codes?
1- red; 2-pink; 3-orange; 4-green

414. Colour the number of bananas as written in the box below.

415. Match the different parts of the face to their names.

Eyebrow •

Ear •

Nose •

Eye •

Mouth •

Tongue •

Hair •

Cheek •

Chin •

416. Can you solve these sums?

 +  = 

9 ÷  3 = 

8 +  4 = 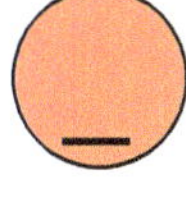

8 -  5 = ___

 ×  = 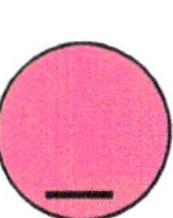

417. Circle the ending letter of each word.

E A T L

W B R A

E C D L

G D O T

418.
Look at the picture in each row and write the name with the given beginning letters.
B______
D______
T______
C______
T______
B______
P______
P______
419.
Encircle all the proper nouns.
Children
Winter
Stories
Tuesday
Cinderella
Months
River
July
Cities
420.
Rearrange these letters to find the name of each fruit. Write their names in the boxes below.
pplea
ngamo
roange
naanab
paayap
moeragtenap
421.
Circle the nouns in the given sentence and colour the picture.
The
boy
is
flying
a
kite

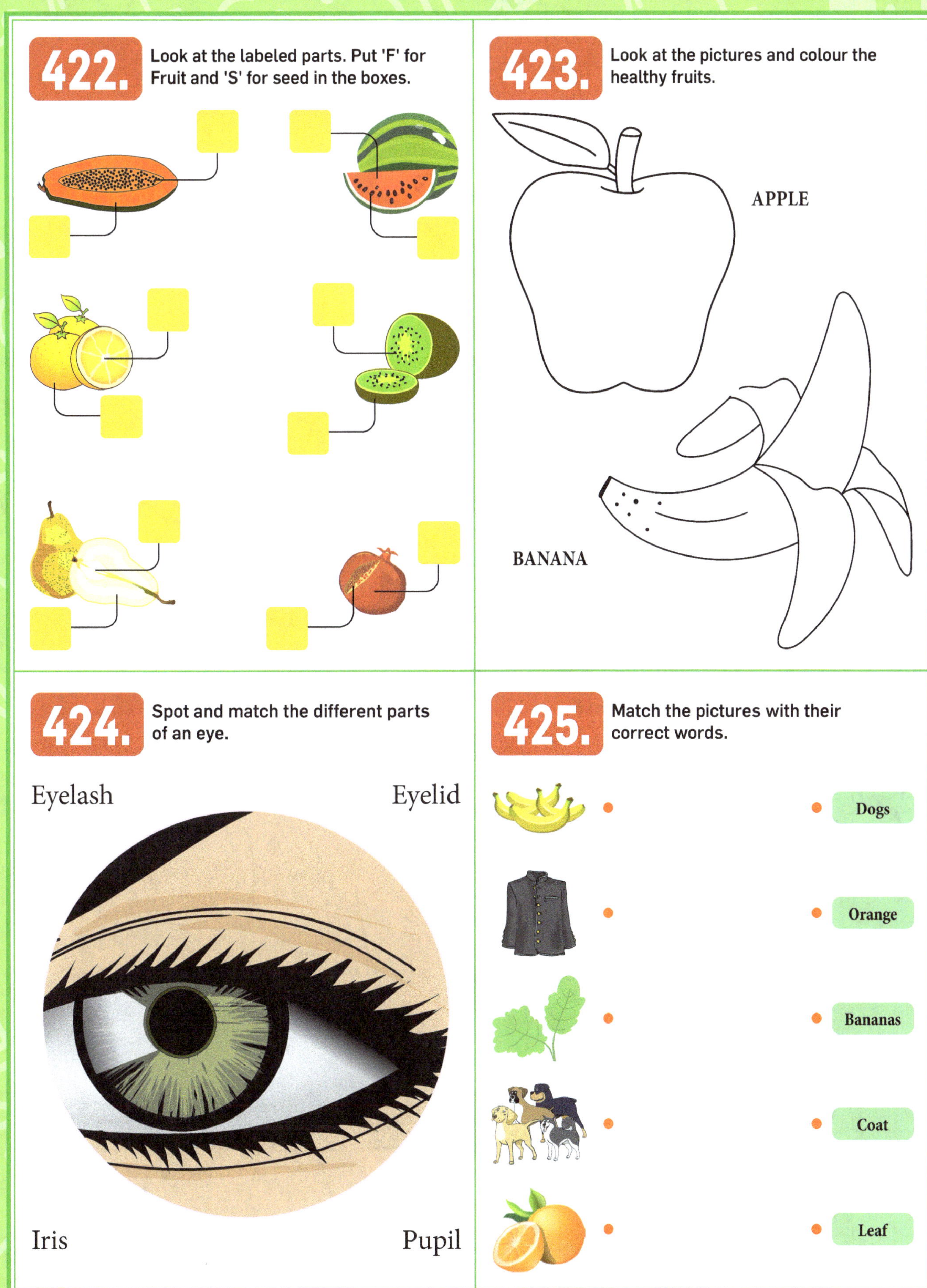

422. Look at the labeled parts. Put 'F' for Fruit and 'S' for seed in the boxes.

423. Look at the pictures and colour the healthy fruits.

424. Spot and match the different parts of an eye.

425. Match the pictures with their correct words.

426. Match the birds to their respective feet.

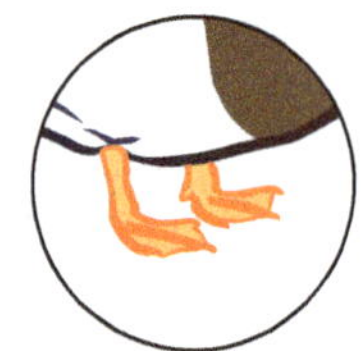

427. Find the names of the birds in the grid below.

S	P	O	R	K	F	I	S	H	B	L
R	E	I	N	D	E	E	R	M	U	E
G	N	L	S	E	A	L	N	O	T	S
O	G	H	E	C	A	M	E	L	T	R
O	U	C	O	P	F	D	A	E	E	G
S	I	K	R	R	H	R	O	E	O	R
E	N	T	N	A	S	A	O	G	F	I
M	O	U	S	E	B	E	N	G	L	L
E	E	B	Y	E	K	R	U	T	Y	H
S	H	E	E	P	S	N	A	I	L	C
E	N	D	A	E	E	M	O	U	S	K

Ant	Bee	Crab	Dog	Fish
Camel	Frog	Goose	Horse	Mole
Mouse	Sheep	Snail	Penguin	Elephant

428. Circle the animals you can keep as pets.

429. Use the instructions to colour the bird and write its name.

1. Pink 2. Red 3. Orange
4.Green 5. Brown

430. Fill in the blanks using the correct pronouns.

it | you | her | me | her | us | them

1. Here are my friends. I am playing computer games with ___________.
2. Kitty has lots of toys. She keeps ________ in a box.
3. We are going to see a movie. Do you want to come with _________________?
4. Paul has a goldfish. He feeds __________ worms.
5. Boys, Miss Less wants to see all of ______.

431. Find the names of all the months in a year in the grid below.

J	M	A	R	C	H	R	F	O	N
U	A	P	R	I	L	E	E	R	O
L	Y	N	A	Y	U	R	B	O	V
Y	E	J	U	N	E	L	R	C	E
N	O	V	G	A	M	V	U	T	M
A	U	G	U	S	R	E	A	O	B
J	L	Y	S	E	P	Y	R	B	E
E	M	B	T	R	M	R	Y	E	R
S	E	P	T	E	M	B	E	R	A
I	L	D	E	C	E	M	B	E	R

432. Look at the images below. Fill each blank with 'can' or 'cannot'.

1. I __________________ swim.
2. My sister____________ swim.
3. She _________________ dance.
4. He ____________ sing.
5. The man ________________ lift the box.

433. Complete the sentences.

Clock Gift Feather Pillow Table

1. The ______ is next to the mirror.
2. My mother got a ______ for me.
3. The ______ are on my bed.
4. The ______________ is ticklish.
5. The _________ is showing lunch time.

434. Match each person with their place of work.

435. Complete the sentences with the correct question words.

_______ will we be going to the park?

We will be going to the park tomorrow.

_______ did you put my toys?

I put your toys in the drawer.

_______ dress are you wearing?

I am wearing the green dress.

436. Circle the first letter of the objects.

t c

p d

d a

g t

437.

Add signs of subtraction and equal between the numbers and encircle various math sums (both vertical and horizontal). Two have already been done for you.

6	5	11	9	3	6	14	4
4 -	3 =	1	7	2	9	6	5
12	4	8	3	2	5	8	9
4	4	8	15	8	7 -	6	2
7	6	14	5	19	4 =	8	0
1	14	5	9	6	3	14	16
3	7	9	3	6	9	6	8
19	7	12	15	6	9	1	8

438.

Help the Dolphin leap forward and complete the sequence by writing the next number in the box.

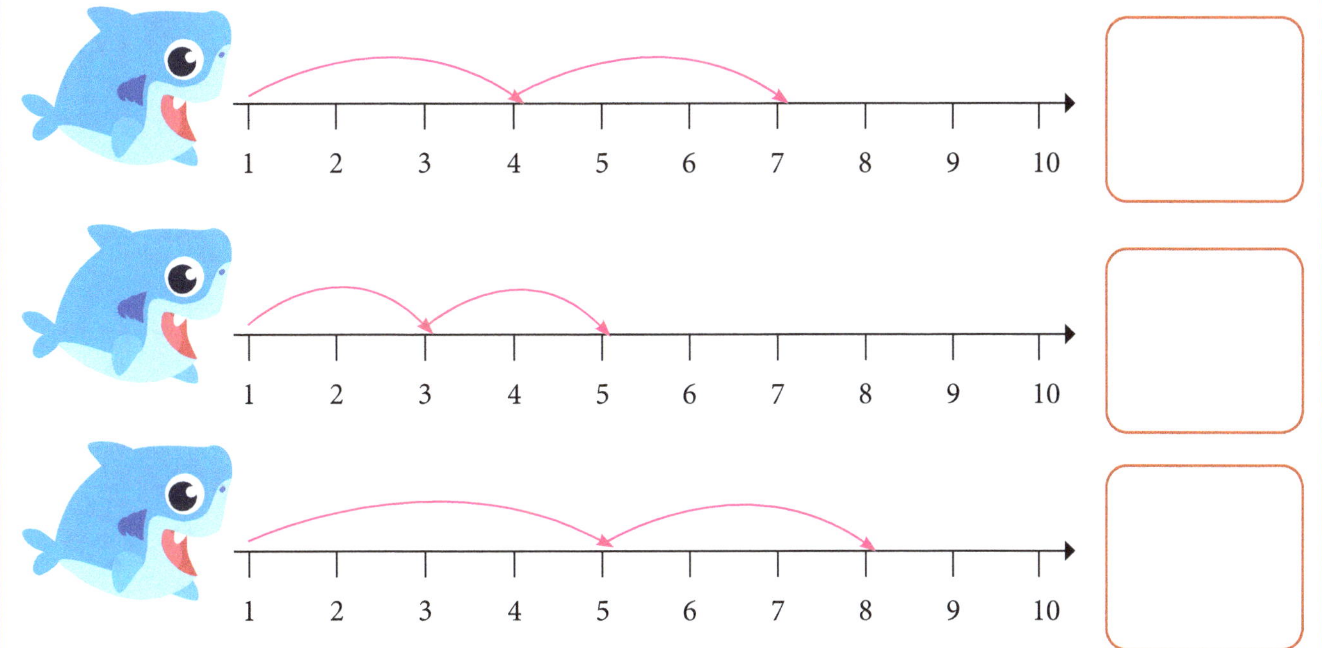

439. Find the right answers for the questions.

(No, he's Indian)(In your bag), (Yes, you are)(No, it's red)(Yes, I'm hungry|)

1. Is your bike black?

____

2. Where's the pencil?

____

3. Is Aman from England?

____

4. Am I late?

____

5. Are you hungry?

____

440. Look at the picture and circle the things you can't find in the garden.

Books

Flowers

Waterhose

Ladybug

Caterpillar

Table

Snail

Chair

441. Fill in each blank with **'where'**, **'when'**, **'what'**, **'who'**, **'which'**, or **'why'**.

1.___________________________ are we going to the playground.

2.___________________________ did you do just now?

3.___________________ is the Principal?

4.___________________ is the baby crying?

5. ___________________ are you?

6.___________________ book do you want?

442. Rewrite these sentences. Remember to use capital letter and full stops where necessary.

1.My brother is riding a horse.

____

2.Mangoes are yellow.

____

3.The cat is in the garden.

____

4. I ate noodles for dinner

____

443. We eat a lot of plants' stems daily. Can you match these edible stems with their names?

Celery

Ginger

Asparagus

Broccoli

444. Can you find out the name of this vegetable after colouring it?

AISHDR

445. Help this little honey bee reach the flowers.

446. Look at the pictures and write their correct names.

H ______________________

T ______________________

P ______________________

O ______________________

S ______________________

447. Solve the following sums and tally the answers with the numbers provided below.

12 + 6 = ☐

20 + 25 = ☐

14 + 25 = ☐

30 + 25 = ☐

45 55 39 18

448. Count the objects and match them with their respective numbers.

5

4

12

9

449. Solve the subtraction sum. Colour the sofas to show the answer. (For instance, if the answer is 2, colour 2 sofas.)

25 - 17 = ○

450. Fill in the blanks with 'a' or 'an'.

________Strawberry

________Bird

________Octopus

________Lion

________Egg

________Truck

452. Say the name of each picture aloud. Next, choose the correct word combination that starts each word: SH, SK, CL, SW.

451. Fill in the blanks with 'he,' 'she' or 'it'.

1. Mrs. Lee is our teacher, ____________ is taking a class.

2. Mr Tan makes things out of wood, __________ is a carpenter.

3. This is a fan, ________helps to keep me cool.

453. See the following codes and colour each word according to its vowels.

a - sky blue   e - yellow   i - pink
o - orange   u - light green

mug	red	ten	had
cab	rob	mob	cap
mat	fog	rip	ten
jet	tab	cat	dog
fig	sat	mit	net
dad	wig	sad	sit
beg	fed	pin	set

454. Using the image as a reference to colour the lion below.

455. Circle the animals with skin that can be made into leather.

456. Colour the image.
Also, can you name this insect?

____

457. Complete the chain below using step-counting!

2	3	 4
4	 6	 8

458. Match each picture with the right answer.

5x6	15	7x4
	16	
4x4	24	3x5
	10	
2x5	30	6x4
	28	

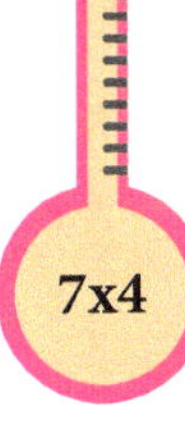

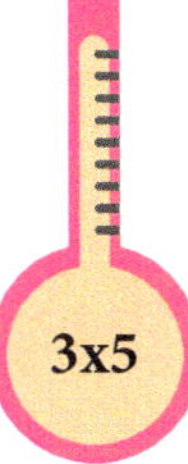

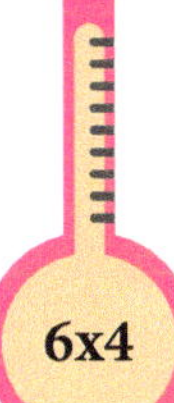

459. Help the teacher reach his notebook by solving the following sums:

13 x 3 = ____

9 x 2 = ____

16 - 11= ____

15 + 24 = ____

17 - 5 = ____

12 + 14 = ____

18 - 11 = ____

16 - 9 = ____

460. Colour the elephants whose numbers sum up to 35.

461. Tanya needs help with encircling the numbers that add up to 7.

462. Fill in bright colours in the given number of butterflies.

463. Join three numbers to get a sum of 10. You can join them horizontally, vertically, or diagonally.

3	7	6	2	6	2	8
1	5	4	4	1	4	2
4	8	4	8	6	7	5
1	7	2	3	4	3	2
6	5	3	5	4	1	7
4	3	5	8	7	3	5

464. Minus 2 from the half of these numbers and write your answer.

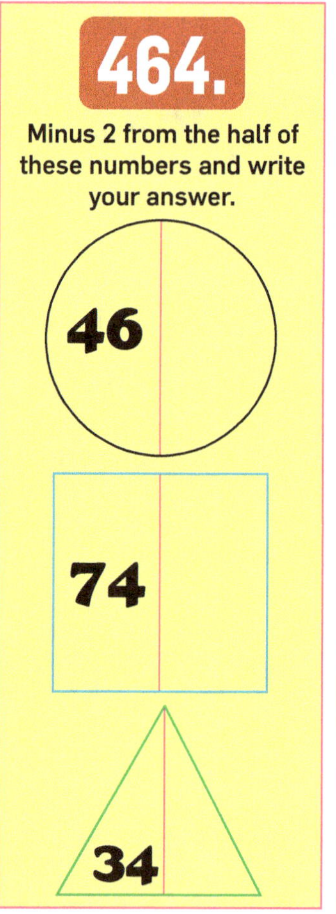

465. Trace the dots to complete the picture and then, colour the tomato.

466. If we eat these food items a lot, they can make us sick. Match the following foods with their names.

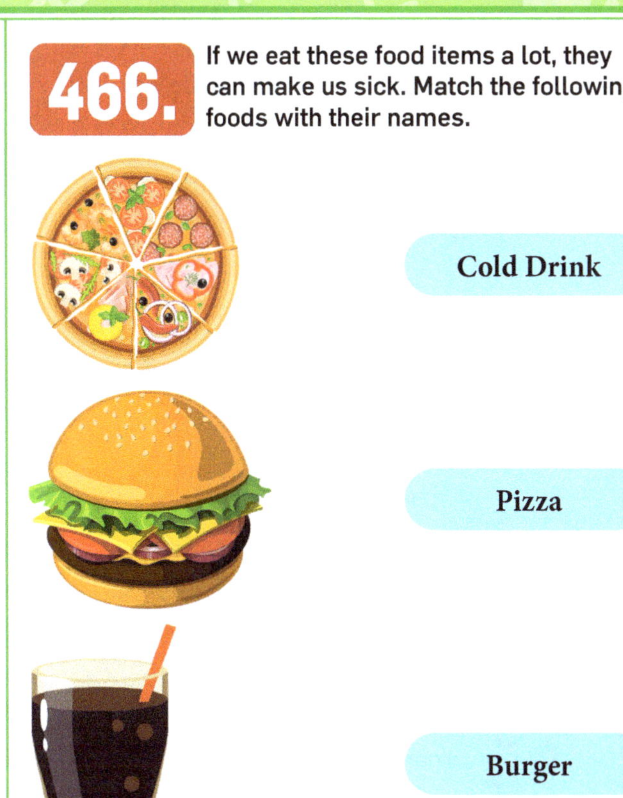

Cold Drink

Pizza

Burger

467. Look at the pictures carefully and circle the odd one out.

468. Circle the sums whose answer is given in the flower.

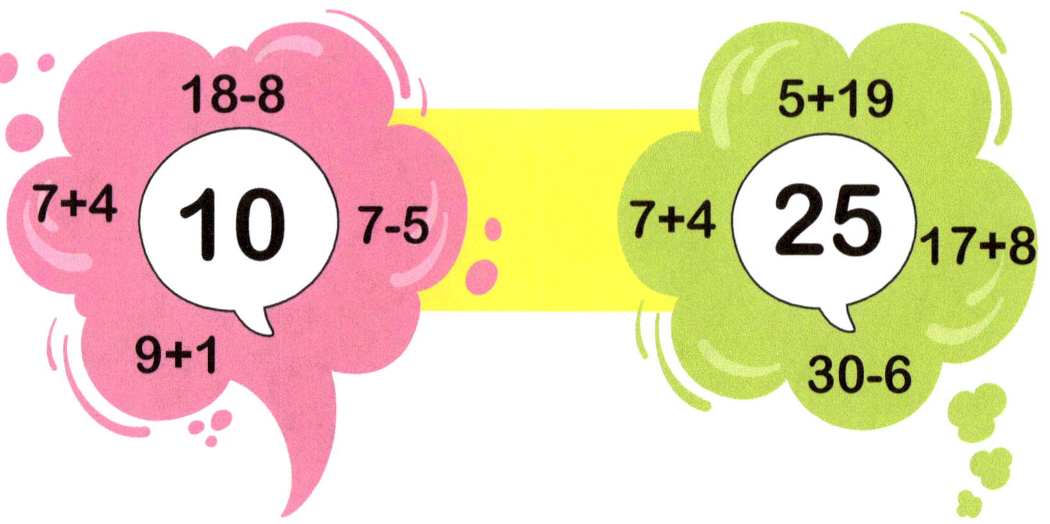

469. Organize these numbers from the greatest to the smallest.

470. The first triangle has numbers placed on its side so that the sides sum up to 12. Can you number the sides of the other triangle so that they add up to 20?

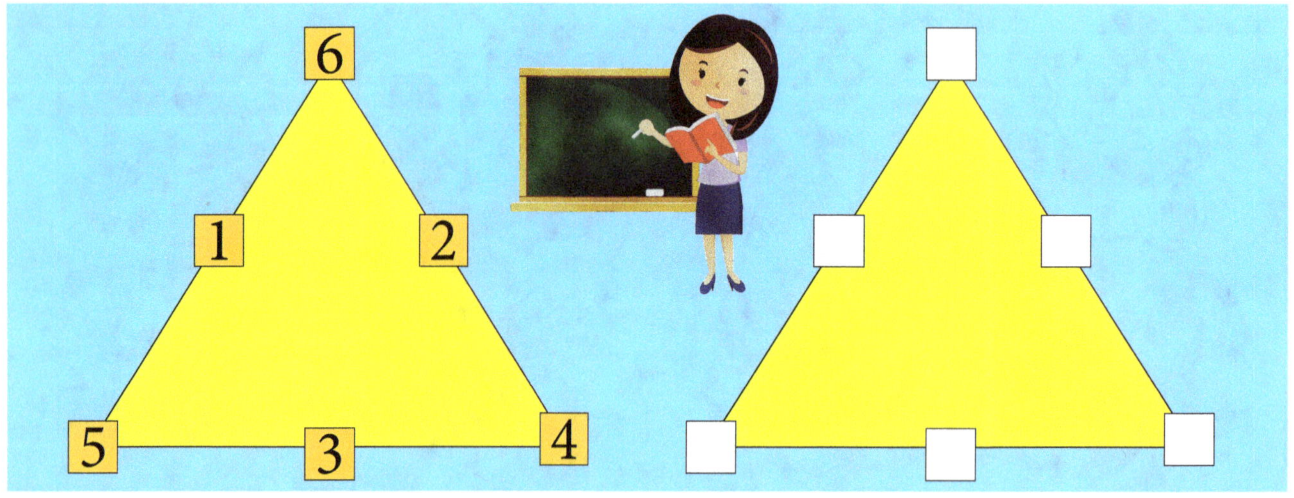

471. Read this poem and write the answer.

In the black, black town, was a black, black road.
On the black, black road, was a black, black truck.
In the black, black truck, was a black, black box.
And, in the black, black box, was a mouse!

Choose the correct answer.

1. The truck was ______ the black road?
A. near
B. beside
C. in
D. on

2. The mouse was ______ black box?
A. on
B. under
C. in
D. outside

3. The truck is a type of_____.
A. aeroplane
B. vehicle
C. bicycle
D. animal

472. Look at the pictures below and fill in the blanks using the word box.

in the box	**behind the box**	**beside the box**
in front of the box	**between the boxes**	**on the box**

1.

2.

1. The puppy is___________
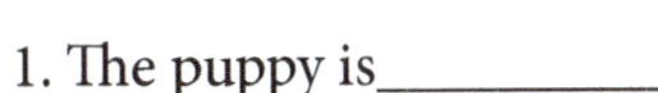

2. The puppy is___________

3. The puppy is___________

4. The puppy is___________
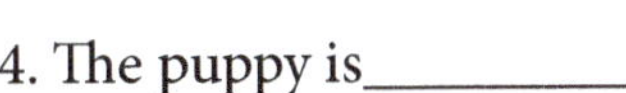

3.

4.

473. Help the mama bird find her way back to her nest.

474. Uscramble the word and name the plant that eats insects.

A T L R P Y F

475. Colour each number with the given colour to find out the name of the insect.

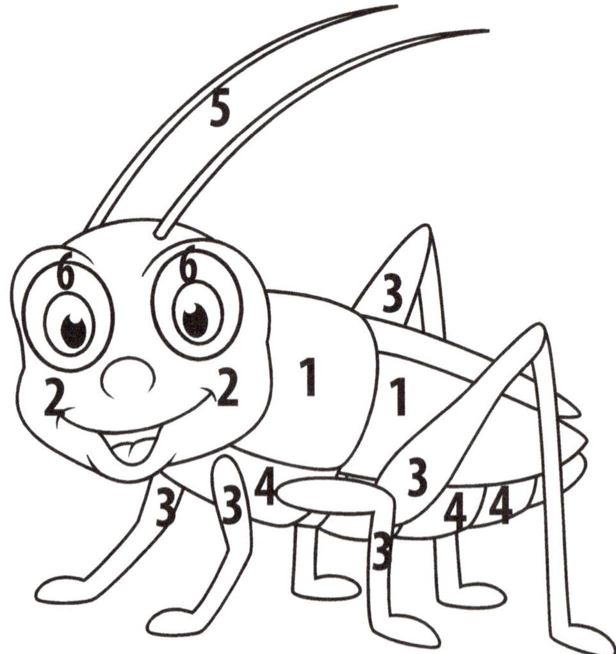

1. Orange	2. Green	3. Yellow
4. Blue	5.Brown	6. Red

476. Write the missing numbers.

	10		20		30
6		18		30	

477. Join the dots to complete the lotus and colour it.

478. Help Tommy reach his dog by following the sum trail of 9.

	5+3	8+1	3+6	8+8	7+8
	5+4	4+2	3+2	8+7	3+7
6+6	8+1	6+3	3+1	5+5	
4+5	7+3	2+7	9+0	5+4	

479. Circle the picture containing the mentioned number of objects.

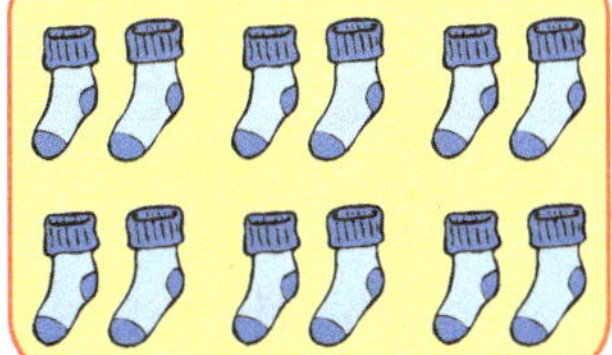

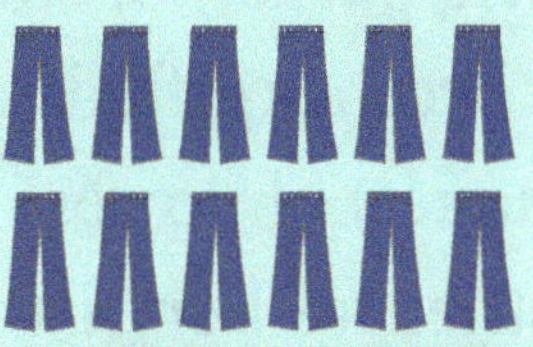

480. Colour the tomato red whose sum is 18.

481. Draw a tick next to the sentences that are correct.

The sun is hot. ☐

A tree can. ☐

The girl bicycle. ☐

I go to school. ☐

The man ate dinner ☐

An elephant animal. ☐

My cat is black ☐

482. Solve the riddles and write the answer in the space below.

I rise in the east and set in the west.

Who am I?

____

We come out at night without being called, and are lost in the day without being stolen.

Who are we?

____

I am round, but not always.

Sometime I am dark and sometime I am light.

Who am I?

____

483. Draw a circle around the things you find in your kitchen.

snow

strawberry

sugar

apron

lion

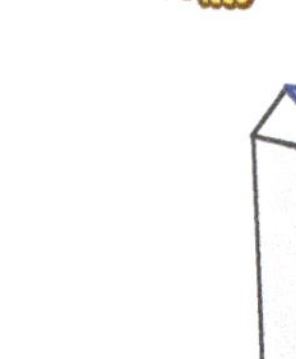

shirt

watch

milk

484. Underline the correct Collective Noun in the brackets.

1. Mr Brown is teaching a (**troop**, **class**) of pupils.
2. The shepherd bought a (**flock**, **packet**) of sheep.
3. My brother gifted a (**group**, **bouquet**) of flowers to my mother for her birthday.
4. My neighbours own a (**set**, **pack**) of dogs.
5. A (swarm, herd) of bees can be found around the honeycomb.

485. Read the clues on the sheep and solve the sums.

4 tens 4 ones

6 tens 3 ones

9 tens 1 ones

486. Colour the boxes that sum up to 9 to find a path from the dog to the food.

	6+3	8+4	3+6	8+8	7+8
	5+4	4+4	3+2	8+7	3+7
3+6	8+1	3+6	3+1	5+5	
4+5	7+2	1+8	5+4	3+6	

487. Colour the correct number of eyed scorpions.

488. There are 8 balls, 2 more balls are added to the group. Draw the balls and complete the sum.

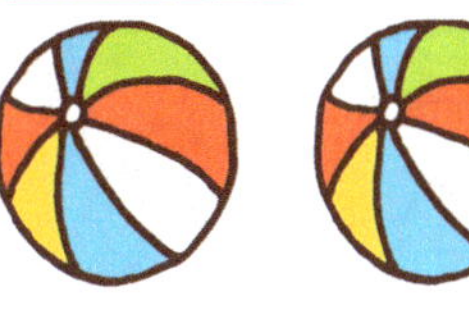
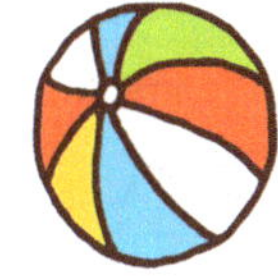

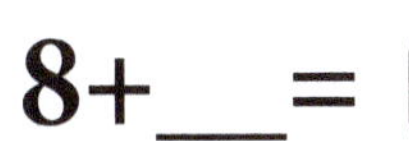

8+___=

489.

Can you write the opposites of these words with the help of word box given below?

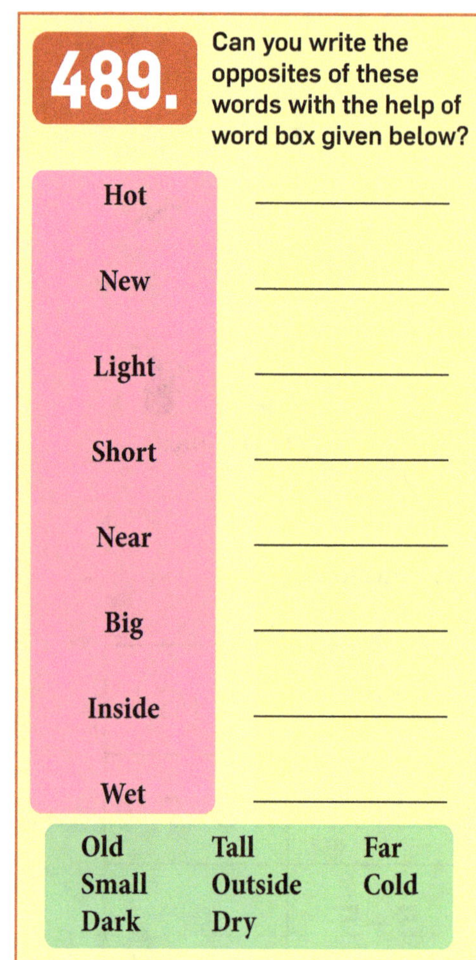

Hot	________
New	________
Light	________
Short	________
Near	________
Big	________
Inside	________
Wet	________

Old	Tall	Far
Small	Outside	Cold
Dark	Dry	

490.

Look at the pictures and complete the pairs with the correct words from the box.

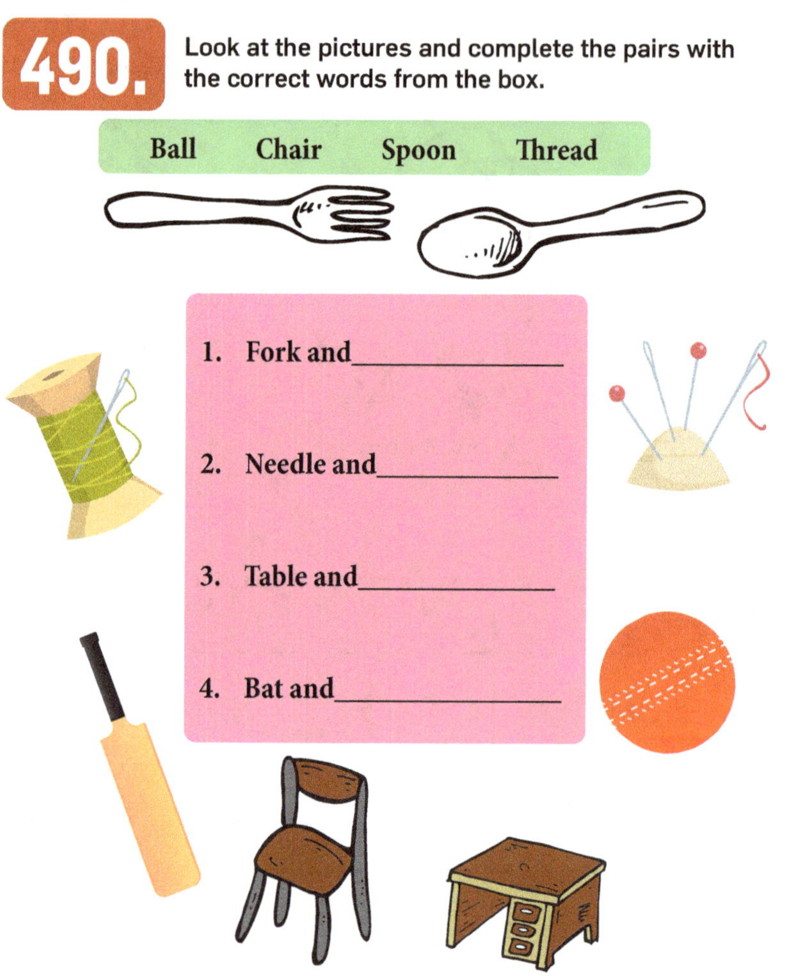

Ball Chair Spoon Thread

1. Fork and________
2. Needle and________
3. Table and________
4. Bat and________

491.

Look at the picture of the objects below. Colour the smaller objects RED and the larger objects BLUE.

492.

Say the word for each picture. Write the letter with the correct ending sound.

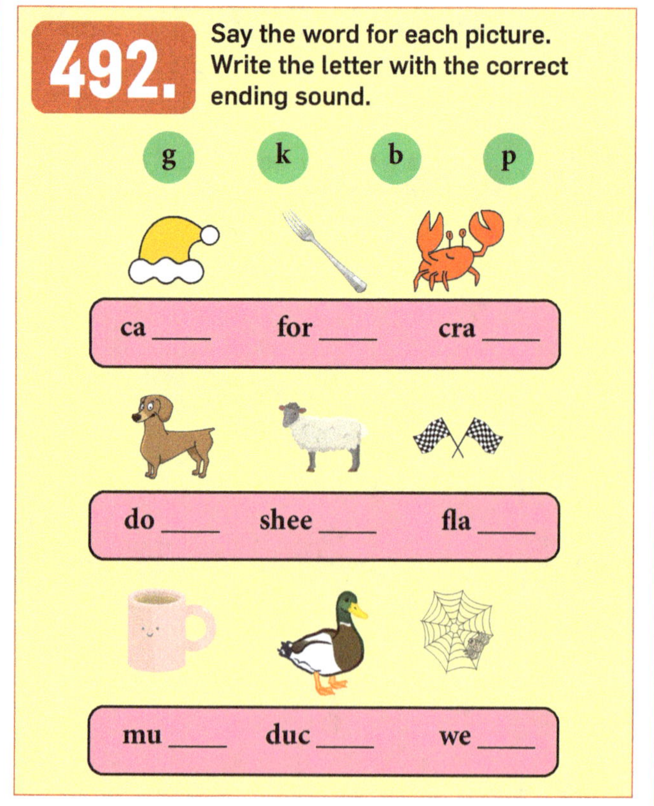

g k b p

ca ____ for ____ cra ____

do ____ shee ____ fla ____

mu ____ duc ____ we ____

493. Cross the two beginning letters of the objects.

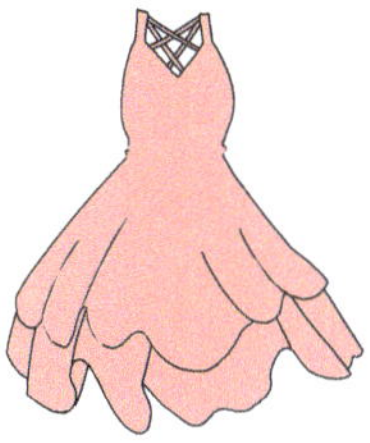

dr / cl		be / st	
ja / st	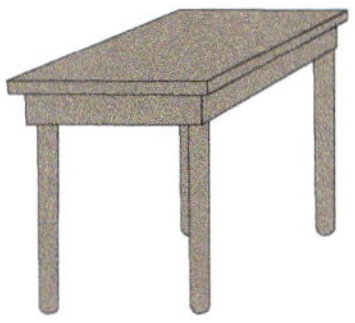	ta / ca	
dr / gu		fl / bu	

494. Arrange these letters in alphabetical order.

Letters	
V B W	
T A M	
O S F	
C W M	
E M B	
Q I L	
J R S	
S K X	

495. Fill in the missing alphabet.

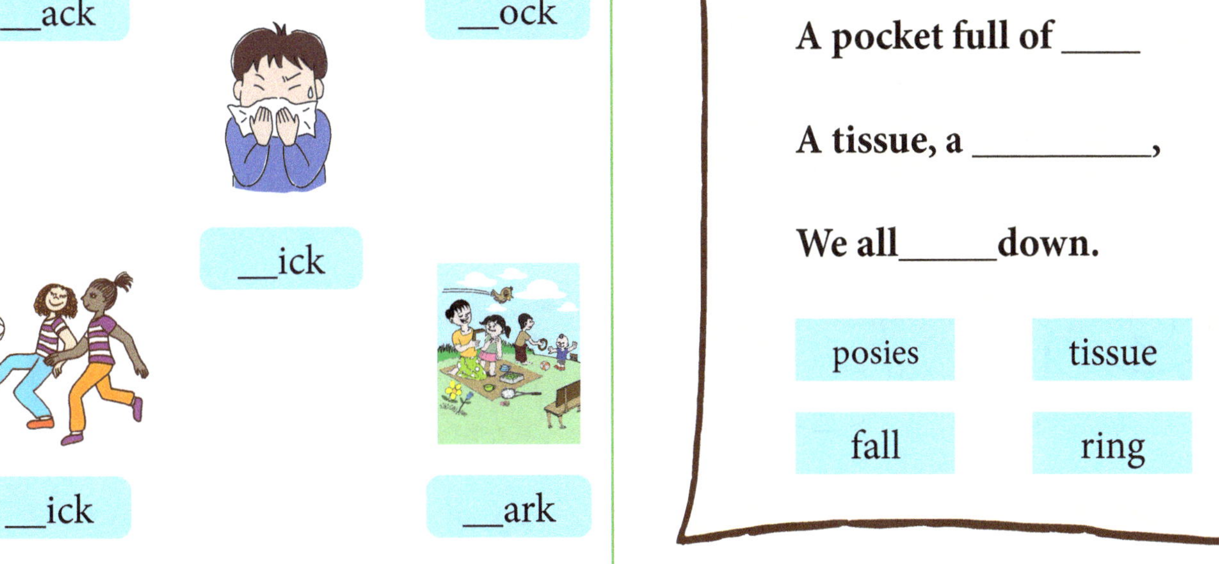

__ack

__ock

__ick

__ick

__ark

496. Fill in the blanks to complete the rhyme.

Ring-a-____a-roses

A pocket full of ____

A tissue, a _________,

We all_____down.

posies	tissue
fall	ring

497. Match the insects with their homes.

498. Colour the picture which matches the description.

ⓐ I have 8 legs.

Octopus

Scorpion

ⓑ I have no legs.

Horse

Earthworm

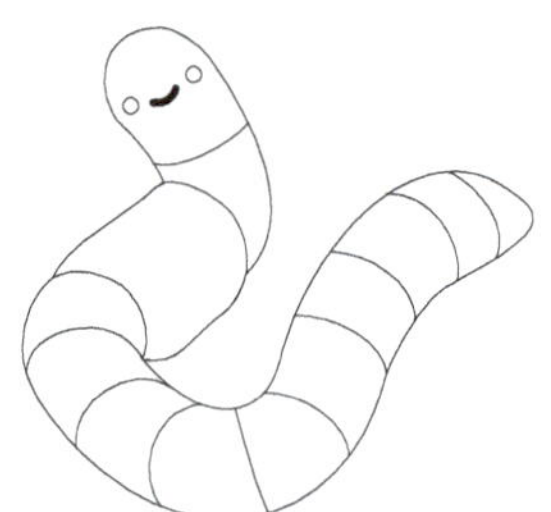

499. Colour the following mushrooms red and orange.

500. Colour the following image. What animal is this?

501. Label the different parts of the insect below using the word bank.

Thorax   Abdomen

Head   Wings

Antennae   Legs

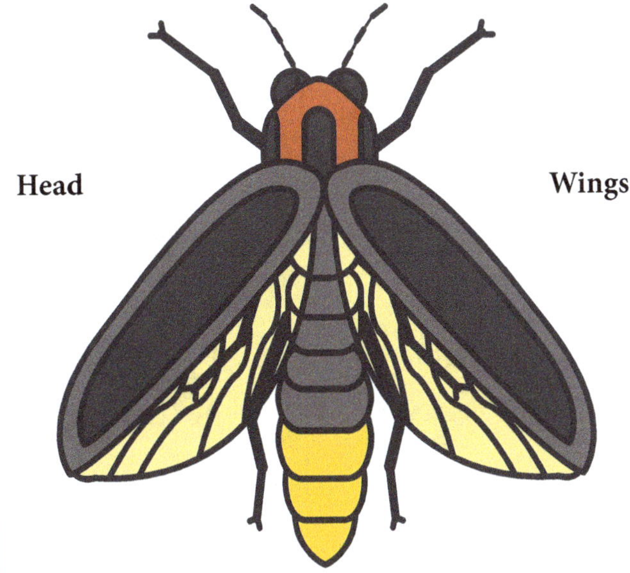

502. What do you know about insects? Fill in the blanks with the help of the word bank.

1. Insects have__________legs.
2. Insects have__________body parts.
3. Insects have 2__________.
4. Insects have a head, thorax and __________.
5. Some insects bite, while some __________.
6. Insects have an __________________.

Three	Antennae	Sting
Adbomen	Exoskleton	Six

503. Label these insects correctly.

Ladybird   Honeybee   Cockroach

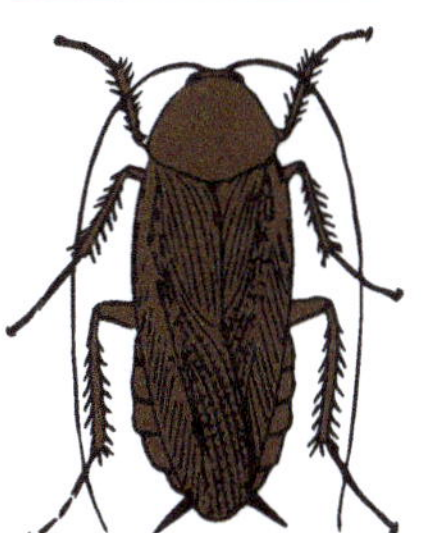

____

____

____

504. Colour the honeybee exactly as the image below.

505. Which of these things melt in the sun? Colour them.

506. Look at pictures and tick the correct word.

This is a cabbage / cauliflower.

It is a fruit / vegetable.

This is an apple / a lemon.

It is a fruit / vegetable.

This is a pea / corn.

It is a seed / vegetable.

These are grapes / melon.

They are fruits / vegetable.

507. Fill in the right number in the given circles to name the body parts of a monkey.

1	2	3	4	5	6
Head	Arm	Ear	Nose	Foor	Ankle

508. Complete the following sentences using the word box.

1. White ______________ falls in winter.
2. The sea at the sunny _________ is warm.
3. A ______________________ is a man made of snow.
4. The _____________________ comes into Dotty's room, it is sunny.
5. Autumn leaves are ______________.

BEACH SNOWMAN SUN-RAYS FALLING SNOW

509.

Look at the table, each number has a value. Using the value solve the puzzle.

1	2	3	4	5	6	7	8	9
A	B	C	D	E	F	G	H	I
J	K	L	M	N	O	P	Q	R
S	T	U	V	W	X	Y	Z	

Calculate and find the worth of the name Spider-man?

_____+ _____+_____+ _____+ _____+ _____+ _____+ _____+_____

S P I D E R M A N

Total =

510.

Use the picture code to solve the sums given below.

511.

Match the numbers with their tens.

512. Solve the following sums.

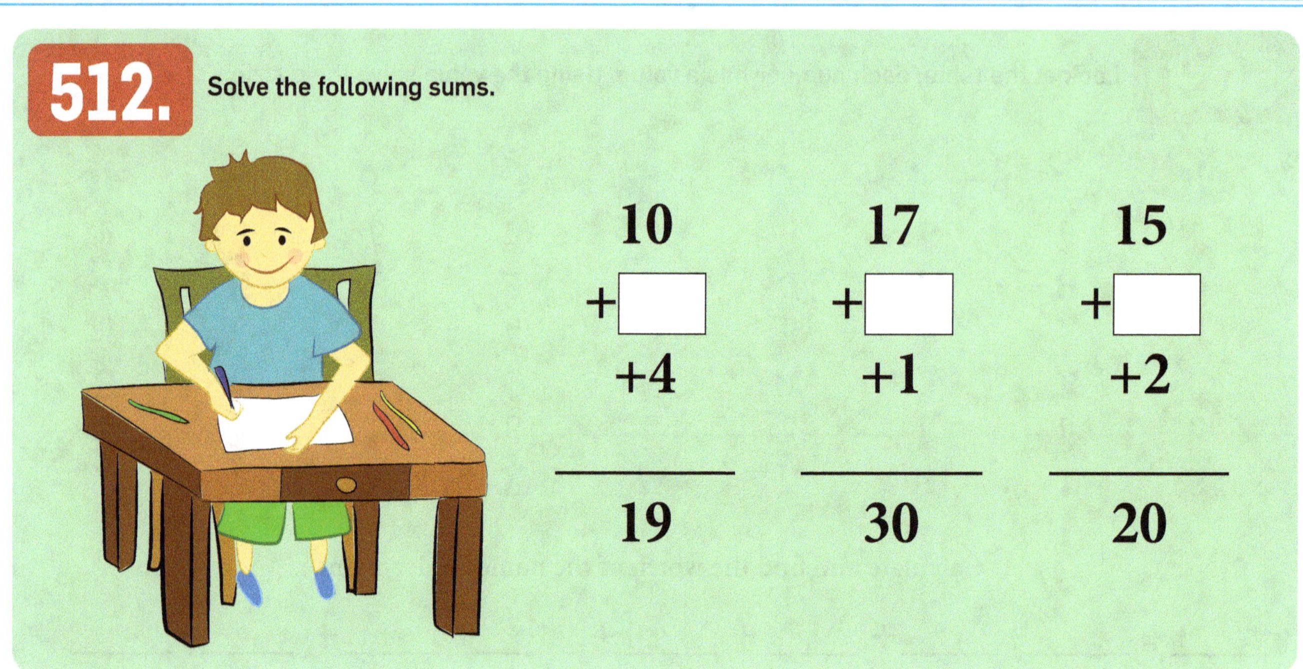

513. Colour the picture of the elephant.

514. Help Sam to solve the sums.

515. Can you create words by summing up these prefixes and suffixes with pictures?

Star + = ____________

Butter + = ____________

House + = ____________

+ Coat = ____________

+ Brush = ____________

516. Where do you find these objects? Match them.

 • • Library

 • • Hospital

 • • Playground

 • • Airport

 • • School

 • • Post Office

517. Can you find out where these people are going from the word box below? Also colour the pictures.

____

____

School Airport Swimming pool

518. Use the word in the centre and make new words. Say these words out loud.

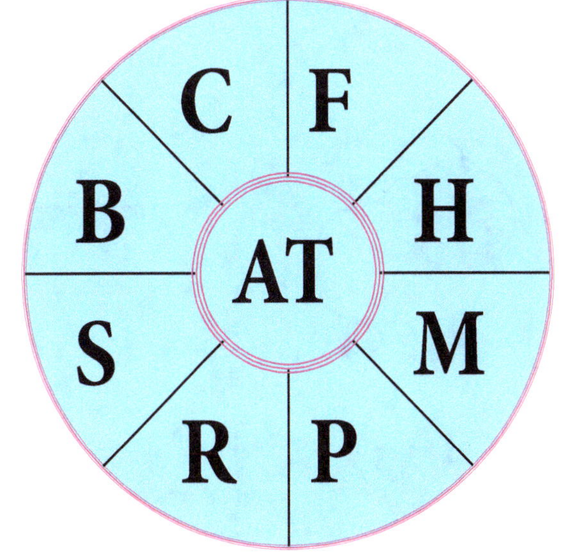

____

____

519.

Given below is an image of a fingerprint. Fun fact: nobody in this entire world has the same fingerprint as yours!

Dip your finger in paint and put your unique fingerprint in the box below!

520.

Unscramble these letters to find the action and colour the picture.

Pagnyil

521.

Write the names of these animals.

522.

Colour the picture and write its name in the given blank.

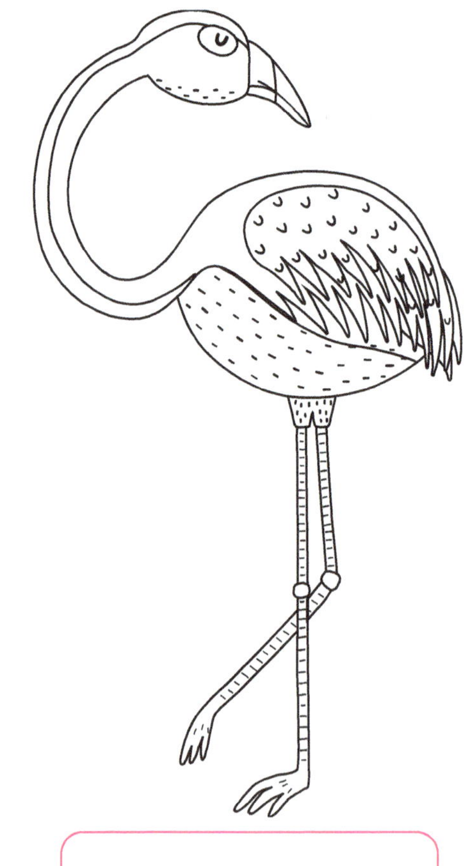

523. Count the number of objects in each set and write the answers in the circles below.

524. Can you find the answers of the sums given from these options?

14	12	14
9	1	2
10	0	6

15-5=	9-5=
9-8=	16-4=
12-12=	20-6=

525. How many objects are there?

526. Solve the sum below.

	+		+		+		+		+	

6 Times 5 = ☐

527. Find out the names of the animals below.

vebaer ____________________

nobir ____________________

oonbab ____________________

sbllelbue ____________________

ukdc ____________________

wcor ____________________

caklaj ____________________

hmuicpnk ____________________

mlfiango ____________________

528. Write 'C' besides the countable nouns and 'U' beside the uncountable nouns and colour the pictures.

Noodles

Ball

Toys

Rice

529. Underline the correct homophone word in the given sentences.

1. Can I go (**to, too, two**) the party?
2. John has (**pain, pane**) in his leg.
3. Nobody (**knows, nose**) what you are thinking.
4. Alicia is going to (**wear, ware**) her boots to work today.
5. The children got (**bored, board**) during the lecture.
6. Martin wants his socks because his (**tows, toes**) are cold.

530. Underline all the gendered nouns.

Boy	Toy
Girl	King
Daddy	Queen
Book	Chips
Computer	Lion
Lady	Jeweller
Man	Clogs
Crayon	Bicycle
Uncle	Chemist
Game	Nurse

531. Colour the beetle.

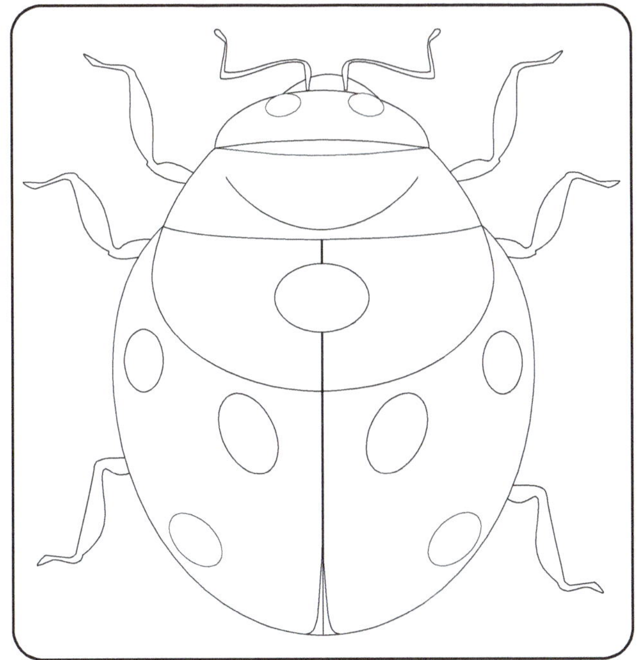

532. Using the words below, label the parts of the bird.

Feather Tail Head Eye Beak Wing Leg

533. Can you encircle the plants that grow in water?

Lotus

Hydrilla

Cactus

Rose Plant

534. Circle the animals you find in a water body.

Tortoise

Giraffe

Honeybee

Fish

Horse

535. Can you write all the possible sums with the given numbers which result in the given answer?

536. Count the total number of objects and write it in the given space.

537. Complete the sequence.

538. Complete the sentences with the correct question words.

______________ are you doing?	I am dancing with my sister.
______________ did you take her toy?	I took her toy because I want to play with it.
______________ are you not going to school?	I am not going to school today because I am tired.
______________ do we need to paint a tree?	We need paints and a canvas.

539. Circle the box with the right answer.

This / That — shirt is red

This / These — is my toy.

This / These — car is blue in colour.

540. Rearrange the words to form a sentence. Write it in the blank.

1. my doll is that
   ______a________

2. girl the happy is.
   ____

3. this red is apple
   ____

541. Place the vehicles in the right category.

boat lorry bicycle aeroplane submarine rocket helicopter

Air	Land	Water

542. Find answers to the following sums.

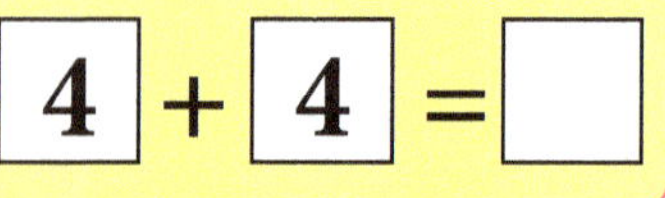

4 x 2 =

6 + 6 =

6 x 2 =

543. Match the frogs with the correct leaves.

544. Write the numbers whose sum equals to the numbers given below.

_______+_______=6

_______+_______=7

_______+_______=8

_______+_______=9

545. Fill in the missing numbers to complete the pattern.

546. Solve the given sums.

17

547. Learn to draw a butterfly in four easy steps!

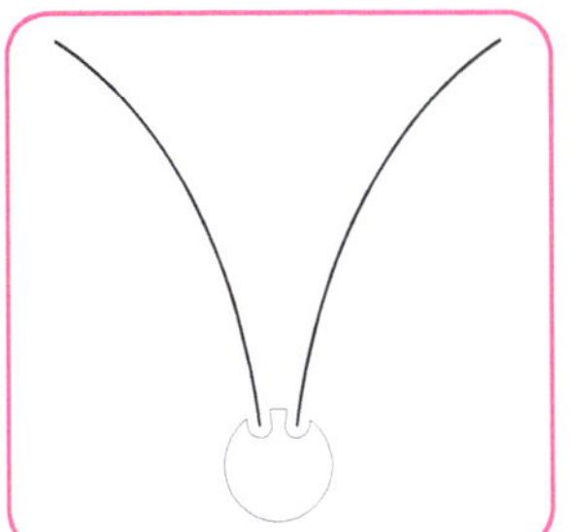

Step_1

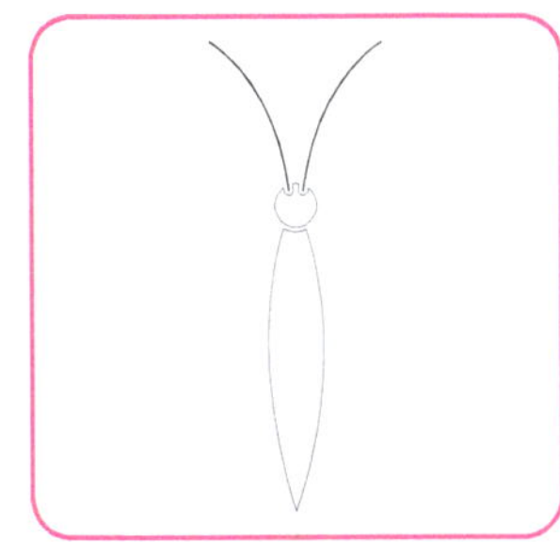

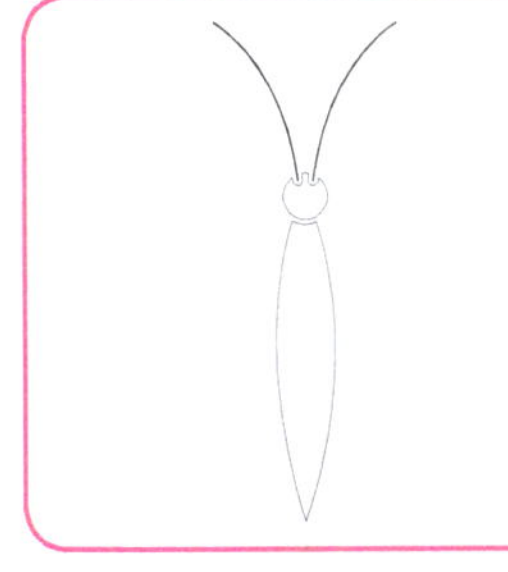

Step_2

Step_3

Step_4

548. Name these Vertebrates.

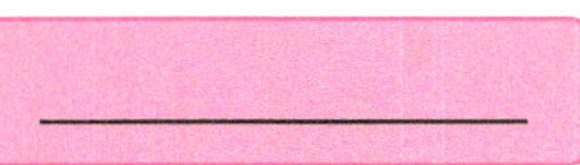

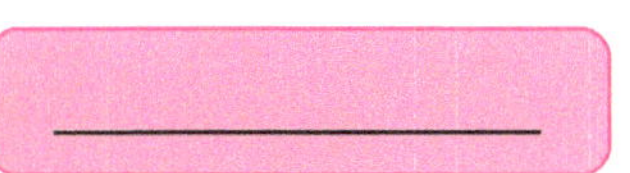

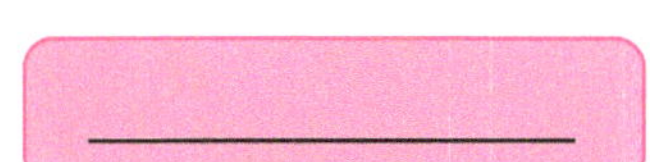

549. Look at the picture and fill in the blanks.

B_ _

W_ r _

_ n _

B_ tt _ _ f _ y

L_ _ y _ _ _

Dr _ g _ _ f _ _

550. Fill in the missing letter in each word.

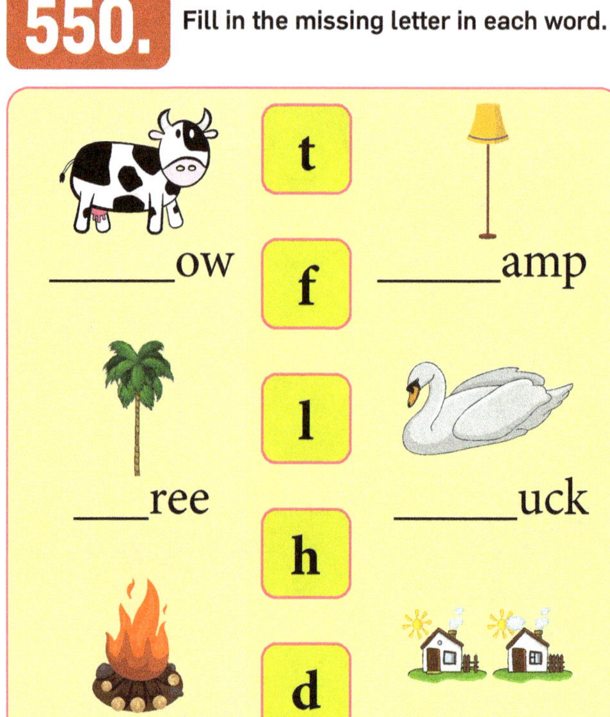

551. Match the rhyming words.

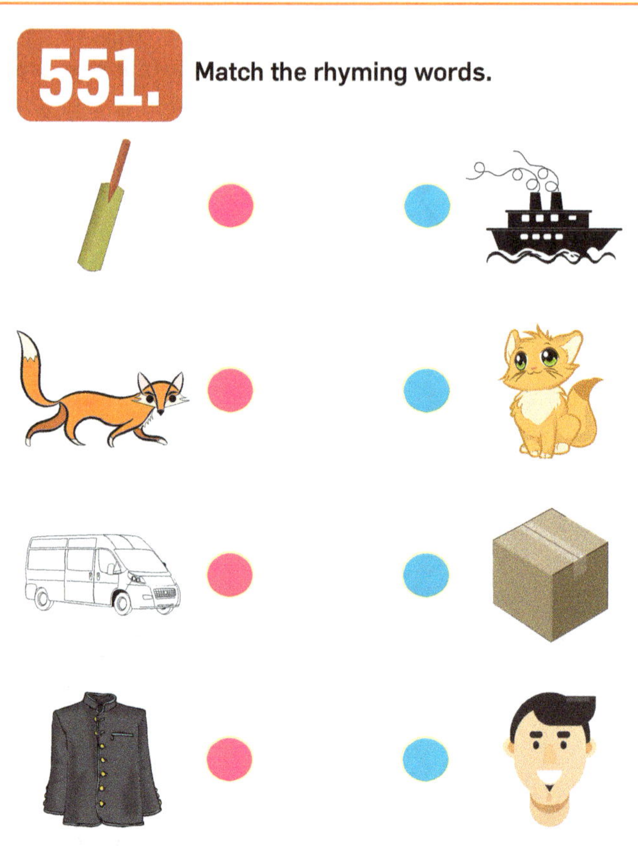

552. Read the nouns and write them in the correct box.

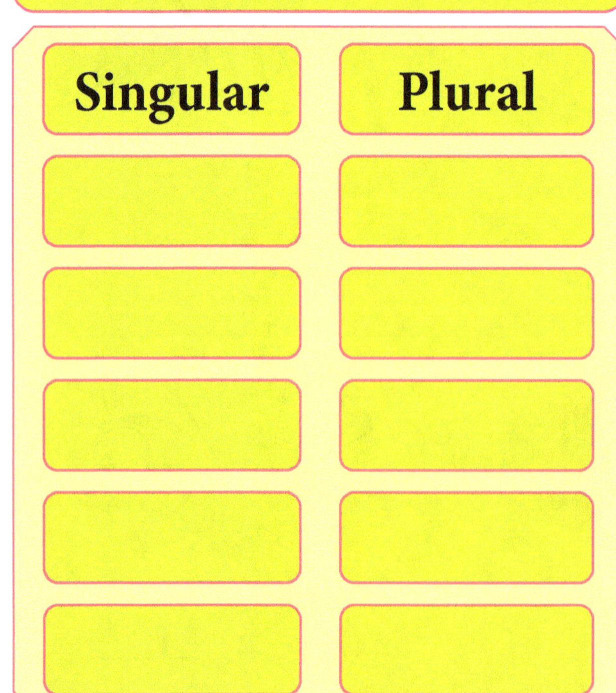

553. Colour the vowel jugs in blue and consonant jugs in yellow.

554. Draw a line to match the pictures to the names of the correct body parts.

NOSE

TEETH

EAR

MOUTH

EYE

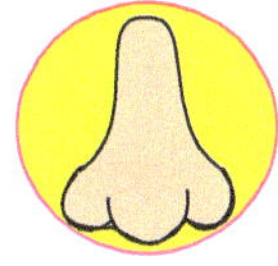

555. Match the feelings with the correct images.

Happy

Scared

Angry

Tired

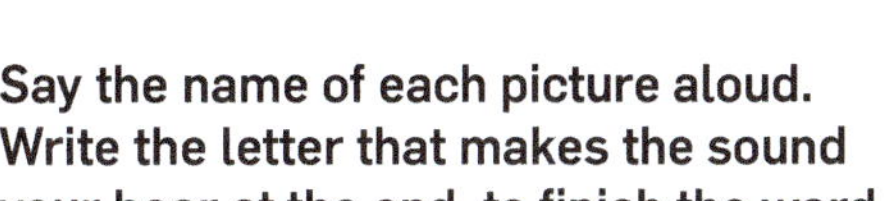

556. Say the name of each picture aloud. Write the letter that makes the sound your hear at the end, to finish the word.

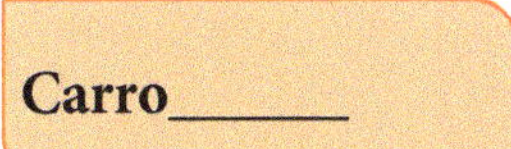

Carro______

Grape______

Pea______

Mil______

557. Fill in the blanks with the correct adverb. Use the words from the box.

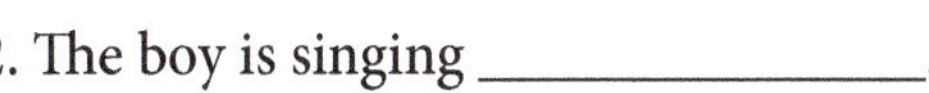

sweetly slowly loudly

1. The tortoise is walking __________.

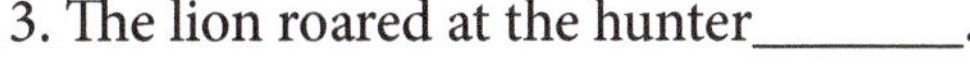

2. The boy is singing ________________.
3. The lion roared at the hunter________.

558. How many Tens and Ones are there in each row?

Tens	Ones

Tens	Ones

Tens	Ones

559. Help Andre to match the sum with the correct answer.

35
05
+0

16
15
+4

10
5
+5

20

40

35

560. Help Tim to complete the puzzle.

		12				
		-				
9	-		=			
-		=				
		6	-		=	2
=						
4	-	2	=			
				-		
		11	-	2	=	
				=		

561. Write numbers that add up to 50.

562. Can you spot four differences between these pictures?

563. Colour the hot air balloon using the colour key below.

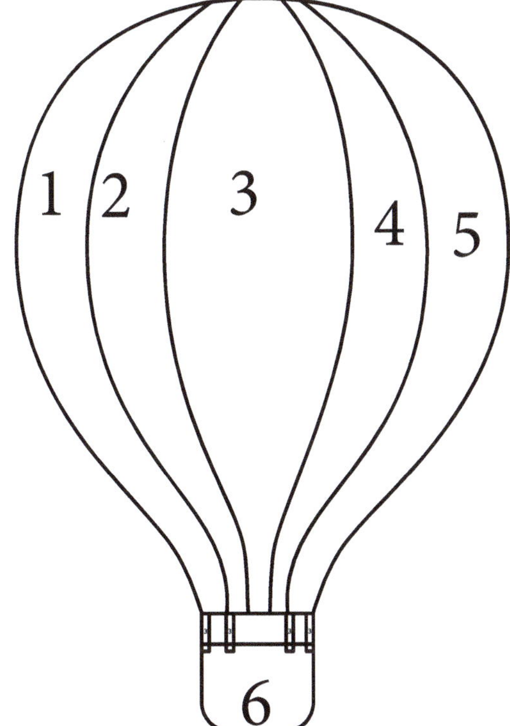

1. Blue	2. Green	3. Red
4. Yellow	5. Orange	6. Pink

564. Write the missing letters to complete these animals' names.

E _ _ P _ A _ T

R _ T

L _ _ N

_ E _ R _

565. How many of each animal are there? Count and write the number.

TURTLES	SEA HORSE
JELLY FISH	OCTOPUS

566. We are vegetables. Do you know our names.

567. Look at the picture and colour the cow.

568. Join the dots and colour the bird.

569. Choose the correct number from the box given below and fill it in the pig's belly.

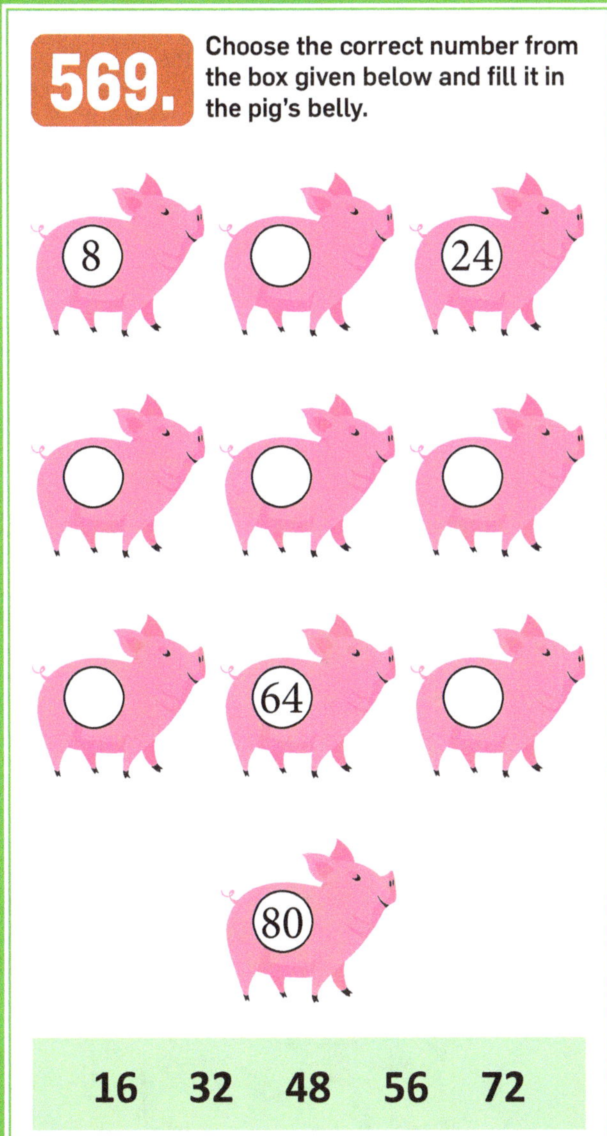

16 32 48 56 72

570. Out of the total dice, 12 had to be kept aside. Cross 12 dices and write the remaining number below.

___ – 12 = ___

571. Solve the maths problems given and encircle the one whose answer is the same as the number of crabs.

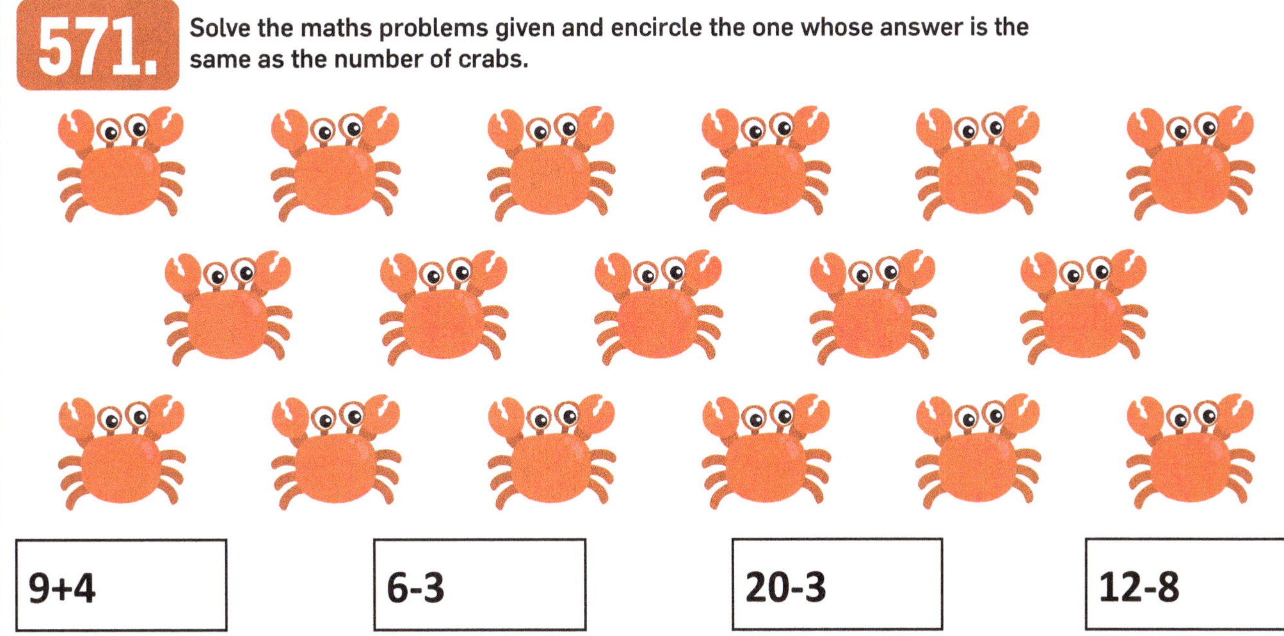

9+4	6-3	20-3	12-8

572. Circle the nouns in the sentence and colour the picture.

she | is | runing | for | the | race

574. Fill in the blanks.

1. My younger brother is a doctor and my ______________________ brother is a pilot.
(Older, Younger, Smaller)

2. ____________find it difficult to behave like an adult and do not feel like children anymore.
(Adolescents, Babies, Infants)

573. Write the rhyming words of the given words.

CAKE	MORE	HUMP	BEST
________	________	________	________
________	________	________	________
________	________	________	________
________	________	________	________

Lake	Core	Test	Jump
Make	Sore	Bump	Rest
Bake	Nest	Bore	Pump
Shore	Guest	Rake	Lump

575. Complete the crossword.

576. Draw lines to show where the clothes come from.

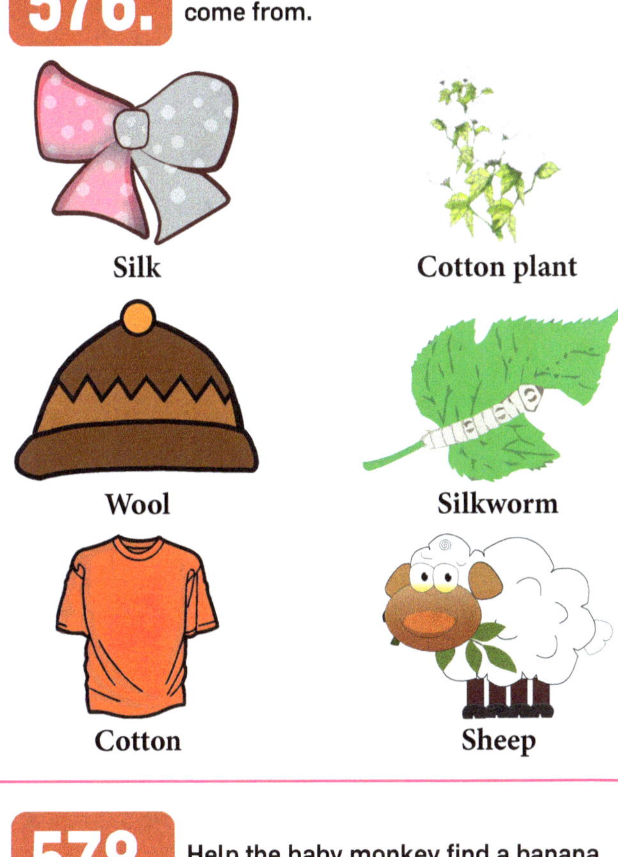

577. Tick the things that are made up of wood.

578. Help the baby monkey find a banana.

579. Colour the image.

580. Colour the ship.

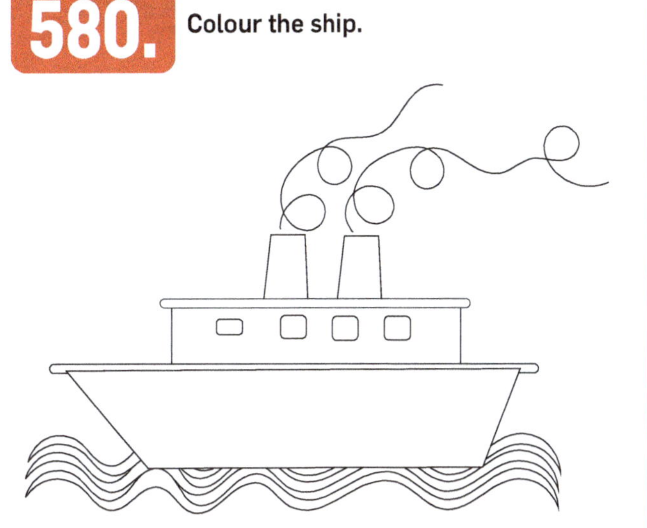

581. Circle the even numbers.

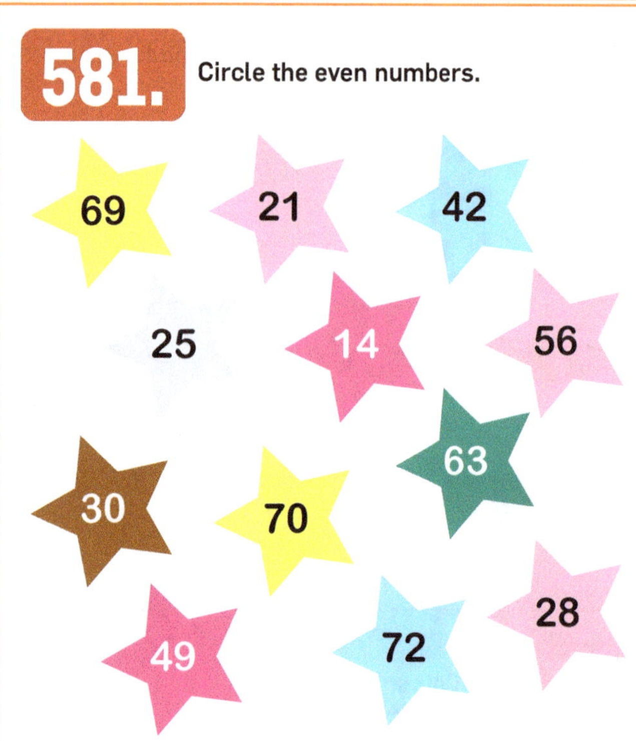

582. Complete the series of numbers in the caterpillar.

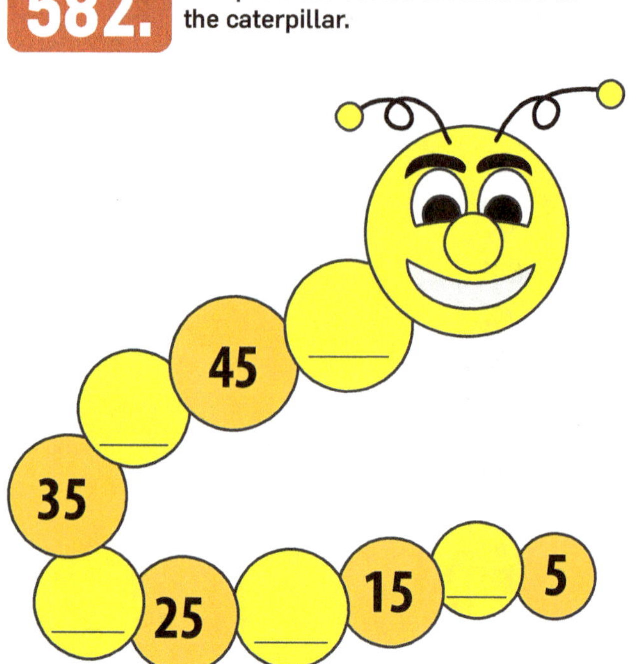

583. Match the cats with the right numbers after subtracting 3 from them.

584. Count the the total numbers of rabbits and write it in the box.

585. Can you identify the insects that are useful to us?

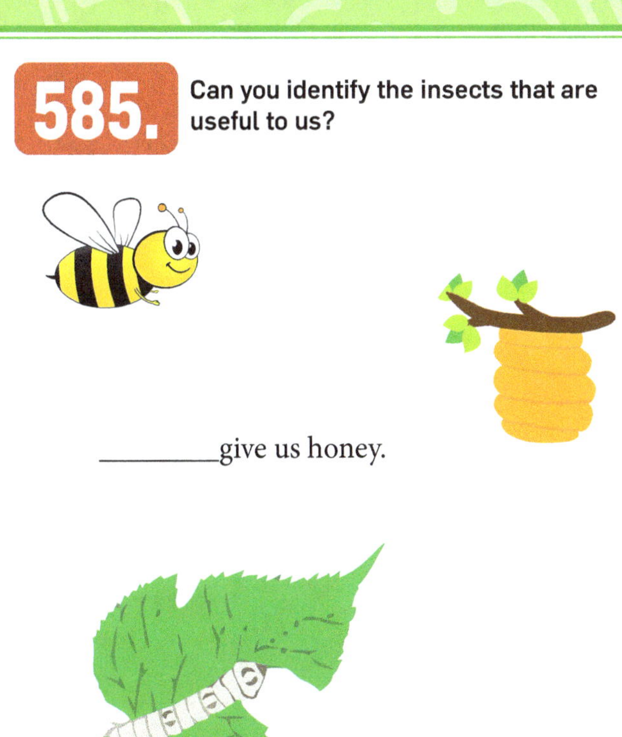

________give us honey.

________give us silk.

586. Underline the adjective in each sentence.

1. Arin is a tall girl.
2. I have a white puppy.
3. I am wearing a pretty dress.
4. Danny is a good boy.
5. This cake is delicious.
6. My grandmother is a kind lady.

587. Write 'F' for animals that move fast and 'S' for those who move slowly.

588. Unscramble these letters to find out the game the boy is playing and colour the picture.

obtoflal ________________

589. Solve the sums given below.

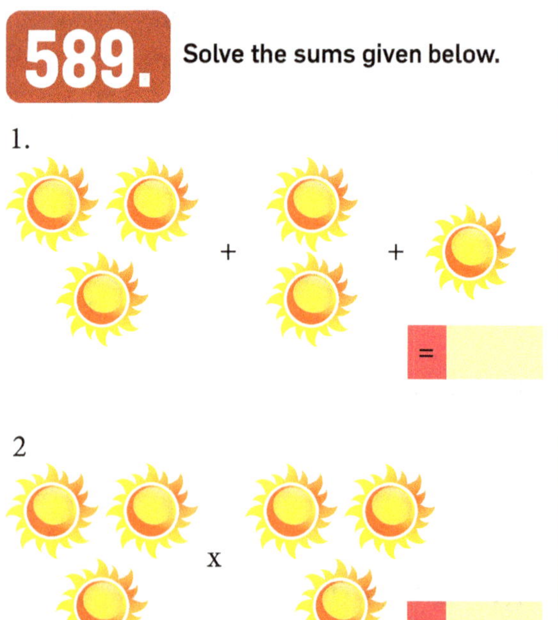

590. Add the following.

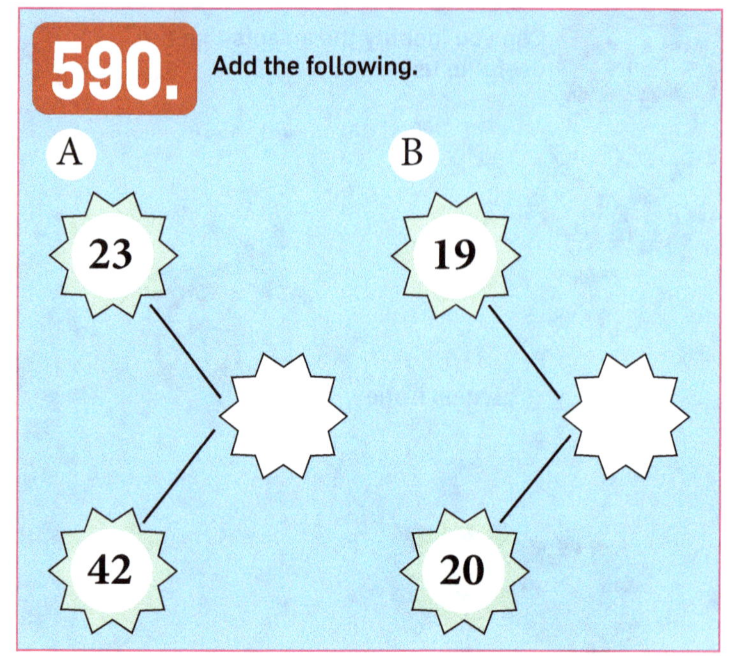

591. Solve the following sum.

592. Solve the equation.

593. Colour the rabbits with even number.

594. Match the following.

COFFEE

CAKE

HEN

CAR

FROG

595. Add the sums with the help of number line method.

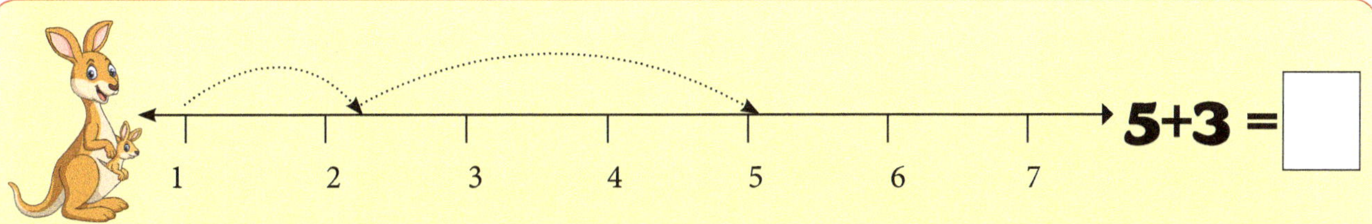

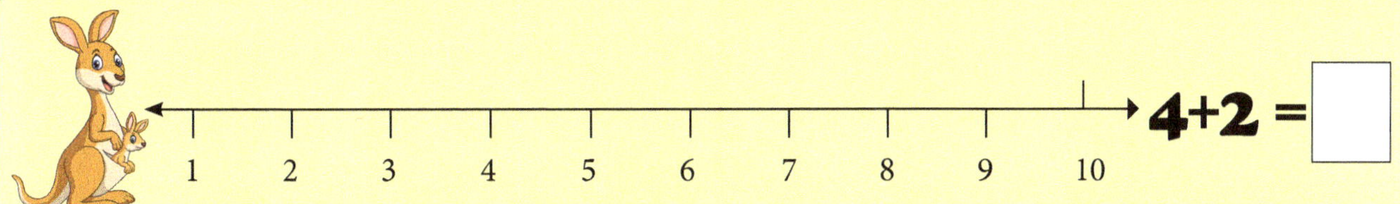

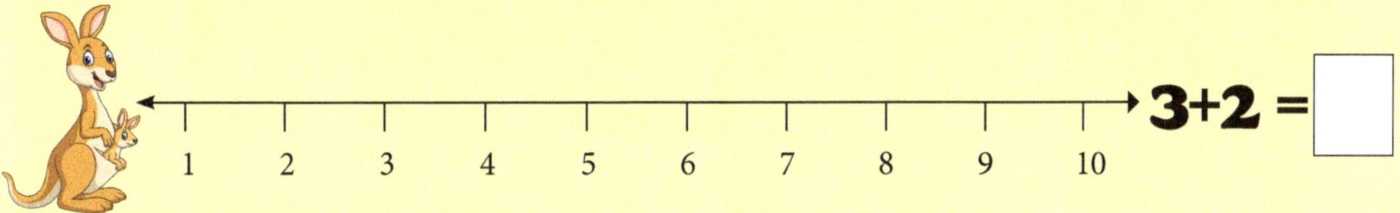

596. Circle the objects that are found in your house.

597. Colour the box with the correct sentence.

- ☐ The dog is running.
- ☐ The dog is sitting.
- ☐ The dog is sleeping.

- ☐ The dog is barking.
- ☐ The dog is running.
- ☐ The dog is eating.

598. Tick the right answer according to the actions that you see.

Draw | Write

Jog | Skip

Throw | Kick

Run | Dance

Clap | Wave

Write | Drink

599. Match the animals with their shadows.

______________ ______________ ______________

600. Find the animals in the word grid.

R	R	F	G	H	I	J	S	K
F	E	T	V	U	H	E	Q	I
D	U	G	O	N	G	A	T	L
O	Q	E	R	T	U	L	D	L
L	T	S	V	V	H	D	X	E
P	R	C	E	J	J	T	O	R
H	D	W	H	A	L	E	R	W
I	C	R	V	E	L	Y	K	H
N	B	H	J	Y	J	I	M	A
T	U	A	M	L	K	I	O	L
S	E	A	L	I	O	N	P	E

KILLERWHALE SEALION DOLPHIN WHALE

601. Complete the sea animal and write its name.

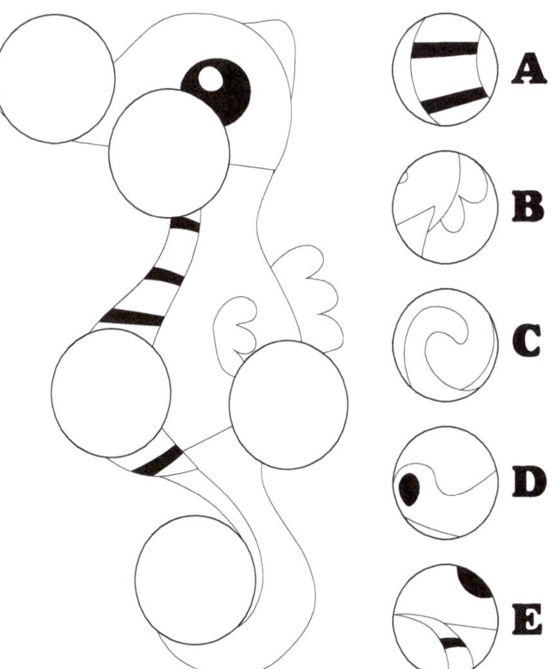

____

602. Write the numbers in increasing order.

14 11 12

10 13

☐ ☐ ☐ ☐ ☐

603. Take Nathaniel to his treat by solving the sums.

6+3 = ____

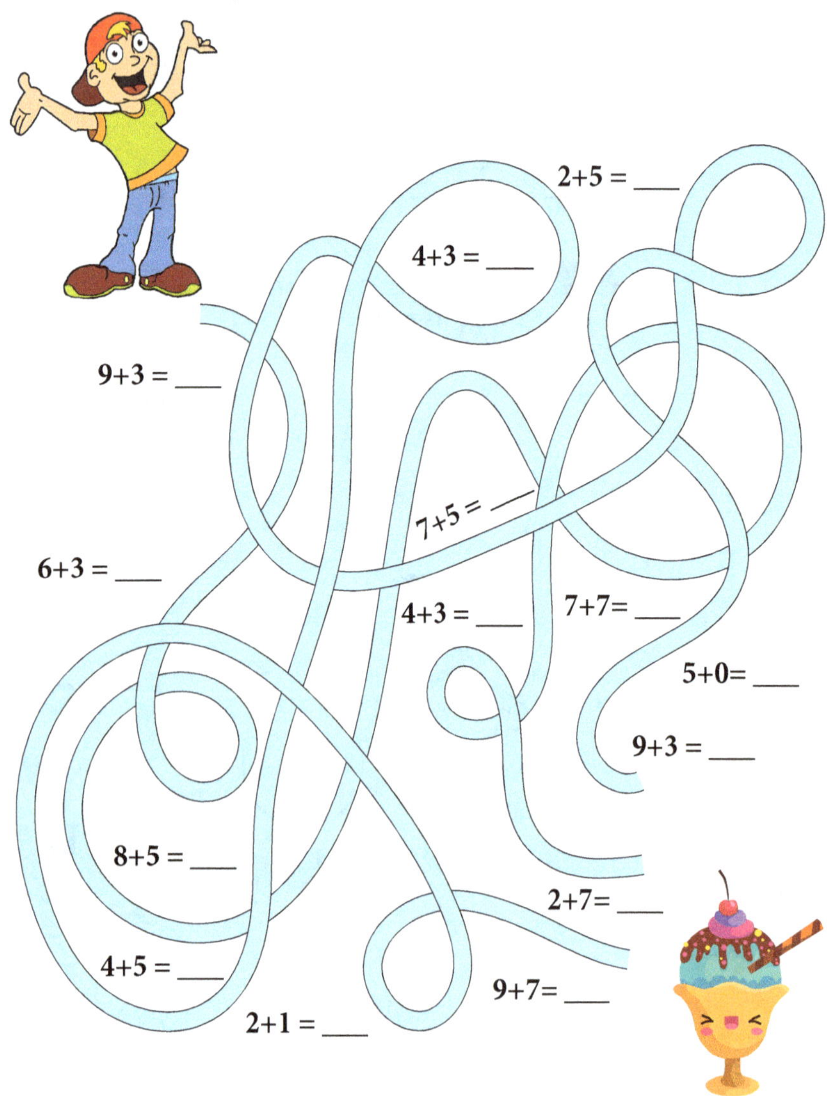

604. Write the double of these numbers.

10 ☐

13 ☐

16 ☐

15 ☐

12 ☐

17 ☐

605. Can you help each girl reach her ball?

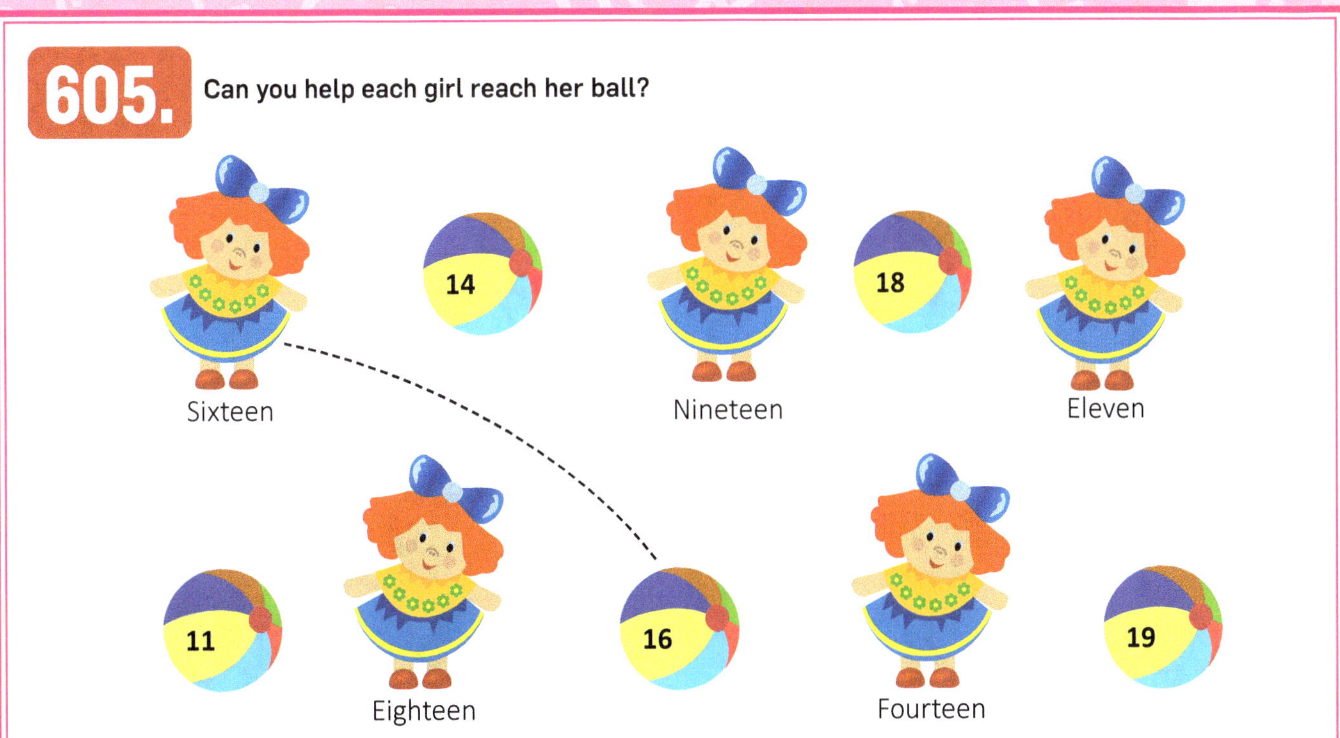

606. Complete the sums using these codes.

607. Colour the circle which has the smallest number.

7	9	18
2	8	3

19	14	15
5	15	8

608. Put the broken images of the elephant in the correct order to complete the picture.

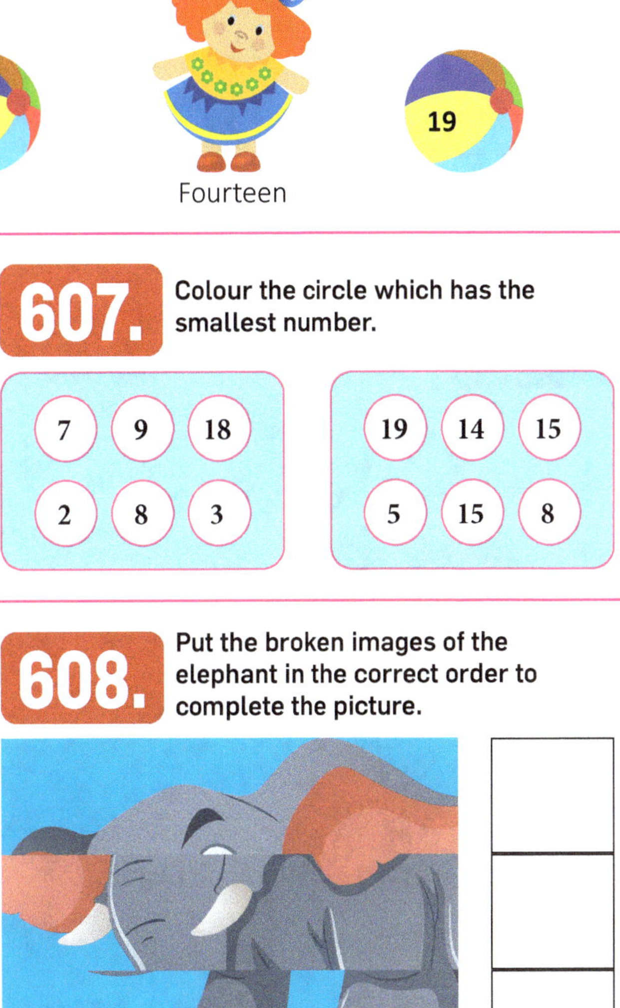

609. Arrange the following numbers in increasing order.

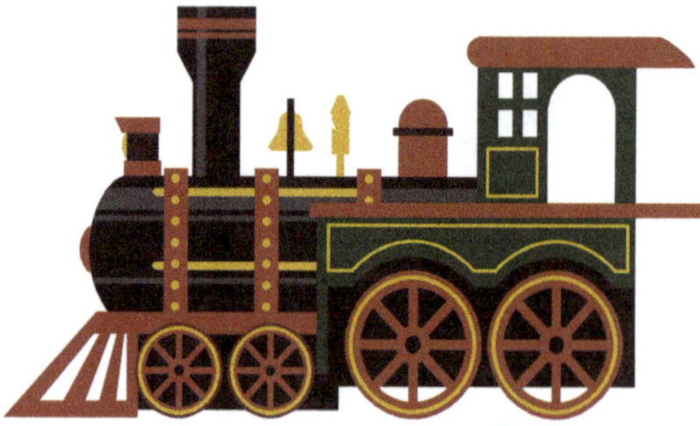

49 — 2 — 61 — 10

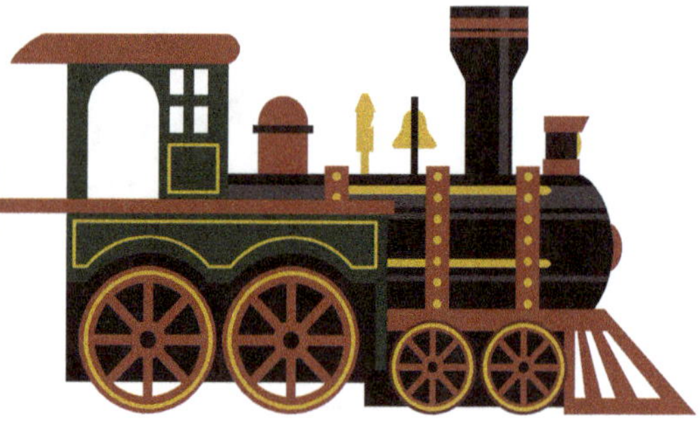

610. Write the correct names of these animals.

noil

____

firegaf

____

nyokem

____

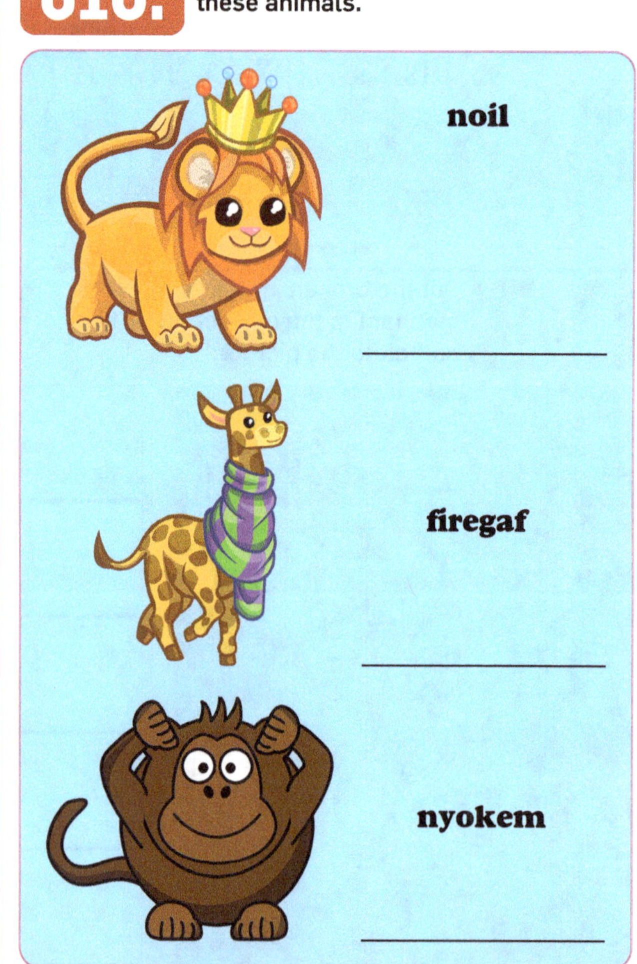

611. Colour this animal baby and name it.

____

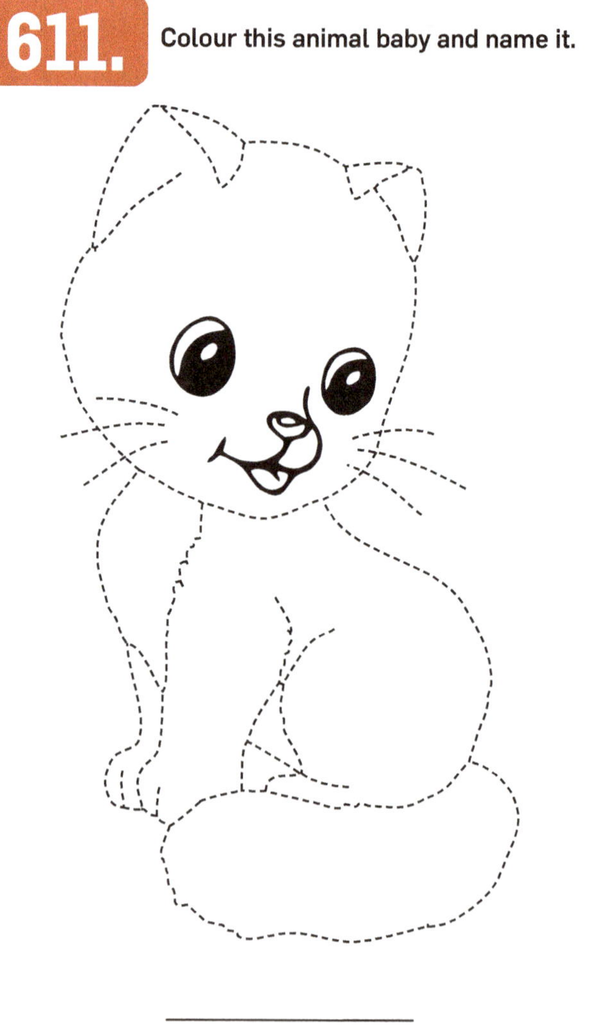

612. Unscramble the letters to form a meaningful word.

MOTCAHS LAIN

____

DNAH EOST

____

NETISNETIS DHEFRAOE

____

613. Complete the sentences.

1. Please op______ the door.
2. Adam is lighting the la________.
3. The scarf is made of si________.
4. I got a gi_________ for my mother.
5. An app ___________ a day keeps the doctor away.
6. Jane lov____to sing.

614. Find the given words in the grid.

Z	Y	A	R	T	I	S	T	X
D	E	N	T	I	S	T	Q	F
O	W	H	L	C	H	E	F	A
C	A	R	P	E	N	T	E	R
T	F	H	I	K	U	R	X	M
O	Q	N	L	Y	R	W	Z	E
R	U	W	O	V	S	G	Z	R
Z	O	M	T	B	E	J	P	L

Dentist Chef Artist Farmer
Doctor Nurse Carpenter Pilot

615. Follow the clues and name the animals.

I have black and white stripes all over.

I am a ________________.

I look like a bear but i am black and white in colour.

I am a ________________.

I am the biggest animal on land.

I am an ________________.

616. Know your months!

January	February	March	April
May	June	July	August
September	October	November	December

1. The first month of the year is ________________.
2. Christmas falls in the month of ________________.
3. The third month of the year is ________________.
4. The month before June is ________________.

617. Match the correct collective nouns and fill in the blanks.

1. A ________ of bananas. String 
2. A ________ of flowers. Collection 
3. A ________ of beads. Bouquet 
4. A ________ of stamps. Bunch 

618. Match these vehicles with their names.

Car

Bicycle

Bus

Scooter

Van

619. Circle the nouns in the sentence given below and colour the picture brightly.

The teapot is on the table

620. Draw a tick sign for the animals you find in a farm.

621. Complete the sentences.

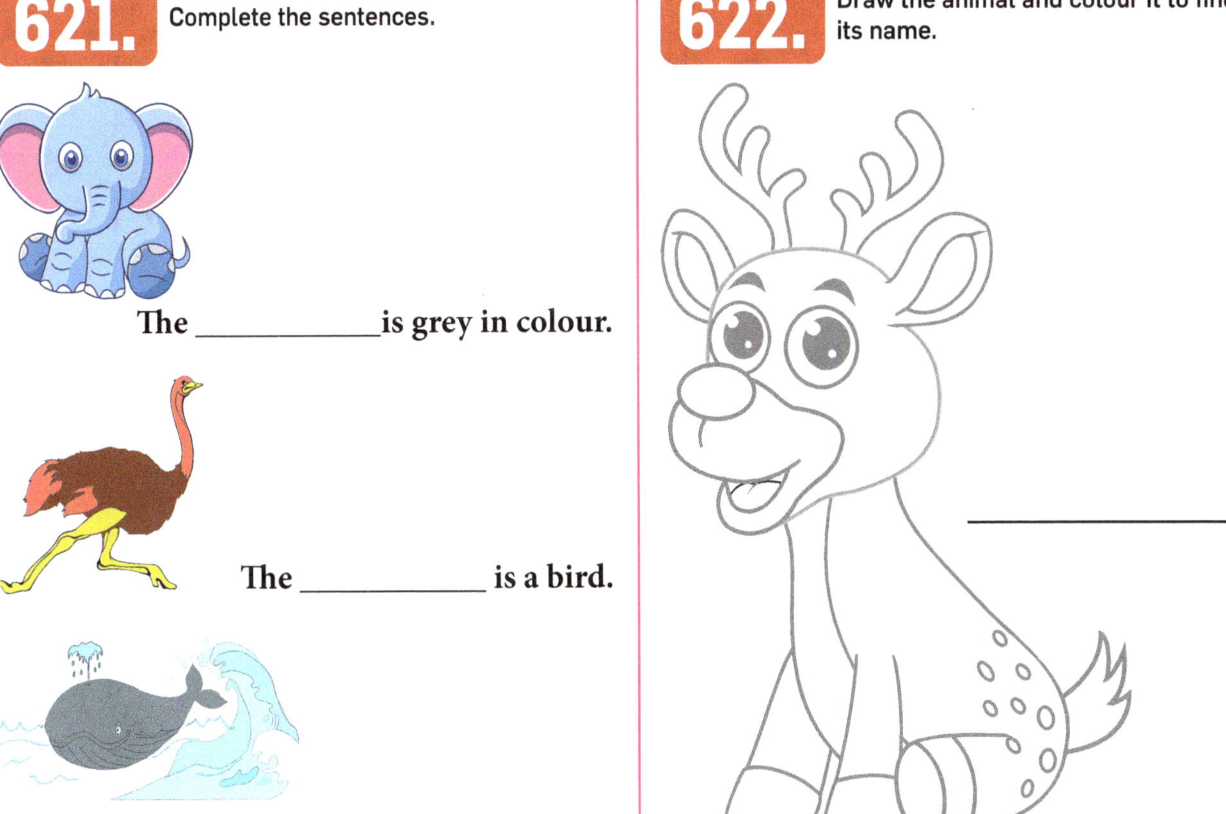

The ___________ is grey in colour.

The ___________ is a bird.

The ___________ is the biggest mammal.

622. Draw the animal and colour it to find out its name.

____

623. Carefully look at the picture codes and then solve the mathematical problems below.

ⓐ  +  −  +  −  = 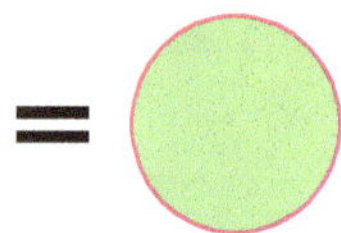

ⓑ  −  +  +  +  = 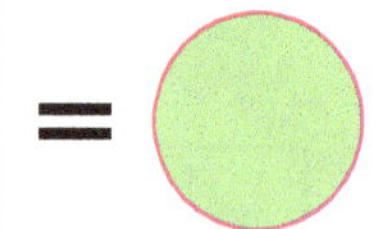

ⓒ  −  +  −  +  = 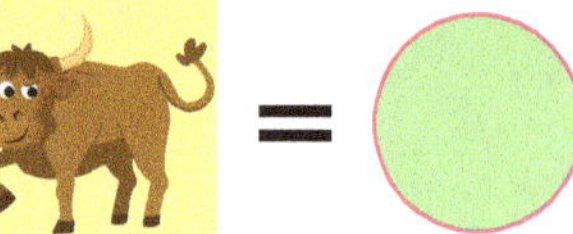

624. Unscramble these letters to find out the names of one of the systems in the human body.

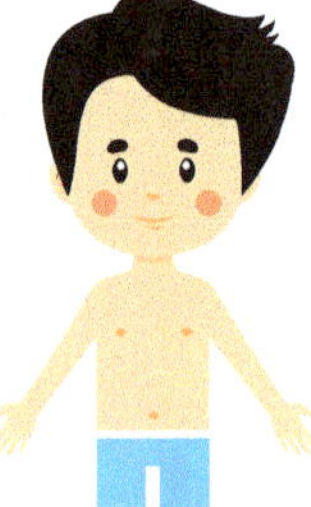

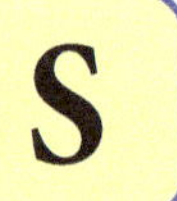
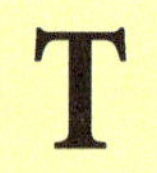
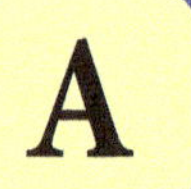

L	K	E	L	S	T	A	E

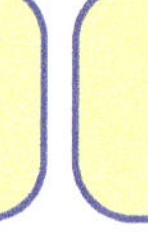

625. Match the laptops with their correct answers.

12       

12	7	5	23	14	15	28	10

18 + 5

20 + 8

14 - 7

17 - 12

18 - 6

Write the names of these amphibians.

Seal, Alligator, Crab, Walrus

Which animal is this?
Colour it to find out.

628. Trace the octopus and colour it.

629. Match the animals with their homes.

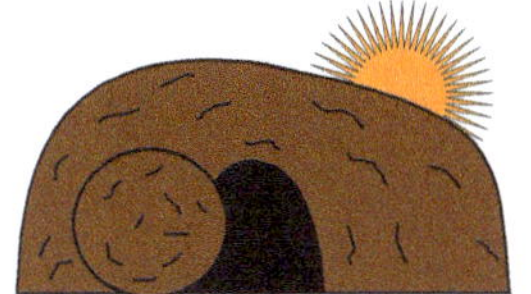

630. Fill in the blanks with the correct vowel.

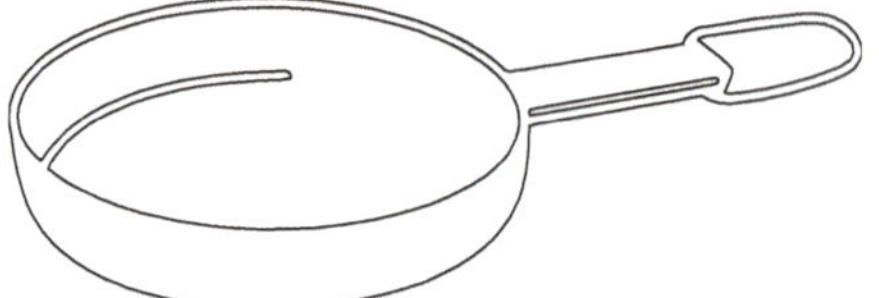

p____n

v____n

b____g

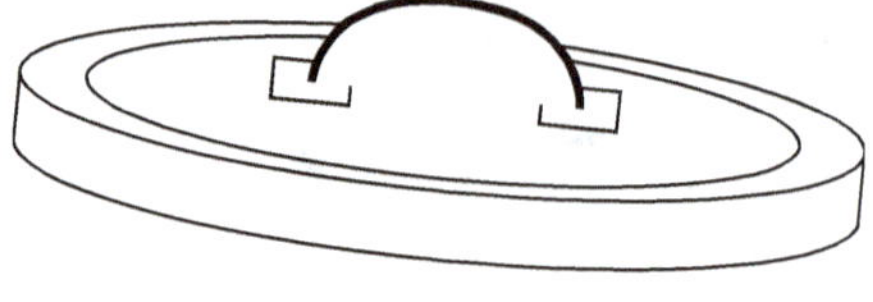

l____d

c____r

s____n

b____d

p____g

631. Fill in bright colours in the scenery below.

A-Red B-Blue C-Green D-Brown

632. Take the duck to her house by following the trail of rhyming words.

main	crane	clean
stale	stain	grain
crane	pain	lane

633. How many of each object are there?

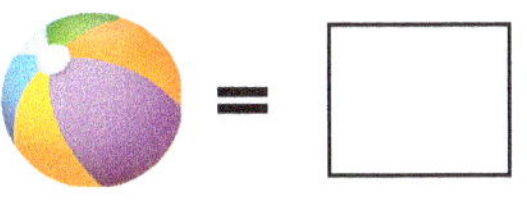

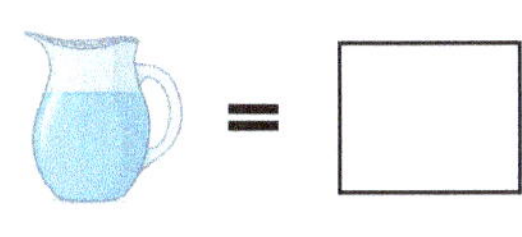

= ☐

634. Circle the sums that add upto the given numbers.

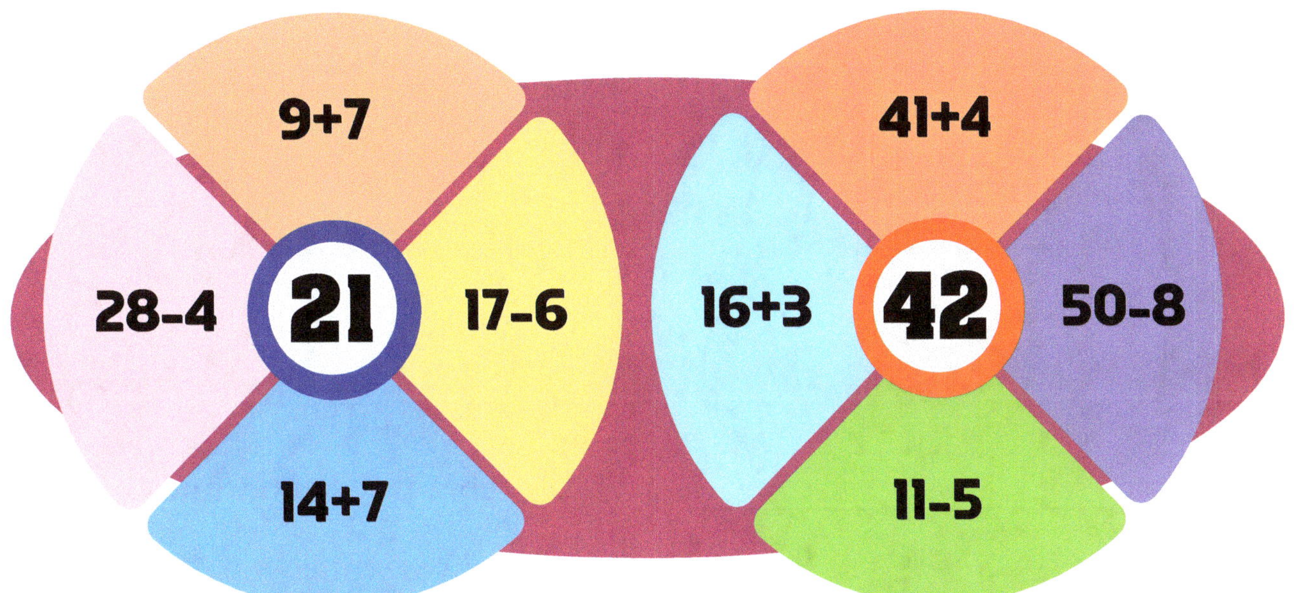

635. Choose the correct helping verb.

1. The cat **(has/have)** pink paws.
2. I **(has/have)** a pain in my stomach.
3. I**(has/have)** a black car.
4. **(has/have)** you done your homework?
5. John ((**has/have)** to play football tomorrow.
6. **(has/have)** your sister finished her studies?

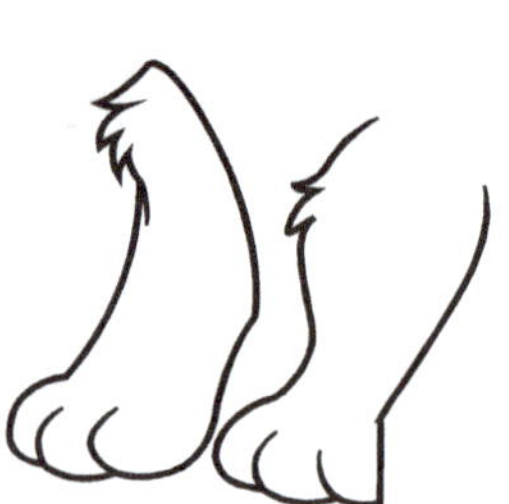

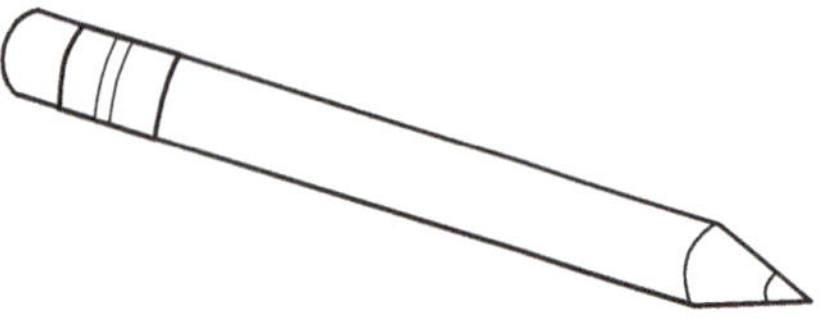

636. Label various parts of the torso using the word bank.

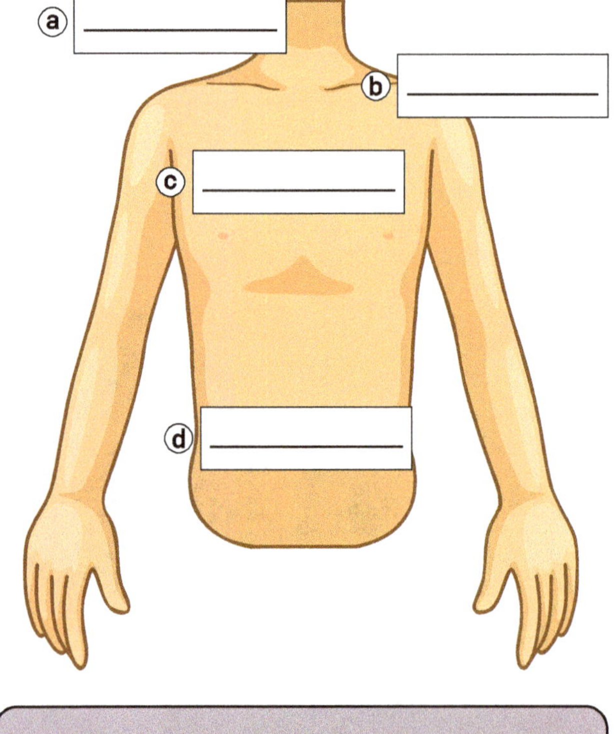

Stomach Neck Chest Shoulder

637. Colour the circles green if the statement is true and red if they're false.

A. An orange is brown. ○
B. Grapes are red. ○
C. A tomato is red. ○
D. The sea is blue. ○
E. A polar bear is white. ○
F.A strawberry is yellow. ○
G. A lemon is yellow. ○
H. Grass is green. ○
I. A zebra is red and white. ○
J. A crow is white. ○

638. Match the animals to the things they eat.

cock

cow

monkey

639. Colour the fruit below and name it.

____

640. What do these animals eat?

641. Solve the multiplication sums below and choose the correct answer from the board.

27		21
	20	
16		18

9x3=

4x4=

3x6=

7x3=

5x4=

642. Count and write the total number of objects.

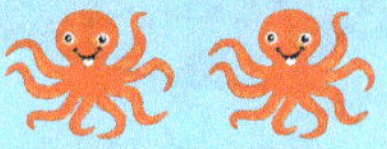

643. Colour the donkey whose multiple is 28.

644. Colour the bear's balloons.

645. Fill in the missing letters in the words starting with consonant blends.

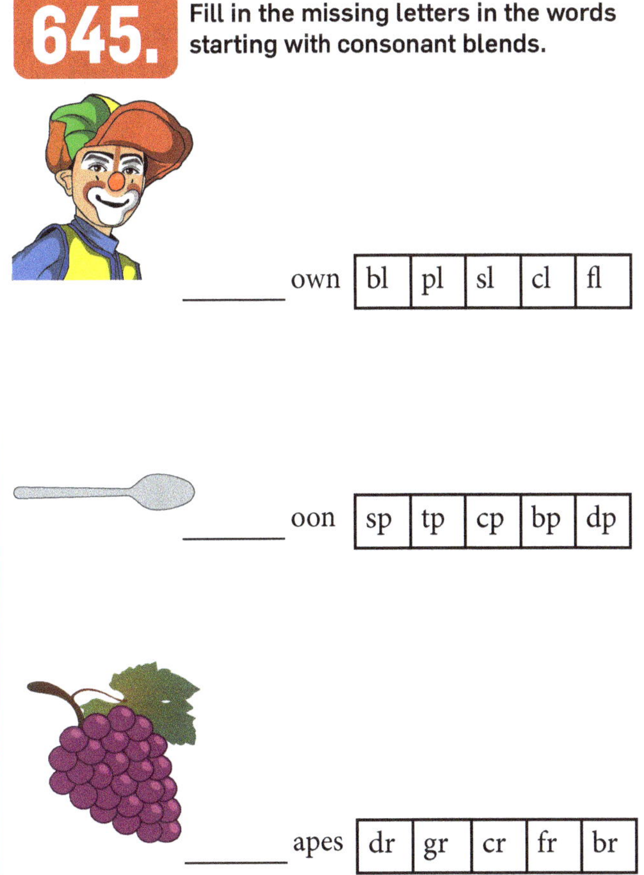

646. Circle the vowels in the lot.

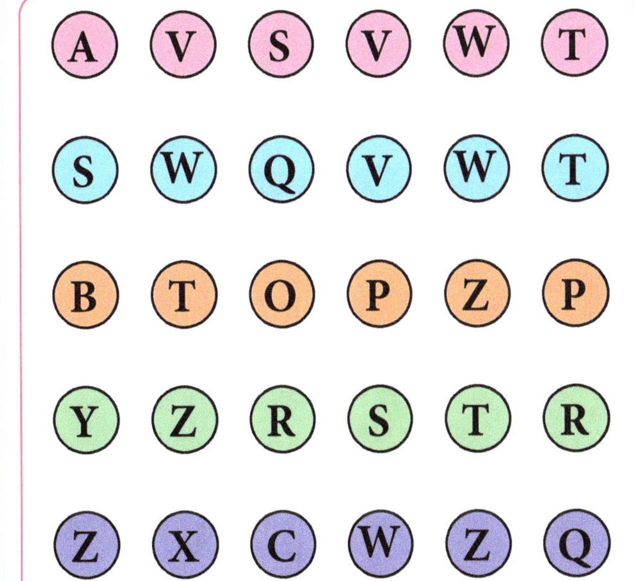

647. Draw a tick for the lots with rhyming words in them.

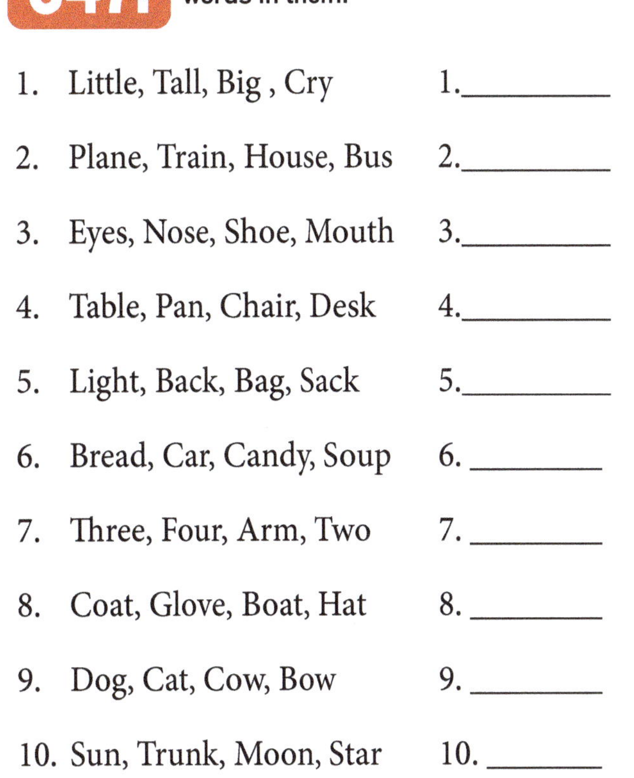

1. Little, Tall, Big , Cry 1.________
2. Plane, Train, House, Bus 2.________
3. Eyes, Nose, Shoe, Mouth 3.________
4. Table, Pan, Chair, Desk 4.________
5. Light, Back, Bag, Sack 5.________
6. Bread, Car, Candy, Soup 6. ________
7. Three, Four, Arm, Two 7. ________
8. Coat, Glove, Boat, Hat 8. ________
9. Dog, Cat, Cow, Bow 9. ________
10. Sun, Trunk, Moon, Star 10. ________

648. Name these aquatic animals.

649. Trace and colour the fish in bright colours.

650. Trace and find the name of the water animal.

651. What is each object made of? Match the objects.

Metal

Wood

Cotton

652. Each dog below has two sticky notes tied to its tail. Colour the sticky note yellow that has the bigger number written on it

653. Colour the words according to the mentioned shades.

Colour 'the' red   Colour 'it' green   Colour 'an' blue

it   an   the

an   it   an

it

it   it

the   the

the

an   an

654. Solve the sums below and fill up the squares.

6	+		=	14
+		+		+
	+		=	
=		=		=
13	+		=	23

655. Fill in the blank space with the right number.

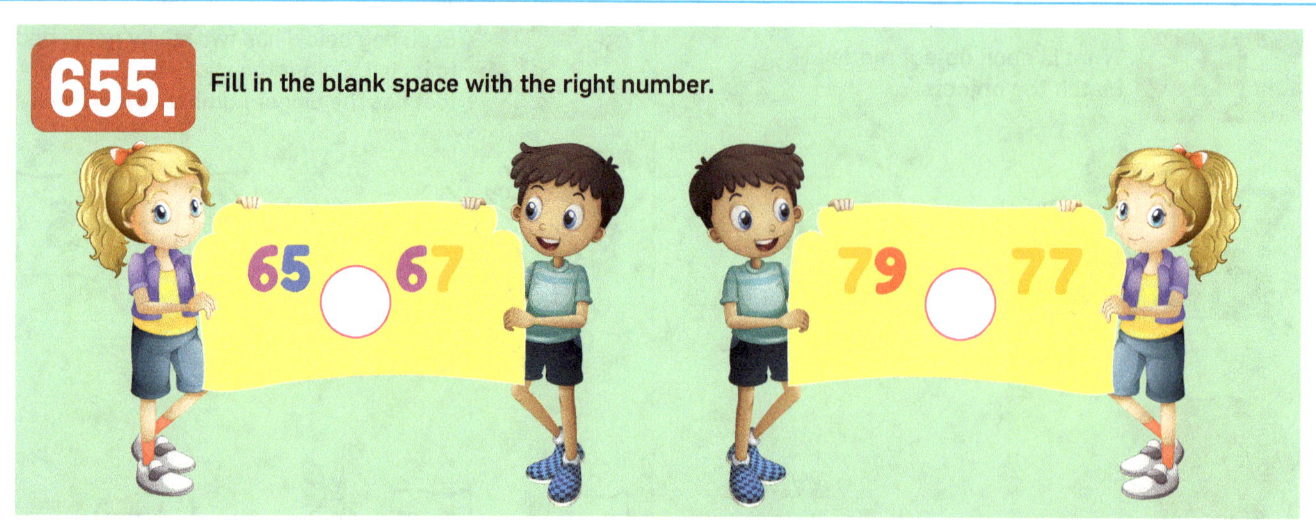

656. How many tens are there?

66 = ________ tens

75 = ________ tens

23 = ________ tens

69 = ________ tens

657. Add the following number

75 + 45 + 15 = ◯

658. What do you get when you add 5 to the below given numbers?

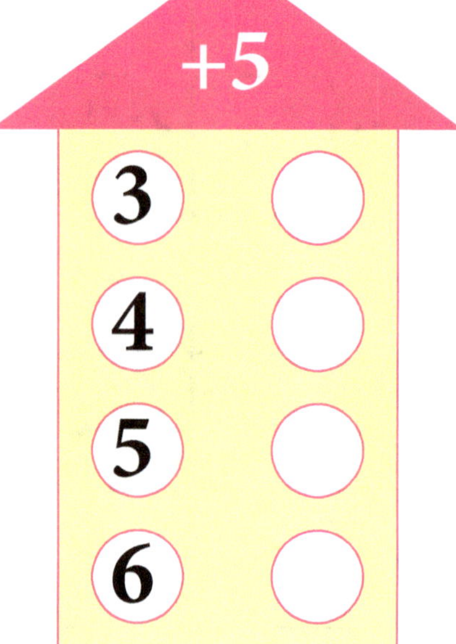

659. Solve the sums and, using the given codes, colour the picture.

10 = ● 15 = ●

660. We may be long or short, but we're very strong. Holding things is what we do. What are we?

Circle the correct answer.

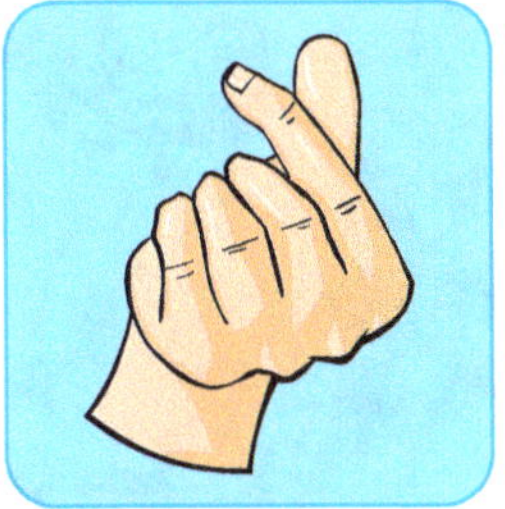
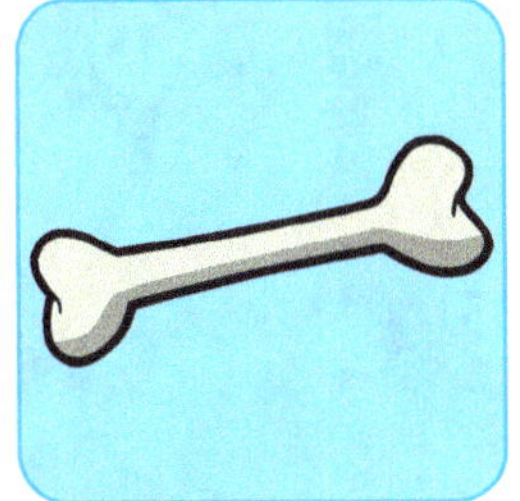
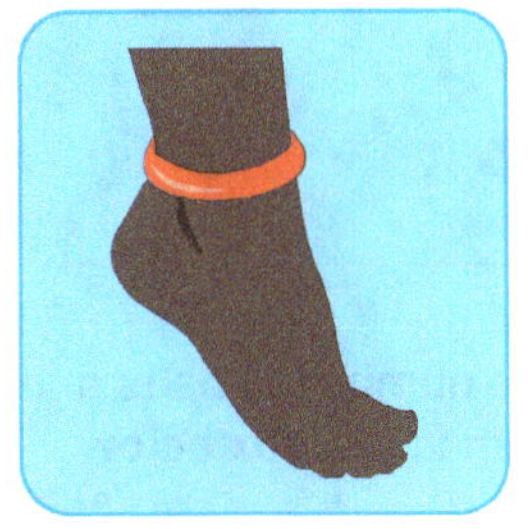
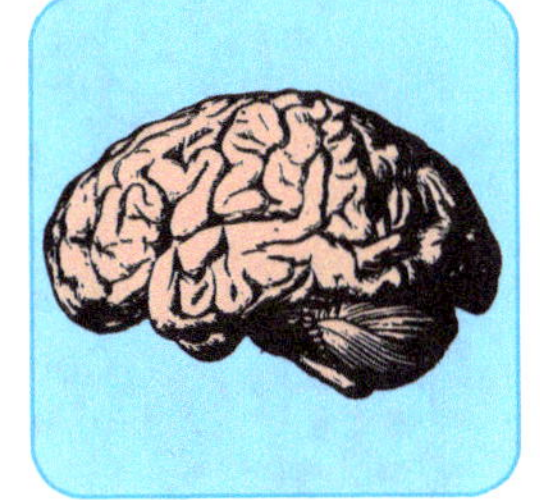

661. Find out the names of these healthy food items.

RRACOT

____

OOATMT

____

EBACBAG

____

662. Colour the following fruits and vegetables according to the shades mentioned.

Potato in Brown | Tomato in Red
Eggplant in purple | Lemon in Yellow

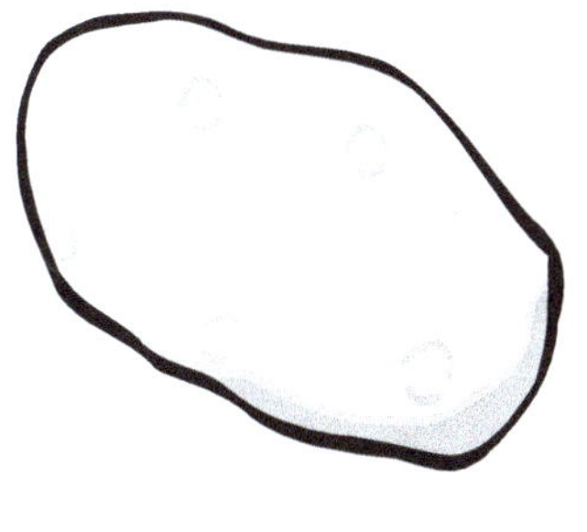

663. Match the pictures that have the same colour.

664. Join the dots to complete the ladybug.

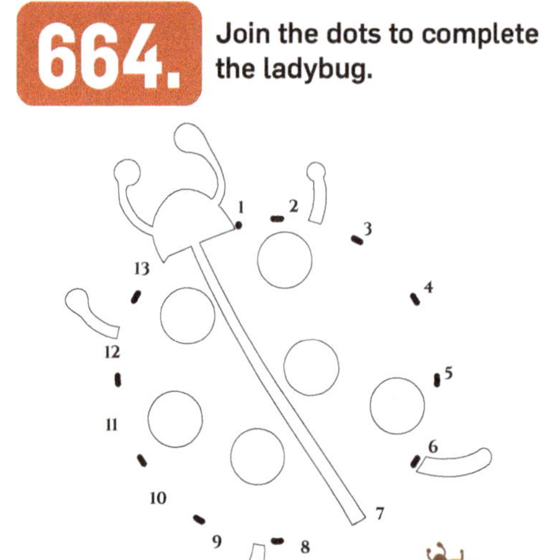

665. Complete the pattern by writing the missing numbers.

666. Colour the odd numbered balloons red and the even ones yellow.

667. Count the number of balls and write them in the box below.

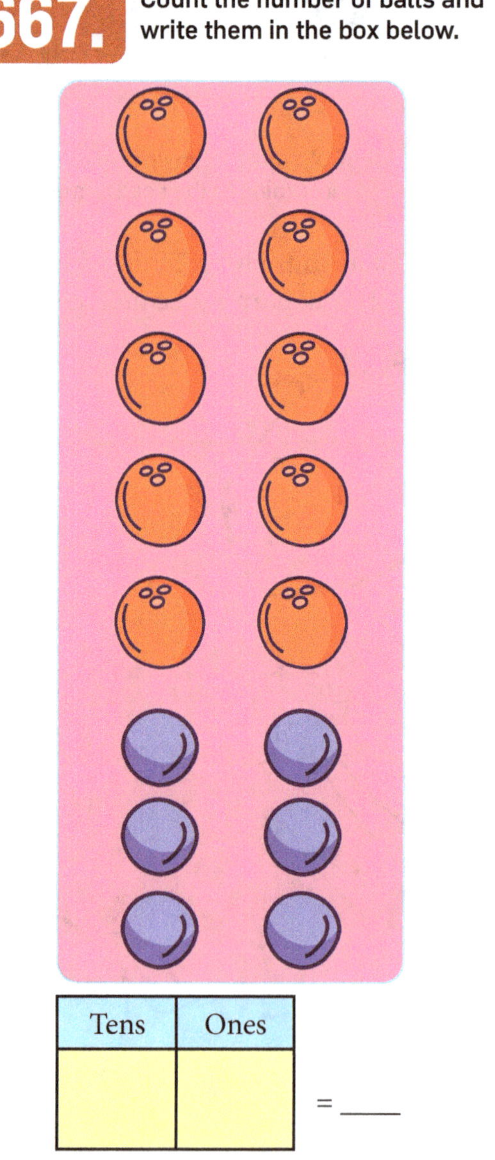

Tens	Ones

= _____

668. Ace the multiplication game!

5x1= ☐

7x3= ☐

4x4= ☐

6x3= ☐

8x5= ☐

669. Colour the circles which sum up to 15.

9+6 = ○

8+4 = ○

11+4 = ○

5+8 = ○

670. Colour the pictures that start with the letter A.

Use the codes below to colour the sunflower.

15=Yellow

20=Red

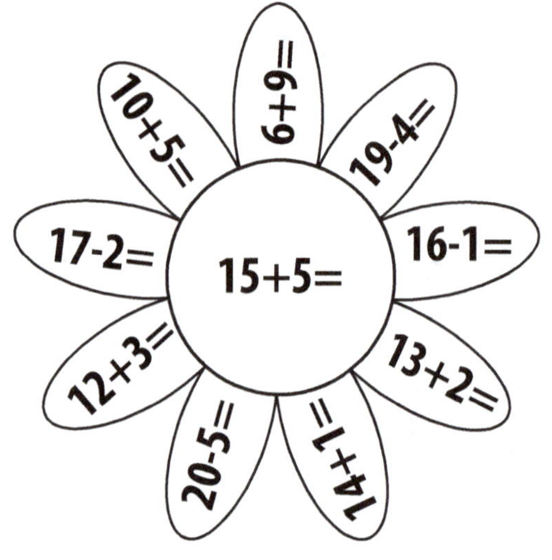

672.

Colour the cute animal.

673.

Take these animals home.

674.

Complete the animal by placing the missing pieces in the right order.

1 2 3 4

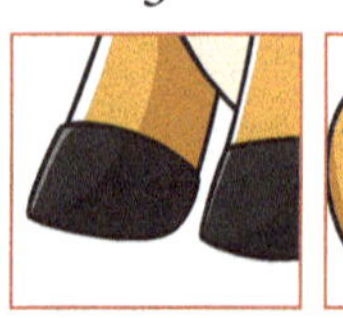

675. Solve the sums.

10 +10 ____	13 +7 ____	14 +6 ____	5 +6 ____	6 +4 ____
17 +3 ____	8 +2 ____	9 +1 ____	11 +9 ____	9 +1 ____
12 5 +5 ____	7 2 +1 ____	18 1 +1 ____	6 2 +2 ____	5 4 +1 ____
4 +6 ____	9 +11 ____	2 +8 ____	5 +15 ____	8 +12 ____
1 1 +8 ____	15 4 +1 ____	14 5 +1 ____	3 6 +1 ____	13 6 +1 ____

676. Complete the series.

677. Look at the numbers given on the board and write the numbers that come after.

678. Animals have lost their body parts. Match them to find it.

679. Colour the picture and name the animal.

----

680. Fill in the missing words to complete the name of the animal.

B_u_ _ _ a_e

_ _l_ _i_

681. Place the life cycle of a fish in the right order.

Fry

○ ________

○

Alevin ________

○ Parr ________

Eggs ________

○ Adult ________

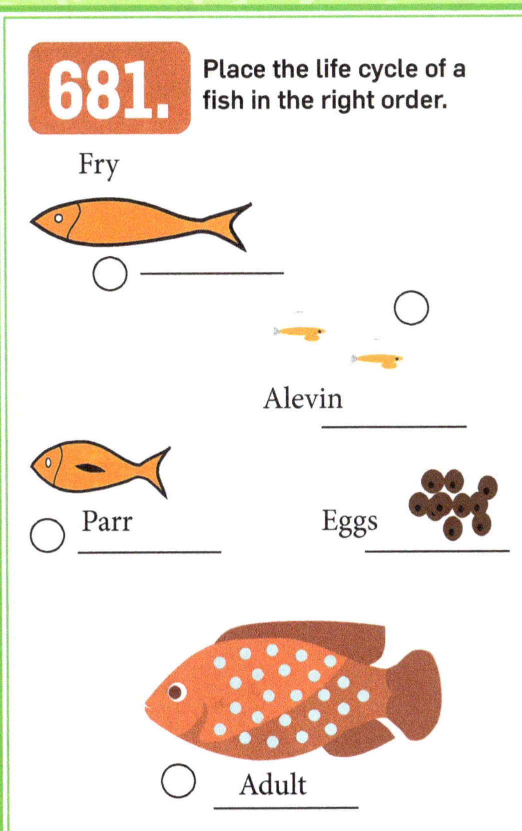

682. Find the aquatic items in the word grid.

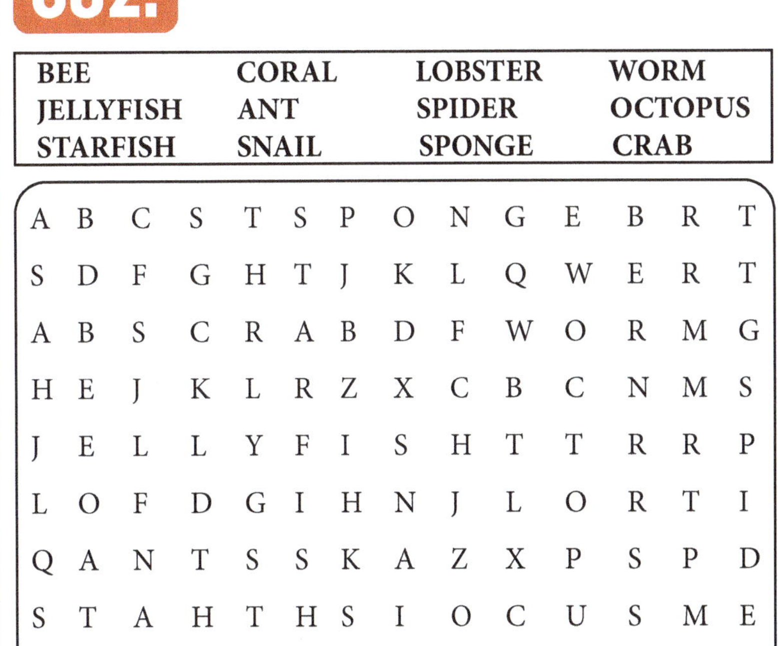

BEE	CORAL	LOBSTER	WORM
JELLYFISH	ANT	SPIDER	OCTOPUS
STARFISH	SNAIL	SPONGE	CRAB

A	B	C	S	T	S	P	O	N	G	E	B	R	T
S	D	F	G	H	T	J	K	L	Q	W	E	R	T
A	B	S	C	R	A	B	D	F	W	O	R	M	G
H	E	J	K	L	R	Z	X	C	B	C	N	M	S
J	E	L	L	Y	F	I	S	H	T	T	R	R	P
L	O	F	D	G	I	H	N	J	L	O	R	T	I
Q	A	N	T	S	S	K	A	Z	X	P	S	P	D
S	T	A	H	T	H	S	I	O	C	U	S	M	E
C	O	B	R	A	B	E	L	O	B	S	T	E	R

683. Write the names of these sea animals.

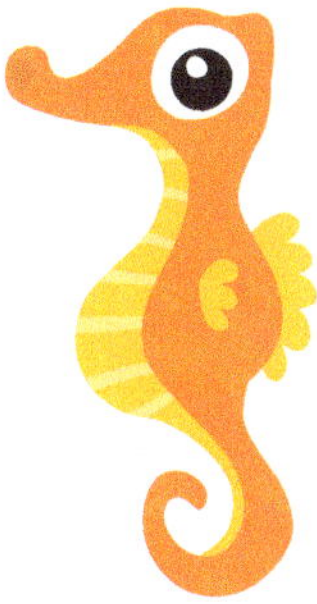

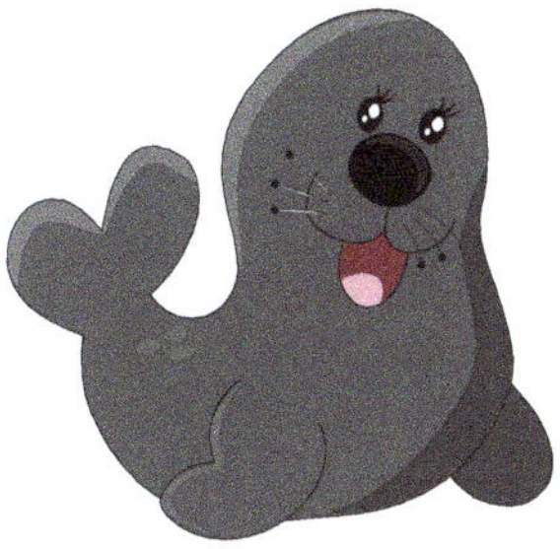

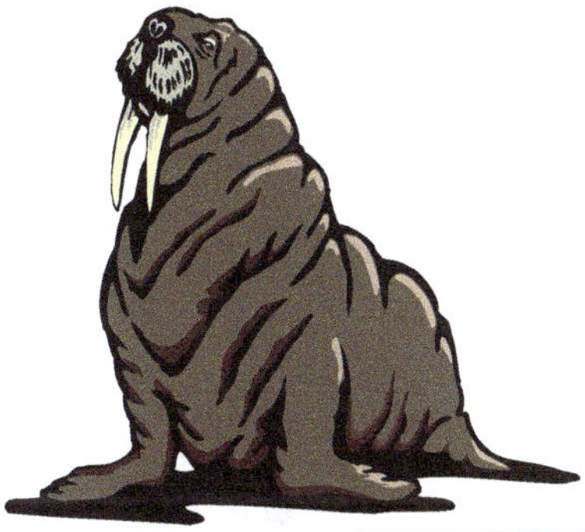

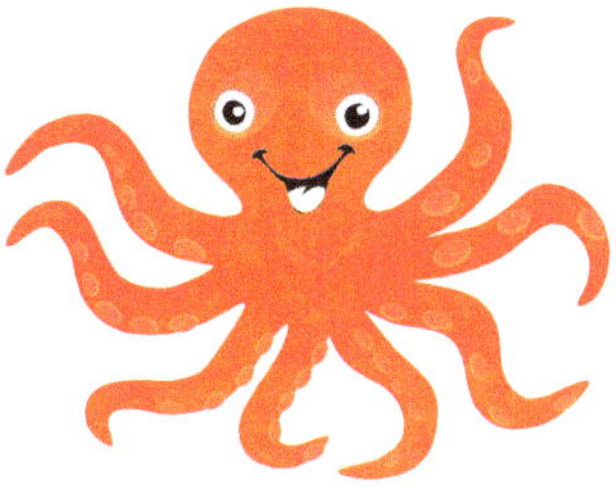

Sea Horse **Seal** **Octopus** **Walrus**

684. What will you add to the following numbers to get the number 60.

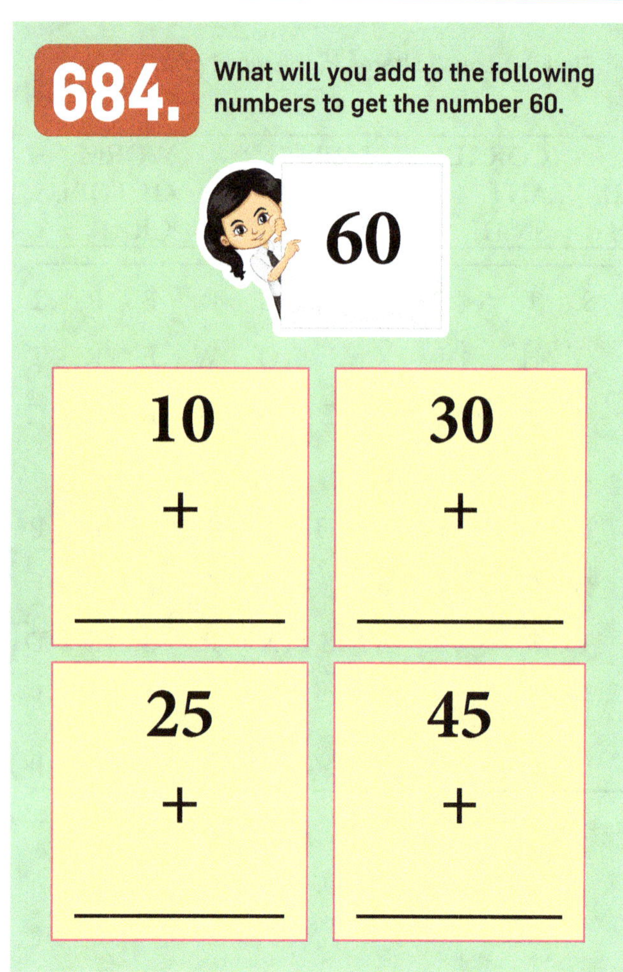

685. Colour the honeybee brightly with the help of the colour codes.

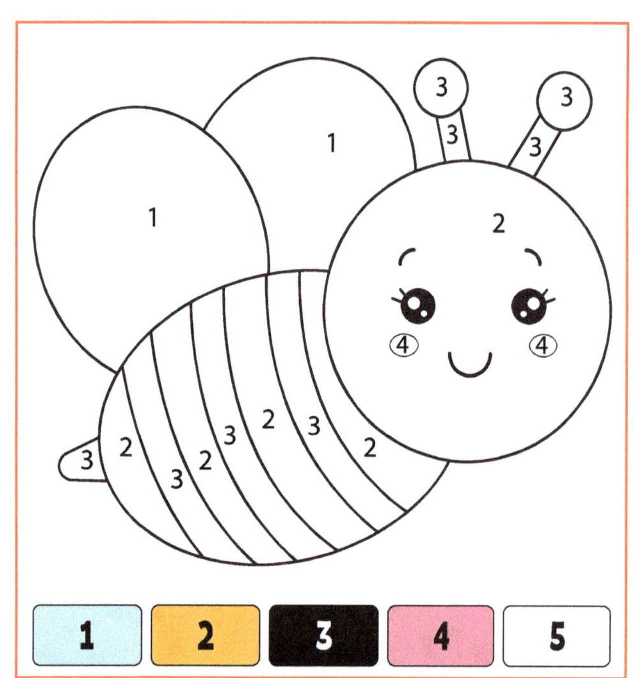

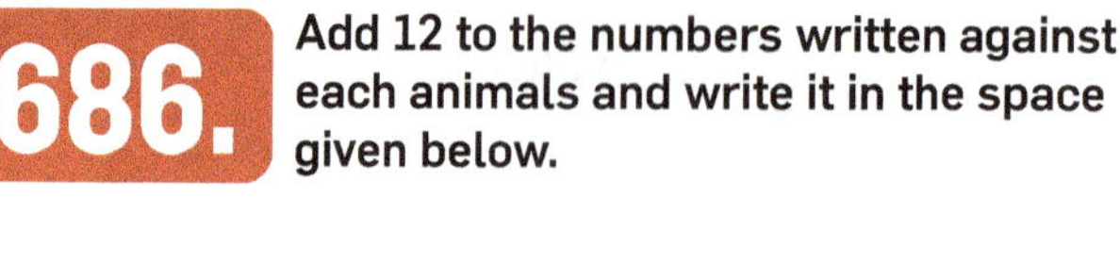

686. Add 12 to the numbers written against each animals and write it in the space given below.

687. Unscramble the names of these food items.

ricemace

prissc

eack

butiscis

688. Know the week days!

1. The first working day of the week is __________.
2. The day after wednesday is __________.
3. Which is your favorite day of the week? ______________
4. __________ lies between tuesday and thursday.
5. The weekend falls on ____________ and____________.

689. Help Ryan draw the star by joining the dots from 1-10.

3

2 4

1 5

10 6

8

9 7

690. Look at the pictures and fill in the blank with 'These' or ' Those'.

1. __________ glasses are full.

2. __________ bottles are empty.

3. __________ children are sitting.

4. __________ children are waiting for bus.

691. Complete the sentences below using words from the Word Bank.

1. The ____________________ consists of hair and face.
2. I taste with my ______________.
3. I see with my________________.
4. I hear with my_______________.
5. I smell with_________________.

Nose Eye Head Ear Tongue

692. Write the name of this water animal.

H A R S K

693. Draw lines to help the babies meet their mothers.

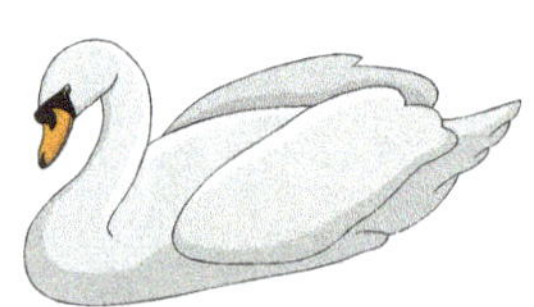

694. Trace the animal to colour and name it.

695. Sam and Dan need your help with this puzzle.

1 2 3 4 5 6 7 8 9 10

			+	2	=	8				
				+		+				
2						1	+	6	=	
+				=		=				
3	+		=	4			+	1	=	
=		+						+		
		=						=		
		6					+	4	=	8

696. Tick the box with odd number of things.

697. Match each picture to the letter with which it begins.

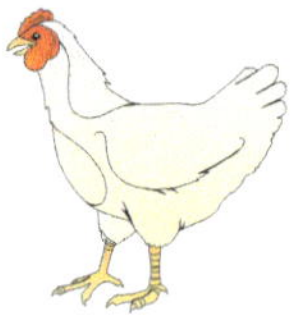

L

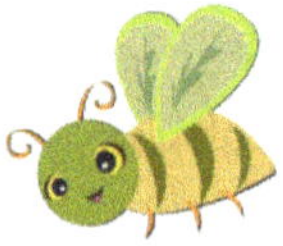

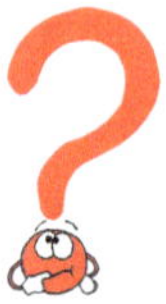

M

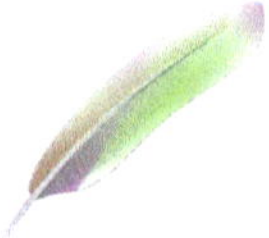

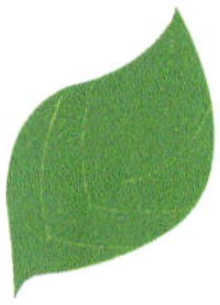

N

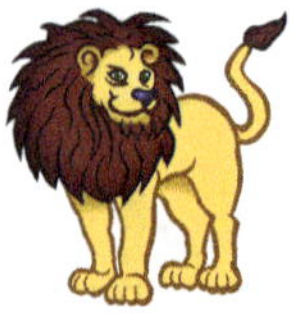

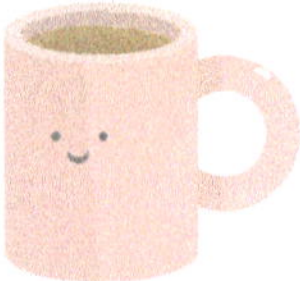

H

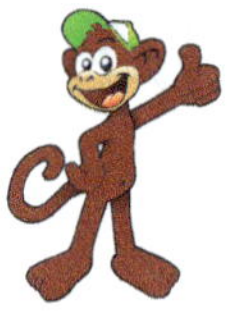

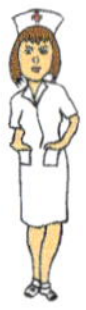

Q

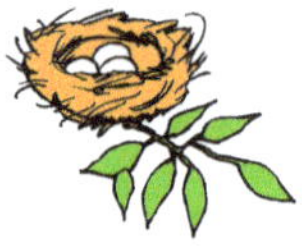

698. Time to get ready for school! Can you identify these useful objects for school? Write their name by taking help from the word box.

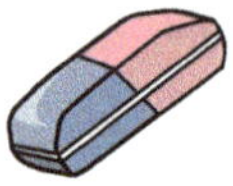

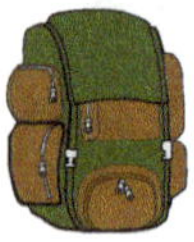

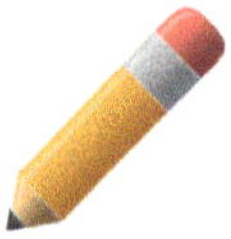

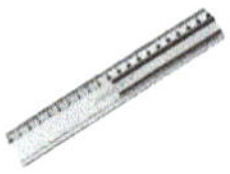

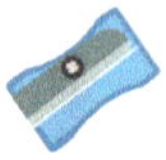

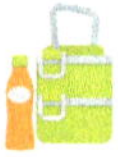

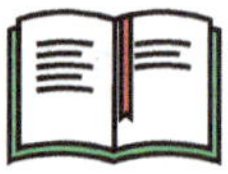

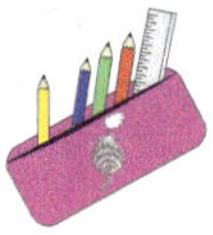

Eraser	Notebook	Backpack	Pencil
Lunch box	Pencil Box	Sharperner	Ruler

699. Choose the correct verb and complete each sentence.

1. A fish __________through its gills. **(talks, breathes).**
2. A whale must ___________to the surface to breathe. **(swim, jump)**
3. A fish uses its fins to ____________. **(breathe, swim)**
4. A bottlelenose dolphin __________ swiftly. **(thinks, swims)**
5. A penguin is a bird that cannot ______________.**(swim, fly)**

700. Fill the given words correctly in the pink crossword.

TALL
SALT
NEST
HEN
HAMMER
APPLE
PLATE
EAGLE

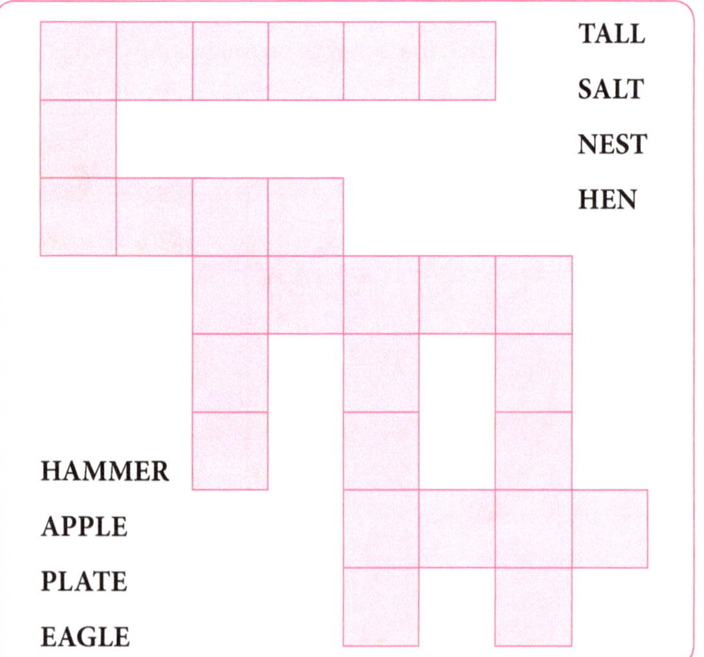

701. Write the different stages of a hen's life cycle. Take help from the Word Box.

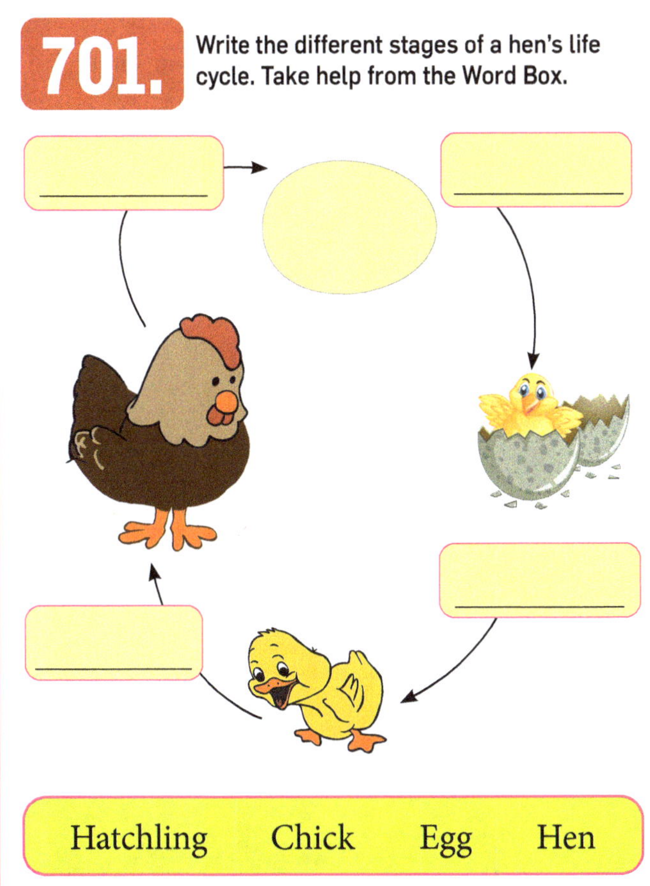

Hatchling Chick Egg Hen

702. Complete the words.

703. Match the animals with the sounds they make.

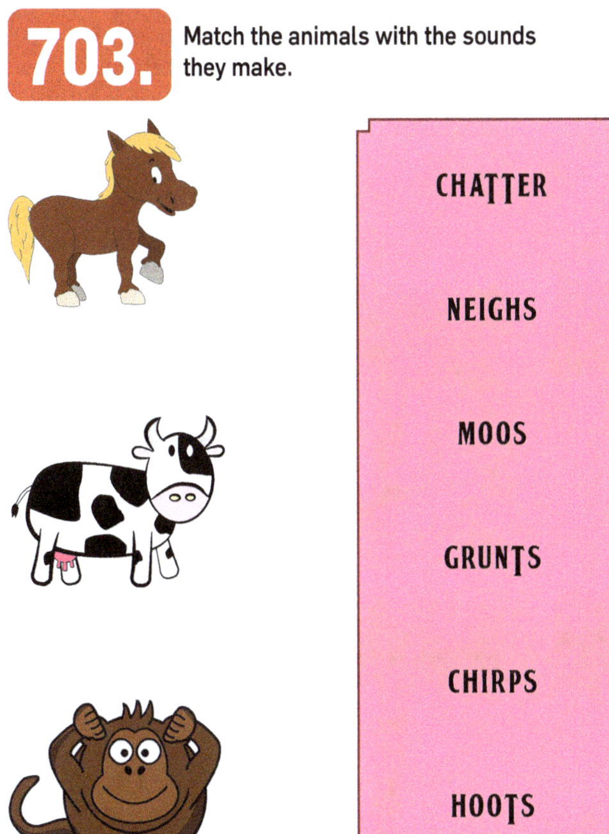

704. Look at the picture of the water animal and colour it.

705. Count the total number of ovals.

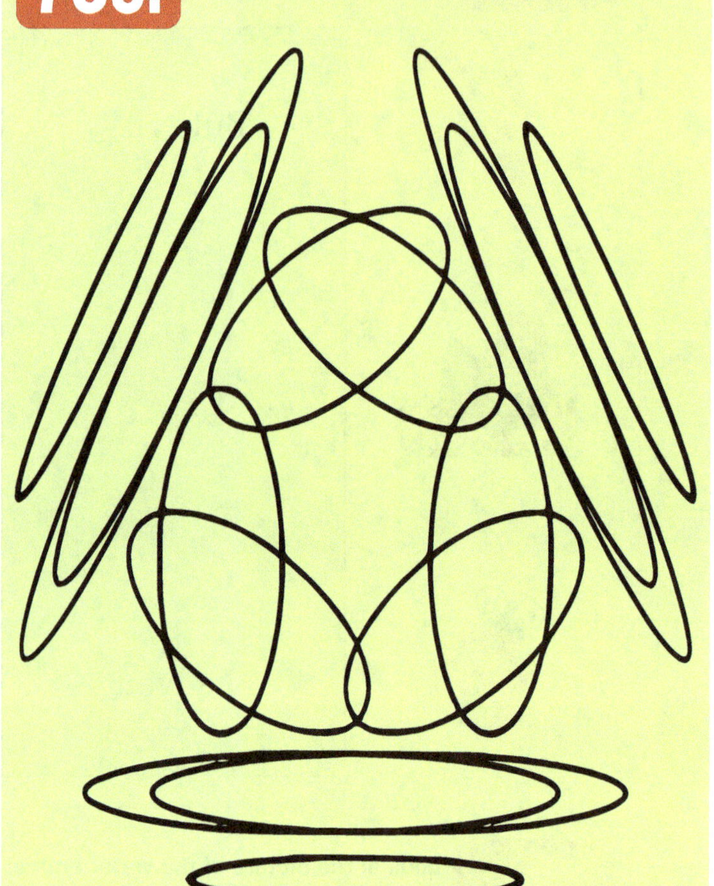

706. Solve the following sums.

a. 6 x 4

b. 9 x 3

c. 6 + 7

d. 15 + 6

e. 18 - 4

f. 32 - 8

a. ______ b. ______

c. ______ d. ______

e. ______ f. ______

707. Complete the series.

12, 24, 36, ___, ___

___, 20, ___, ___, 50

708. Draw a circle around the images that start with the letter D.

709. Unscramble the words

BAER ________________

PLEEHANT ____________

LMUBAELRA ___________

OMUNATNI ____________

710. Solve the sum.

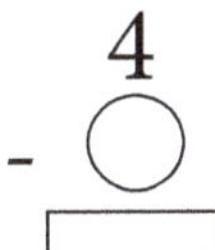

4

- ◯

▭

711. Fill in the blanks.

I You He She It

1. My mother in in the kitchen. __________ is baking a cake.

2. ________________ am listening to The Beatles.

3. Jane has a lot of books. ________ keeps them in her shelf.

4. I have a table.________________ is next to my couch.

712. Colour the animal to find out its name.

NAETLEHP ____________________

713. Write the names of these animals.

______________ ______________

______________ ______________

714. Fill in the missing capital or small letters according to the pattern in the blank spaces below.

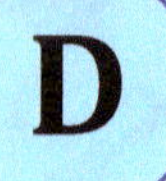

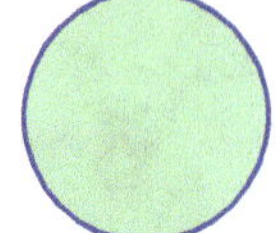

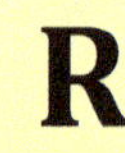
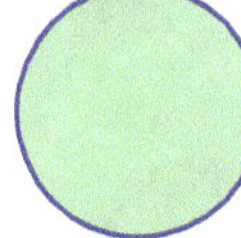

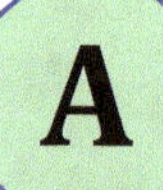
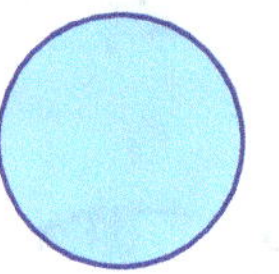
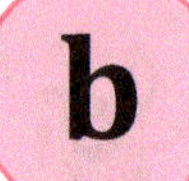

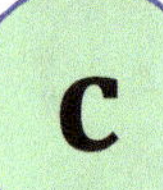

D		Q	
P		R	
O			A
	b		c
n		t	

715. Circle the wild animals in every lot.

716. Circle the correct letter with which the names of these animals begin.

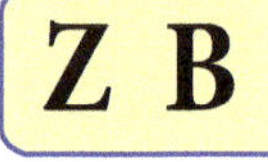

Z B

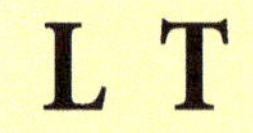

L T

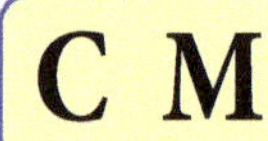

C M

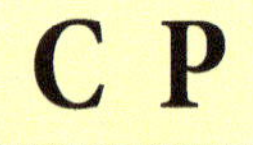

C P

Colour the given vegetables and count them.

718.

Add the numbers given the bowling pin.

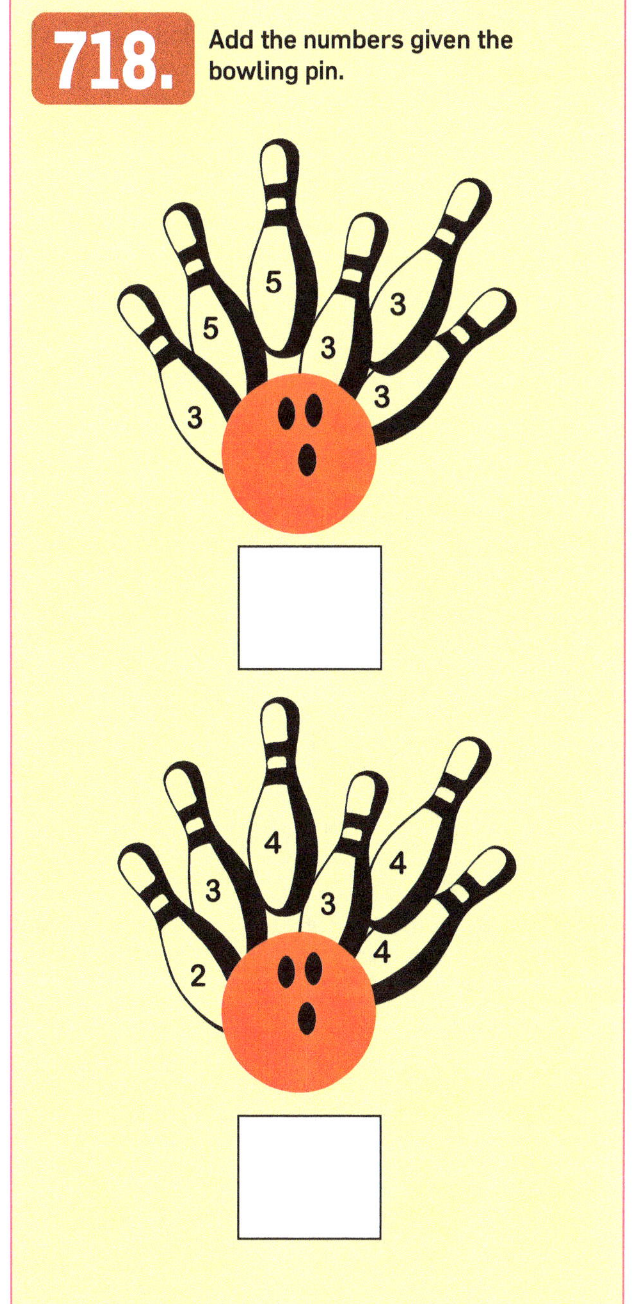

719.

Add up all the pencils of the same colour, and write the answer.

720. Circle the images you find in your living room.

721. Solve the sums on the flowers to know which group of butterflies will hover over it.

722. Colour the picture of tiger.

723. Which of the following actions are done using hands?

Reading

Cooking

Bathing

724. Match the animals to their food.

ZEBRA

CARROT

RABBIT

INSECT

FROG

HAY

725. Connect the star to complete the table of 6.

6 18 30

12 24

54 36

48 42

60 66 72 78

726. Draw the picture of the animal on the grid. Colour the picture and write its name.

727. Count the spoons and find the answer.

24-8 =

728. Solve the sums given below:

24-8 =

2 + 5 =

4 x 4 =

7 x 8 =

7 - 2 =

9 x 3 =

729. Solve the sums and write the answers in the crab's belly.

730. Match the images to their respective names.

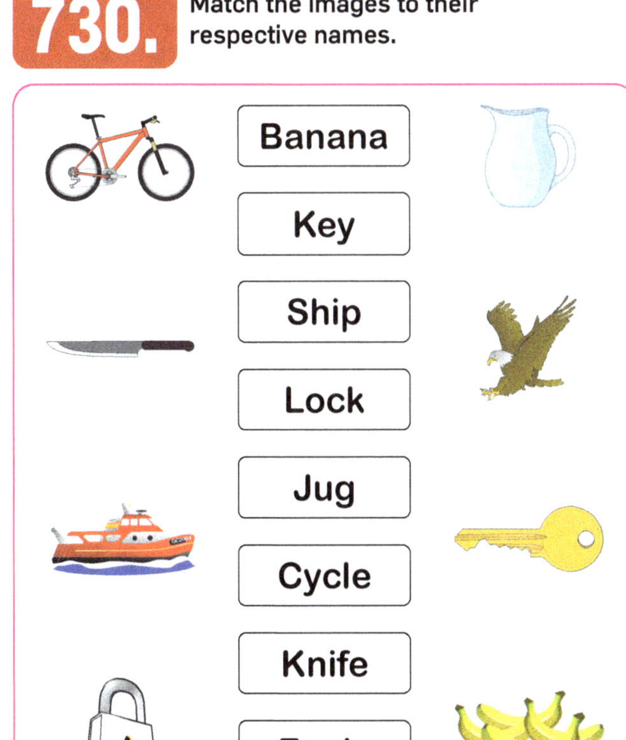

731. Match the following to form a word.

732. Encircle the words in the row that begin with the same sound as the picture.

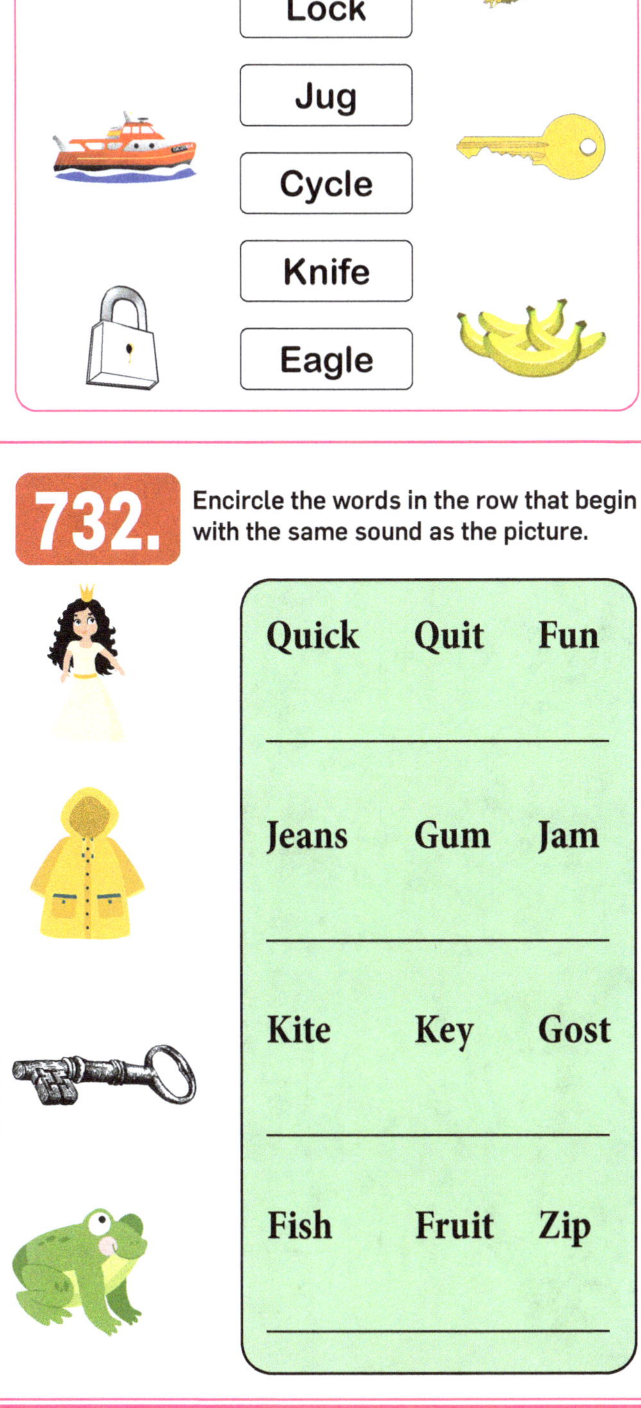

733. Write the beginning letter of each object.

D M B J W S

734.
Help the baby tortoise meet its mother.
735.
Colour the picture and write the name of the animal.
736.
Trace the animal and colour it.
737.
Write the names of the desert animals.

738. Fill in the blanks with numbers that add upto 80.

5 7 3 6 4 8

80

_ + _ = 80

_ + _ = 80

_ + _ = 80

739. Count the pictures and write the correct answers in the box.

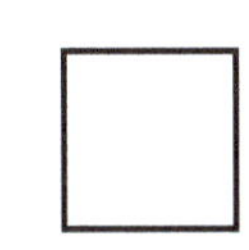

740. Note the time.

☐ o' clock

 o' clock

 o' clock

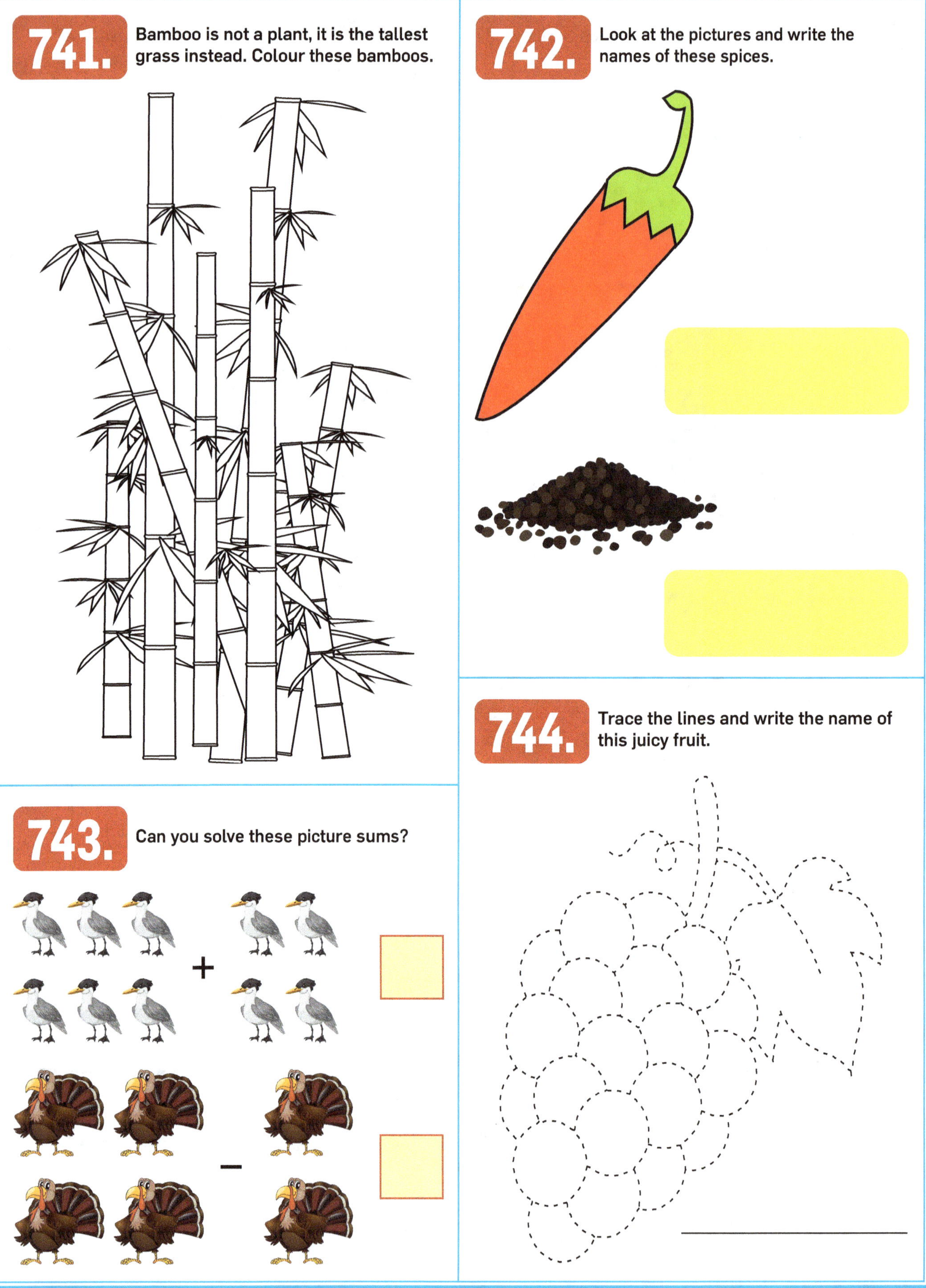

741.

Bamboo is not a plant, it is the tallest grass instead. Colour these bamboos.

742.

Look at the pictures and write the names of these spices.

743.

Can you solve these picture sums?

744.

Trace the lines and write the name of this juicy fruit.

745. Fill the grid with the correct answers.

5	+		=	12
+		+		+
	+	2	=	
=		=		=
8	+		=	

746. Can you colour the grid below according to the sums below it?

7	9	5
6	3	1
2	8	4

20-19 10-1 13-6

16-10 13-8 12-4

747. Solve the sums given below. You can count with the help of butterflies given.

8 + 4 = ☐

7 + 2 = ☐

7 + 5 = ☐

2 + 3 = ☐

748. Can you calculate the number of objects and write them below?

749.

Circle the numbers that are a divisible of 5.

750.

Write the numbers of the given number names.

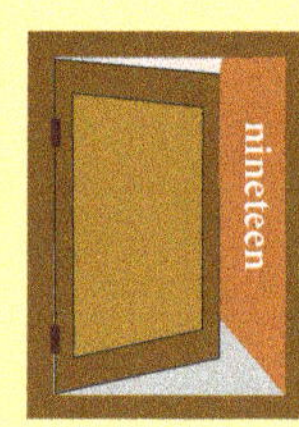

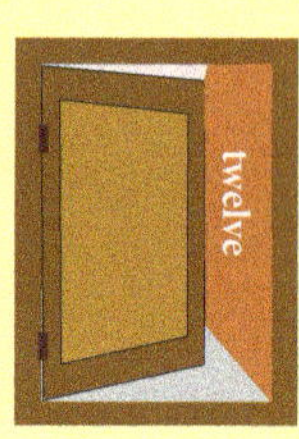

751.

Match the flowers to their respective vases.

752. Underline the nouns in each sentence.

1. My mother is a teacher.
2. The tiger is looking for deer.
3. My father is sitting on his chair.
4. A pilot flies an aeroplane.
5. The painter is painting a picture.
6. Tom has bought a new car.
7. The cat jumped onto the box.
8. The doctor is working.

753. Find the tools used in gardening.

C	A	I	W	P	T	A	T	R	I	D	R
W	A	T	E	R	I	N	G	C	A	N	F
O	R	K	O	U	S	P	E	D	H	E	P
R	U	W	S	N	E	K	E	O	R	F	A
K	E	S	P	E	A	H	S	H	O	O	P
L	S	G	A	R	D	E	N	C	A	R	T
T	R	E	D	G	E	R	O	E	L	K	G
A	S	H	E	A	R	S	R	D	F	K	T

Pruner, Fork, Watering Can, Shears, Edger, Spade, Hose, Garden Cart, Rake, Trowel

754. Complete the picture by joining the dots.

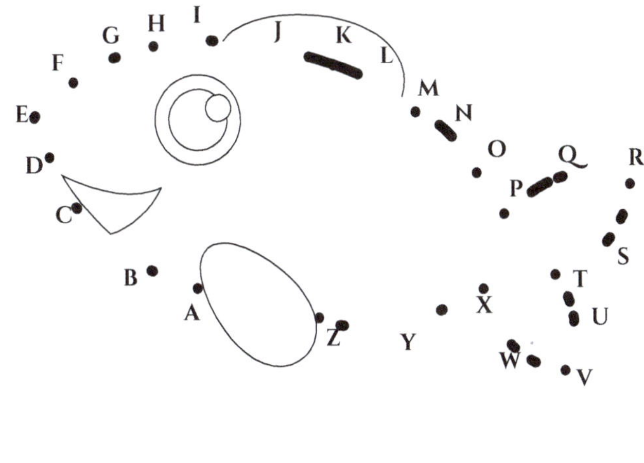

755. Use the following words to frame sentences. One has been done for you.

Egg **Watermelon** **Sweets**
Book **Bottle** **X-phone**

1. *I like sweets*
2. ______
3. ______
4. ______
5. ______
6. ______
7. ______
8. ______

756. Write the last letter for each animal.

LIO ______

BA ______

CA ______

BEA ______

757. Fill in the blanks using the letters given in the box.

d c b m h t s l r p

__at

__uck

__en

__onkey

__ird

__ent

__hip

__ion

__abbit

__ear

758. Circle the farm animal.

Koala

Sheep

Tiger

Dog

Lion

Fox

759. Colour the picture of the bird.

760. Solve the multiplication sum.

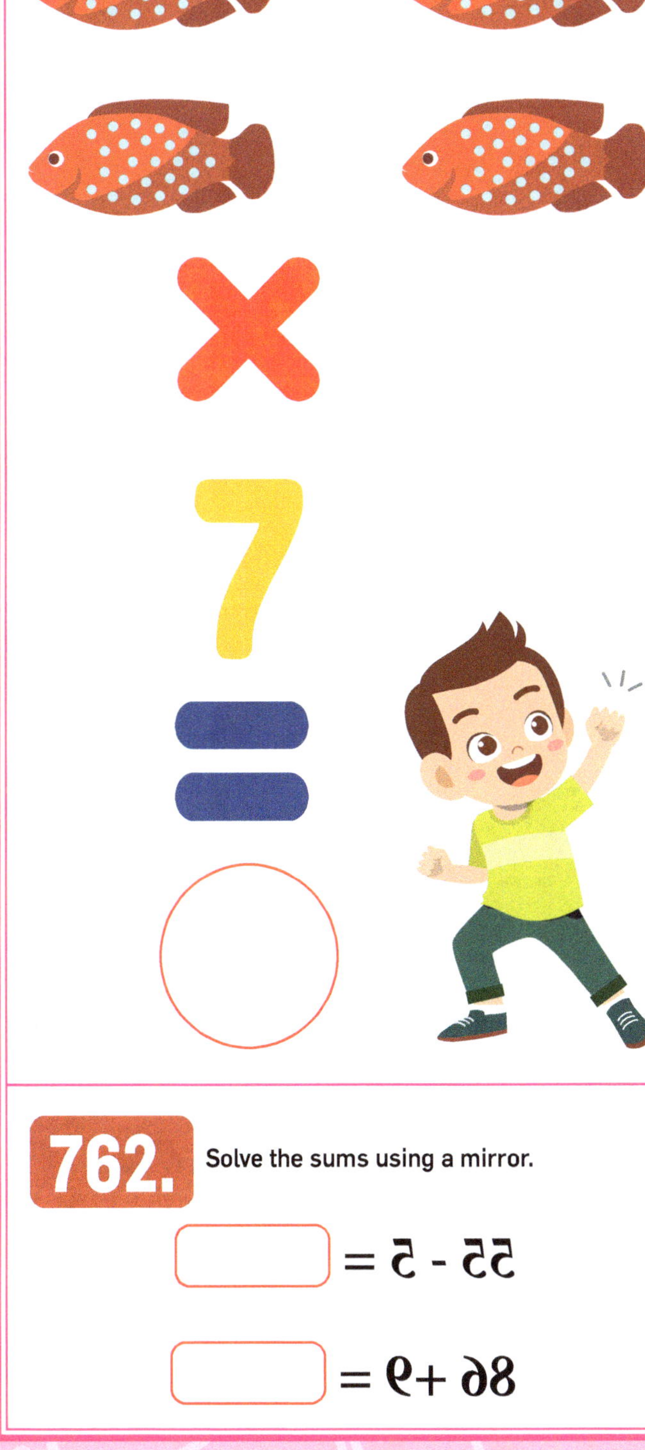

761. Can you number the sequence of a seed growing into a plant from 1-4?

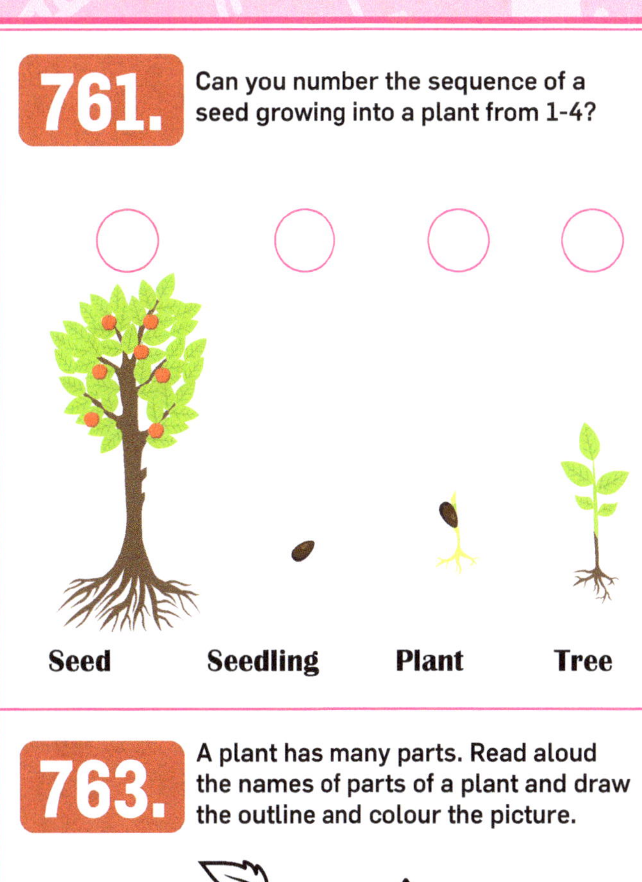

762. Solve the sums using a mirror.

55 - 5 = ☐

86 + 9 = ☐

763. A plant has many parts. Read aloud the names of parts of a plant and draw the outline and colour the picture.

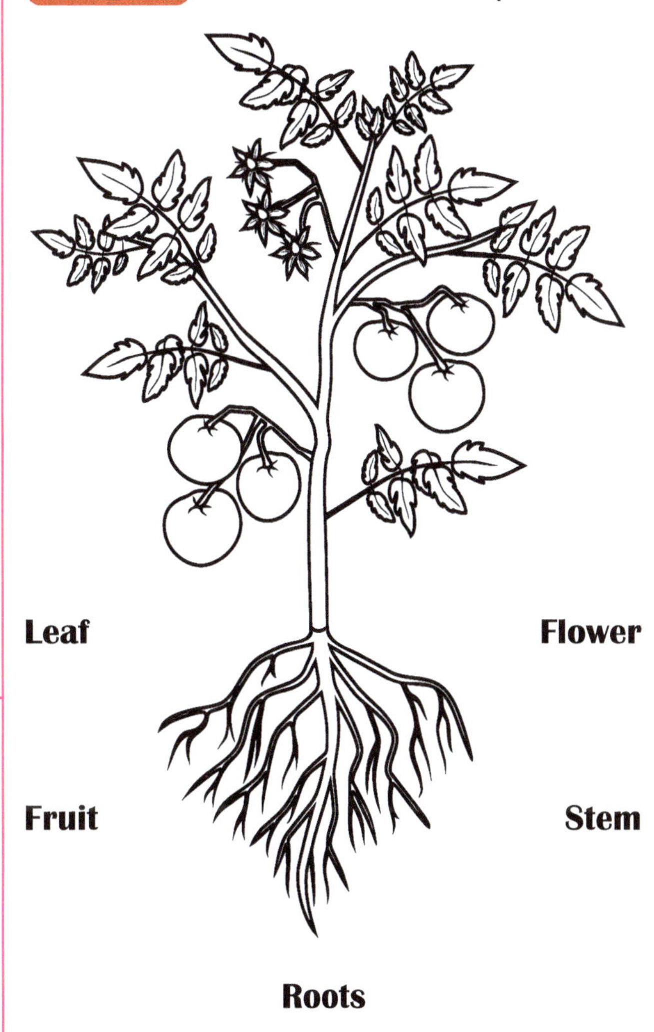

764. Complete the sentences.

lk ft lt lp mp

1. The qui __________ keeps the cold away.
2. Anne got a gi ____________ from Martin.
3. Silkworms make si__________.
4. David will he ____________ me with complete my assignment.
5. We ate marshmallow at the a __________.

766. Unscramble the letters to form words.

iahcr ____________________

utckr ____________________

lccye ____________________

fkine ____________________

765. Circle the images that start with the letter 'C'.

767. Circle the ending sound of the images given.

G T

K D

R T

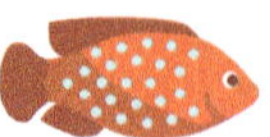

H F

D R

768. With the help of the word box, complete the life cycle of an insect.

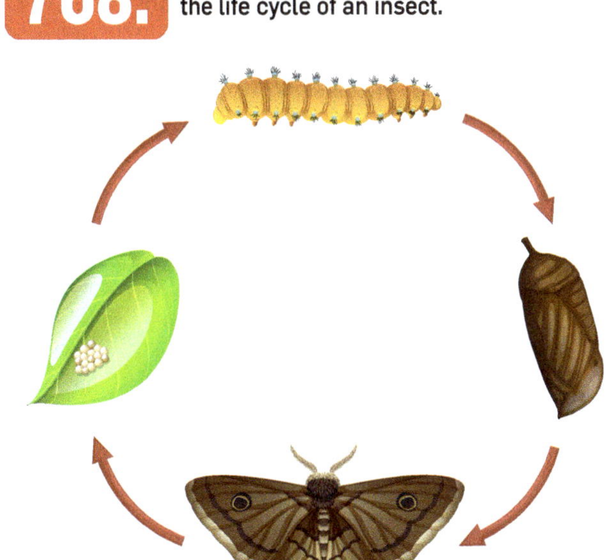

Egg, Larva, Pupa, Insect

769. Fill in the blanks with the correct words from the box.

COLD	ROUGH	SOFT
SHARP	HOT	

1. The ice feels____________
2. The nails feels___________
3. Thr feather feels __________
4. The kettle feels __________
5. The stone feels___________

770. Finish the crossword using vowels.

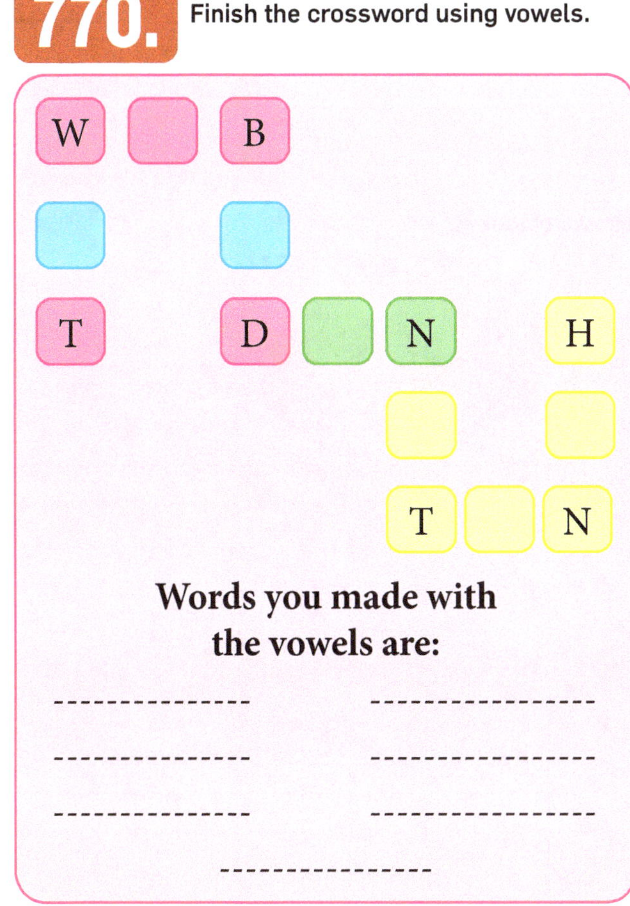

Words you made with the vowels are:

______________ ______________

______________ ______________

______________ ______________

____

771. Solve the sum.

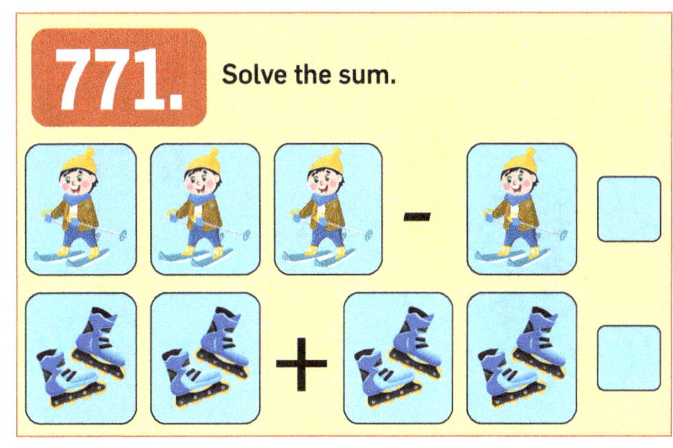

772. Categorise the animals into domestic and wild.

__________ __________

__________ __________

773. Count the owls and circle the correct answer.

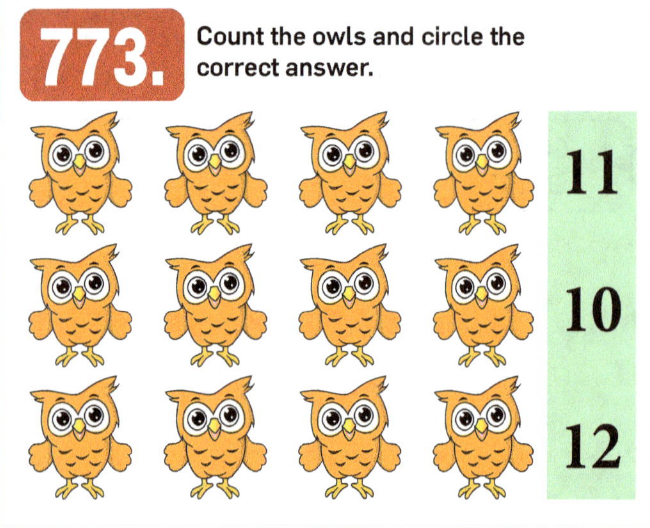

774. Colour the shapes in each column using the given instructions.

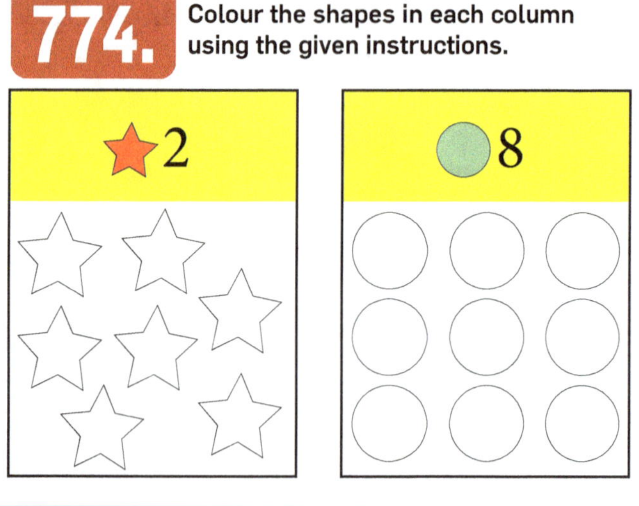

775. Add 2 to each number and take the butterfly to the other side.

776. Join the numbers to complete the rhinoceros and colour it.

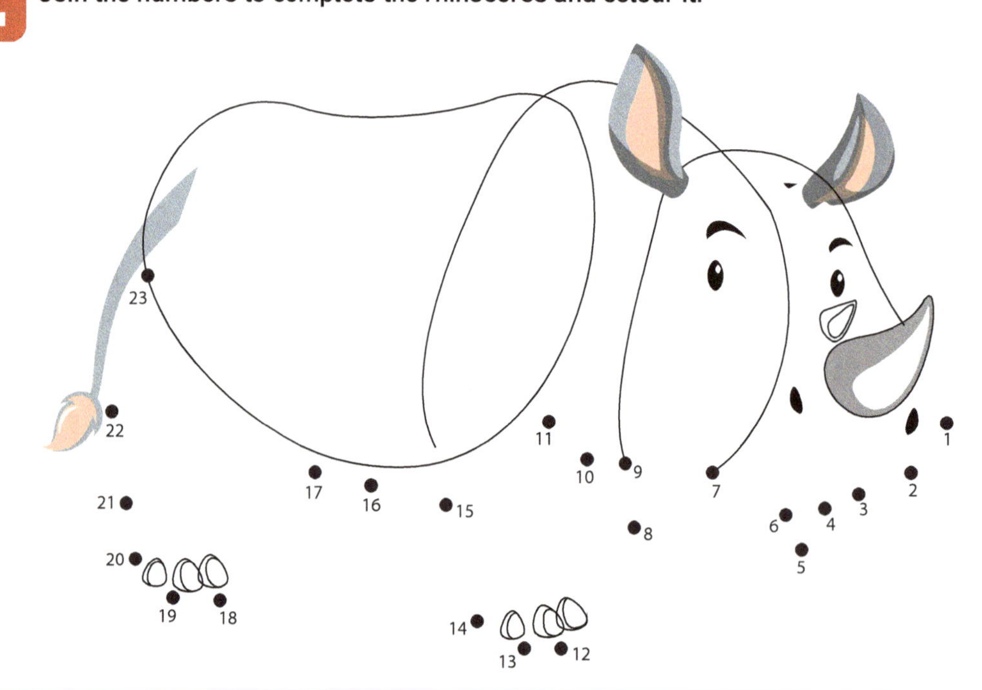

777. Solve the riddles given below.

1. I look like a lady's fingers.

   I am a ______________________________

2. You cry when i am cut.

   I am an ______________________________

3. I am a flower that looks like broccoli.

   I am a ______________________________

4. I begin with 'egg'.

   I am an ______________________________

778. Match the activities to the days on which they are done.

Rainy Day

Winter Day

Summer Day

779. Which of these animals can be seen in the water?

780. Write C for for cold and H for hot, in front of the following food items.

781. Draw a line to match the animals with the adjectives that best suit them.

Brown Hair

Big Teeth

Speed

Transport

Meat

Grass

Help the animals find their skin pattern.

783. A plant needs, air, water and sunlight to grow. Number the pictures from 1-4 to label the process of a plant's growth.

Colour the picture and write the name of the man below.

_ _ O _ MAN

785. Encircle the odd numbers.

3	4	6	1	3
2	8	4	9	7
9	5	5	7	8
1	4	3	1	5
5	9	6	2	10
1	8	10	4	7

786. Colour the number of dices.

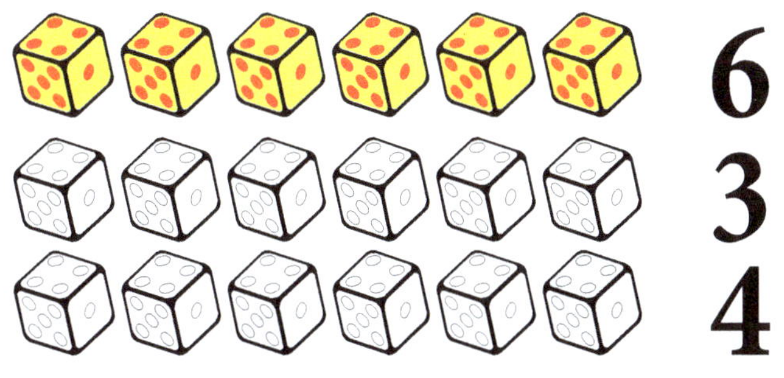

6

3

4

788. Help the girl reach her books by drawing a path through the numbers that show a difference of 8.

	2-1	2-1	2-1	2-1	2-1
	8-4	15-7	20-12	9-1	16-8
10-2	12-4	14-6	5-2	7-5	11-3
7-5	8-6	6-1	9-5		

787. Join the dots to complete the chick and colour it.

789. Add the following images.

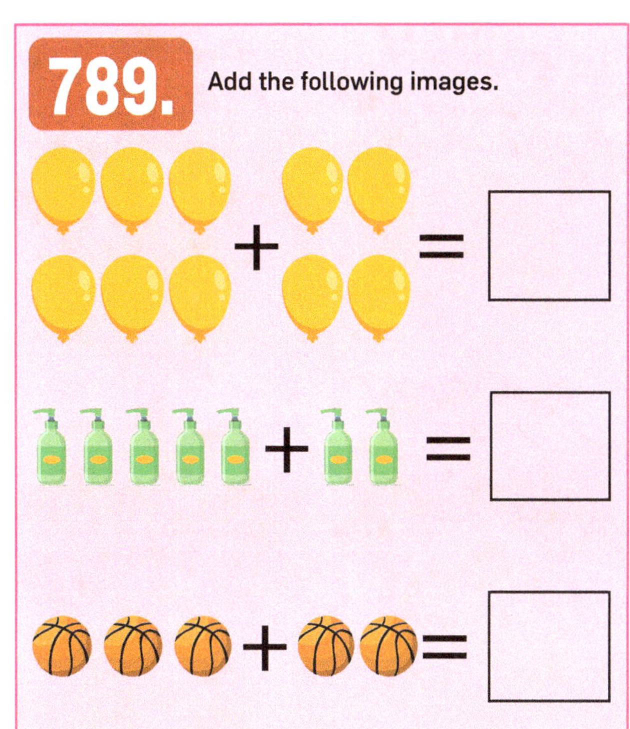

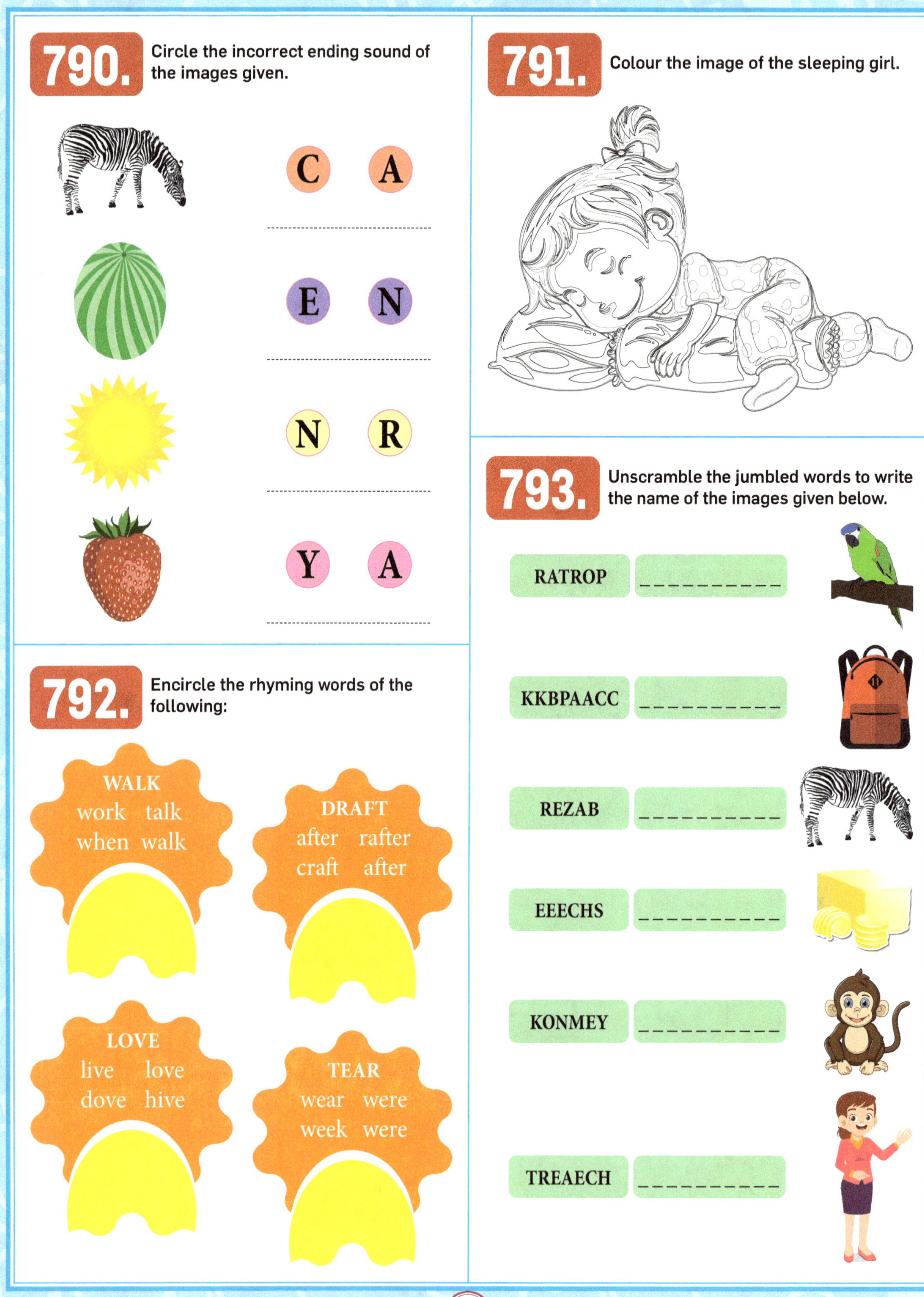
790.
Circle the incorrect ending sound of the images given.
C A
E N
N R
Y A
791.
Colour the image of the sleeping girl.
792.
Encircle the rhyming words of the following:
WALK
work talk
when walk
DRAFT
after rafter
craft after
LOVE
live love
dove hive
TEAR
wear were
week were
793.
Unscramble the jumbled words to write the name of the images given below.
RATROP
KKBPAACC
REZAB
EEECHS
KONMEY
TREAECH

794. Draw circles around the insects.

Frog

Gecko

Honeybee

Tortoise

Caterpillar

Snail

795. Find the animals in the word grid.

IGUANA ALLIGATOR TURTLE CROCODILE
SNAKE LIZARD DENTIST NEW

A	S	D	F	L	K	J	G	H	Q	P	T
L	C	E	L	U	E	T	E	O	O	T	A
I	G	U	A	N	A	P	C	S	T	E	L
Z	U	M	S	O	N	Y	K	U	O	N	L
A	E	P	S	O	L	A	O	S	N	O	I
R	D	E	N	T	I	S	T	A	G	U	G
D	O	O	A	H	F	R	Y	S	U	H	A
T	Y	C	K	B	A	I	T	N	E	W	T
S	A	T	E	R	T	U	R	T	L	E	O
L	A	R	M	S	R	L	C	I	S	O	R
C	R	O	C	O	D	I	L	E	N	G	U

796. Did you know turtles are amphibians? Draw a turtle in the space given and colour it.

797. Write the ending letters of these words.

s h s e e k r r h

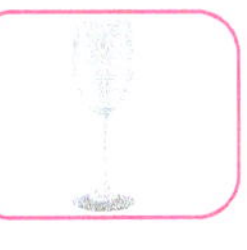 ______

 ______

 ______

 ______

 ______

 ______

 ______

 ______

 ______

798. Put the images in the correct order to complete the picture.

799. Write the number that when added to 10 gives the given result.

800. Count the number of pigs in the picture and write the correct answer.

801. Fill in the missing numbers to complete the puzzle.

	+	6	=	9
+		+		+
6	+		=	
=		=		=
	+	8	=	17

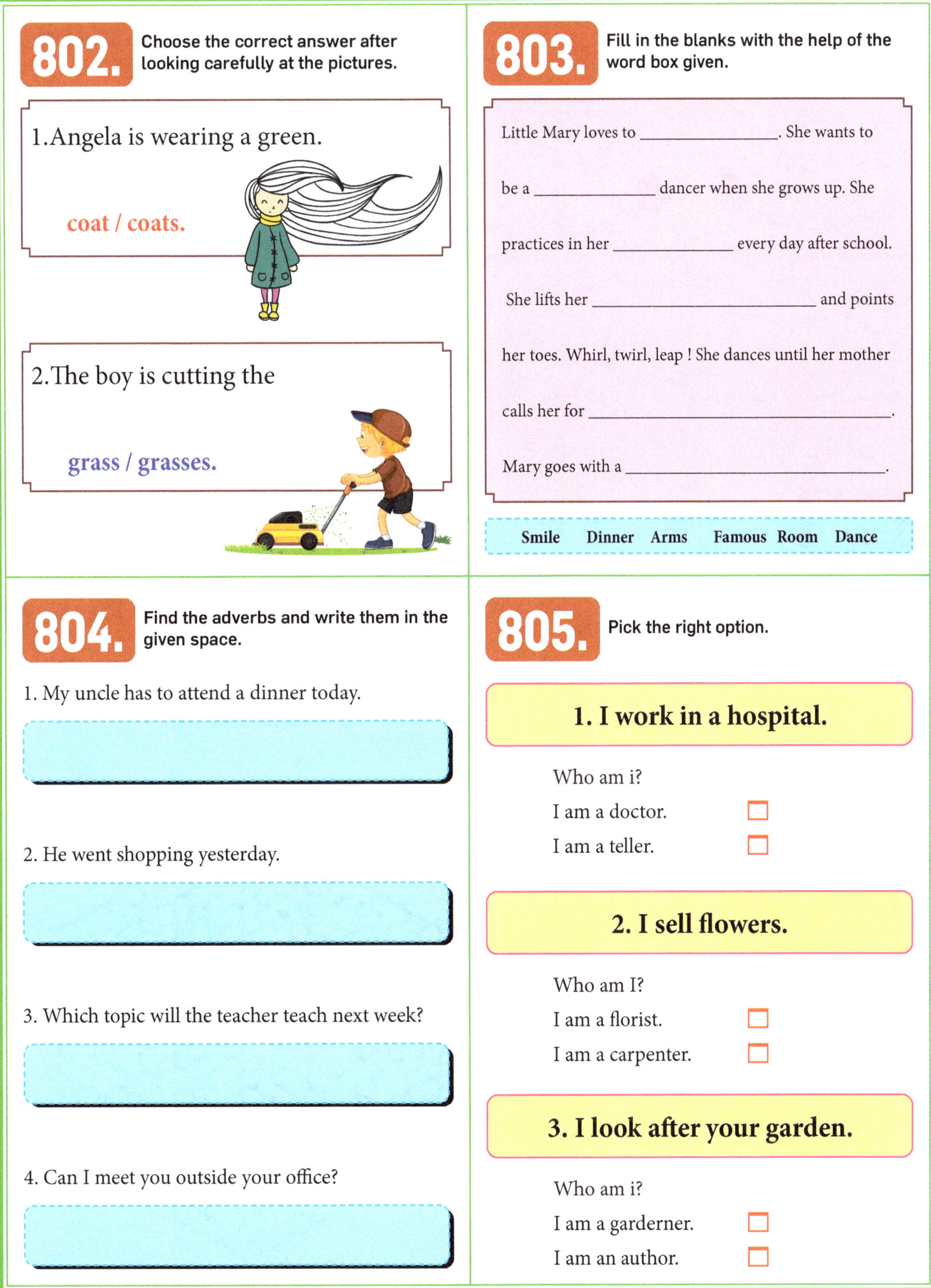

802. Choose the correct answer after looking carefully at the pictures.

1.Angela is wearing a green.

coat / coats.

2.The boy is cutting the

grass / grasses.

803. Fill in the blanks with the help of the word box given.

Little Mary loves to ______________. She wants to be a ______________ dancer when she grows up. She practices in her ______________ every day after school. She lifts her ______________ and points her toes. Whirl, twirl, leap ! She dances until her mother calls her for ______________. Mary goes with a ______________.

Smile Dinner Arms Famous Room Dance

804. Find the adverbs and write them in the given space.

1. My uncle has to attend a dinner today.

2. He went shopping yesterday.

3. Which topic will the teacher teach next week?

4. Can I meet you outside your office?

805. Pick the right option.

1. I work in a hospital.

Who am i?

I am a doctor. ☐

I am a teller. ☐

2. I sell flowers.

Who am I?

I am a florist. ☐

I am a carpenter. ☐

3. I look after your garden.

Who am i?

I am a garderner. ☐

I am an author. ☐

806. Complete the sea animal and colour it.

807. Learn about the life cycle of a jellyfish. Take help from the word box.

Planula, Polyp, Polyp(with buds), Eyphra, Medosa, Planula Larva

808. Colour the insects in different colours.

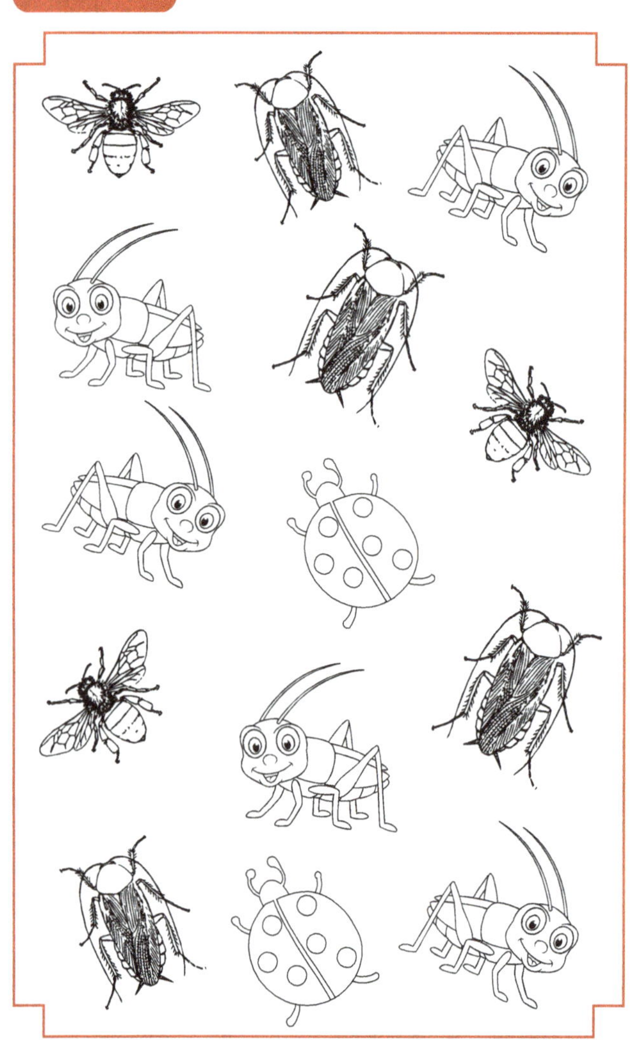

809. Solve the maze puzzle to help the bee reach the honeycomb.

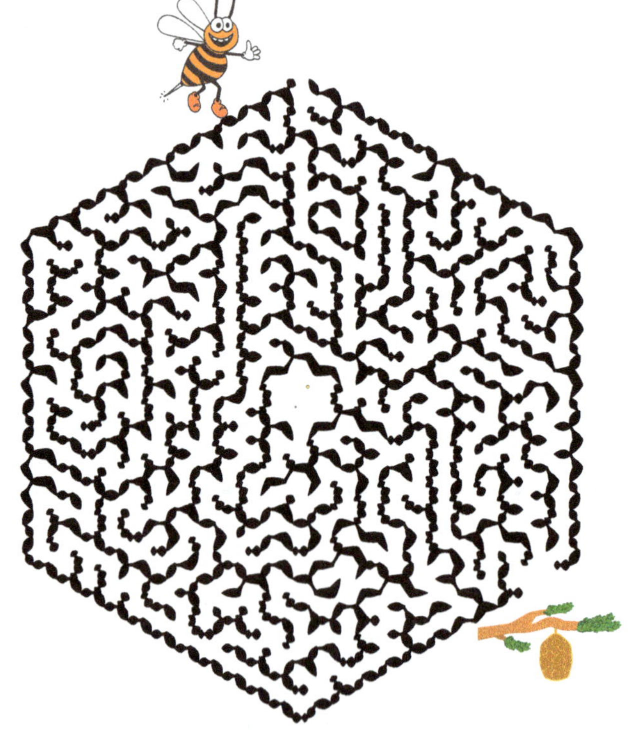

810. Solve the following.

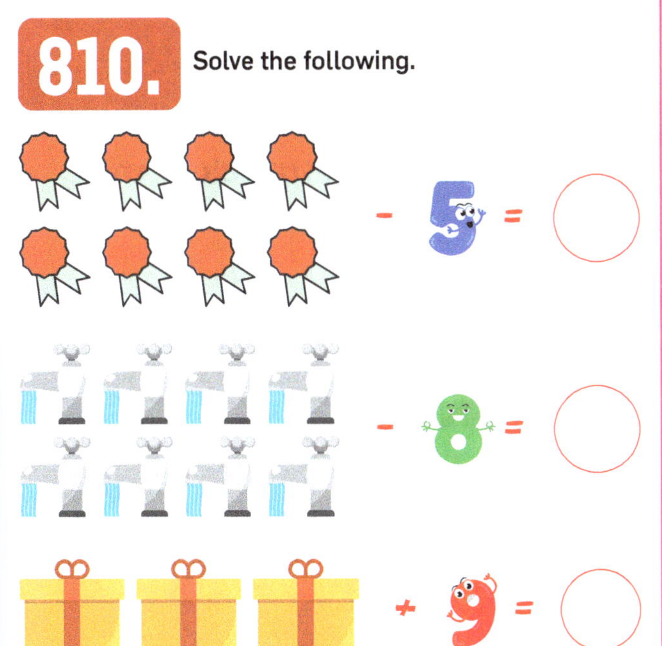

811. Join the dots and colour the picture.

812. Colour the turtle using the given colour codes.

1	2	3

813. Find the words of the word box in the grid below.

S	F	R	U	I	T	J	B	G
I	E	S	S	R	W	L	I	R
S	U	V	E	H	E	K	R	E
N	E	T	A	V	A	C	D	E
D	A	E	O	E	O	D	S	N
W	I	H	R	O	L	V	E	N
Z	S	G	L	T	L	I	O	S

BIRD	FRUIT	SOIL	COOL
GREEN	SUN	DIG	SHADE
TREES	LEAVES	SHOVEL	WATER

814. Write the correct Adverbs.

yesterday, next to, below, this morning, everywhere

1. I will park my bicycle ____________ the garden.
2. My mother looked ______________ for her necklace.
3. We could see everything ____ from the roof of the hotel.
4. Teddy called me at 7 a.m_____.
5. Tom celebrated his birthday _________________.

815. Change the following words into plurals by removing the -y and adding -ies.

One Copy — Seven _____________

One Butterfly — Six ________________

One Lady — Five ______________

One Fairy — Nine _____________

One Cherry — Four _____________

One Berry — Two ______________

One Lorry — Seven ______________

One Country — Seven ______________

816. Fill in the blanks with 'he', 'she' or 'it'.

1. Mr Rory is eating. ____________ is busy.
2. Martin is not well. ____________ will see the doctor today.
3. Have you seen my watch? ____________ was on the table.

4. My mother gifted me a dress. ____________ love it.
5. The rabbit looks sick. May be ____________ is hungry.
6. Archie won the race yesterday. ____________ is a good runner.

817. Solve the mathematical problems to complete the grid.

7	+		=	11
	–	4	=	9
4	+		=	10
	–	2	=	18
14	+		=	21

818. Know the life cycle of a frog with the help of the word box given below.

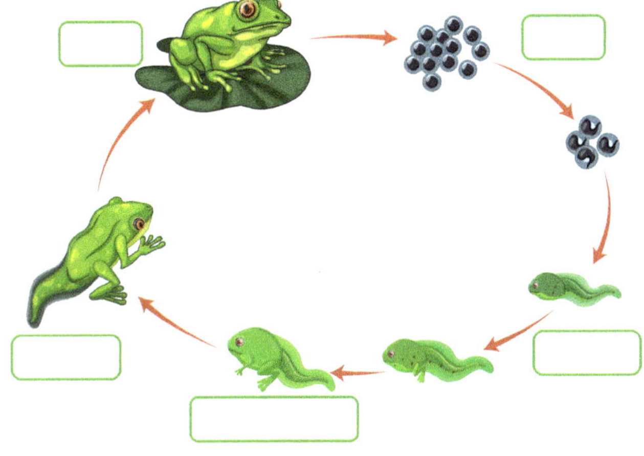

Eggs, Tadpole, Tadpole legs, Froglet, Adult

819. Name the following amphibians correctly.

____

____

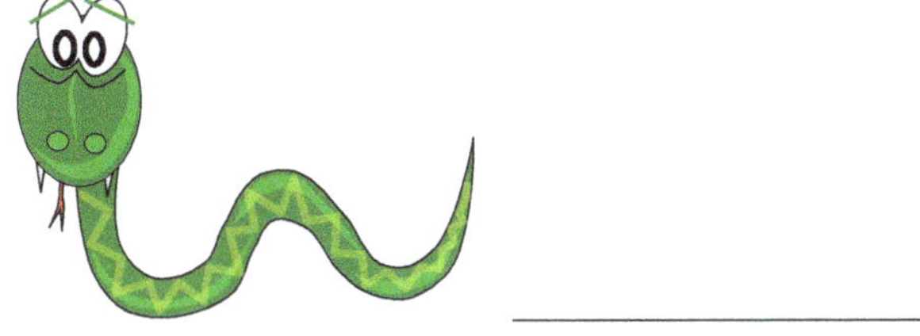

____

____

820. Colour the picture of the frog in bright colours.

821. Solve the sum with the help of BODMAS.

2 + 8 - 5 × 3 + 5 = ____

7 - 3 × 1 + 5 - 3 = ____

822. What time do these clocks show?

☐ o' clock   quarter past ☐   half past ☐   quarter past ☐

823. Write the number of tens in the blank space.

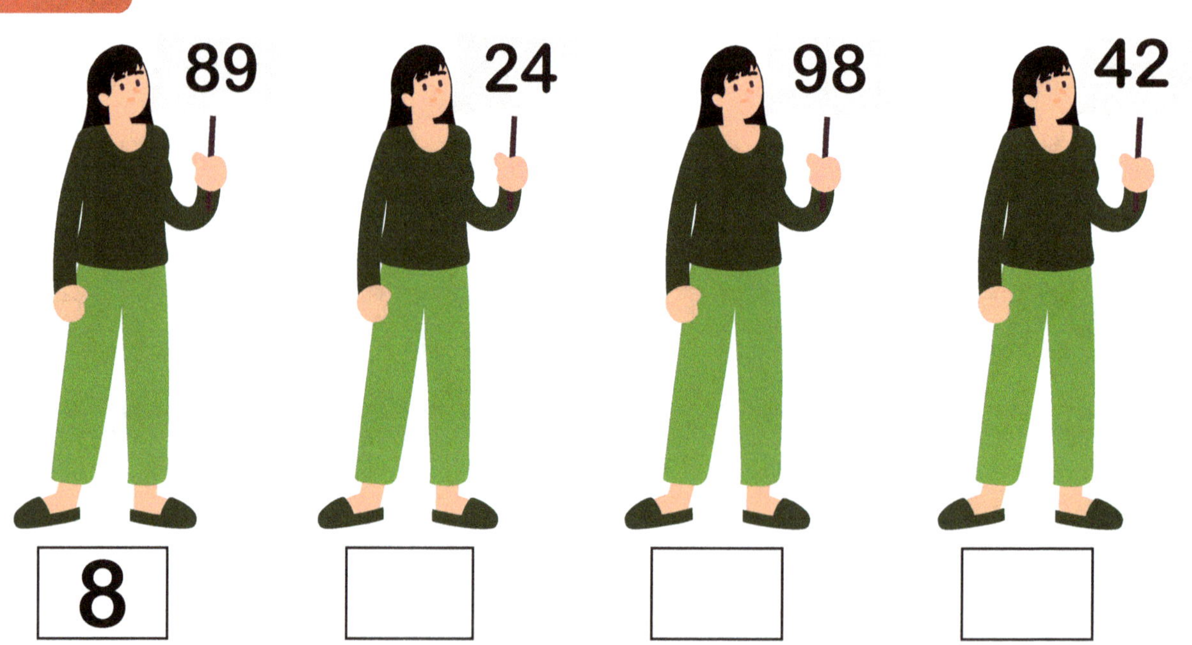

824. Fill in the blacks with the correct pronouns.

1. This is my computer. It was gifted to ____________________ by my father.
2. I am looking for my mother. Have you seen ____________________?
3. Debbie and I are busy. Please don't disturb ________________.
4. I want to speak to Carter. Can you please call ________________?
5. This belongs to Teddy and his brother. Please return it to ________________.

825. Paint the nouns 'yellow' and the verbs 'green.'

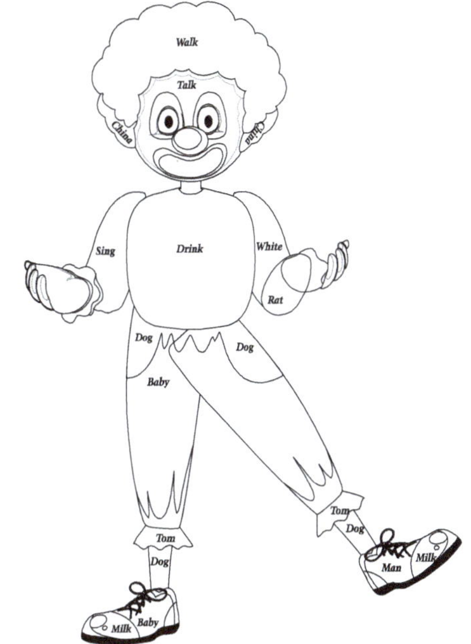

826. Fill in the missing alphabets to complete the words and colour the image.

um __ re __ a

h _ t

_ o _ k

_ o _ t

827. Colour the image and name it.

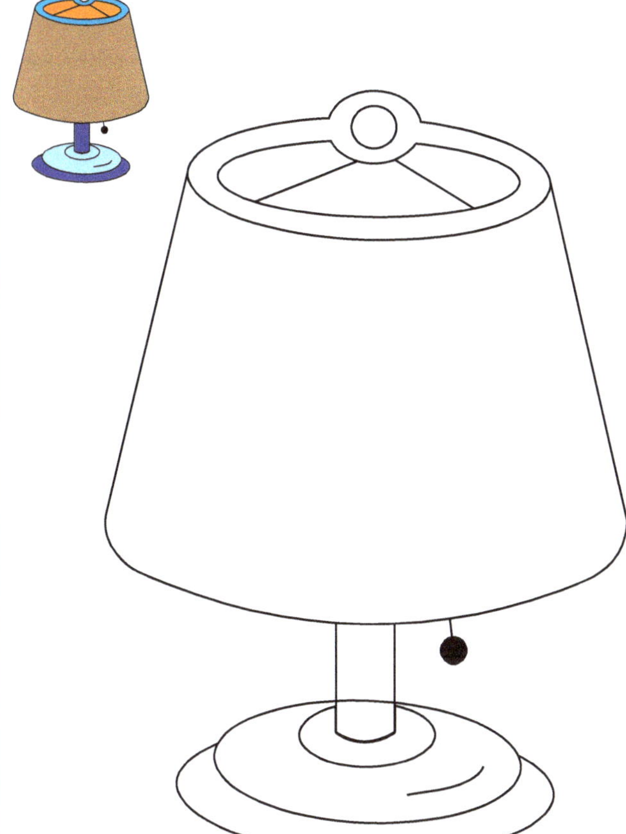

828. Fill in the crossword with the help of the images given.

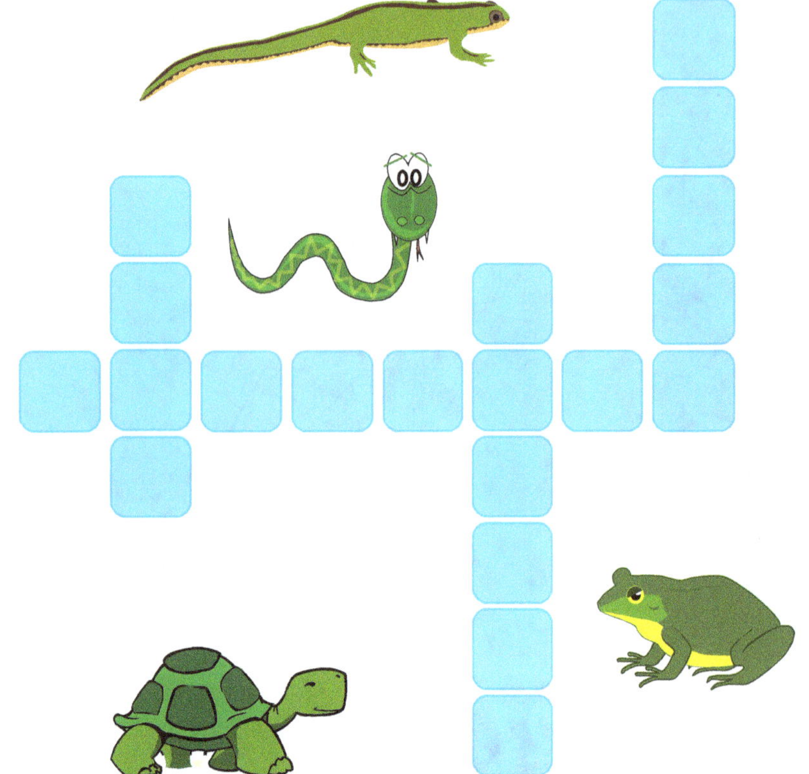

829. Cross the odd one out.

830. Colour the picture according to the key given and find out the hidden insect.

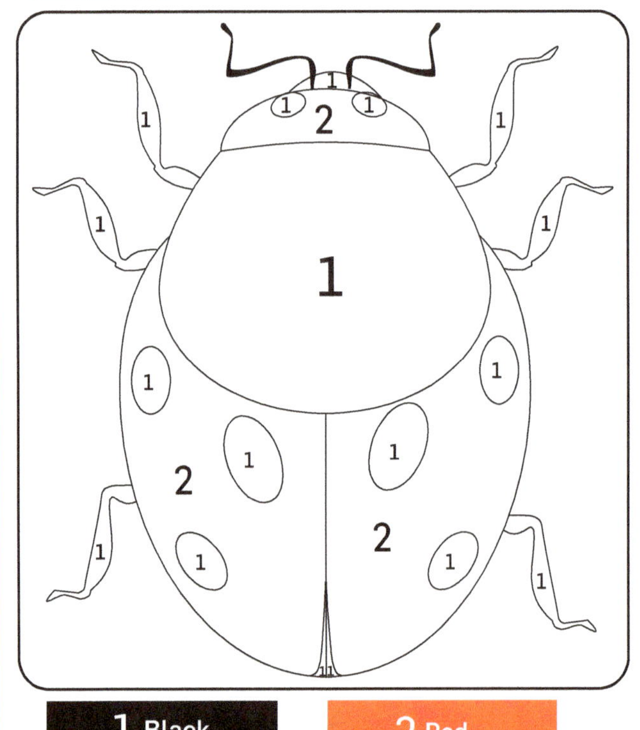

1 Black

2 Red

831. Trace along the dots and colour the animal.

832. Multiply the numbers in the wheel with 2 and write the correct answer in the space given.

7 8 1 2 3 4 5 6

2

833. Count the images and draw a circle around the correct number.

834. Solve each sum on the train and colour the train green which gives the answer 10

45-15

25 + 25

835. Teddy needs your help to match the numbers with their names.

836. Circle the first letter of each image.

b c a

e a t

j e p

b g k

n c k

q p c

837. Draw lines to match the picture with their correct names.

watermelon

watch

wheel

wall

window

well

838. Pick the right sentence that corresponds with the image.

1. I am made by bees.
2. I am red in colour and good for health.
3. You can see me in the sky at night.
4. I am round and have many spokes.
5. It is my job to keep you dry when it rains.
6. I give you knowledge.

839. Help Maurice solve her sums and match them with the correct answer.

840. Some animals give us food. Match each animal to the food it gives.

841. Fill in the correct consonants of these words.

____at

____eet

____oat

____elly

____acket

842. We come across many weathers throughout the year. Write the correct name below each picture.

____

____

____

____

843. Circle the objects that help you on a rainy day.

844. Look at the pictures and encircle the correct number.

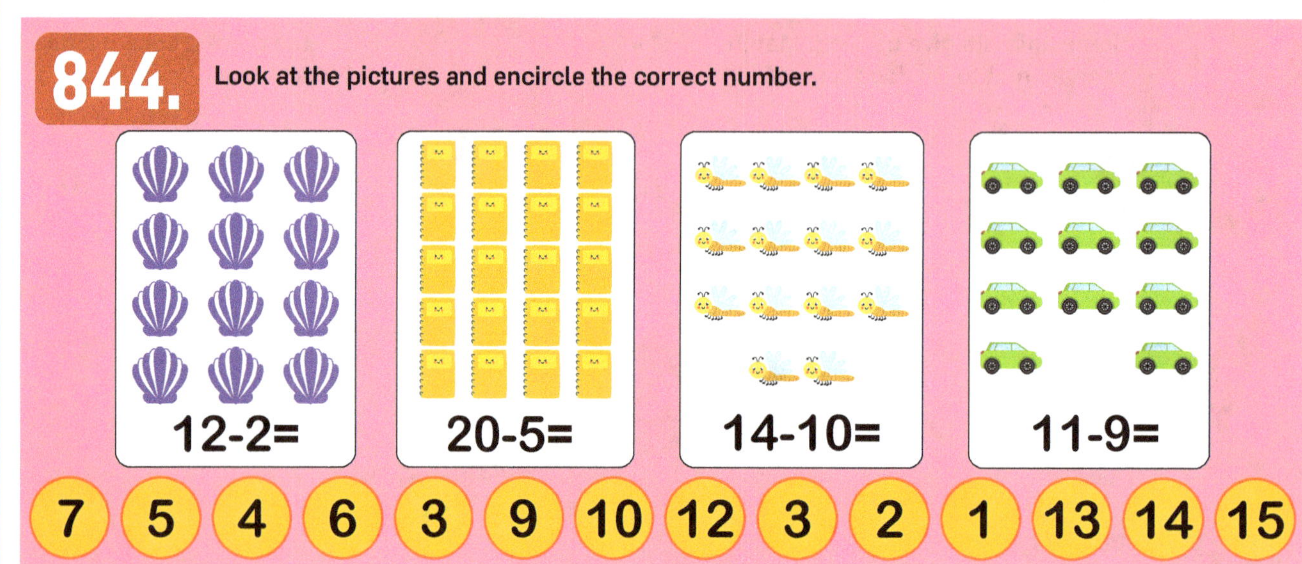

845. Help Martin and Jamie to do the sums.

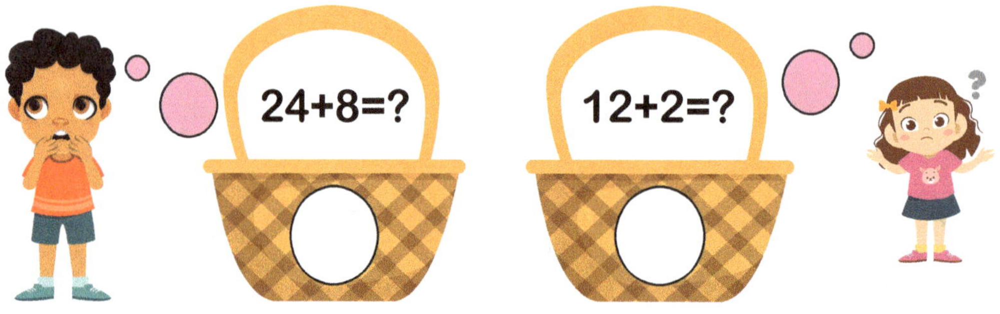

846.

How many rockets are there?

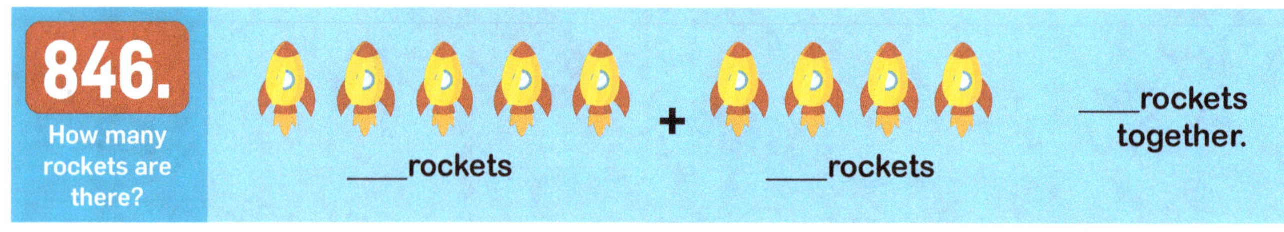

847. Help the boy complete his math homework.

848. Form a new word by changing one letter in the word given. For Example - Hat and Mat.

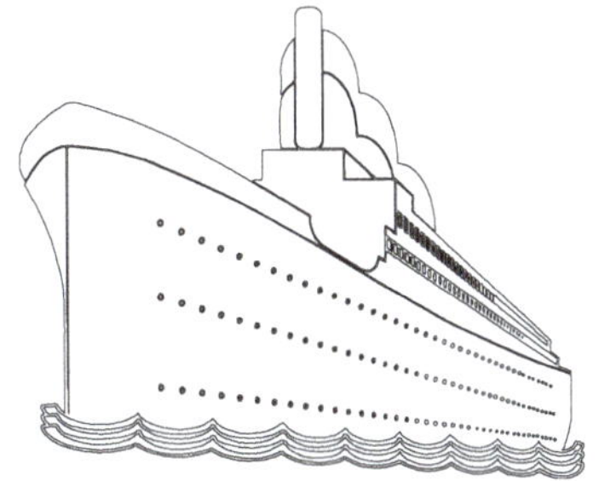

Ship

Car

House

Shop

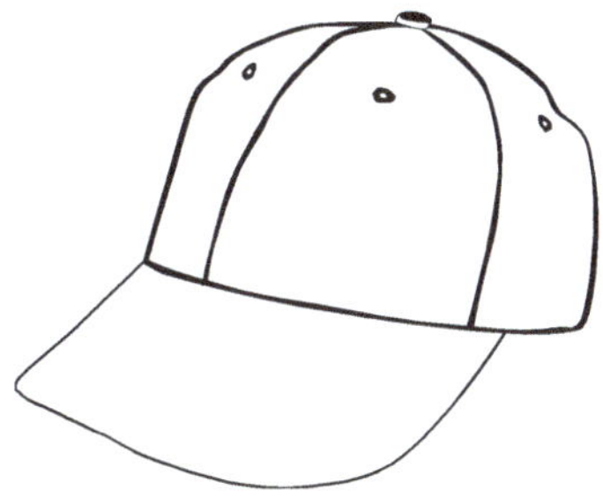

849. Match the animals with their babies.

Chick Puppy Lamb Calf Kid Foal

850. Complete the following sentences.

1. Please op__ the door.
2. John is lighting the la___.
3. The scarf is made of si____.
4. I got a gi____for my parents.
5. An app___a day keeps the doctor away.
6. Alisha lov____to sing.

es en ft le lk mp

851. Draw a line to the image that best denotes the weather.

Windy

Rainy

Sunny

852. Match the following.

Snow

Sunny

Stormy

Cloudy

Rain

Windy

853. Fill in the blank with the correct word from the box.

closed cold small soft

1. Wood is hard, but feather is ______________.
2. Elephant is big, but dog is __________.
3. This door is open, but that door is ___________________.
4. Tea 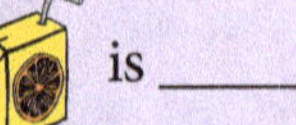 is hot but, juice is __________.

854. Solve the sums and help the puppy reach its house.

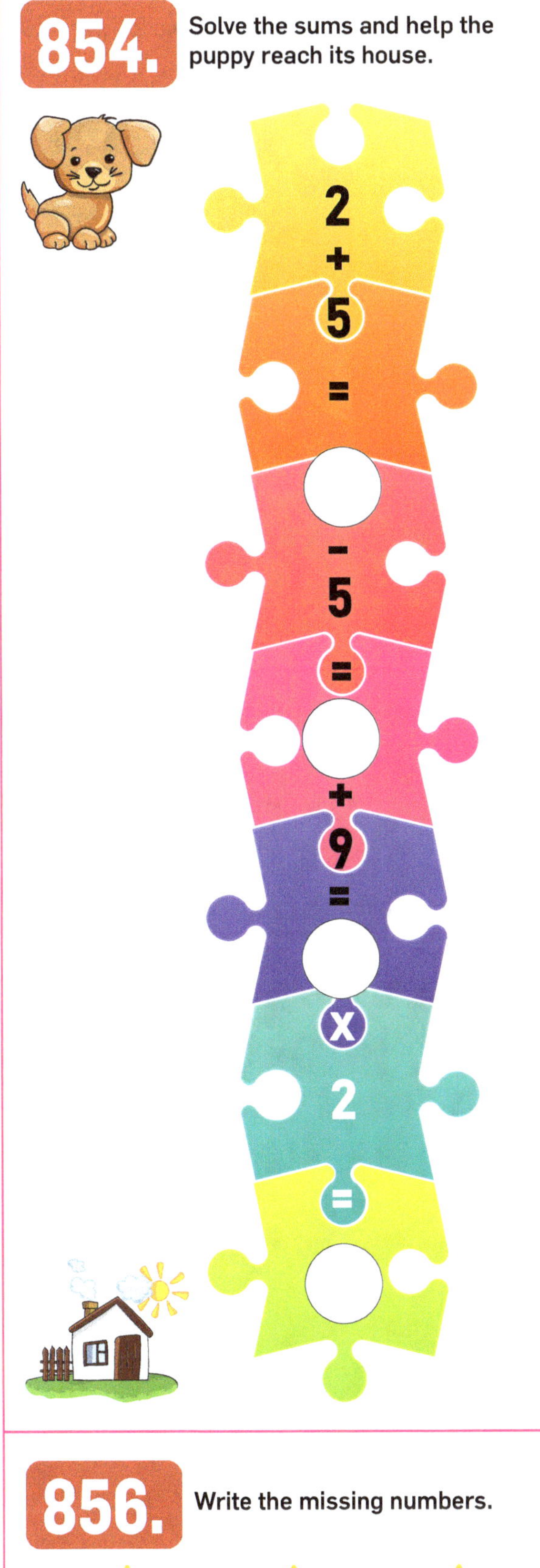

855. Write the correct answers of the sums given below.

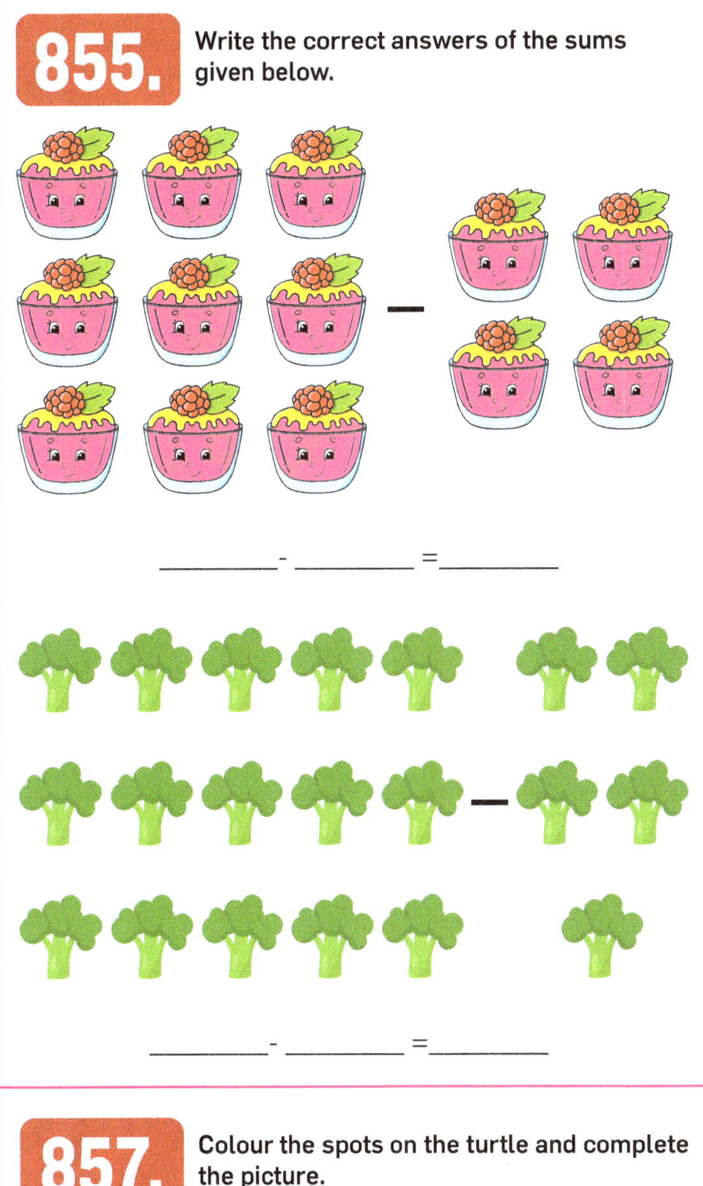

________- ________ =________

________- ________ =________

856. Write the missing numbers.

46

857. Colour the spots on the turtle and complete the picture.

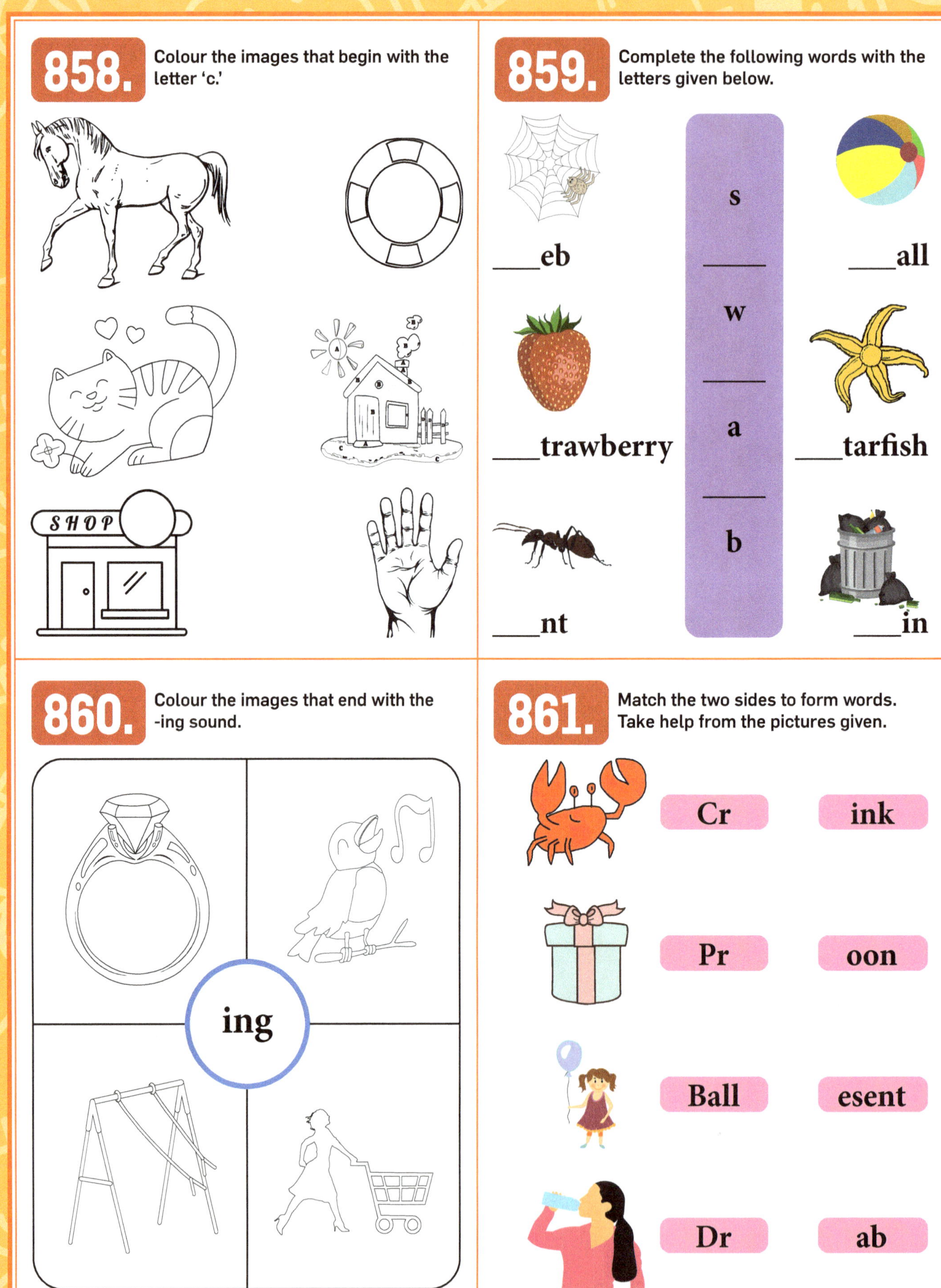
858.
Colour the images that begin with the letter 'c.'
SHOP
859.
Complete the following words with the letters given below.
s
w
a
b
___eb
___all
___trawberry
___tarfish
___nt
___in
860.
Colour the images that end with the -ing sound.
ing
861.
Match the two sides to form words. Take help from the pictures given.
Cr
ink
Pr
oon
Ball
esent
Dr
ab

862. Which of these activities do you do in summers?

Bonfire

Cycling

Wearing Woollens

Picnic

863. Colour the objects that come in handy during the winter season.

864. Join the dots to complete the picture. Colour it in bright colours.

865. Find out the correct word of the weather and colour it.

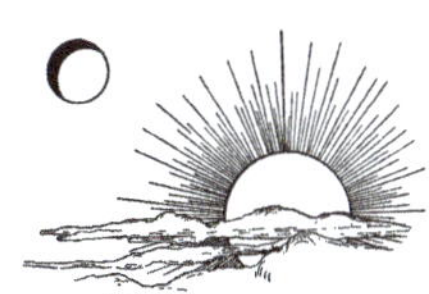

memsur

inydw

olucdy

inary

866. Add the following.

2 Socks	9 Socks	5 Socks	=	___ Socks altogether
5 Pens	7 Pens	2 Pens	=	___ Pens altogether
4 Boards	8 Boards	3 Boards	=	___ Boards altogether
6 Flowers	9 Flowers	4 Flowers	=	___ Flowers altogether

867. Divide the following sums.

5 7 9 2 6 3

12÷2 16÷8 25÷5 21÷3 18÷6 27÷3

868. John had 10 ice creams. He gave 2 to his brother. How many does he have?

____

869. Circle the dices that give the following results when added.

7

10

9

12

8

11

870. Circle the alphabets with which these images begin.

L Y N E

Y U M S

A F S Z

871. Fill in the blanks to complete the rhyming words.

sleep __eep

wink __ink

house __use

872. Use **have** or **has** to fill in the blanks.

have has

1. Our cat ____________ six kittens.
2. We ________________ bought a new dog this year.
3. My brother _____ a red car.
4. This garden ______________ a large pond.
5. My board ___________ lots of beautiful sketches.
6. My neighbours _______________ two children.
7. Darwin and his brother _____________ a lot of video games.

873. Cross the odd word out.

I our my

he her his

my it am

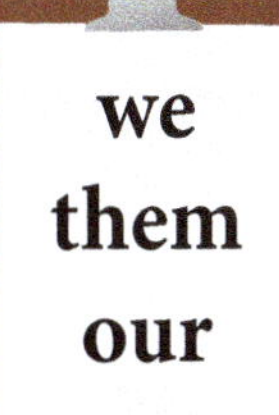

we them our

they you their

she we her

874. Tick the object that you will need when you go for the following activities.

876. Guess the season each picture is showing.

875. Look carefully at each thermometer and write the temperature each one of them is showing.

877. Draw the missing parts of this image. Colour and name it.

878. Solve the following sums with the help of the given example.

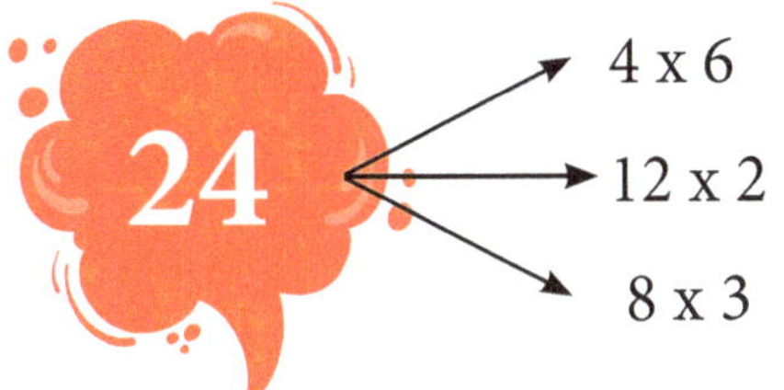

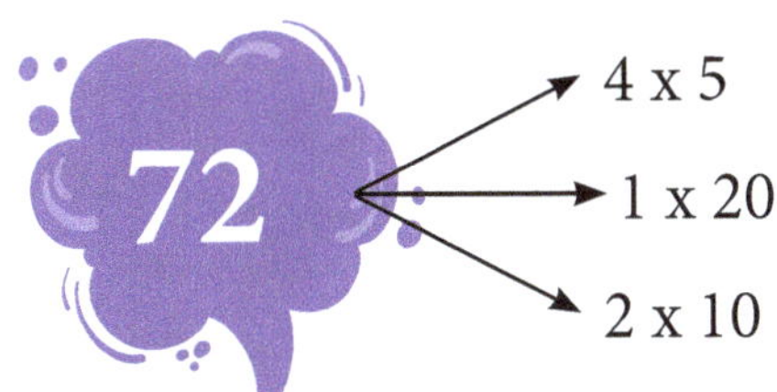

879. Write the last letter to complete each word given below.

CA__

CA__

RA__

BU__

DO__

HE__

JU__

EG__

BO__

880. Count and write the number of vegetables.

881. Write the combinations of numbers that multiply to give 100.

100

882. Pick the right colour to fill in the blanks.

White Pink Red Green Orange Brown
Blue Yellow Black Purple

1. The colour of apple.
2. The colour of spinach.
3. The colour of the sea.
4. The colour of the sun.
5. The colour of orange.
6. The colour of the night sky.
7. The colour of milk.
8. The colour of tree bark.

883. Pick the right adjectives to complete the sentences.

colourful, cold, juicy, low, interesting, famous, large, hot

A. Ice is very ________________.

B. Donna is wearing a _____________ dress.

C. I like _______________ oranges.

D. My garden has a____________tree.

E. He is a ____________photographer.

F. Ken ordered a ____________ pizza.

G. I have an _______________ comic.

H. The pollution is _________in areas sur rounded by trees.

884. Fill in the blanks with the correct comparative adjectives.

	Thinner	
Good		Best
Quick		
	Softer	Softest
Fair	Fairer	Fairest
	Happier	
	Harder	Hardest
	Wider	Widest
Fast	Faster	
Dirty	Dirtier	
Hot		Hottest

885. Write the correct helping verbs.

am is are

1. Superman _____________very strong.
2. Mary _________________ the youngest girl in the class.
3. My mother ___________________ a teacher.
4. I _____________________ good at dancing.
5. His father ____________ 56 years old.

886. Write the name of the season in which the leaves fall off the trees.

____

887. Draw lines to show which clothes you wear in which season.

888. Take Tommy to his kite.

889. Find out the names of the following weathers.

toh _______________

yiran _______________

looc _______________

dywin _______________

mraw _______________

wyson _______________

romsty _______________

ggyof _______________

nnuys _______________

dolc _______________

890. Find out the names of the following weathers.

1	3 + 1	2	3 + 2	3	3 + 3
4	1 + 0	5	1 + 1	6	1 + 2

891. Join the dots to complete the picture of the owl given below. Colour it.

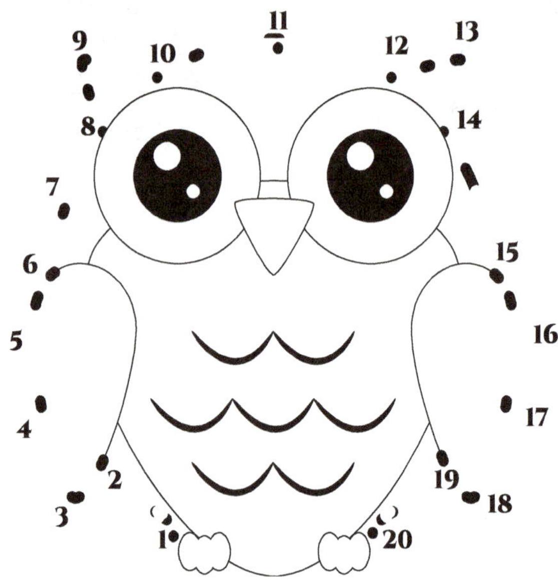

892. Add the following.

893. Fill in with the correct symbols: <, >, =

6 __ 9	10 __ 10
11 __ 8	16 __ 19

894. Complete the puzzle.

5	+		=	18
+	■	+	■	+
20	+		=	
=	■	=	■	=
	+	25	=	50

895. Follow the pattern to complete the series.

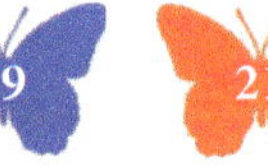

896. Complete the sentences with the right form of the verb.

1. Jane *likes / like* to dance.
2. My mother likes to *eat / eats* healthy food items.
3. My dog *enjoy / enjoys* chicken curry.
4. Henry *need / needs* to complete his homework.
5. The stars *shine / shines* bright in the night sky.

897. Encircle the rhyming words in each sentence.

1. The frog is sitting on a log.

2. There is a pin inside the bin.

3. My rat was under my hat.

4. Do you see the man in the van?

898. Tick the right answers.

Athena is going to the library. She is going with her aunt, Jane. They want to read books. Jane likes to read comic books. Athena likes to read fairy tales. They enjoy going to the bookshop.

1. Where are Athena and Jane headed?
   - to the bookshop ☐
   - to the library ☐
   - to the school ☐

2. Why are they going to the bookshop?
   - to buy ice cream ☐
   - to borrow books ☐
   - to sleep ☐

3. Athena likes to read _______.
   - fairy tales ☐
   - adventure ☐
   - comics ☐

4. Jane likes to read _______
   - comic books ☐
   - adventure books ☐
   - fairy tales books ☐

899. Search for the weather names given in the word box.

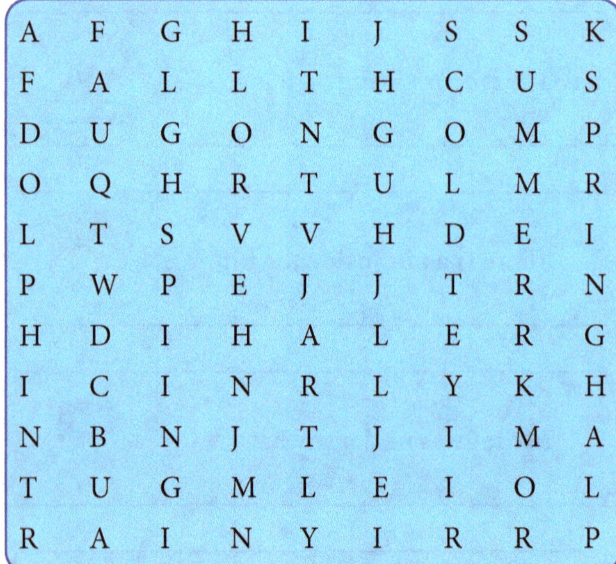

A	F	G	H	I	J	S	S	K
F	A	L	L	T	H	C	U	S
D	U	G	O	N	G	O	M	P
O	Q	H	R	T	U	L	M	R
L	T	S	V	V	H	D	E	I
P	W	P	E	J	J	T	R	N
H	D	I	H	A	L	E	R	G
I	C	I	N	R	L	Y	K	H
N	B	N	J	T	J	I	M	A
T	U	G	M	L	E	I	O	L
R	A	I	N	Y	I	R	R	P

HOT FALL COLD RAINY
SPRING WINTER SUMMER

900. Categorise the seasons into Spring, Summer, Fall and Winter.

__________ __________

__________ __________

901. Leaves are beautiful in Autumn. Colour them yellow, red, and orange.

902. Match the drinks with the correct seasons.

903. Solve the subtraction problem below.

-

9 - 4 = ◯

There are_____________books.

904. Solve the following sums.

______X______=_______

______+______=_______

______+______=_______

905. Follow the sequence in the example and complete the second pyramid.

32	4	8
16	2	1

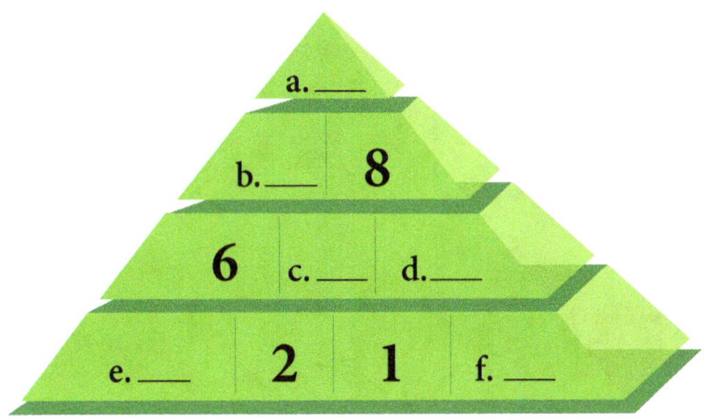

906. Tick the boxes with the correct sentences.

1. Kate is crying. ☐
   kate is crying. ☐
2. The lion roared. ☐
   the roared lion ☐
3. There are ducks in the pond. ☐
   ducks in the pond there are. ☐
4. I have a black dog. ☐
   black dogs have i ☐
5. The night sky is beautiful. ☐
   Sky night beautiful the is ☐

907. Write the plurals of the following words.

DOG	DOG__
Fan	Fan__
Coin	Coin__
Candy	Candie__

908. Match the words in the column A to the best available answer in the column B.

A	B
SLEEPING	SCENERY
PAINTING	WATER
CARRYING	BABY
DRINKING	BOOKS
CRAWLING	BOY

909. Find the insect below in the word search.

B	B	T	R	I	C	H	M	R	F
H	U	E	B	O	R	O	O	R	L
R	O	T	E	X	C	P	T	R	E
B	E	U	T	T	R	A	H	Q	A
E	S	F	S	E	L	K	A	U	S
E	F	O	F	E	R	E	K	D	W
W	A	S	P	S	F	F	A	H	O
T	N	O	H	G	U	L	L	E	R
E	M	U	W	S	J	K	Y	Y	C
H	O	N	E	Y	B	E	E	N	P

BUTTERFLY MOTH FLEAS WASPS HONEYBEE

910. Find out how the water travels from the skies and reaches the Earth. Colour the images as you go.

The heat from the sun evaporates water from sea, river etc.

Water evaporates to form clouds.

Water from the clouds fall on the earth as rain.

Rain water goes into rivers and other water bodies

911. Complete the following weather related terms.

W__ATH__R

C__OU__Y

H__T

R__I__Y

__O__L

W__N__Y

W__R__

__N__W__

S__OR__Y

F__G__Y

C__L__

S__NN__

912. Write the names of the different types of water bodies.

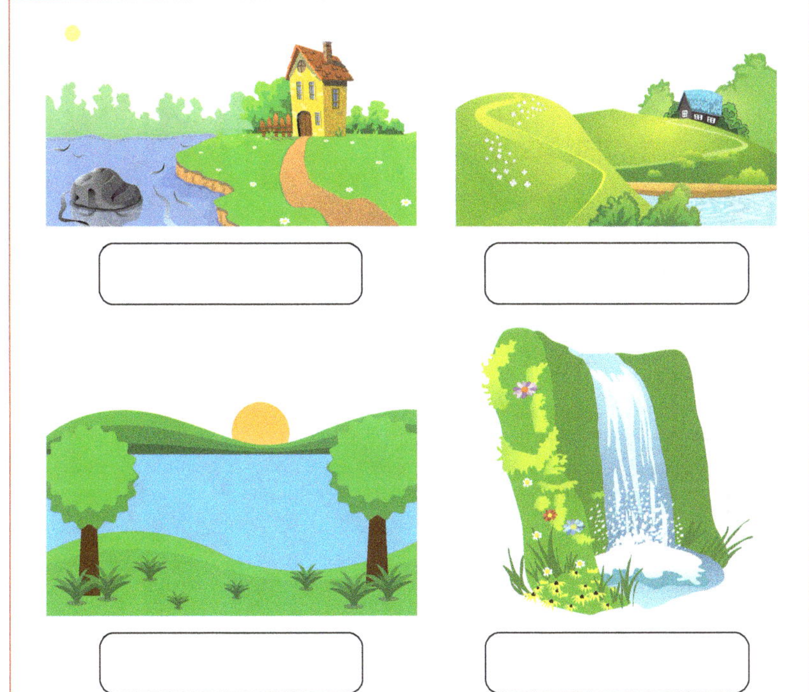

913. Colour the Earth with shades of green and blue to denote land and water.

914.

Solve the multiplication sums and match them with the correct answers.

915.

Help Superboy reach his bowl of warm soup.

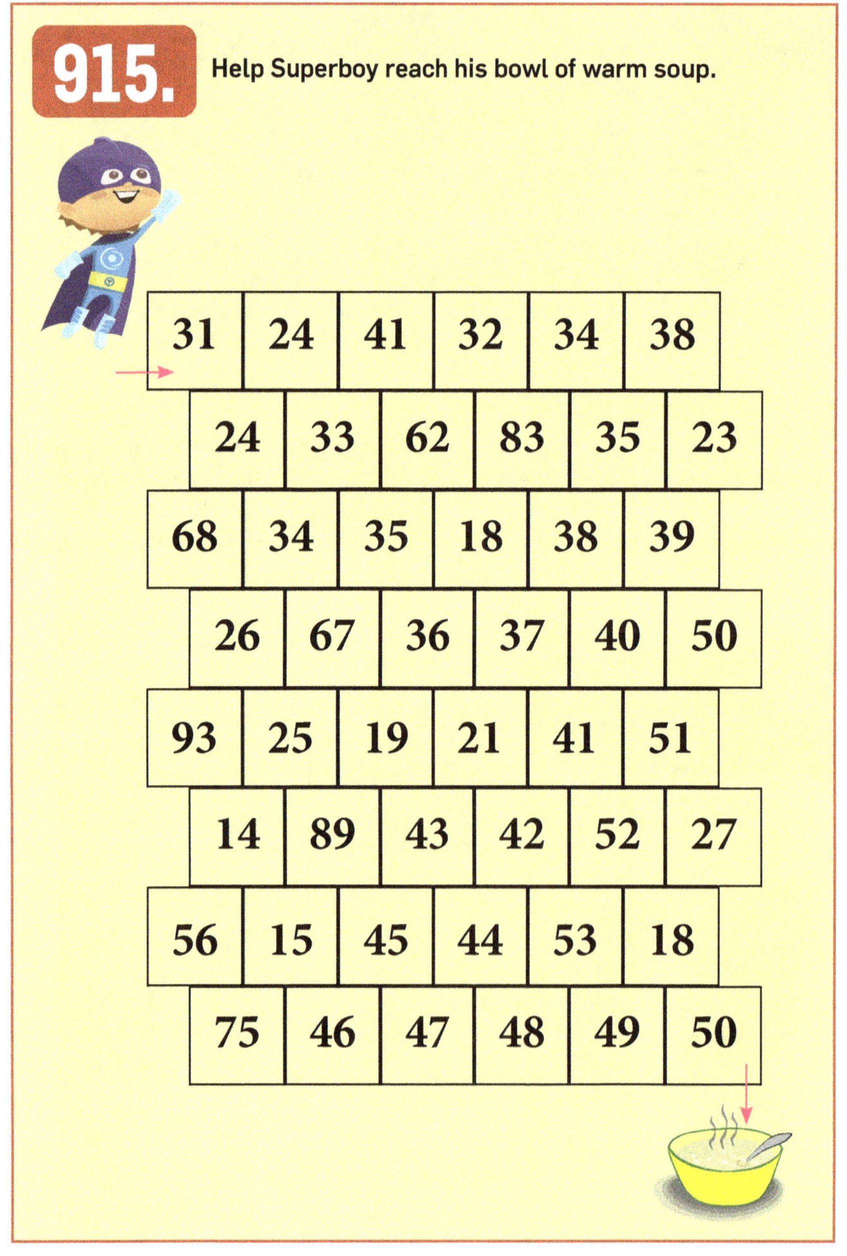

916.

Write the missing number to complete the multiplication sum.

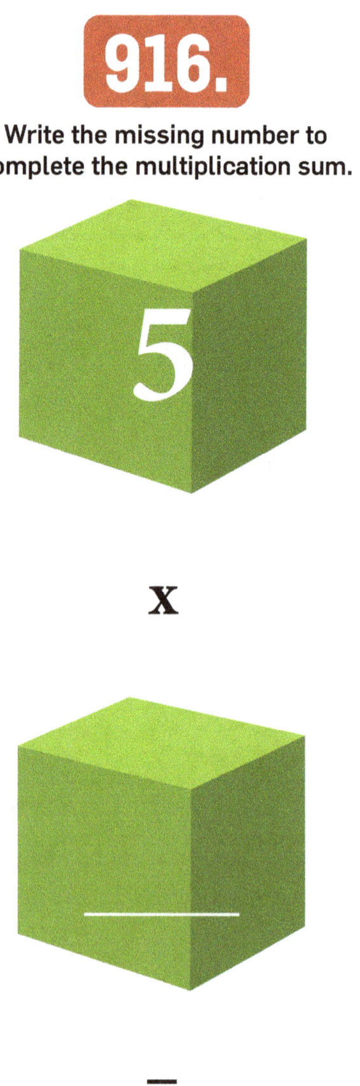

917. Solve the crossword with the appropriate masculine and feminine nouns.

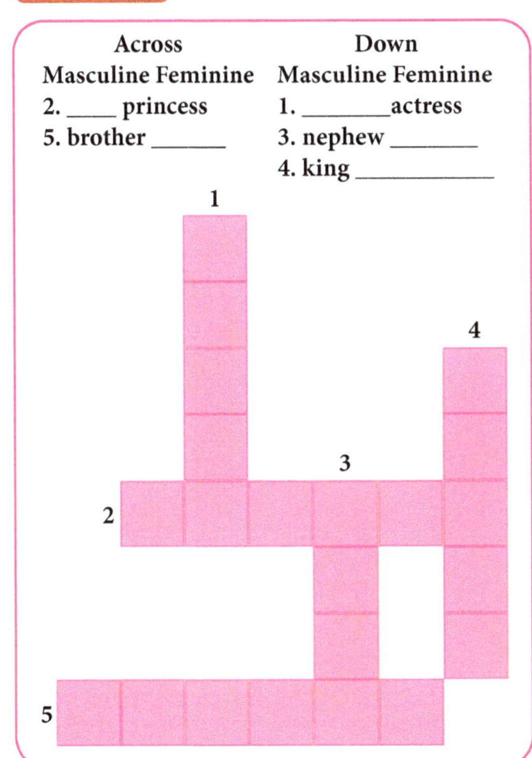

918. Write the correct number names of the following.

919. Write the names of the images along with a word that rhymes with them.

920. Form a word with the help of the beginning letters of the given images.

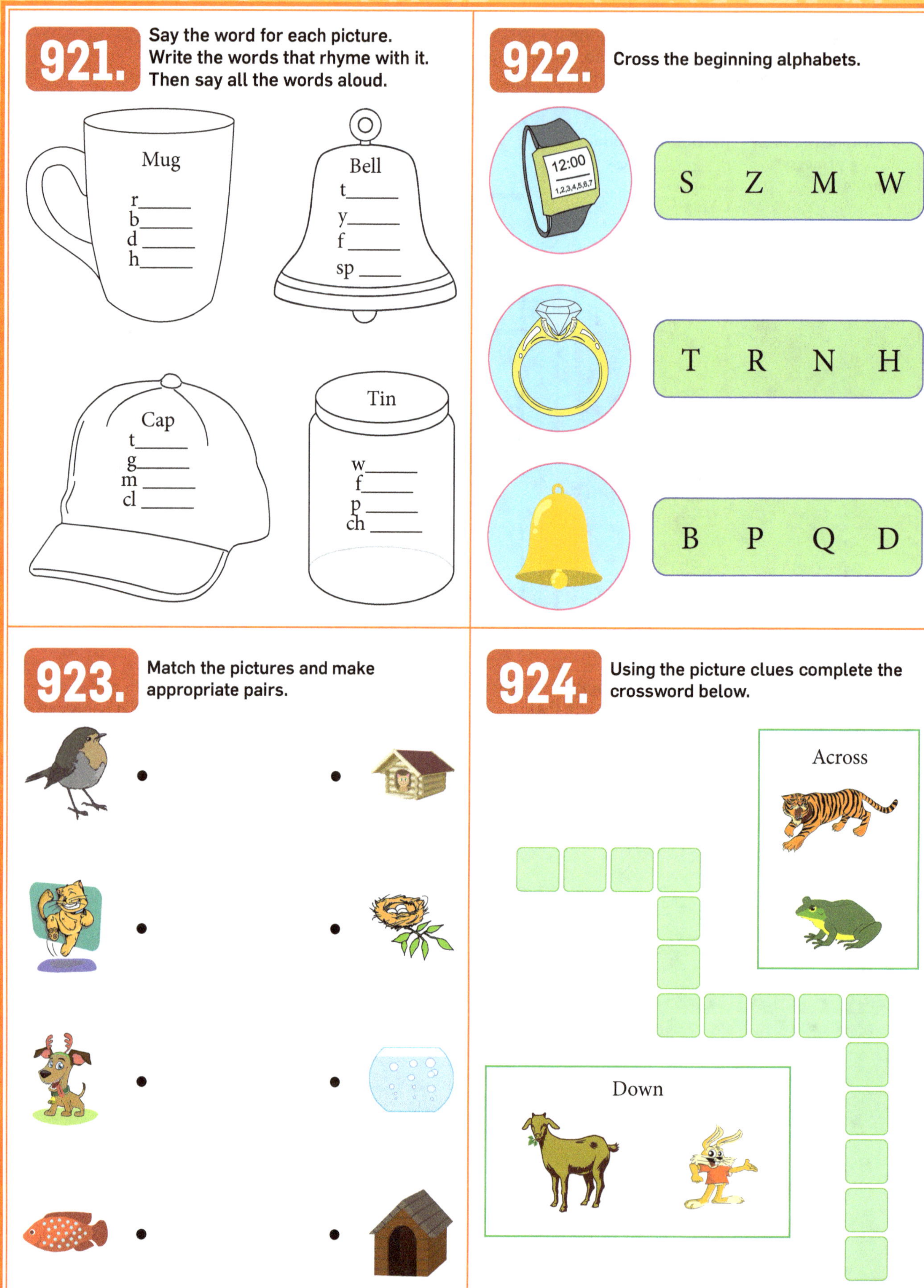
921.
Say the word for each picture.
Write the words that rhyme with it.
Then say all the words aloud.
Mug
r
b
d
h
Bell
t
y
f
sp
Cap
t
g
m
cl
Tin
w
f
p
ch
922.
Cross the beginning alphabets.
12:00
1,2,3,4,5,6,7
S Z M W
T R N H
B P Q D
923.
Match the pictures and make appropriate pairs.
924.
Using the picture clues complete the crossword below.
Across
Down

925. Solve the sums by colouring the marbles according to the given instructions.

Add 1 blue marble to 3 red marbles.	◯ ◯ ◯ ◯	____+____ = 4
Add 2 blue marbles to 2 red marbles.	◯ ◯ ◯ ◯	____+____ = 4
Add 4 blue marbles to 0 red marbles.	◯ ◯ ◯ ◯	____+____ = 4
Add 1 blue marbles to 3 red marbles.	◯ ◯ ◯ ◯	____+____ = 4

926. Solve the division sums.

927. Multiply the following:

x 10 =

928. Divide the following:

2 ÷ 2 = ______

8 ÷ 2 = ______

9 ÷ 3 = ______

12 ÷ 3 = ______

15 ÷ 3 = ______

20 ÷ 2 = ______

18 ÷ 3 = ______

21 ÷ 7 = ______

929. Multiply the given numbers.

3 x ____ = 0

3 x ___ = 12

3 x ___ = 18

3 x 5 = ___

3 x 8 = ___

3 x ___ = 30

3 x ___ = 33

3 x ___ = 21

930. Circle the things that do not begin with the same first letter as the 'frog.'

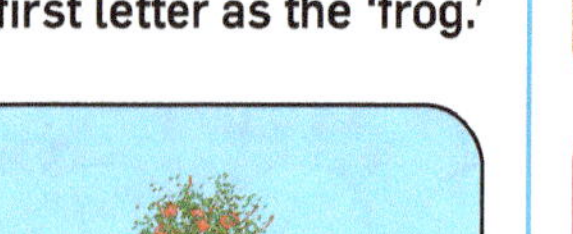

931. Match each word with the right image.

DOG

DOGS

FAN

FANS

BAG

BAGS

CLOWN

CLOWNS

932. Draw a line from each picture to its beginning letter.

933. Match the pictures with the answers.

16

10

28

934. Colour the gas balloon.

935. Write the name of the activities given below. Take help from the word box.

Drinking	Cooking	Bathing
Washing	Blowing	

936. Did you know? Bats are happy to sleep upside-down in a variety of places. Colour the bat.

937. Draw a line to match the fruits with their shadows.

938. Help Tony with his homework.

$24 \div 4 =$ ______

$3 \times$ ______ $= 24$

______ $\div 3 = 7$

$3 \times$ ______ $= 21$

$15 \div$ ______ $= 3$

$3 \times$ ______ $= 15$

939. Can you fill in the missing numbers?

8	+		=	12
+		+		+
	+	8	=	
=		=		=
11	+		=	

940. Circle the number of cupcakes you see.

21

22

23

24

941. Fill the boxes with bright colours on each side to get a sum of 15.

2	5	12	3
7	4	3	9

6	7	4	10
2	14	4	5

942. Use addition, subtraction, multiplication, and division to attain the number 90.

___ + ___

___ - ___

___ x ___

___ ÷ ___

943. How many cherries are there in the jar?

____

944. Join the words that have similar meanings.

Old	Happy
Glad	Beautiful
Shy	Easy
Silly	Wicked
Simple	Quiet
Silent	Stupid
Small	Tiny
Bad	Timid
Attractive	Elderly

945. Write one short and one long answer.

1. 

Is it a fish? ______

What is it?______

____

2. 

Are these books? ______

What are they?______

____

3. 

Is it an aeroplane ? ______

What is it?______

____

4. 

Are these fruits? ______

What is it?______

____

946. Look at the pictures of different liquids and write their names.

____

____

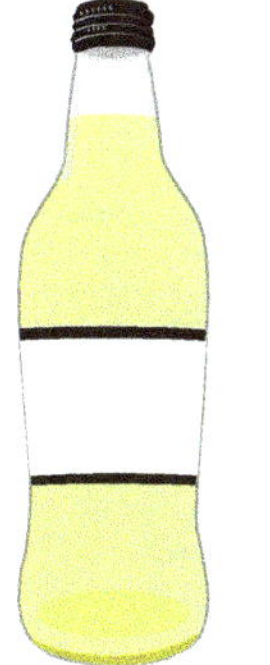

____

____

947. Take the butterfly to the flower.

948. Protect the Earth and paint only the green parts to plant trees.

949. Spell the name of the flower.

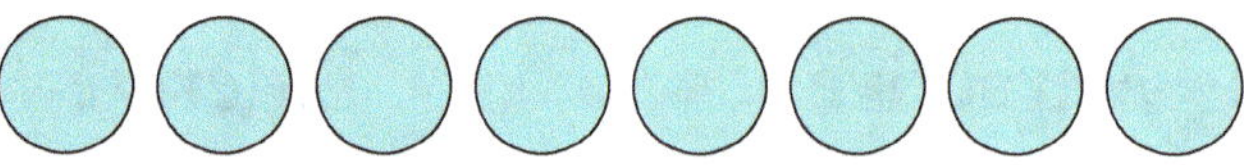

950. Colour the different things you find on Earth and around you.

951. Which of these means of transports have you used?

____

____

____

____

952. Circle the boxes which give the answer 16.

12 + 12	10 + 7		2 + 14	18 + 6
8 + 9	3 + 14		8 + 8	4 + 9
19 + 5	6 + 11		20 + 2	4 + 13
6 + 9		16		2 +15

953. Match numbers that add upto 19.

A	B
04	09
06	07
10	11
08	12
03	05

954.

There are 5 snack packs in the picture. Add 3 more snack packs to it. How many snack packs are there in all?

5 + ______ = □

955. Which two flowers when coloured give the answer 11?

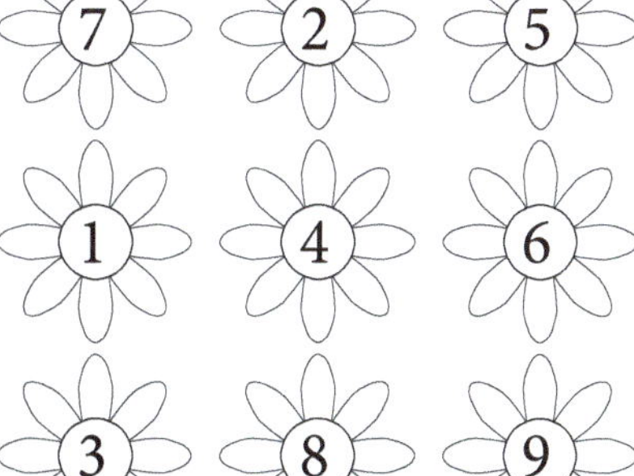

956. Pick the right answer.

15 18 21

10 + 5

16 19 22

9 + 13

957. Complete the sentences using helping verbs.

1. This tree _____ very few apples.
2. My mother _____ five watches.
3. The boy ____________ playing with the leaves.
4. Martin _____ going to school.
5. The cow _____ looking for its baby.
6. I _____ a big car.

958. Match the opposite words.

sweet	few
big	sour
many	slow
fresh	small
fast	awake
sleeping	stale
new	short
long	old

959. Homonyms are words with the same sound. Match them.

Week	Steal
Steel	Weak
Dear	Fair
Fare	Deer
Male	Tail
Tale	Mail
Sale	Hare
Hair	Sail
Son	Some
Sum	Sun

960. Unscramble the letters and tick the ones you see in your kitchen.

veon ____________

feigretroarr ____________

kisn ____________

nibas ____________

blas ____________

evorcimwa ____________

sga rliycnde ____________

961. Complete the sentences by filling in the subject words.

1. ____________ ran down the hill.

2. ____________ flew over the tree.

3. ____________ ate carrot.

4. ____________ took bath in the pond.

5. ____________ sleeps a long time.

962. Circle the thing made up of wood.

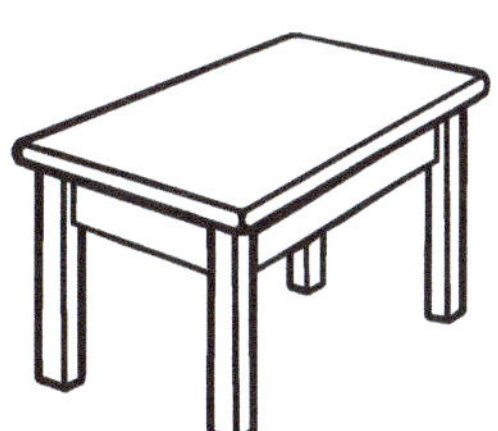

963. Match the following vehicles with the correct means of transportation.

AIR

LAND

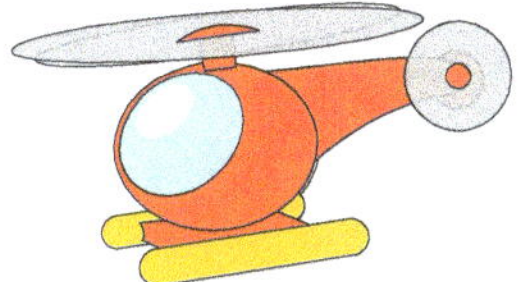

WATER

964. Find the shown fruits in the grid.

C	K	O	L	I	M	E	A
H	I	R	E	G	E	P	P
E	W	A	M	R	L	E	R
R	I	N	P	A	O	A	I
R	F	G	L	P	N	R	C
Y	N	E	U	E	L	G	O
T	L	E	M	O	N	E	O

965. Which of the two bears will give the answer 12 when coloured?

966. Complete the series.

14 ☐ 16 ☐ 18 ☐ 20 21

967. Solve the addition sum.

968. Which of these sums are wrong? Draw a cross in the box.

8 + 3 = 9 ☐	14 + 45 = 9 ☐	16 + 12 = 14 ☐
6 + 5 = 14 ☐	18 + 15 = 13 ☐	45 + 23 = 16 ☐
5 + 7 =12 ☐	14 + 16 =30 ☐	19 + 23 = 10 ☐
7 + 8 = 17 ☐	15 + 22 = 17 ☐	14 + 22 = 36 ☐

969. Complete the crossword.

GRASS	MOUNDS	ROOM	TUNNELS
LODGE	RABBITS	FLOODING	BEAVER

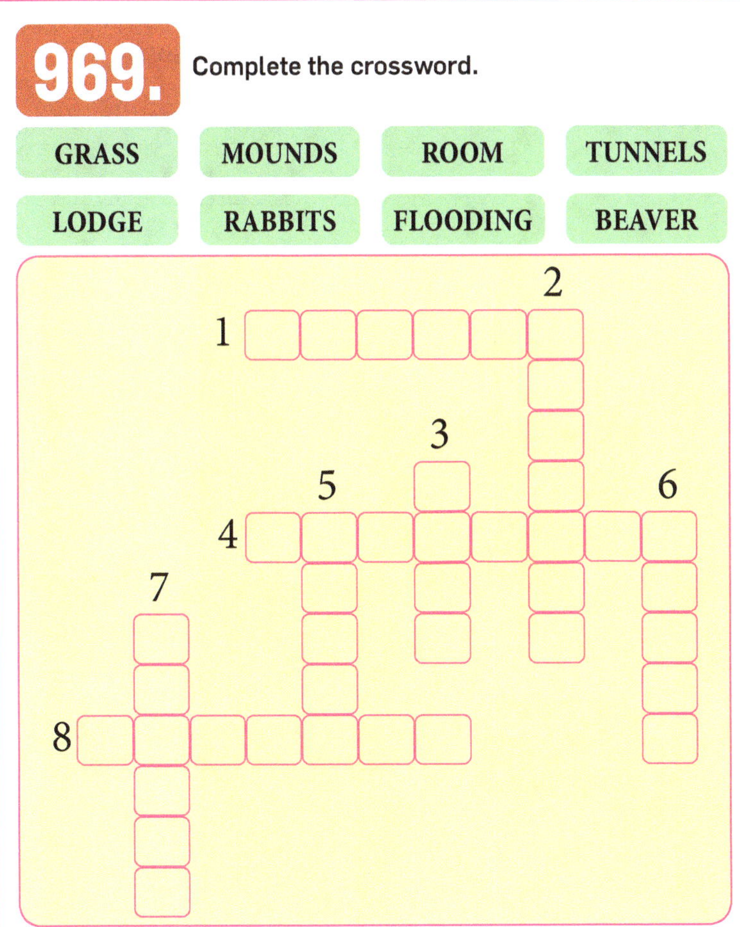

970. Colour the words that rhyme with each other in one shade.

971. Fill in the blanks with the help of the pictures given.

1. The man drives a 

   ________________.

2. I can pick an  from a tree.

   ________________.

3. I like to drink for lunch.

   ________________.

4. The likes to eat corn.

   ________________.

5. The is very slow.

   ________________.

972. Name the object and circle the word that rhymes with it.

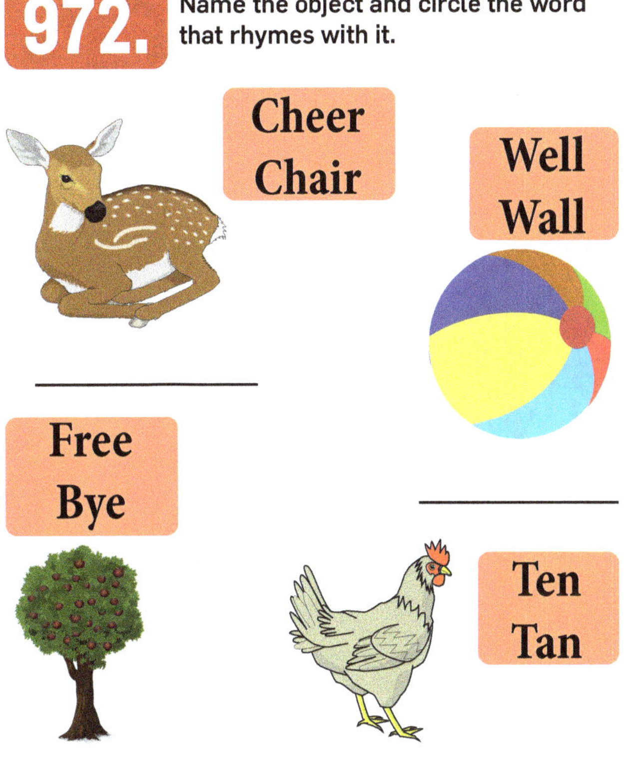

973. Colour the shell.

974. Write 5 adjectives to describe the plant.

975. Draw a circle around the edible items.

976. Colour the flower given below and write its name in the given space.

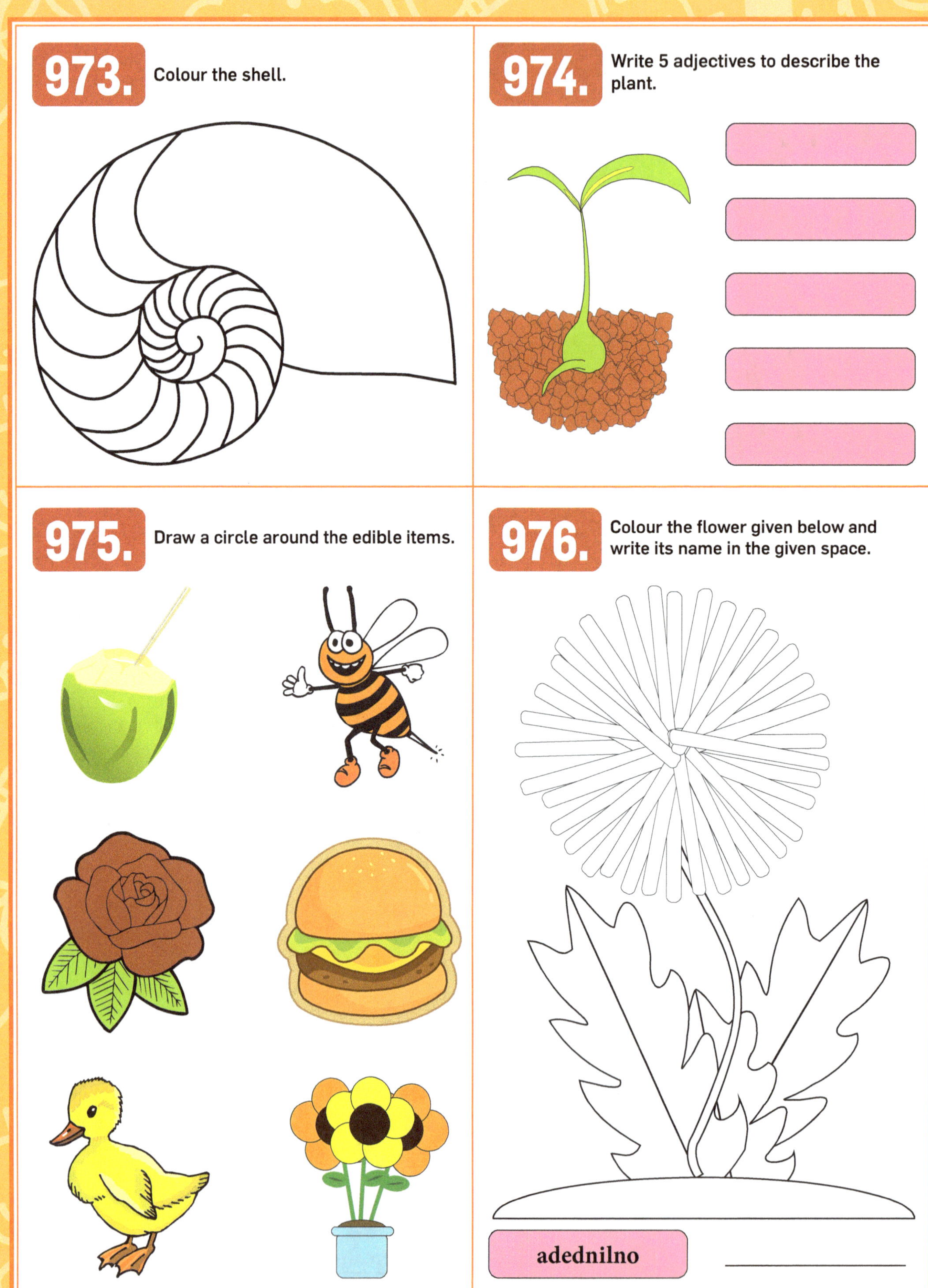

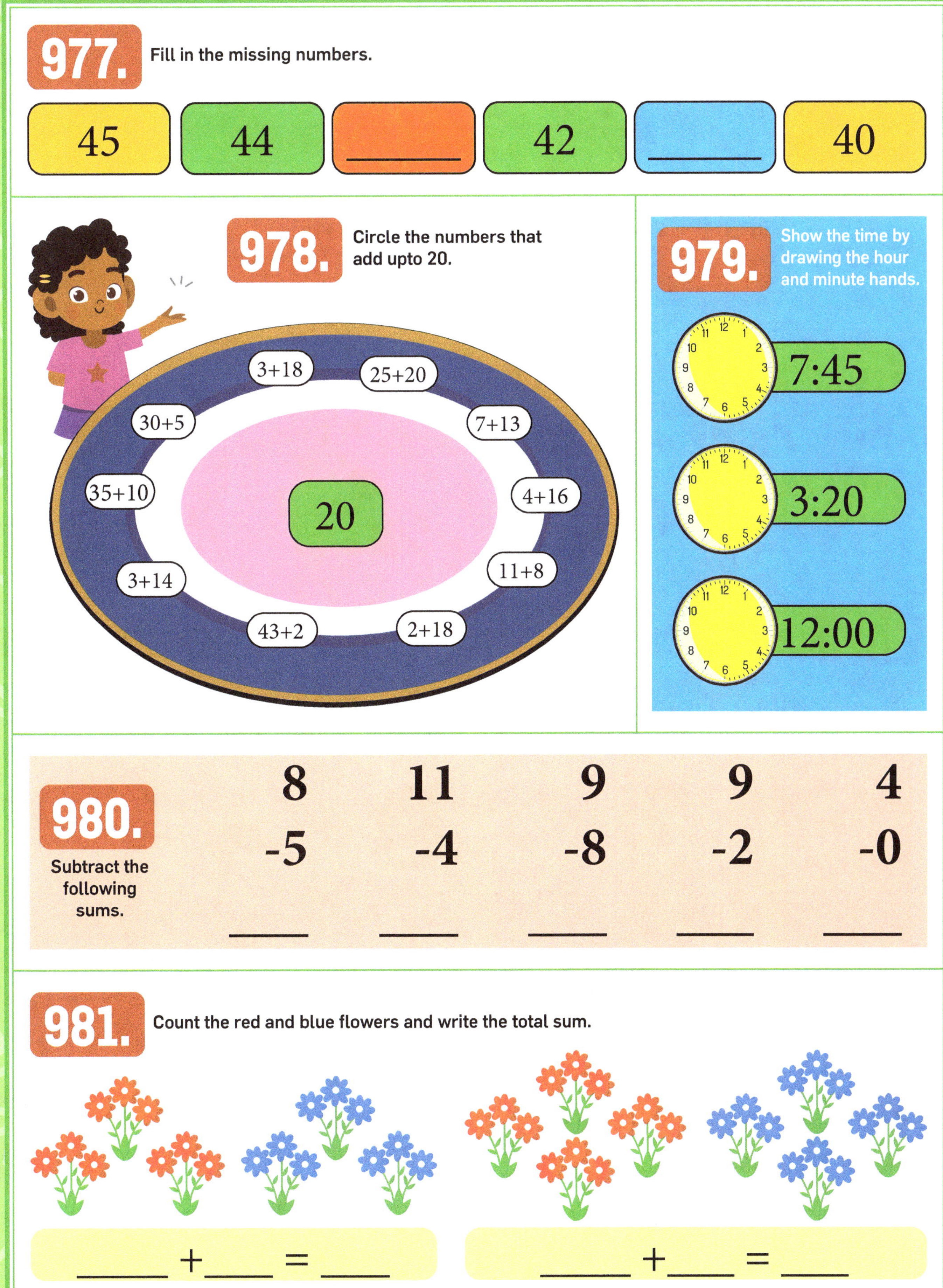
977.
Fill in the missing numbers.
45
44
___
42
___
40
978.
Circle the numbers that add upto 20.
3+18
25+20
30+5
7+13
35+10
20
4+16
3+14
11+8
43+2
2+18
979.
Show the time by drawing the hour and minute hands.
7:45
3:20
12:00
980.
Subtract the following sums.
8 -5
11 -4
9 -8
9 -2
4 -0
981.
Count the red and blue flowers and write the total sum.
___ + ___ = ___
___ + ___ = ___

982. Match the animals to their homes.

Horses	Bees	Dogs	Rabbits	Sheep	Birds	Fish	Lions
Kennel	Burrow	Nest	Aquarium	Pen	Den	Stable	Hive

 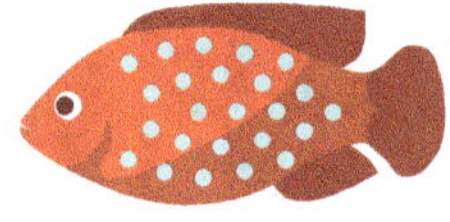  

983. Using the picture clues, choose the best word from the bracket that completes each sentence.

1. My mother is in the kitchen.
   She is ________
   (baking / Frying) fritters.
2. Nate is ________________
   (playing / lying) football.
3. Maria has a lot of books.
   She is __________
   (putting / throwing) them in a box.

984. Complete the sums using the codes.

 =14  =25  =19

 +  = ☐

  -  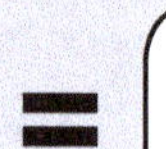 = ☐

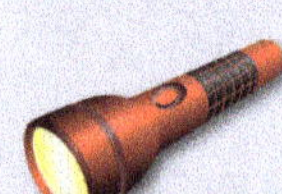 +    = ☐

 +    = ☐

985.

Below are the pictures of a mountain and a beach. Colour the two pictures.

986.

Colour the volcano.

987.

Cross the animal that has spots.

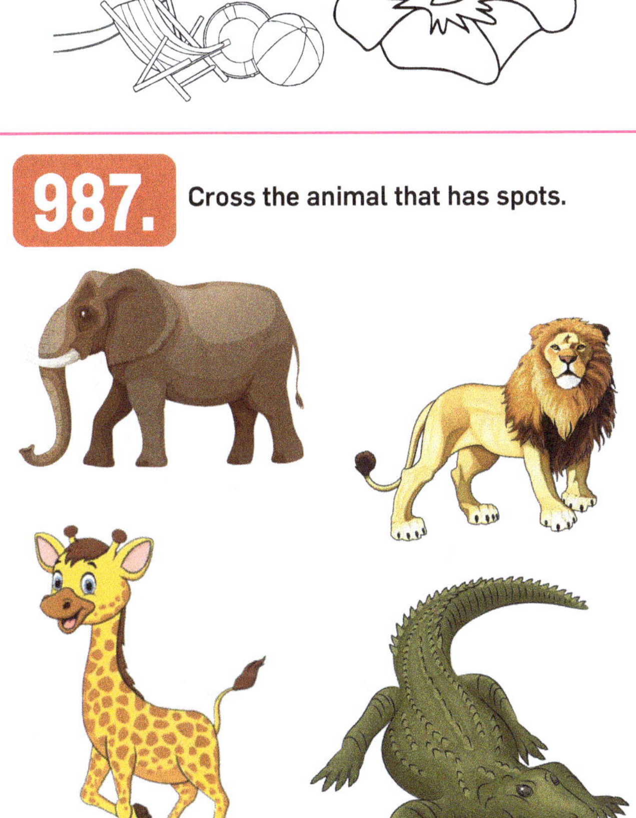

988.

Write the names of the given food items and categorise them into healthy and unhealthy.

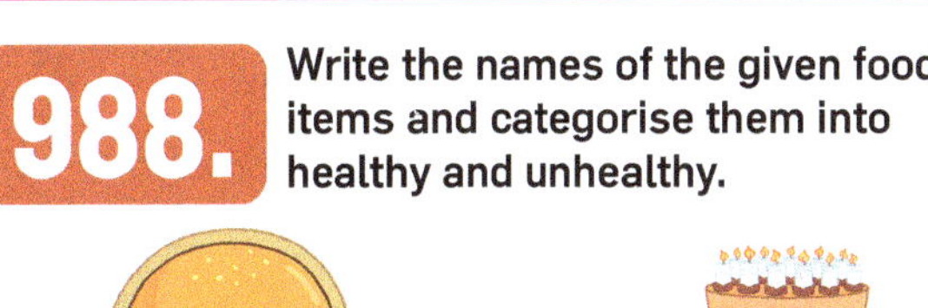

989. Solve the sums using number lines.

If I add 2 and 3

1 2 3 4 5 6 7 8 9 10

If I add 3 and 6

1 2 3 4 5 6 7 8 9 10

If I add 4 and 5

1 2 3 4 5 6 7 8 9 10

990.

Solve the sum.

6

x

3

+

☐

=

30

991. Add 7 to the following numbers.

23 +7 ◯

992. Write the missing Alphabets in the series.

D, E, F, ______, ______, ______,

O, N, M, ______, ______, ______,

I, J, K, ______, ______, ______,

V, U, T, ______, ______, ______,

993. Fill the grid below by solving the sums.

24	+	8	=	
+		+		+
12	+	6	=	
=		=		=
	+		=	

994. Look at the puzzle pieces carefully and write the name of the fruit.

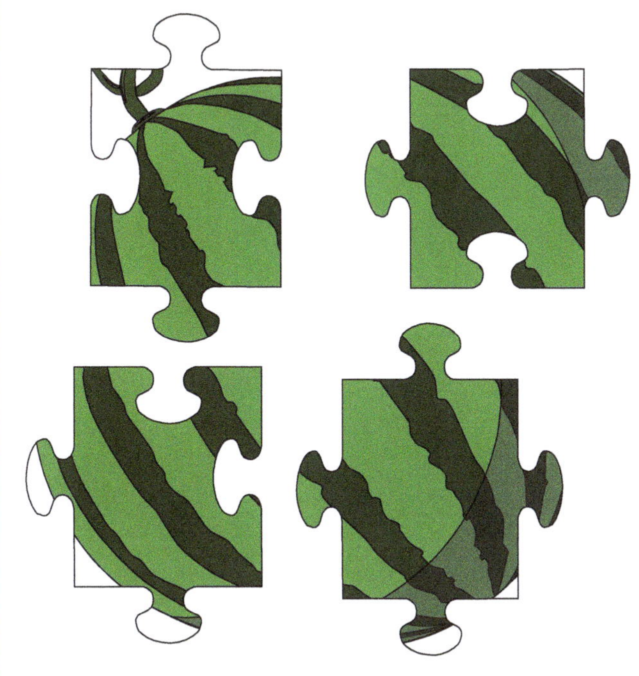

_ A _ E _ _ E _ O _

995. Solve the word equation to find out the name of the vegetable and colour it.

CAB-AB+A+BB-B+B+AGE

____

996. Fill in the blanks with This or That.

1. ____________ is red paint. I will use it to colour the flowers.
2. ____________ textbook belongs to David.
3. ____________ is my new dress. My mother gifted it to me.

997. Fill in the blanks with the correct vowel.

SN __ KE

D __ ER

C __ W

GO __ T

998. Write 'H' for healthy and 'U' for unhealthy against the following food items.

999. Draw a portrait of your family and colour it.

1000. At what time do you sleep and have your breakfast? Show it by drawing hands on the clock.

Bedtime ______

Breakfast _____

Bedtime ______

Breakfast _____

Bedtime ______

Breakfast _____

1001. Swimming is fun in summers. Colour the fun summer activity.